LEDGER OF THE OPEN HAND

Ledger OF THE
OPEN
HAND

LESLIE VRYENHOEK

P.O. BOX 2188, ST. JOHN'S, NL, CANADA, A1C 6E6
WWW.BREAKWATERBOOKS.COM

COPYRIGHT © 2015 Leslie Vryenhoek
ISBN 978-1-55081-604-4
A CIP catalogue record for this book is available from Library and Archives Canada.

We acknowledge the support of the Canada Council for the Arts, which last year invested $153 million to bring the arts to Canadians throughout the country. We acknowledge the financial support of the Government of Canada through the Canada Book Fund (CBF) and the Government of Newfoundland and Labrador through the Department of Tourism, Culture and Recreation for our publishing activities.

PRINTED AND BOUND IN CANADA.

Canada Council
for the Arts

Conseil des Arts
du Canada

Canadä

Newfoundland
Labrador

Breakwater Books is committed to choosing papers and materials for our books that help to protect our environment. To this end, this book is printed on a recycled paper that is certified by the Forest Stewardship Council®.

FOR BILLIE AND RALPH,
WHO TAUGHT ME ABOUT MONEY
AND ABOUT LOVE

Each one according as they purpose in their heart, so let them give, not grudgingly or of necessity; for God loves a cheerful giver.

2 CORINTHIANS 9:6-7

An anthill increases by accumulation.

OVID

I.
ASSETS AND LIABILITIES

1.

LONG BEFORE WE rolled over the railroad tracks that, even then, marked the divide between here and after, I felt like I'd swallowed a pound of gravel. I guess I'd expected some kind of big deal—my big deal, for a change. But we were running late, then Dad was called back to the dealership to negotiate a sale and the only thing even close to a big-deal moment was the single, silent squeeze he gave my shoulder.

"Business first," he said as he moved my luggage from his trunk to Mom's new car. She'd refused to just swap the keys.

Business as usual.

As we drove through Calder, no one marked my departure, not a single neighbour out on a single porch. Only the poplars lined up between the ditches and the fields offered a flickered farewell as Mom coddled her brand new, metallic blue Cavalier down the gravel access road. She rolled slowly over the tracks, then hesitated for what seemed like much too long before turning, unhurriedly, onto the highway.

Then she started up again. It was her first-impressions speech, the one I thought was over when I'd changed out of my jeans and into her version of more presentable. "I just don't want you to spend your university years on the outside too, Meriel-Claire."

We'd covered this ground before.

"Mom, can you drive a little faster?" There was almost an hour of highway ahead and I didn't want to miss the welcome meeting at the dorm.

In my side-view mirror, I caught a last glimpse of Calder through the trees. The town looked like a kid's pop-up book laid open on the prairie. Then the road curved and Calder closed up behind me.

Mom was saying, "You'll meet people who can shape your whole life."

If Dad had been behind the wheel, at least the conversation would have played to my strengths, would have focused on hard work and following a true line.

The sun moved into the centre of the windshield. Mom reached behind my seat for her purse and her foot came right up off the accelerator. She dug out her sunglasses and used both hands to clean them on her shirt, letting the car drift across the centre line. When I reached for the wheel, she brushed me away and took control again. She was at the point in her speech where my real life begins, where everything changes today.

But I already knew that. I was the one, after all, who'd been gearing up for rebirth since the guide had pointed out that old stone residence on my campus tour. Over and over I'd imagined arriving, stepping across the threshold into a new life, my faded Levis making just the right impression.

I lowered my visor against the sun, startled to find my own image staring back. Years later, the face caught in that little mirror clipped to the visor would come back to me—a face so unguarded, so utterly uncreased by compromise or caginess. If I'd recognized then just how defenseless I appeared, maybe I'd have found a way to protect myself. But all I saw that evening was my wretched blandness. And I had a solution for that.

I sorted my mouth into just the hint of a smile, sparked a deliberate light behind my eyes. I'd learned from a magazine how to appear instantly more interesting, and I'd been practicing for weeks. I was getting good at it, too. When my brother, Gord, had come to pick up his new car—Mom's old car—I'd lit up my face in the kitchen.

Gord was on his way out, keys in hand, but the transformation stopped him in his tracks. "What's up with you, MC?" he'd asked. "You in love or something?"

Mom removed her sunglasses as soon as the sun pulled off to the right of the highway. She turned a naked gaze on me. "You could be a beautiful social butterfly, Meriel-Claire. You just have to get out of your—what's it called? Your—"

"Chrysalis."

"Exactly. Good, I'm glad you know what I mean."

She shut up after that and I stared at the dashboard clock, watching the digital numbers steadily shift. I felt the rise and fall of the overpass, then I realized she hadn't moved left into the turning lane.

"Mom, it's the other way!"

"I know where it is. We have to buy you some new towels first."

"What? I don't need towels. I already have some." She knew that—she'd seen me pack them, watched me tuck the frayed threads along the edge into my suitcase. She'd spent the whole day watching me pack, trying to unload her crap on me: framed photos and quilted cushions and a stupid blue vase with a chip at its mouth that she'd pulled from some deep cupboard somewhere. I'd refused it all.

"You can't use those old rags, Meriel-Claire, you'll look like a street urchin." Mom affected a tight smile. "Relax dear, I'll pay for them."

2.

I USED MY suitcase to prop open the door while I levered my overstuffed backpack into the room. Then I looked up and saw her—saw first just the mass of curls, her long neck. Her head had turned to crane at us coming in but the rest of her stayed put, posture perfect at her desk. She was backlit, silhouetted against the window, a cigarette poised between two fingers. Behind her, the low sun burned like a false fire pretending to be warmer than it was.

"Oh, you're finally here," she said, more accusation than statement. An apology might have leapt right out of my mouth if she'd left another beat of silence. "Do you smoke?"

"No—but I don't mind." My voice like a dog wagging its tail. "It's great that you smoke!"

Still caught in the hallway, my mother made a noise like she might say something disapproving. I grabbed my suitcase and stepped over the threshold, letting the door swing against Mom.

"I'm Meriel-Claire. I guess we're roommates." Obviously. Only my baggage, which blocked the path between us, kept me from reaching out to shake hands like my father would.

"Daneen Turner." Her name rolled toward me in a cloud of smoke. The air was already thick with its blue-grey haze.

Mom pushed her way into the room, flicking the light switch as she passed it. A fluorescent fixture on the ceiling shuddered to life, bringing everything into sharp relief. The room was a narrow rectangle with a bed and a desk pushed flat against each longer wall. Ballpoint blue bedspreads unravelled at their polyester edges. On her bed, Daneen had piled silky red cushions; above it, she'd hung a large painting, black and crimson slashes of paint bulging from the canvas.

I hated that painting on sight, and then I hated everything about that suffocating space. I hated my long-necked roommate in her black T-shirt and jeans and I hated the skirt my mother had forced me to wear. Most of all I hated coming in last, hated not getting to choose which side of that little room would be mine. I kept my faux-interesting face in place and hoped none of that showed through.

Mom squeezed past me, leading with a plastic bag that bulged with new towels, Kmart logo stretched taut across the front. I took in her nodding approval of that hideous painting and the silk pillows, the way she turned her attention toward my roommate's slender profile.

"I'm Meriel-Claire's mother, and I'm surprised they let you smoke in these rooms." Mom dropped the towel bag onto my empty desk. "Does that window open?"

I tried to catch Daneen's eye, to send a message that said I wasn't at all like my mother, but Daneen had turned to look at the window. It stretched up the back wall almost to the ceiling. A fine checkerboard of cracks scored the casement's thick layers of paint.

"Great idea," she said. She crushed her cigarette in the fat bowl of her ashtray and stood. Unfurled, really. She was several inches taller than me.

When Daneen grasped hold of the brass handles at her waist and tugged, the window didn't budge. My mother stepped in to help, reaching up to brace her hands at the top edge of the lower sash, her feet in their rubber-soled slingbacks spread wide, knees bent like she was Sisyphus pushing that rock up the hill. She bounced her whole stocky self up and down, up and down, but the window refused to move.

"Maybe it's painted shut," Daneen offered, turning to fish something from her desk drawer. "That happened once at our cottage." A long pair of scissors flashed in the fluorescent light. She spread the blades wide and used one to carve around the window's perimeter, wriggling and sawing where the blade jammed.

My mother, still braced, looked over her shoulder. "Your roomie's resourceful, dear. I think you're going to learn a lot."

Daneen laid down the scissors and took her place at my mother's side, her long white fingers next to Mom's tan, squat hands. There was no space for me between them.

They jostled and shoved until finally, the window gave slightly. Daneen reached down to hook the handle again and succeeded in pulling her side up by an inch. My mother followed suit, grasping and wrenching until her side was twice as high as Daneen's—but just for an instant before Daneen yanked again. The seesaw battle kept up for eons while, from the sidelines, I considered hurling myself right through that stubborn pane.

When the window was finally open a foot they stepped back, satisfied. My mother held out her hand to my roommate. "Well that was certainly—" was all she managed before the window began to descend and the two of them, synchronized, leapt forward to grab its base. No one moved for a long few seconds. Then Mom said, "For God's sake, Meriel-Claire, hand us something to hold this up!"

I had nothing—nothing but shut-tight luggage and an ineffectual bag of towels—so I just hovered, empty-handed, trying to think. Then Daneen executed a graceful corkscrew, twisting and bending to reach a thick textbook on the floor beside her desk without losing her grip on the window.

They stood back again to admire their achievement and for the first time I caught sight, obliquely, of Daneen's beguiling smile. "Thanks for your help with that, Mrs. Claire."

"Elgin, Mrs. Elgin," my mother offered, leaving me to explain about the hyphen I lugged around. Then, after just enough of a pause to make it obvious she'd thought about it, Mom added, "But call me Doris."

I dug deep and found my voice, reminded Doris about the meter, that we'd only had one quarter, that she'd better be going. She kissed me goodbye and there wasn't much I could do about that.

3.

I WAS STARING down into the folds of familiar clothing in my suitcase when Daneen said, "I think we need a few rules. You know, to avoid conflict in such a small space."

She'd been writing on a piece of loose-leaf paper ever since my mother had left. I thought maybe she'd been writing down rules, but she looked straight at me, not at the paper, when she said, "First, no dirty clothes or wet towels on the floor. We can put that shit in the closet."

I'd already discovered the closet, walk-in huge and more than half full of Daneen's things, though I couldn't really complain since I'd brought so little.

I lifted a neat stack of shirts from my suitcase while she laid down the second rule. "Neither party—" her exact words—"can take something of the other's without permission."

It surprised me, a rule so basic. Maybe if I'd asked right then about the terms of such an agreement, about just what, exactly, was off limits, Daneen would have revealed more. But I was only eighteen and my world was still so absolute. I had no understanding of the shifty nature of ownership, so I just nodded dumbly and went back to sorting through my meagre belongings.

Daneen lit another cigarette and I thought the rule-setting was done, but she had one more pronouncement. "If one of us is having sex in the room, she has to tie *that*"—she pointed with the lit end of her cigarette to a cherry-red bandana—"to the doorknob outside, so the other person knows not to come in."

I considered that bandana, wound around the inside of the doorknob.

"What's the other person supposed to do, the one stuck outside?" Maybe it was the way the smoke was starting to burn my throat that made me sound so hostile.

Daneen considered my question like she actually believed it could be her on the other side of that door. Finally, she said, "There's a lounge at the end of the hall to hang out in. But you're right, we need a time limit." Her head tipped backwards, her eyes scanning the ceiling as if she was reading a text only she could see. "Let's say three hours."

Three hours sounded like a very long time, but I didn't exactly have personal experience to draw on so I shut my empty suitcase and I went down the hall to find the bathroom.

4.

DANEEN WAS PEERING into the full-length mirror she'd hung on the closet door. She held a skinny gold belt to the waist of her all-black outfit, let it drop, then brought it back up again. She'd been doing that for a while, for long enough that the repetition had pulled me out of *The Great Gatsby*, which I had to finish for class on Monday.

It was a rare occasion, both of us in the room at the same time. Most days I left for class before Daneen was awake, creeping into the hallway to zip up my jeans. Late at night, I kept my eyes shut when she clattered in. The rest of the time, we brushed past each other, Daneen in high-heeled boots and big hair heading out for the evening as I came in from the library, where I went to escape the shouting and squealing and slamming that went on in the dorm.

Without meeting my eye in the mirror, Daneen asked if she should wear the belt. Her question, the fact that it seemed to be directed at me, took me by surprise. When I didn't respond, she turned, the belt still riding her hips. "I mean, is this something a person *here* would wear?"

Daneen was from Toronto. She'd gone to private schools all her life and sometimes she acted like she'd landed in a completely foreign culture. And maybe she had—I didn't know. I'd never been to Toronto.

I wracked my brain for local belt customs but came up blank. "People wear stuff like that here," I offered, adding, "I think" as a kind of insurance against being held accountable. When she fastened the belt, I felt triumphant, like I'd solved world hunger with just a bit of sophisticated knowledge. The success made me bold. "So why did you come here anyway, Daneen?"

She left the mirror and sat down on the edge of her bed. "You mean to Nowhere Prairieville?" Her green-gold eyes, the kind of eyes that can never settle on being one colour, looked me over before turning to the invisible text on the ceiling. "I guess I wanted to get away from big city constraints, to meet people with real values." It sounded like she'd read this answer off before. "Small town people are so much more genuine, you know, so much less concerned with status and showing off. Besides, I knew the air here would be more salubrious."

She reached for her boots while I tried to think of a single thing to say that wouldn't make me sound like a small town idiot. I knew what salubrious meant—we'd done vocabulary building in public school, too—but it wasn't the kind of word I'd ever heard anyone just drop into a conversation. Anyway, this wasn't a small town and I knew she was dead wrong about those. I'd lived in one my whole life—a town with fewer than six thousand people—and as far as I could tell, every single one of them was obsessed with status and showing off.

Daneen drove her right foot into a tall black boot, extended her leg to draw the zipper shut, and repeated the manoeuvre with the left. She was checking the boots' effect in the mirror when someone pounded on our door. Daneen made no move to answer it. Instead, she turned back on to the mirror, head wrenched around to inspect the view from behind.

The second round of pounding was more intense. I put my book down and went to the door, hauling it open to find the spongy side of a fist heading for round three. The fist was attached to Kathy, a friend Daneen had made the instant she'd stepped onto campus, hours before I'd even made it out of the driveway in Calder. At the sight of me, there in my own room, Kathy reeled back so abruptly the stiff, frothed-up top of her hair jiggled.

"Hi," I said.

She looked past me. "Come on, D. Let's make like babies and head out."

Daneen hooked a hand through her purse strap, slipped past me without a glance and they were gone, the door shut, their laughter getting louder as it moved away.

I picked up my book again but I didn't open it. I just stared at the cover, thinking how people take their same selves along wherever they go—how no one ever emerges a totally different creature from their chrysalis.

5.

I STEPPED OUT of the shower and all my things had vanished. My clothes, my towel, my keys—all gone from the bench where I'd left them. I backed up into the stall and drew the industrial-strength shower curtain across me like a stiff toga.

"Hey—hello?" My voice was hollowed by the hard, empty room. I held my breath, listening for someone else's, wishing I hadn't adopted the habit of showering in the afternoon when there was no one else around.

Behind me, the shower nozzle dripped.

Finally, arms crossed tight against my breasts to make me less obviously naked, I searched inside the other stalls, then scurried back to my still-wet one. After a long pause, it dawned on me that this might be some kind of hallway hazing, a dormitory rite of passage. Maybe it happened to everybody. Maybe they'd explained the whole thing at the welcome meeting I'd missed.

I stuck my head into the corridor like a turtle poking out from its shell. At the far end of the hall, a long, naked walk away, all my stuff was rolled into a tidy bundle. By then, a chill had puckered not just my nipples but every square inch of my skin.

Ours was a co-ed dorm, risqué for the 1980s, and while my floor was all girls, the ones above and below were all guys, like the planners had designed a gendered layer cake for maximum titillation.

I listened to be sure no one was nearby, then I made the dash.

A lucky person would have made it easily from the bathroom to her stuff and into her room before anyone saw her. I wasn't lucky. I was squat down, digging around in search of my key when three older guys from upstairs came around the corner. I tried furtively to cover my naked gooseflesh with the wad of a Kmart towel. Two of them allowed a one-syllable laugh; the third just looked away. Not one of them looked back in my direction once they'd passed.

I never mentioned the incident to Daneen, but when it happened to her, she told me all about it. She acted like it was just the chance she'd been waiting for to stroll down the hallway naked. I couldn't tell if someone had warned her or if she was just ready for anything, like that time in the dining hall when someone had asked what classes we were taking. I'd listed mine off—Intro this, Intro that—but Daneen had just said, "Oh you know, the Arts sampler platter." Offhand, dead on, and everyone around the table smiled in the way that pretends to be applause but actually means, "Damn, I wish I'd thought of that."

A handful of weeks into our association, I already regarded Daneen as a deep pool, one that reflected back all the things I wasn't. Where she was lithe, I was lumpy; where I felt awkward and alienated, she was always so sure of herself.

6.

GORD AGREED TO pick me up and drive me home for Thanksgiving dinner. I waited for him on the sidewalk in front of my residence, a breeze swirling the leaves in mini-cyclones. It was cold enough for gloves. I'd left mine inside but I wasn't sure Gord would stick around if I was out of sight when he drove up, so I just shoved my hands deep into my pockets. My knuckles collided with the quarters I'd brought to help pay for gas, which Dad had pointed out was only fair.

When I gathered the coins into my cold fist, the ridges

pressed into my palm and triggered a memory—coins glinting against the blue tile bottom of a fountain. I didn't know where it was, that fountain, what city we'd been in or why, but I knew I'd been about six years old. Since Gord was older, he might remember. I could ask him when he finally showed up.

A gust of wind shut my eyes and that fountain rose in my memory—not its bottom now but the blue-green body of a mermaid arcing over its basin, her carved hair a cascade, her tail curled. Water came from somewhere between her wrists and tumbled out from her cupped hands and her expression, up close, said she had a wonderful secret.

We were dressed up: Gord wearing a blue blazer, Mom slicked with pale pink lipstick and me in a dress that felt slippery and not warm enough. I'd never even seen a real wishing well before. My mother had told us each to take out a penny. Gord stuffed his hand into his pants pocket while I dug through the little purse slung across my shoulder. The purse was full of coins, probably the sum total of my saved allowance, and a hum of anticipation coursed through them. I had some special purchase in mind, I guess—a coveted toy, maybe, or a mound of candy.

"Try to get it right in her hands, Gord. That's extra lucky."

I was still searching through coins when I heard my mother say that—heard *extra lucky*, the dazzle in her voice. I looked up just as Gord let go. His wish arced perfectly and landed in those cupped hands. The mermaid smiled like an angel and my fingers emerged holding a single round penny.

I stood as close to the same spot as Gord's unmoving self would allow me and imitated his toss. My penny canted, dropping with a splash into the lower basin, joining the other unlucky ones on that blue bottom.

"I want to try again," I said, my fingers already rooting around. My mother didn't object as I pulled out a dime and flung it, harder this time, toward those hands. The dime barely made a sound as it disappeared into the pool below.

I went for another coin but Mom said, "That's enough."

"I forgot to wish," I protested.

Mom held up her hands in surrender, the way she did when she was letting us make our own choices. Gord whirled and walked away from both of us then, like he'd suddenly become aware of some terrible danger we couldn't see.

I found a shinier penny and its gleam felt lucky enough, but the result was just the same. No luck. I looked down at my fancy shoes, the white patent leather smearing through my tears. When my mother put her hand on my arm, I shook her off. "No!" People nearby looked over. Mom stepped away again.

I threw a quarter next, hoping its heft would carry it higher, and then another and another—all in rapid and failed succession—and then I stepped in closer for the nickel. Gord had come back and he was right behind me. He caught my wrist. "Hold it like this," he said, his fingers shaping mine, "and open up. Let go earlier."

He demonstrated the motion for me. Even at that age, I understood his expertise. I'd been made to sit through enough Little League games to know that Gord was the only boy his age who could consistently deliver a ball to its destination. Of course he and Dad had been playing catch in the yard ever since I could remember, and the slap of a ball against leather was the sound of summer to me.

I followed Gord's advice, positioned my fingers and mimicked his motion, even let him guide my wrist, but none of it mattered. The next coin and the one after that missed their mark, though at least they got closer. Frustrated, I flung a quarter hard at that mermaid's smiling face.

It bounced off her eye.

"Enough! Stop it!" Mom was yelling now, though it hardly mattered. I was down to my last coin, fished from the dark corner of my little purse and tucked in my palm. I might as well have traded in my party dress for the lead apron they put on me in the dentist's chair as I moved to retrieve my coins, my bad fortune flashing up at me from the fountain's bottom. A fine mist cooled my cheeks as I plunged one arm into the water, but my fingers hadn't reached the money before my mother grabbed me by the other arm and yanked, hard.

"What do you think you're doing?"

"I'm getting my money. I know how many are mine," I told her. "I counted."

"You can't have them back." Mom pulled me out of reach of the fountain, just far enough away to make her point. "You threw them away."

Hot tears blinded me even to the mermaid's equanimous smile. In my tight little fist, the grooved edges of my last dime bit into my palm, leaving a mark.

7.

BY THE TIME Gord pulled up, twenty-five minutes late, my fingers were white from the cold and I'd decided not to mention the mermaid fountain at all. Instead I handed him that fistful of quarters for gas and I told him every single thing that had happened to me in the past two months—more words, probably, than I'd said to Gord in two years. I bombarded him like he was the first human being I'd seen after years of wandering alone in the woods. I even told him about the shower incident, only I renamed it the Disappearing Clothes Caper like it was a Nancy Drew mystery and I was its damp and unlikely heroine. Gord laughed so hard I thought we might crash into a pole.

When I finally got around to asking what was new with him, he blew out a stream that sounded like a long F punching the air. "Nothing. I don't do anything, remember?" He cranked the stereo and sped up on the overpass. "Here we come, home sweet home."

Gord thought even less of our hometown than I did, if that

was possible. Calder, back then, was a mean little strip mall of a town, separated from Highway No. 1 by a railroad track and cupped in a wide turn of the snaky Auberge River. When I was little, Gord told me it wasn't even a real town, that Calder had been built just in case someone driving from the city to their cottage had a Big Mac attack and needed a McDonald's, fast. Calder had a McDonald's, and a Burger King and a Dairy Queen too, and they all kept a respectful distance from the Prairie Peacock Chinese Restaurant and Lounge where people dined on special occasions.

I'd believed Gord, too—believed that Calder had just popped up, suddenly and recently, to be somebody else's burger stop. I was gullible like that, where he was concerned. But then the Calder centennial celebrations rolled around and Mom, who organized the displays and practically everything else, covered our dining-room table in grainy images of Main Street when it was still a dirt path. There was even a picture of the family dealership on its first corner—a picture so old my grandfather was a young man leaning on a '47 Chevy and there was no fast food in sight.

And then I understood that Gord wasn't entirely trustworthy—and worse, that Calder was mutable.

8.

THE HOLIDAY SERVING dishes were still making their first go-round when Dad asked if I was learning anything interesting. I was learning fascinating things, and it was thrilling how all the pieces fit together, how political systems mirrored what I'd just learned about in anthropology, how the threads of early psychology wove their way through twentieth-century literature. But I couldn't explain any of that, not sitting at our dining-room table in Calder staring at a bowl of mashed potatoes. Instead, I just said, "It's as interesting as the Arts sampler platter can be, I guess. But it's a lot of work."

Dad laughed, then turned solemn. "I'm glad you find it interesting. That's what makes hard work worthwhile." He reached for the salt shaker. "How about you, son—anything interesting on your horizon?"

Gord was on a seasonal layoff, same as last year, and Dad knew his son planned to collect unemployment insurance until his lawn-care job resumed in the spring. It was the same every year and it was the reason Gord had moved to the city— to escape Dad's daily disapproval.

Gord put the turkey platter down with a thunk. I held my breath, waiting to see if he'd swing his arm and launch half the holiday feast across the room. He'd done that sort of thing when he still lived at home. Once, he'd sent a bowl of peas off into the sunken living room, each small green sphere taking its own path. For weeks afterward, we discovered them under chairs or poised delicately on Dieffenbachia leaves.

But Gord just looked at Dad and said, "Pass the gravy, please."

Mom shot Dad a castrating look and started in on me: What about my social life? Had I made any lifelong friends?

I looked down at my plate, at the food so carefully arranged on it. In the residence cafeteria, the food was soggy and indistinct, the flavours tangled up like everything had been cooked in one greasy pot. Still, since the meal card came with the room, I never went anywhere else to eat. I'd come to Calder so hungry for real food, but with Mom interrogating me—Was I taking advantage of all the activities? Were there, um, any boys showing an interest?— I forgot to savour anything. I just shovelled food in on automatic pilot until Mom said, "I see you've still got your big appetite, Meriel-Claire."

I was afraid she'd go dig out pictures of her at my age, like she had the last time my big appetite had become an issue. "I'm a middle-aged mother now," she'd said that time, "but this is how a young woman is supposed to look, Meriel-Claire."

By the time I laid my fork across my empty pumpkin pie

plate, my insides felt bruised. It was such a relief to be back in the car with Gord, to sit next to someone who was just as happy not to say anything, who wasn't weighing my worth and finding me both too much and too little. As we neared University Crescent, I wanted to say, "Don't turn, just keep driving. I'll pay for the gas."

Gord would have, too—he'd have just kept driving. We didn't talk much, but sometimes we got each other.

9.

THREE STEPS INTO the building, I heard it: Eddie Money, one of Daneen's favourites, wailing down the hall. I must have seen the red bandana tied to the knob but it didn't register until I reached the door, key clasped in my hand, turkey and gravy congealing in my belly. For a while I stood dumbstruck, considering, then I trudged to the lounge and lay down on the couch and watched the second hand on the clock crawl forward. Eventually I turned on the TV. There was nothing but football and religion, so I clicked it off again.

After half an hour, it occurred to me that maybe Daneen and her—well, whoever—had been behind that locked door for a long time. Maybe she was tying that red bandana to the doorknob while I was still spooning carrot wheels onto my plate. Maybe their time was up.

I went back down the hallway. Someone in the room had stopped whatever they were doing long enough to change the cassette tape. Even with my ear right against the door, I couldn't hear anything over Elton John and in the short silence between songs, there was just a faint rustling that might have been anything.

"Daneen?" My voice barely above a whisper; the only response the next song kicking in.

I skulked back to the lounge and turned on the TV again, opting for a sermon. A corpulent man in a silvery suit glared out at me. "The Lord," he told me, "does not want you to have a hard heart against your poor brother." I thought about Gord, about how he'd had time to drive a million miles since dropping me off. I imagined him as a small speck moving away from me in the night sky, blinking faintly.

A sharp bark brought me back to earth. "No!" The TV preacher had thrown his arms out on either side, meaty fingers spread like he was holding two watermelons. "No, he does not. The Lord wants you to freely open your hand!" Zeal emerged in beads of sweat that trickled from his hairline and ran down his round cheeks.

Worried that someone in the dorm might overhear, I turned the volume down low. I guess I dozed off then because when I resurfaced and edged the volume up, sweat had soaked through the reverend's silver suit and he'd moved on to asking viewers to open their wallets. A toll-free number blinked green on the bottom of the screen. It was almost ten o'clock. My neck was kinked from being bent against the arm of the couch and I didn't care about the time limit anymore.

When I rapped on the door, Daneen opened up right away. She was fully clothed, absolutely alone and a thick book was turned face down on her pillow.

I released one finger from my fist and pointed to the bandana.

"Oh—sorry. I just wanted to be left alone. I didn't expect you back so soon." She plopped down on her bed and picked up her book.

It was a hardcover novel, not even from the library. Daneen bought a lot of books and whenever she had nowhere better to be, she spent her time reading, though never from a textbook. I was the opposite, reading only what was on a course list. I'd long before lost the habit of reading for pleasure. It wasn't worth suffering through my mother's exasperation over my choices, wasn't worth worrying she'd find the science fiction paperbacks buried in my bottom dresser drawer.

Daneen held her book in her lap but didn't start reading

again. Instead, she placed a finger on the page and asked me how dinner was.

"The usual—" I told her, struggling to remove a boot that had fused to my foot. "Turkey and disappointed parents." I lobbed the boot toward the closet.

"Really? What did you do?" She laid the book aside.

"I didn't *do* anything." I threw my second boot more emphatically. "It was just a typical family dinner—you know, parents asking questions, hoping you'll finally turn out how they want you to be."

Daneen looked me over the way she did an outfit she couldn't quite put together. "Interesting." From the edge of her bed, she leaned forward like we might actually be starting a conversation. "I'd love to have a family that sat down for family dinners. I don't think the three of us ever had one of those, not without company."

I leaned forward, too. "Never? Not even on holidays?"

She reached for her cigarettes. "Dad worked most of the time, and my mother had hobbies. She was out a lot. They really only showed up for the highlights, so they could applaud."

"At least they were proud of you."

"They were just proud of themselves for having me. I'm like one of my mother's paintings—she admires them for a few days and then she gives them away like she can't stand to look at them anymore." Daneen scanned the ceiling. "To Daddy, I'm like one of his expensive cars. He pays a lot of money to keep me shiny and stored away, but occasionally he wants to show me off."

I thought about my father and the cars at the dealership. Dad didn't even seem to like cars—he just liked to sell them off. He said things like, "I'll be late tonight, Doris. We're overstocked so I've got a lot of tin heaps to move."

Daneen pointed the fiery end of a cigarette at me. "You should have seen their faces when I told them I was enrolling here, instead of going someplace they could brag about."

I watched the smoke spread from her mouth and considered her comment. Just planning to go to university had been such a big deal at Calder Collegiate. It had never occurred to me that there were universities you didn't brag about.

"Why'd they let you come here, then?"

Daneen bundled up her face and turned her head away. "They didn't let me. I didn't give them a choice—" The phone rang and she snatched it up before that first ring even finished.

After Daneen had gone, I went down the hall to brush my teeth. In the harsh bathroom light, my face looked as muddled as a bowl of mashed potatoes. I stared in the mirror and I thought it was about time I took charge of my life, did what I wanted. Whatever that was.

10.

GORD ONCE TOLD me that anything worth doing should at least be easy. The only thing easy for me was math. When my grade-four teacher caught me making up complicated long-division problems just for something to do, I was moved to Independent Acceleration. Every morning I took my math book down to a small room where the only other person was a boy from grade three. I never even spoke to him, but my best friends, Chelsea and Lisa, started calling him my Special Ed boyfriend. Then I found out they were having sleepovers without me.

I begged my parents to tell the school I wanted to stop going to that special classroom. Dad refused, even after Mom said he didn't understand how bad it was for a girl to be labelled smart. But Mom didn't argue hard, didn't use her low and absolute voice like I hoped she would. Even when I told her about the sleepovers, she just shrugged and said a threesome of girls was impossible, that someone always got left out.

Finally, I started making math mistakes, just enough to get moved back into the regular class. The stain of smart gradually faded and things with Chelsea and Lisa went back to normal. After that, we huddled in our threesome for years. Maybe we didn't have a choice. No other group wanted us—not the popular kids or the jocks or even the burnouts. Certainly not the farm boys and the 4-H girls, who stuck together and talked about their horses and could beat the crap out of anyone, and who always looked sunburnt, even in the winter.

For a few years in junior high, Lisa and Chelsea got into ridiculous fights and it fell to me to make the peace. But that turned out to be easy, too, once I realized that every fight was really just about hurt feelings, that fixing it was as simple as talking to one and reporting a nicer version of what she'd said back to the other. Dad overheard my half on the phone one night—Lisa, then Chelsea, then Lisa again—and he told my mother, "That girl's going to be a diplomat."

My career aptitude test in high school, however, disagreed. It pointed straight to engineer. I didn't know anything about engineering, but the guidance counsellor said it was a tough choice for a woman, that I'd be a target for sexism, that I'd really stand out. Since I'd learned early that the spotlight wasn't for me, I figured I'd have to find my calling somewhere else.

I wanted, like I suppose maybe everyone does when they're young, to do something important. Something worthwhile. I was still mulling over my options when Chelsea and Lisa shifted together, in the last year of high school, from the academic stream to trades. For girls at our school, trades meant cosmetology. They found new friends, then they got boyfriends from the welding program, and they talked a lot about hair dye and perms and made snickering jokes about blow jobs and I couldn't join in. I couldn't even go for a cheap haircut, since that would mean choosing between them.

With no friends to distract me, my grades shot sky-high. I had no idea what I was shooting for, but I won a scholarship that covered my first year's tuition. I was ecstatic. My parents expected me to pay half of my university costs, and that award counted on my side of the ledger.

11.

DANEEN WAS STILL sleeping so I turned the heavy pages of *Western Civilization* as quietly as I could. Caesar was crossing the Rubicon and I must have flipped a page too energetically because she suddenly rolled over and fixed her bloodshot eyes on me. "I have to talk to you."

She'd already made it clear she thought I was too studious. She said grades only mattered if you wanted to go to med school, and she could tell that wasn't for me.

But it wasn't my intense studying that Daneen wanted to discuss that morning—it was her friend Kathy. "She is so caustic. And constantly telling me what to do." Daneen's hair fanned out like flames across her white pillowcase. "Why would a friend act like that?"

I thought it must be a rhetorical question, but she repeated, "Why?" and peered at me so expectantly that I offered the obvious: "She's jealous of you."

Anyone could see it. Daneen was so much more interesting than the rest of us. Even at that age, she knew how to pull people into the warm pool of her voice. But halfway through any story she tried to tell in the dining hall, Kathy would jump up and interject something asinine—something like, "Let's live, not re-live!" Then she'd hurry off, jostling the table on her way like some gangster movie thug.

"Jealous?" Daneen sat up in bed. "I guess so. You know, you're absolutely right. She's certainly not good at being a friend." She twisted the word *friend* so it sounded like a photograph being torn, and then she stared at me. "You have such x-ray insight. You're the only person in this place I can trust."

She laid back down and rolled to face the wall, leaving me

astonished and kind of fluttery, like I'd just been named the most valuable player. Like I'd been crowned Miss Congeniality.

12.

WHEN THE SCHOLARSHIP letter had come, my father had announced that we needed to talk. He made a big production of taking me for a drive instead of just talking to me in the kitchen, like what he needed to tell me was so important, so expansive, it required the open road, scrub oaks and furrowed fields standing witness.

"You have an opportunity here that should not be squandered," he began. By this time he'd left the highway. "A university degree is like scaffolding. If you build it right, it will be a secure place from which to create your masterpiece, which of course is your career and your life."

I wondered where Dad got this stuff. He didn't have a degree, he just had a car dealership. But maybe if you inherited your career—if your path was emblazoned on a sign that said *& Son* from the day you were born—then scaffolding was intriguing since you never have to build any yourself.

We were five miles down a gravel road when I admitted that I didn't have a clue what to study, what direction to head. Dad slowed and executed a perfect three-point turn before he spoke again.

"If you're lucky, Meriel-Claire, you'll find yourself on the right path, and no one and nothing will pull you off it."

13.

I FINISHED EXAMS on a piercingly bright December day, the kind of day that announces winter is about to get serious. In that light, it was impossible to ignore the condition of our room. Garbage spilled over out of the can; an amalgam of dust and crumbs and soot coated every surface. While Daneen wrote her last exam, I hauled garbage to the big bin out back, then swung by the bathroom for a sheaf of paper towels and the only cleaner I could find—a little shampoo mixed with water and shaken to a froth. I wiped down every surface, hoping the sharp green-apple scent could mask the stale smoke. The paper towels turned caramel when I washed the window, black when I turned next to Daneen's desk.

I knew I shouldn't be doing it, invading her space, but it was like I couldn't help myself. Or else I didn't want to. I wanted to make a point, take a stand, and I practiced how that stand would sound when she confronted me, how I'd calmly tell her I was sorry in a way that's not really an apology at all because it's glued so tight to a *but*—but I couldn't take it anymore. But it was disgusting.

Her desk was a morass of papers with a term essay on top. Along the margin, the question *Reference?* repeated in scalding red ink. I flipped to see the grade at the end. *Elegantly expressed but I'd like to see more substance behind your arguments. Always cite your references. B+.* An almost A for an unsubstantiated argument, a paper I knew Daneen hadn't spent more than two hours writing.

A small scrap of paper fell out from between the essay's pages. On it, Daneen had scrawled *turkey and disappointed parents.* I tucked it back in fast, pushed all the papers into a neat pile, and grabbed her ashtray.

Daneen kept a giant coffee can she'd taken from the cafeteria under her desk and that's where she dumped her cigarette butts, but she never wiped out the ashtray. The bowl was caked with a thick rug of soot that came off in chunks in the bathroom sink, an acrid stench rising in the steam. I had to stand as far back as my arms would allow while I soaked and soaped and scrubbed until even the gold stains in the crevices of the cut glass were gone and the only things that still reeked were my fingers.

I thought about how I might use the word *revolting*, how I could interject something about *my* rights. I tried to imagine her response—"Meriel, I'm sorry. But..."

And that was another thing. Daneen called me Meriel, never Meriel-Claire, like she didn't have time for the final beat. Like she'd deemed it superfluous. I wasn't crazy about the four syllable weight of my name and the anchor of that hyphen, but when you start kindergarten in a small town with a particular name, that's the name you're stuck with. Same kids, all the way through, and their parents have known you since before you were born. You can't suddenly abbreviate or swap or unhyphenate. If you're lucky, someone might slap you with a not-terrible nickname, something closer to your actual self, and you can ride that nickname right through graduation. But that didn't happen to me. Chelsea and Lisa tried—they called me MC for a while after they heard Gord say it, but there weren't enough people listening, I guess, for it to catch on.

When Daneen came in, I was organizing my class notes. I didn't look over, didn't acknowledge her, hoped she wouldn't pick up on how agitated I was. Instead, she picked up her ashtray.

"Hey, this looks great!" She held it up to the window and peered through the bottom, turning it like she was surprised to find cut glass could sparkle. "We should do this more often." She set the ashtray down and cleared her desk by pushing the papers I'd stacked into the empty garbage can. Then she unzipped her makeup bag and dumped its contents. "Hey, are you sticking around tonight or going home? There's an end of term bash."

I wasn't going home until Sunday—my mother's edict, "a chance to enjoy your friends"—but I certainly wasn't going to any party. I told her I just wanted to stay in and rest and then, because that sounded ridiculous, I invented a headache.

She didn't reply, just started in on her eyeshadow. I'd seen her do it plenty of times: dab dab with a little wand, then whisk and blend with the pad of her ring finger until the colour was almost gone. Her eyes moved from the mirror to me. "Do you ever wear makeup?"

"Not unless I have something to cover up."

She uncapped an eyeliner but paused, purple tip hovering, and looked me over. "You know, you could really bring out your eyes. And some contouring would do wonders."

Criticism couched as concern—so familiar to me. I told her exactly what I always told Mom. "I just think it's phony."

Daneen didn't respond right away. She was too busy holding her mouth open, lips rolled over her teeth while she lined inside her lower lid. Finally she put the mirror down and turned back to me. The purple liner did its magic trick, making her eyes emerald. "I just think it's smart to use all the tools at one's disposal."

I wondered if it was deliberate, the way she shifted to a neutral pronoun to deflect malice. I tried it out. "With or without it, one is still the same underneath."

She picked up her mirror. "Whoever sees your underneath? People only see how you let them perceive you." And after a coat of mascara, "Even you only see how you perceive yourself."

I wondered again if she spent a lot of time thinking up her lines, or if they just popped into her head when she needed them to.

"Besides, Meriel, everybody else uses makeup to make an impression. If you don't, you're giving them the advantage."

I didn't have an argument for that.

"We'll have to get you some. We can go shopping tomorrow."

14.

I HAD THE same bare face I'd always had, but sitting at the cosmetics counter in Eaton's department store waiting for the first round of my reinvention to begin, I felt conspicuously flawed. Daneen had pointed me to a stool—"Start there and move down the line"—and gone off to shop. While the cosmetologist assembled her brushes and bottles, I watched a clump of traffic-darkened slush slide off the side of my boot and plop onto the shiny floor. Then I closed my eyes and succumbed to the rub rub, pat pat of a stranger's hands, to the possibility of metamorphosis. I was trying to pay close attention to what was being done to my face, to the techniques I'd need to know.

When told to, I opened my eyes to the mirror. A wave of nausea replaced my excitement. I looked like my grandmother had when she'd kept up with the rouge long after her eyesight failed, smearing gobs of it across her cheeks. I said thank you too ardently.

At the next counter, my face was cleansed and exfoliated and toned until it seemed like this cosmetologist couldn't stand to do anything but erase the last one's work. When that was finished, the rosy cheeks were all mine but just as much a trick, and just as temporary.

Daneen returned while I was sitting at the third counter, drifting on the gentle touch of a makeup sponge. "She could use a little contour under her cheekbones," she said. And then, "This shadow will work best with her eyes."

It embarrassed me, Daneen talking like that to someone so much older, someone who wore a lab coat and did makeup for a living. I started to feel like a prop in Daneen's show. But when the woman spun me around to the mirror, my irritation fell away. I looked amazing—my eyes bigger, my skin flawless, my face defined. I looked like somebody else.

Daneen put a hand on my neck and smiled at me the way the 4-H girls back home smiled at their horses. "We'll take everything you put on her."

I tore my gaze from my reflection. "Daneen, I can't afford all that—I still have to buy Christmas presents!"

She waved off my protest. "It's my present to you."

It was the first time she did that, subsidized me, and maybe if I'd said no right then, I'd never have become so beholden. So mired. Maybe my acquiescence that afternoon was the first mistake, the error that multiplied over the years. Or maybe that's the wrong way to think about it. Maybe everything is about accumulation, about how things add up and liability compounds, day after day, year after year.

I let Daneen pay for those cosmetics. Two desperate hours later, when I could find nothing in the entire department store that felt like the right reciprocal gift, I offered to buy her dinner downtown.

The restaurant was dimly lit with carved wooden chairs, heavy and serious. We sat at a small table along the back wall. Daneen ordered a carafe of wine and told me how much she dreaded going home for Christmas, dreaded having to spend time with her frosty parents and dreaded, even more, the inevitable obstacle course of old boyfriends. I nodded like I had the same problem.

Every so often, she detoured from talking about life back home to tell me again how amazing—how different—I looked. But while I was figuring out how much to leave for the tip, she took a harder look and saw something else. "You're like a sponge, Meriel," she said, "absorbing everything but holding your own shape exactly."

15.

ON NEW YEAR'S EVE, a flu climbed onto my chest like a big dog with hot breath. For days, it kept me pinned to my mattress. Even after I was up again, feverless, my mother made me stay in Calder to regain my strength. I'd missed the first day of classes before Dad agreed to give me a lift to the university.

I felt fine until we were almost there, until I flipped down the visor and saw how drained I looked. A hot heaviness fell over me again, reminding me that Daneen was going to ask how I'd spent the past few weeks and I'd have to admit I'd split them watching *Another World* and practicing my makeup techniques.

"I'm so glad you're finally paying some attention to your appearance," my mother had said when she'd caught me at it. Five minutes later Dad had come in from outside, his shoulders slumped from shovelling snow. "You're trowelling that stuff on pretty thick, aren't you Meriel-Claire?"

The next day, Mom suggested a good haircut. After she'd left the room, Dad said, "You want to be careful you don't spend too much effort on things that have so little value."

I'd always known I couldn't please both my parents, at least not simultaneously. Normally I was inclined to Dad's way of thinking, but not this time. How could he possibly understand what was valuable for a woman?

As Dad pulled into the right lane to turn onto University Crescent, I took out my makeup bag. Dad glanced over, but I shot him a look that stopped him from opening his mouth. He didn't say a word after that, not until he said goodbye to me on the sidewalk in front of the residence.

Our room, when I stepped inside, was dark except for a narrow band of light that escaped the closet and bisected the floor. I would have flicked on the fluorescents if a swallowing sound hadn't pulled my gaze to the wall beneath the window. I could barely make her out—Daneen on the floor between the beds, knees bent, beer in hand. She didn't glance up, didn't see my great haircut. She just stared at a spot near her toe and muttered, "I thought you weren't coming back."

When I explained about the flu, complained about my mother making me stay home to recuperate, Daneen fixed me with a hard stare. "Just be glad you have a mother who acts like one." Her beer bottle collided with the edge of my bed and bounced back to hit her leg, leaving a trail of foam that disappeared fast in the dim light.

Daneen made no move to wipe up her spill. Someone more socially skilled might have known what to say, but I just perched on the edge of the bed and waited. Finally: "My mother packed up and left last week. Apparently she's been planning it for years, waiting for me to grow up. Now I don't have a mother."

16.

"LOVE IS ONLY measurable, and therefore only exists, in tangible behaviour." This was my psychology professor, eight thirty on a February morning.

I thought I must have missed something. I'd skipped the last class. Mornings were hard when I stayed up half the night with Daneen after one of her parents' phone calls—calls that sounded nothing like caring to my eavesdropping ears.

Eavesdropping was what Daneen wanted me to do—to lean into the phone and catch every nuance so we could analyze the conversation. For hours afterward, we held flakes of her parents' personalities up to the light, looking for signs of disease. We poured over past transgressions and then we delivered our best amateur diagnoses. My only experience came from talk shows and magazines, from Intro Psych, but Daneen didn't care. It was as if she was untangling a giant ball of yarn and she just needed me to hold parts of it, to keep her from getting lost in the threads.

I didn't know it at the time—maybe she did—but we were both rehearsing for our future careers.

The professor repeated his pronouncement: "Love is only measurable, and therefore only exists, in tangible behaviour." There was a long minute of silence during which we all, every student in that lecture hall, wrote down what he'd said.

Then he rephrased it. "Love only exists in overt behaviours. Actions, not feelings."

I got it then. He was trying to start an argument. He wanted to trot out some research to shatter our Disney-planted, pop-music enhanced ideas about love. He stood there expectantly, but no one raised their hand in defense of feelings. No one took love's spiritual side. I certainly didn't feel qualified—I'd never been in love. Besides, I had a crush on the professor so I couldn't make a sound in his class.

Finally he moved back behind the lectern, picked up his

notes and launched into his lecture, which turned out to be about Harry Harlow and baby monkeys who bonded with cloth-covered wire when robbed of their mothers, and not about love at all.

17.

GORD SPILLED A pool of beer around his glass when he poured from the full pitcher. He used the side of his hand to sweep the liquid off the table and said, "I saw Wendy on the weekend."

"Are you two back together?" I loved Wendy, loved how she'd made Gord better, shinier somehow, when they'd dated in high school. I still had a picture I'd taken of her on my dresser in Calder. In it, she's cross-legged on the floor, hands folded in her lap, head tipped to one side watching Gord. Adoring Gord.

"She was with some fucking campus football star. They showed up at a party at Saw's." Saw—Bill Sawyer—had been Gord's best friend since forever.

"Are you upset?" Obviously he was upset. It was Monday night and he'd called me for the first time ever to meet him for a drink.

"I guess. I mean I was at the time. I wish I'd left as soon as they came in but—" He slammed his mouth shut.

"What? What happened?"

"I kind of called her a slut." He was looking at the smear of beer on the table. "I kind of screamed it at her, actually."

The little sister part of me wanted to tell Gord it was okay, that he couldn't help himself. All the rest of me wanted to smack him. He'd acted crazy stupid when Wendy had broken up with him, too, punching walls and making desperate phone calls it was impossible not to hear, no matter where you were in the house. My mother kept saying, "What's wrong with that girl?" while Dad just shook his head like it was all beyond his comprehension.

"Felt pretty stupid after, especially since I stormed out without my jacket and my wallet. I had to go back for it yesterday."

"What did Saw say?"

"I doubt he even remembers. He was pretty loaded." Gord refilled our glasses. "Anyway, I called Wendy to apologize."

"And?"

"And she said it was okay. She told me to leave her alone." I couldn't tell in the murky bar-room light if there were actual tears forming in his eyes, but I looked away fast just in case.

The only other people in the bar were two old guys sitting alone at tables in opposing corners. They both had that slumped, watery-eyed look of regulars and it was easy to think they staked out those tables every night and never once walked across the floor and sat together.

"Anyway, sorry, MC. I don't know why I made you come all the way here so I could tell you this. I guess I just needed to see a friendly face." When Gord smiled with his lips shut, only one side of his mouth succeeded. He drained his glass. "So what about you—you got a boyfriend? Somebody I should be checking out, big brother like?"

"Of course not."

"Why not? Are they all idiots?" I could feel my face burning and I busied myself with rolling back the arm on my sweater where it had soaked up some beer.

"Seriously, MC, you look fantastic. Life away from Calder is way better for you." And after another minute: "So how is it—is it fun?"

I couldn't come up with an example of fun, exactly, but I told him about Daneen and her family, how screwed up they were, how I spent all my time helping her sort it out.

"Sounds like a big drag." Gord poured the rest of the beer into our glasses.

"It's actually really interesting." After I said it, I couldn't explain it, not even to myself, so I pretended I meant school in general.

"Hey, I've been thinking about going to school, too."

That was more surprising to me than his story about Wendy. Gord had always hated school. He couldn't sit still when he was young and as he got older, he just didn't care enough to try. He lost interest in everything so fast.

"What would you take?"

He shrugged. "What do you think I should do?"

"Gord, I don't even know what I'm gonna do."

He lifted up the empty pitcher, then set it down again. "You're gonna ace it like you always do. And then you'll do whatever Mom and Dad tell you to. Because you're the good kid."

I looked down at my watch. The numbers wouldn't register. "I have to go," I told him.

"You can't stay for another pitcher?"

I was on my feet, shrugging into my coat. I laid down a five dollar bill on the table—more than my share but I didn't want to wait for change. Gord threw another couple of bucks in and followed me outside.

It was brutally cold, no bus visible in the distance, so I asked Gord if he'd drive me back to school. He shook his head. "Got pulled over last week for drunk driving. Ninety day suspension. Sorry." I guess I gaped at him. "Jesus, MC, it happens. And don't run and tell Mom and Dad, okay?"

At the bus stop, I cupped heavy calfskin mittens over my aching ears and watched Gord cut a path through the snow in an empty field. At least he still moved like an athlete, loose hinged and agile as he clambered over a chain-link fence and into a parking lot, where I lost sight of him.

18.

"WHY ARE YOU telling me this?" Daneen had the phone wedged between a lifted shoulder and her jaw so she could refill her plastic cup from the box of wine she'd set up on the window ledge—four litres in a foil bag, a spigot for easy pouring.

Between refills, she paced the room with the phone on her hip so I couldn't position myself to hear what her mother was saying, but I could tell it was worse than usual.

"That's nice. Very nice." Daneen's voice dropped low. "I guess we're done for good then. Goodbye." She set down the phone as quietly as she'd spoken, but the receiver didn't settle right in its cradle. A dial tone filled the room. Even when the tone turned to the terrible squawking, the warning that says things are off-kilter, Daneen made no move to set it right. Her attention was fixed on the red and black painting above her bed.

Finally I crossed the room and hung the phone up myself, which seemed to remind her I was there.

"Can you believe she called to lecture *me* about being self-centred? She wants me to be grateful for the life she gave me—" She'd started digging through her desk drawer. "Apparently the doctor told her pregnancy could be dangerous. She said, if it had been a few years later, she probably would have had an abortion."

A small burst of laughter, the unfunny kind. "Now she wishes she had."

"She said that?"

"That's what she meant." Daneen came away from the desk with her scissors wide open, long blades flashing. "I guess I turned out to be a bad risk after all."

She reached over her bed with those yawning scissors and drove a blade through the stiff canvas.

"Jesus, Daneen, what are you doing?"

"She painted this when she was pregnant with me. Fitting, isn't it?" Her arm pulled straight down. The scissors were surprisingly effective.

"But do you really want to wreck it?" I hated that painting, but it was the only thing we had on our walls.

Arm in ascent, she paused. "Don't worry, it's not worth anything. It's just a bad copy." She drove a blade in again. "Hey, pour me some more wine." Slash.

I filled Daneen's big cup and a smaller one for me. Outside, fingers of loose snow were blowing free from the drifts along the side of the road. Behind me, thick red and black hanks of canvas were falling away.

19.

THAT SUMMER, MY father decided I was ready to take over the bookkeeping at Elgin & Son Chevrolet. His long-time bookkeeper was taking an extended holiday. I resisted until Dad told me extended holiday meant cancer, and then there was no way at all I could refuse.

"Bookkeeping is the same as balancing your chequebook," he insisted. I pointed out that I'd never had a chequebook. Dad swore he could teach me everything I needed to know in an hour. Then he spread the general ledger on his desk and spent about ten minutes explaining it. Bookkeeping, I was relieved to see, was all about straight lines and even columns.

I felt secure in the rise and fall of numbers until I spotted the column called Allowance for Doubtful Accounts. I pointed to it. "What's that mean?"

"That's just an estimate of what's owed but will never get paid."

I traced my way down the column, trying to find the logic of it. The sun blasted through streak-free windows and ricocheted off the glass-topped desk, making me squint. Finally, I admitted I didn't understand.

Dad flexed his fingers on his desk like they were doing calisthenics. "A certain number of accounts never get paid, so this is where we factor in the shortfall." He could see I still wasn't getting it. "Look, all you have to do is subtract this percentage and move on, Meriel-Claire." Dad closed the ledger. "It all gets reconciled eventually."

He told me to ask him if I had questions, but when I did,

Dad just glanced at the number next to my finger and told me it should all add up. If it didn't, he said, it was my job to fix it. And it turned out I could fix it—could locate the problem, though sometimes I wasted too much time trying to figure out what faulty logic or subtle misperception had fouled things up in the first place.

That first summer with the books, I had so much faith in evenhanded rationale. I still believed everything could be neatly reconciled in the end.

20.

WHILE I WENT to work every morning, Daneen slept in as late as she wanted—and she was sleeping in Gord's old room. She'd moved to Calder with me for the summer because her father had gone to Europe with his girlfriend, and there was no way Daneen would stay with her mother. When I'd mentioned it at Easter dinner—"Her parents are getting a divorce and they don't want her around"—Mom had insisted Daneen could live with us.

I liked having her there, but I worried about how my parents would behave. When I found out my mother had started making Daneen help out, washing windows and planting snapdragons along the back of the house, I apologized. I let Daneen know I'd tell my mother to stop treating her like a servant.

"What are you talking about?" Daneen looked genuinely surprised. "I'm having a great time—it's like being part of a real family."

At night, we prowled the streets of Calder so Daneen could smoke far from the disapproving eyes of Doris. We covered the main drag four or five times, looping around on side streets and popping out again on Main, heading in the opposite direction. Sometimes we stopped in at the McDonald's for a hot apple pie or to share a fistful of fries, the calories allowed, Daneen said, because we'd walked for so long.

And every night, a craving for something to happen sizzled and popped like hot grease under my skin. I wondered if expectation might be contagious, if I'd caught the desire for some greater fate from Daneen. My desires were never grand or clear—I just didn't want to be embarrassed about the lack of excitement my life had to offer. No gang of friends, no past lovers driving fast cars. The closest we came to excitement was at McDonald's one June night when we ran into a guy from my graduating class—someone who brightened up like I was a long-lost friend, who hugged me and said, "God it's great to see you!" with a surprising amount of enthusiasm.

Walking home, Daneen said, "I hope you don't feel like you can't hang out with your old friends. I don't even have to come along if you don't want me to."

The infinite number of possible responses stayed just out of my reach. To stall, I asked for a drag of her cigarette. I'd been trying to learn to smoke since Daneen had mentioned that smokers were always thinner. Though I could think of a hundred examples that proved it wasn't true, I tried anyway. So far, my attempts to inhale had all ended in sputtering coughs.

I held the smoke in my mouth until she looked away, then released it in one heavy clot. Finally I said, "I guess I sort of feel beyond them now."

A week later, the shock of Lisa's voice over the phone made my skin constrict. We hadn't spoken since high school. At first I thought maybe she wanted to get together, catch up, get back to being best friends and my mind scrambled around, trying to figure out how to fit Daneen into that equation.

But that wasn't why Lisa had called. She just wanted to sell me tickets to the wedding social in August that she was organizing as Chelsea's maid of honour. As soon as we'd worked past my surprise over Chelsea and Darrell Taggart getting married—the obvious pregnancy finally dawning on me—and we'd arranged for Lisa to put two tickets aside, she said, "Okay, well I guess I'll see you there."

The conversation was over in a minute. A month of apprehension yawned wide in front of me.

21.

I HAD ANOTHER question for Dad and it wasn't about the numbers this time. It was about his brother.

Uncle Stewart had left Calder at a young age, maybe younger than I was that summer. I'd only ever met him twice—the first time when I was eight, at my grandfather's funeral, and again when I was eleven and my grandmother died.

Stewart had stayed longer that second time because there was the estate to settle. I remember him poking through boxes in the basement of my grandparents' old brick house until he came across one labelled *Pieces of string too small to be of use.* He'd made a production of that, then surrendered to the futility of finding anything valuable that wasn't already accounted for. He packed just two small cartons, shook my father's hand and disappeared again. As far as I knew, the only time he'd been in touch was a few years later when he'd phoned to say he'd gotten married to an American woman he'd just met.

So what was he doing in the dealership's books?

Dad was standing at the window in his office, arms crossed, staring up at an empty sky. I had to clear my throat to get his attention.

He motioned me in. "Meriel-Claire, credit is going to ruin everyone faster than this weather." This was one of Dad's regular sermons, delivered more frequently that summer because it was so dry, the crops gasping, topsoil turning to fine powder that took to the air and settled on every surface in the dealership and at home. "Everybody putting their faith in the bank's money. It's all well and good until the bank turns off the tap."

Dad had a complicated relationship, equal parts affection

and obligation, with the customers who kept his dealership in business. He'd grown up with them or watched them grow up, knew them by name and wanted the best for them. He personally approved every deal and he had a reputation for driving a hard bargain, but I knew he felt let down if a buyer gave in too early, paid a higher price than what my father would have eventually accepted.

I didn't want to hear the full sermon on debt, so I cut him off. "Dad, why does Uncle Stewart get a salary?" Salaries came just before Sales Commissions in the Payables section.

Dad took his seat before he answered. "Stewart owns half the dealership. It's the deal we cut so I wouldn't have to borrow to buy him out after Grandpa died."

"But he doesn't actually do anything here. He's not involved, right?"

Dad smiled like he was half proud of me for seeing it and half annoyed I'd brought it up at all. "That's just family business, Meriel-Claire."

22.

WHEN WE WERE kids, we had a job board mounted to the wall beside the refrigerator. Poster-sized, divided into two sections: one for me and one for Gord. Every Saturday, Dad made a new chart at work with a black felt marker and a T-square, then brought it home and conferred with my mother about what tasks to put in the top row of blocks. When he had it ready, Gord and I wrote our names on the chart. It's one of my earliest memories, struggling my way through *Meriel-Claire* long after Gord had scribbled his four letters and gone.

Under our names, the days of the week were written, and next to those, a grid of little boxes waited to be filled with shiny stars—if we just did the things we were supposed to do: *Make bed; Put dishes in sink; Brush teeth*. Some tasks changed week to week, season to season, while others remained across the years.

I never got tired of it, that expectant pause before bedtime when my father got out the stars and said, "Let's see who earned their way today." Then the negotiations began: Did you really put your dishes in the sink? Is your homework done right? Are you sure? Finally, the doling out of the day's reward, the thick sweet taste of glue on the back of those stars.

They were worth something, those stars, beyond their simple glittering proof that we were worthy. They were the source of everything—of allowance and ice cream and even our new school clothes. On Saturday evenings, Dad would sit down with the chart from the week before and calculate our scores based on his special formula: the number of stars multiplied by our ages equalled our allotment of cash for the week.

After Dad paid us, he pinned up the blank chart for the next week.

There's a picture of me standing in front of the job board in grade two. I'm wearing my new school clothes, the purple plaid vest over the ruffled blouse I loved so much, and holding my arms like a model on *The Price is Right*. I'm grinning to beat hell, my front teeth missing, and every box on my half of the job board is filled with a star. Every single one.

There's no picture like that of Gord. Gord didn't care much about star stickers, and his not caring hardened over time until it was absolutely unyielding. The summer before I started grade five and Gord started grade seven, he was tanned the same colour as his baseball glove and his supposed-to list had dwindled to almost nothing: *Put uniform in hamper; Be home for dinner on time; Put bike in garage.* Still, he messed up about half the time and lost out on his stars. When I tried to help by taking his dishes to the sink, he'd just admit that I'd done it and lose out again.

Dad's lectures about responsibility and teamwork only seemed to make it worse. Gord would yell that he was sick of those stupid stars and sick of that stupid chart, and he'd storm off to his room before anyone could send him there.

That year, he didn't earn enough stars to get new school clothes. And he claimed not to care about that, either, but he'd grown a lot over the summer. Even Gord couldn't pull off pants that short. A few weeks into the school year, I guess Mom couldn't take it anymore. She went out and bought him new clothes, then stood in front of Dad with her hands on her round hips. "Our son cannot go out of this house anymore looking like that."

Dad didn't say anything.

"And no more charts. You're just making him miserable."

My mother wore the same expression years later, when she told my father that Gord was absolutely not going to wash cars all summer at Elgin & Son, that he had to be free to find his own path. After that, Gord worked on nearby farms and down at the lumberyard. He got hired, I think, because he was Don and Doris's son, and he probably got away with coming in late and screwing up for the same reason—or maybe just because every job along his path, all the way up to that summer when Daneen took over his room, was seasonal.

23.

I CAME HOME from the dealership one afternoon and found Daneen standing at what used to be Gord's bedroom window, watching him cut the grass. She told me that he'd just moved back, that there'd been some unspecified trouble with his roommate so he was living in the basement.

"Just for a few months," she said. "And by the way, you never told me your brother was gorgeous."

"Gord?" I had never, not ever, considered that. I joined her in looking out, but the seal between the panes on my side of the window had failed, leaving the glass permanently fogged. Daneen had a much sharper view of Gord out there in only his jeans, his skin bearing a pale impression of the T-shirt he had to wear at work.

24.

BY JULY, MOM was calling Daneen her Other Daughter and it was as if she'd made Daneen into one of her special community projects, the kind with so much *potential*. They had matching tans from lawn-chair afternoons spent passing novels back and forth, talking them over. And when they weren't talking about books, they were talking about the rest of us.

Daneen and I had stopped strolling around Calder. Instead, we spent our evenings sitting on the riverbank where the ground sloped so we were out of sight of the house. There, perched on a log, Daneen would puff away and talk about my family like we were fascinating characters in a television show. A show I didn't even watch.

"Your mother doesn't understand why you're so—what did she call you?—so austere." It was dusk, her cigarette the brightest light around. She held it out to me. "Of course Doris understands Gord better, because they're so much alike."

Suddenly I could see the similarities: the blue eyes and the shape of their mouths, the way Mom and Gord both just did what they wanted without meaning for it to be a provocation. The way they reacted if you challenged them, cupping a hand behind the neck so the elbow jutted pointedly forward.

I took a drag from Daneen's cigarette and pulled the smoke into my lungs. When I exhaled, a ribbon of smoke came out just like it was supposed to.

She had more to say. "I think your mother's just afraid you'll turn out like your father."

I never responded during these conversations. I didn't want to contribute to the dossier she seemed to be keeping. I just wanted my family to stay who they were in my head, unanalyzed.

I flicked her cigarette toward the muddy Auberge water, hoping to hear its small, fast fizzle but the butt landed on the muddy bank. For several seconds I could make out its glowing ember. I stood up and brushed the grass from my pants, hoping Daneen would see it was time to go in.

25.

IT TOOK US hours to get ready for Chelsea's social. My anxiety deepened as the day wore on. I knew it was ridiculous, getting worked up about people from high school and how I might seem to them now. And it wasn't just that. I had to factor in Daneen. I worried she'd finally get a whiff of what a misfit I'd been, that I wasn't at all who she thought I was.

But maybe that wouldn't matter at all. Maybe Daneen would be too busy sweeping through the community hall, seducing the whole town. Or maybe they wouldn't get her. Maybe they'd think she was weird and I was weirder for bringing her. And then Daneen would realize that I was a total loser for having hung out my whole life with these morons.

Late in the afternoon I gave up on trying to make my hair look luxurious and moved on to another round of mascara. My hands were shaking. Daneen, perched on the floor, looked up from painting her toenails hot pink and saw right into my raw nerves. I covered with a cryptic remark—someone who might be there, someone from my past. Nothing I wanted to talk about. Daneen nodded like this was what she'd expected all along.

"Someday you'll have to tell me the whole story, Meriel." Then she asked again if I was sure Gord was coming with us and I said yes, I was still positive. She dug for more. Would his friends be there? Did he like to dance? Did I think he was interested in her?

I don't know, I don't know. Lately, it was all I could say. The only useful answer I'd had in weeks was, "No, no girlfriend." I could have told her about the Wendy torch, but I didn't think Gord would want me to. Besides, for all I knew that torch had burned out.

Daneen capped the bottle of nail polish. "Do you think he's insecure? Maybe I just need to be more aggressive."

Before I could respond, my mother rapped on the open

door. She was holding two small boxes, one in each hand, and she extended her arms wide to pass them to us simultaneously.

Spermicidal suppositories. Someone must have told her about Chelsea.

Neither Daneen nor I spoke. We just looked from the boxes to Mom, waiting. Finally, she delivered a line that sounded even more deliberate than usual. "I'm not saying you should go out and have sex. I just don't want you to take chances."

Daneen smiled. "That's really great, Doris. Thanks!"

After my mother was gone, Daneen opened her box and held up one foil-wrapped bullet. "What, does she think we're having sex with werewolves?"

26.

NOTHING EVER GOES like I think it will. In grade five, my class staged an adaptation of *A Christmas Carol*. I memorized the script—all of it, everyone's part—but then my mother explained acting involved so much more than just knowing the words. She'd once had the lead in a community production of *The Glass Menagerie*, so she was happy to share what she knew. She taught me how to pretend so hard to feel things that it showed on my face and came through in my voice. She said the most important thing of all was to be convincing.

I knew I'd mastered it when Miss Graham, sitting on a stool at the back wall of the otherwise empty gym, said, "Listen to how Meriel-Claire puts *feeling* into her lines by changing her voice."

Miss Graham had been elevated that year to our grade. She'd also been our teacher in grade two, and so she was the first adult I'd ever suspected of making stuff up. A number line stretched right across the front of her grade-two classroom, corner to corner, even wider than the chalkboard, zero at its dead centre. I spent a lot of time eyeing up the negative numbers, trying to get a clear fix on them. I was already a whiz at adding and taking away, but there'd been marbles and wooden blocks and sometimes even Smarties to help us master those obvious tricks. Negative numbers were another universe, one in which there weren't just no marbles—there were no marbles minus some marbles, like holes cut right out of the air.

Not satisfied with shaking us up mathematically, Miss Graham caught up to us in grade five to coerce a whole new vocabulary into our inadequate throats. From a tiny stool island in the middle of that ocean of gleaming hardwood that was the Calder Elementary gymnasium, she badgered us about inflection and demanded enunciation. For months afterward, Darrell Taggart would yell out, "Please *e-nun-ciate*!" at inappropriate moments, cracking up the whole class.

My performance in the afternoon dress rehearsal was flawless. While I doubt the grade-four audience appreciated it, Mr. Noble—grade four, best teacher ever—came over after the show to tell me how professional I'd been. That's what he said, *professional*, and somehow it sounded like a promise of things to come.

Wriggling into my Ghost of Christmas Future costume for the real show, I imagined how impressed my parents and everyone else would be with me. Then I imagined Amy Miller forgetting her lines again—imagined how I would whisper them just loud enough, just directed enough at her that only those of us on stage and maybe a few people in the front row would know I'd come to her rescue. And Amy Miller and Miss Graham and the entire class would be so grateful.

But that's not what happened. Amy remembered her lines, even if she stumbled on some of them, and when it was time for me to cross the stage, to take the spotlight and deliver the best performance of the play, I tripped over the hem of my costume. Tripped on that treacherous stage and went down hard on one knee. My palms slammed the wooden floor. I had trouble standing back up. After that, instead of gliding ghostlike I could only limp through my performance. I still got my lines off, with inflection, but I couldn't make my face register anything but anguish.

27.

OUR TICKETS WERE waiting at the door just as Lisa had promised, but it turned out Daneen didn't expect to have to pay for them or for her drinks either. I had to lend her twenty dollars and explain the concept of wedding social as a fundraiser for the couple.

On either side of the vacant dance floor, the long tables sat mostly empty, but there was a knot of people in the back corner by the bar. I saw grey hair, thick necks and then I knew we'd arrived too early. Even the lights were still on full blast. Getting ready, I'd pictured the hall dimmed the way it would be when the dancing began. I guess that's all I could remember from other socials, baseball team fundraisers where I'd sipped lemon gin and ginger ale and been startled when anyone asked me to dance.

Crossing that empty floor under those bright, bright lights, I knew my flowered panties must be blaring through the transparent fabric of my white skirt. I tried to pace myself so Gord was ahead of me and Daneen behind for cover, but she kept stepping up alongside me, her head swivelling to take in the whole room. Just as we reached the centre of the dance floor, I heard a faint rustling overhead. I looked up to see blue and white crepe paper arcing diagonally, corner to corner along the high ceiling. Except one corner had just let go, the tape-heavy end spiralling right for our trio.

It missed us, or maybe we all deked sideways and missed it, but its swan dive caught every eye in the room and delivered them all right to our little band: to mysterious Daneen, familiar Gord, and see-through me. A whoosh ran through the room, as if every person in the hall had inhaled at the very same instant. Then there was a loud squeal.

Lisa, squealing, hurtled toward us in the same peach-coloured, high-shouldered dress she'd worn on grad night. I remembered it by the neckline's plunge and the double row of rhinestone buttons that spilled like runway lights all the way to the split hem. She looked the same as she had at graduation, too, except she looked so much happier to see me.

She hugged me tight. The full complement of those buttons pressed against me. "I'm so glad you came." The force of her enthusiasm stabbed at my eardrum. "My god, you look so different!" I was glad, finally, that I'd let Daneen goad me into buying the overpriced, fitted teal T-shirt with the scoop neck.

Lisa rushed to catch me up, told me about her breakup with Blair and I nodded as fast as she talked while trying to remember just who he was. I thought about introducing Daneen, but then Lisa was telling me that she worked at A Cut Above in the Calder Mall and that I should come see her, that she'd do my hair for half-price the first time. And then she saw someone else she had to greet and she was gone.

So were Daneen and Gord—gone. Vanished, and it was just me alone in the centre of the dance floor, transparent and deserted. I couldn't be sure anyone was still looking, but I flicked the switch anyway, sparked up the light behind my eyes and pretended to be harbouring some divine intrigue. Fortunately, Daneen and Gord emerged from the crowd by the bar, foamy plastic cups of beer in each hand, before I had to figure out my next move.

I trailed them to a table, watched Daneen follow Gord around the far side and sit next to him. The place was starting to fill up and I couldn't hear a word the two of them were saying— which didn't matter, since except for asking me to slide over a paper plate of pretzels, they weren't talking to me.

Eventually, Chelsea and Darrell made their big entrance. She didn't look pregnant, not the way I'd imagined. Her ruffled dress was enough to hide any sign of her not-so-secret pregnancy, but she looked thicker and softer and bigger-boobed than she had in school, and her hair was also bigger, sprayed up and away from her face. Her very round, very beaming face.

"She looks like—" Daneen's words were swallowed by a swell in the music. I tore my eyes from the happy couple and strained toward her, cupping my ear. Daneen leaned over the table, the line between tan and breast revealed inside her blue sundress. Her hair, untethered, slid over one shoulder to make a curtain between her and Gord.

"I said she looks like a giant piñata!"

But I didn't think so. Not at all. I thought Chelsea looked beautiful. I couldn't believe how happy she looked—how happy they both looked as they stepped into their first slow dance. Not that they really danced. They just did that thing everybody did in Calder: arms looped around each other and a slow shuffle of feet, a little sway, a quarter turn if the music absolutely insisted. Someone finally dimmed the lights.

When Daneen saw Gord was heading back to the bar, she drank up and followed him. I wanted a drink, but I stayed where I was, mesmerized. I hadn't expected happy. I'd expected some kind of tragic, forced march to the altar. After all, we'd been led to believe in school, in Sex Ed, and by our parents that getting pregnant was the worst thing that could happen to a girl, the best way to ruin your life for sure and forever.

After that first waltz, after the wedding party had joined the dance and the father of the bride had cut in on the groom, Lisa spotted me sitting alone and headed over. She was wondering if I would help in the hall kitchen.

My job was cutting spears from homemade pickles, two giant jars of them, and the smell of garlic and dill and vinegar reminded me of every event I'd ever attended in Calder. Across from me, Lisa was absorbed in cubing cheese, struggling to keep the knife straight and force it through an enormous block of orange cheddar. Next to me, Chelsea's brother Sam was making perfect sausage coins out of a roll of kielbasa, and maybe it was just the dark suit he wore but he didn't seem at all like Chelsea's little brother anymore.

I'd been too anxious to eat all day. Now I couldn't stop popping pickles and lopsided cheese rejects into my mouth. Between mouthfuls, I answered Sam's questions about university—about how hard it was and how long it took to figure out the campus. I told him how nervous I'd been, and that I'd be happy to show him around before classes started. Then Darrell's mother brought in two big bottles of sparkling wine. She poured us all gigantic glasses and when "Old Time Rock & Roll" came blasting, Sam whipped off his jacket and started dancing goofy so I did, too. Lisa barked at us to put down the knives and Sam and I shouted, "Before someone loses an eye!" and that was it, we were in league, joined by crazy high spirits and the smell of garlic on our hands.

Even after everything was cut up and Saran wrapped, I stayed in the kitchen with Sam and the wine. There was no point going back to Daneen—she had Gord pinned deep in conversation. And just before eleven thirty, when we carried the midnight supper to the side table, she had Gord up on the dance floor.

Sam, Lisa, and I headed there, too, to a far corner where we tried to outdo each other's stupid moves. I laughed until I ached, until a slow song wrenched us from hysteria. Sam put his hand on my arm then and it felt like being chosen. I stepped between his rolled-up shirtsleeves. We danced in that undancing way to "Against All Odds," my left hand loose on his shoulder and his hand tight in the small of my back and moving in circles. As Phil Collins sang, "Take a look at me now," those circles grew progressively larger and lower.

28.

I DIDN'T SEE any of it. I was outside, out behind the hall where it was very dark, my hands under Sam's suit jacket and our tongues twisting around. I didn't see Wendy arrive and I didn't see Gord spot her and just stop talking, mid-sentence. I didn't see him walk away from Daneen. I missed it all because Sam's hands were sliding up under my bra and my hips were churning.

I didn't see Gord's happy hello before he realized Wendy wasn't alone, or how he stood, stunned and swaying as Daneen tried to drag him back to the dance floor. I didn't see him shove Daneen, or see her fall, or see how things got out of control when Wendy's boyfriend stepped forward to block Gord's path.

I didn't see Gord take the first swing, but I absolutely knew he had.

Daneen described the whole scene in livid detail, everything I'd missed because my skirt was up around my hips and my hand was down Sam's pants. And then my name was everywhere, over and over again in Daneen's urgent voice.

I pushed away from Sam, pulled my clothes back to an approximation of where they were supposed to be. I didn't even think to tell him to call me. I just hurried around the hall to Daneen. When I got there, Gord's shirt was torn and Chelsea's dad was holding his arms just firmly enough to be the idea of restraint.

Sam came after me but when he popped out the side of the building and saw his father, he withdrew into shadow. I gave him what I hoped was a rueful look.

Daneen fixed me with a glare. "We have to go. *Now!*"

Gord, released, stumbled his way toward the car. He barely even argued when I told him to give me the keys.

29.

DANEEN AND I were sitting on the floor in my bedroom, each holding a copy of the university calendar, the thick-as-a-phone-book listing of every single course offered. Between us, we'd positioned a sack of Scrabble tiles. The game was Daneen's idea: pick a letter then pick a course that starts with that letter. But it wasn't that easy. When I picked an S and blurted, "Statistics!" Daneen shook her head. "Come on, nobody would voluntarily take statistics. Try again."

I had a soft spot for statistics, for the way they told a story without the clutter of too many words, but I reached for a new letter anyway. I drew a blank.

When she got bored with the Scrabble tiles, Daneen started looking for course descriptions that sounded like horoscopes. It didn't seem to matter to her what courses she ended up taking. She already knew what she wanted to do—getting through a degree, any degree, was just a pre-requisite for accessing her trust fund.

I was just happy to be spending time with her that didn't include hearing how Gord had humiliated her, that didn't involve tears. Even after we'd picked a full slate and sorted out our best schedules, we went on reading the course descriptions out loud, sending each other into hysterics over just how pornographic they could be made to sound.

I read out, "Various forms of deviance will be explored."

Daneen closed her calendar without laughing and uncrossed her legs. "I'm not living in residence again. I hate it there."

The tiny print in my calendar went fuzzy. Of course she was moving on.

30.

MY FATHER STOOD watch over the barbecue while Daneen and I set the patio table. She laid down the last steak knife and announced, more to the air than to anyone specific, "Meriel and I are getting an apartment this year."

She said it like we'd talked about it, like we'd already agreed on the particulars.

Mom placed the salad at the centre of the table. I could see this news was no surprise to her.

When Dad turned, his focus fell on me. I pretended to fish something from my eye. After a long second he asked, "Can you afford that, Meriel-Claire? You know we agreed to pay for you to live on campus, not in some luxury suite."

He never used that tone with me at the dealership.

Maybe Daneen was right—maybe Dad was callous and stingy. I'd disagreed when she'd called him that, made excuses, argued that he was just a bit ham-handed. But looking for evidence to counter her critical view I'd looked too closely and seen all kinds of things that made me like my father less.

"No one said anything about luxury, Dad, and I—"

Daneen cut me off. "I can pay for it."

Dad turned his back to us and flipped a steak, his next line barely perceptible over the hissing of fat. "The rich ruleth over the poor, the borrower is servant to the lender."

When he was really riled, Dad liked to rattle off a bit of Bible verse. It drove Mom crazy. She referred to his upbringing as churchy, by which she meant Dad's family attended services more out of community expectation than any conviction.

"I'm not an idiot, Dad. I'm sure we can find something affordable." I wanted to sound firm but only managed to sound defensive.

My mother leapt in and took charge. To me she said, "You can work out a budget." To my father, "It's exciting. It'll give them a chance to learn how to run a household." And then to Daneen, in an altogether more congenial tone, "September is only a few weeks away. We'll have to start looking tomorrow."

31.

I SPENT AN hour figuring out just how much rent I could afford, leaving aside enough for utilities and groceries. When I presented the number to my mother, she said, "Oh for heaven's sake, give us some leeway," so I topped up my budget a bit and we agreed—nothing over four hundred a month, split equally between us.

Dad and I arrived home from the dealership that night to an empty house. After he'd changed into his at-home clothes and opened the mail, I saw his mouth start to squirm like it was warming up to say something big, but the apartment hunters marched in carrying Burger King bags and looking triumphant. Over dinner, they regaled us with horror stories of basement suites with concrete walls and filthy olive carpeting. Finally, they got to the apartment they'd chosen, described all its space and light.

Dad set down his napkin. "Sounds pricey."

"It's very reasonable for what it is." Mom and Daneen responded in unison, so I knew they'd practiced in the car. My father opened his mouth to say something else but my mother muzzled him with a thunderous exhale.

I told Daneen I thought we should go for a walk. Now.

At the bend where the street follows the river into downtown Calder, she told me the truth. Four eighty-five a month, plus electricity.

"Daneen—that's way more than we agreed on!" I'd stopped moving so I was talking to her back. She walked on a little further before she understood I wasn't going to budge. Then she turned but she held her ground.

"It's perfect. You are going to love it."

"I can't afford it."

She put out a hand and that hand joined her tone in saying calm down, you're being ridiculous. "Your mother thought it would be fine. She figured you were just being overly frugal."

"Overly frugal? I won't be able to eat!" Suddenly I was shouting, short of breath. I'd never been so mad at someone who wasn't related to me. "You have to cancel it!"

She stepped back. "I can't. I already signed the lease. Look, it was the only decent place we saw." We stared at each other for a long time. Finally her face settled into something like remorse. "Don't worry, I'll pay the difference. I'll pay all of it, in fact. Really, you don't have to worry."

I hated the way she did that, threw her money around like it was worthless, like money had no value at all. "Forget it, Daneen. I'll just live in residence." I whirled and started stomping toward my house.

"Jesus, Meriel-*Claire*, what is your problem?" It was like being hit in the back of the head with a rock. "I said I'd pay for it!"

A shriek rose through my chest—a shriek louder than any sound I had ever made—but before the noise left my throat I noticed the houses all around us, windows yawning open to catch an evening breeze. I clamped my jaw and barrelled back toward her and snarled, "I need to be able to afford where I live."

"Alright." She pulled out a cigarette. "How about this. I'll pay more than half—hang on!—I'll pay more but take the bigger room. You can do all the cleaning to make up for your share. That's fair, right?"

She closed the distance between us, walking slowly enough as she exhaled that smoke formed a soft cloud around her. "I really want this to work out, Meriel. You're the best friend I'll ever have and I don't want to live with anyone else."

The setting sun was in her face; her eyes were bright and maybe filled with tears. I took the cigarette she offered and inhaled, experiencing for the first time the way nicotine could feel like relief. "Okay," I said. "I'm sorry. I don't know why I got so mad. That's fine."

I couldn't see it clearly, the deal I was making, but I hoped that when I calmed down, it would all look perfectly reasonable.

32.

ON MY LAST day at the dealership that summer, Dad walked me over to a used Pontiac Sunbird—a silver two-door with a sunroof and a cigarette burn on the driver's seat—and he handed me the keys. Before my surprise had worn off, he reminded me that gas and insurance and parking downtown weren't cheap. I hugged him for the first time in a long time and his cordial dealership face softened into Dad's version of happy.

I loaded the trunk of that Sunbird with our clothes, a box of old dishes and the coffeemaker I'd bought, which seemed both lavish and necessary. My mother handed me a Foodway bag she'd filled with dishcloths and kitchen implements—a gouged wooden spoon, a ladle with a rust stain at its centre.

"Gord's going to help you move in. That way he'll know where to find you girls." Mom winked at Daneen and I realized my mother was salivating at the idea of her perfect match. Of course she didn't know what had happened at the social. I'd begged Daneen not to tell her.

And if she didn't know that, she also didn't know that when Gord had finally crawled up from the basement the next day and Daneen had made another move on him, he'd rejected her flat out, shaken her hand off his arm and said, "I'm just not interested."

After that, Daneen made a point of never being in the same room, which wasn't hard since lately Gord was either at work or lurking in the basement.

33.

GORD FOLLOWED MY car to the city in a pickup truck Dad loaned us from the dealership. Everything fit in one load— everything being just my bedroom furniture and a floor lamp that had watched the world from a dark corner of the basement for years. I left Gord untying the ropes and hurried up to see where I lived.

It was just as they'd said—big rooms with big windows, vintage radiators and thick, solid doors that creaked on their hinges. There were gouges in the plaster; the pattern in the linoleum had worn away in front of the kitchen sink.

It was true, I loved it.

Daneen missed my first reaction. She'd taken refuge in her bedroom so she wouldn't have to see Gord. I raised my arms toward the high ceilings and started to spin like I was some graceful, jubilant dancer, but I stopped dead when Gord appeared in the doorway, his hand clenched around that old lamp.

I pointed him toward my bedroom. There was no place for anything of mine in the living room. Doris had taken Daneen on a shopping spree earlier in the week, so our living room was already stuffed with a huge black couch and shiny brass tables with glass tops.

In silence, Gord wrestled my mattress up four flights of stairs like some epic penitent. I hadn't spoken a word to him in the weeks since the social, and every day that Sam didn't call, my resolve to never speak to my brother again grew stronger.

Setting up my bed, he smacked his knee off the corner of the frame. I didn't ask if he was okay and he didn't utter a sound, not until everything was in its place. Then Gord said, "I guess that's it then."

"I guess so."

"Hey, MC—"

"What?" I didn't look at him.

"Nothing. Never mind."

I didn't give him anything. I just let him limp away.

34.

DANEEN DECIDED TO skip Thanksgiving dinner, claiming Gord's cruel rejection still stung. When I showed up in Calder alone, my mother looked crushed. But when I explained Daneen was working hard, buried in her studies, Dad was so impressed he wanted to know why I wasn't hard at it, too. I thought of Daneen as I'd left her, standing beside the VCR deciding whether to watch *Footloose* or *St. Elmo's Fire* first. I wished just once there could be a conversation in which I got to be the superstar.

Anyway, Daneen could have come to dinner. Gord was nowhere in sight. Mom told me he wasn't feeling well enough to come upstairs, then she loaded up a plate for him and placed the feast on a glossy red tray embossed with black roses.

"Let him get hungry," Dad said. "Maybe he'll rejoin the living." Mom just scowled and carried the tray downstairs.

Dad and I filled our plates. Finally, he filled me in. "Your brother's been charged with drunk driving and now he can't seem to show his face above ground." Dad said it quietly, like he didn't want anyone in Calder to find out—like he thought the whole community didn't already know.

"Again?" I tried to suck the word back in as fast as it had flown out.

Mom's head appeared at the top of the stairs. "Gord's sorry he's missing your visit, Meriel-Claire. He says hello."

She took her seat and I tucked a forkful into my mouth, but not before I saw my slip register in Dad's eyes. "What do you mean *again*, Meriel-Claire?"

I pointed to my mouth, exaggerating its fullness, chewing deliberately. He watched me the whole time. Eventually I had to swallow. "I just meant about Gord hiding away when he's upset, like he used to."

The flat of my mother's hand on the table made the tomato juice jump in our glasses. "I will not have the two of you sit here and pass judgment. Gord needs our support."

Dad's jaw kind of twitched but he kept quiet, and there wasn't much point trying to make conversation after that.

35.

STRETCHED OUT ON Daneen's big couch, I decided two things. One: I could do nothing about the trouble in Calder, Gord wallowing in the basement and my parents sniping overhead. And two: I was the one with a car and a driver's license and I drove Daneen everywhere, so I absolutely did not have to feel beholden to her for this amazingly comfortable couch. I was sunk deep down in it, congratulating myself on my logic, when I heard Daneen dial the phone in the kitchen. I knew who she was calling, but the couch's heavy embrace wouldn't let me up fast enough to stop her.

She asked, "How are you?" with far too much urgency. Then: "I know, I heard." After that, she went silent so my mother could fill in all the details.

Daneen and I were in the habit, then, of telling each other everything, unfiltered—but that afternoon I pressed a pillow to my ear so I couldn't listen to what I didn't want to know, and I wouldn't have to hear Daneen get more tangled up in the weirdness of my family. When she tried to report the phone call back to me, I held that same pillow out as a shield.

After that first, there were many more calls, all of them long and wide-ranging, but Daneen respected the boundary I'd drawn. She never told me what my mother told her. Instead, she scribbled it all down inside the coil-bound notebook she was never without. And I was grateful she kept it all to herself—at least until she didn't.

36.

WHEN DANEEN AND I arrived in Calder three days before Christmas, I headed straight downstairs to find Gord watching TV. He didn't have much to say, but he didn't seem to mind that I sat next to him for a little while. Later, though, my mother said it would be better if I left him alone, that my company might upset him. After that, Gord was like a ghost in the house, just the distant sound of water running or music playing, and the only company he got was when Mom took down his meals, always on the same glossy tray. At supper, Dad gritted his teeth until Christmas Eve. Then he barked, "Good God, Doris, what's wrong with that boy?"

Mom looked at my father like he'd spit in the soup. She leaned right into his face, eyes molten. "He's *depressed* is what's wrong with him. What's wrong with you?"

Then she picked up the tray and headed for the stairs. I tried to catch Daneen's eye but she was staring after my mother's disappearing head. "The tray's a nice touch," she said. "It adds a bit of elegance to the basement experience." I wanted to laugh but I knew Dad didn't think it was funny. He glowered at Daneen. Her face stayed unnervingly content, and my appetite vanished.

In the morning, my parents were already drinking coffee and eating tangerines when Daneen and I slid down the hall into the living room. The house had that weird-light spangly, breathless feeling that only ever happens on Christmas Day. Through the big picture window, I could see the air holding its breath.

Mom was beside the fireplace, where gas flames flickered weakly in the daylight. "Let's open our stockings."

For the first time, there was a fifth stocking hung from the mantle. Daneen's name was glue-glittered on its cuff. And for the first time I realized that families were not fixed, that they could change their shape and size.

"Wait!" It seemed so obvious I couldn't believe I had to say it out loud. "I'll get Gord."

"Meriel-Claire, don't! I can take him..." Mom's voice faded as I descended the stairs.

I knocked twice before I opened the door to Gord's room. The door was a joke anyway—the last wall of the room had never even been finished; it was still just a wood stud outline. Someone—probably Gord himself—had tacked up a crooked blanket across most of the opening.

"Leave me alone, Mom." He shifted and pulled the comforter up over his ear as if there was some ongoing, deafening ruckus.

"It's not Mom, it's me."

He rolled over and opened one eye. His hair was overgrown,

sticking up all around his face in the same moppy way mine did. "Hey." I waited for more, but there wasn't anything.

"It's Christmas morning, Gord." No response. "You have to get up."

"Christmas? Yeah, I guess—"

"Get up, there's presents!" I flopped down on the bed, near enough to feel the heat of him. When we were really little, it was always Gord who woke me up on Christmas morning. Sometimes it was still dark. Once, he'd actually pried my eyelids open.

Gord half sat and looked kind of interested, but that disappeared fast. "You guys go ahead. I didn't buy anything for anybody." His head smooshed back into the pillow.

"Just come. Please—I got you something you'll really like." I'd bought him a stupid set of bongo drums at an international craft sale. I had no idea if he would like them at all. "All I want for Christmas is for you to come upstairs, Gord."

"Okay." He said it like he was mad about it, but he got out of bed and went into the little bathroom Dad had put in downstairs when we were teenagers. I stood outside the door like a sentinel, and when he emerged I took Gord by the wrist, pretending it was a friendly gesture. He came along easily then, all the way to the living room, and sat on the floor looking at the fire. He kind of nodded like he was saying hello.

Mom looked as if some stranger had been hiding in the house for days and had just leapt out. Daneen stiffened and looked out the window.

But Dad looked like I felt—relieved. Just relieved, and even though Gord went back downstairs right after the presents, before we ate scrambled eggs, and even though he didn't come up again the entire time I was there, it was as if, for those few hours on Christmas morning, everything was okay. Everything was back to normal.

37.

GROWING UP, I thought my family was poor, and I kept thinking it right up until I was twelve and my mother took me to the skeleton of our new house, where we threaded our way between pallets of creamy beige brick to get to the door. Inside, the walls weren't up but Mom gave me the tour anyway—the divided kitchen, the family room with its fireplace, a sunken living room, another fireplace. And down what would become a long hallway, bedrooms, all so much bigger than what we were used to.

After her tour, Mom left me standing near the idea of my room, still trying to grasp it, and she went to talk to the foreman. He was a foot taller than her, with a tool belt and a sombre forehead that said he knew what he was doing, but Mom wasn't put off. She told him her ideas, what she thought should happen just as if she was organizing the Calder centennial parade. I was about to turn away in embarrassment when I realized he was taking her seriously—seriously enough to pull a pencil from his tool belt and jot notes on a sheet of plywood.

As we drove away from the construction site, from our new house sprawled along the bank of the Auberge River, Mom told me it was being built on the last plot left of the original Elgin homestead, the land granted to Dad's great grandfather when he'd arrived, twenty years old, from Scotland. He'd cultivated enough of the land to be allowed to keep it, but his only son, my grandfather, had sold almost all of it to finance his car dealership.

What Grandpa kept, a stretch along the river, sat untended for decades until Dad and Stewart inherited it, split it into several plots and sold all but one. "Your grandparents never wanted to share the wealth while they were alive," my mother said.

And then she confirmed it: we weren't poor. We were just thrifty, which was an impersonation of poor that didn't allow for a wide selection of breakfast cereals, creamy brand-name peanut butter, or the kind of orange juice that came ready to drink so you didn't have to stir for ten minutes to dissolve the last core of concentrated ice. At Lisa's house, they weren't thrifty at all. They had all those things in their kitchen, and on the fridge they kept a picture of a foster child in Africa who they sent money to every month.

If my mother had shopped liked Lisa's mother, Dad might have refused to build the house she wanted. He considered orange juice of any kind in the middle of winter opulent enough, and money was the one area where Mom let Dad be in charge.

I wasn't poor in university either, not by real-world standards, but I felt like I was. I couldn't afford to go to the clubs like Daneen and our other friends did so often. Even our Sunday afternoon ritual, nachos and a pitcher of Caesars at Murph's Place down the street from our apartment, stretched my budget. I became a master at living on next to nothing, at buying on sale and finding the best bargains. I bought shampoo in family-sized jugs and Dippity-Do by the two-dollar tub. Daneen laughed when she saw that throwback pink jelly, but she had to agree it did the trick. It made my hair glossy and kept my cowlicks in check.

When Daneen set out to revamp her wardrobe at the vintage stores so she could look unique, I tagged along. While she slipped in and out of dressing rooms in increasingly complicated outfits, I pawed through the dollar bins. Daneen spent a month's rent on old clothes that afternoon. I came away with three silk scarves for five dollars.

Then I discovered the Salvation Army Thrift Store, and I bought wool cardigans that smelled of pipe smoke and old man. Daneen said they'd almost certainly belonged to people who were dead, but when I wore them with tight jeans and a scarf at my throat, I felt like a golden age movie star on her day off.

38.

SPRING FINALLY ARRIVED. The air smelled like wet sheets hung on the line and the sun's light fell evenly over everything. But you couldn't see any sunlight from the lower level of the Student Centre where I first met him. Where I met him first.

A ridiculous thing to think—that I met him first, that it mattered—but I did. I met him in the long line that snaked from the used bookstore out into the Student Centre. I hadn't expected such a line with two weeks of exams still to go. I thought people would need their textbooks to study.

I'd only brought the ones I could spare: two I'd already summarized in my notes, and two that were on class reading lists but had nothing to do with what we were expected to know. I also had three paperbacks from Daneen's Victorian Lit class, which I wasn't even sure they'd take.

Every so often I looked back at the growing line, comforted that it was getting longer behind me as if that meant I was moving forward instead of practically standing still. Some students were clutching books to their chests like I was; others were nudging along a box or bag or naked stack with their foot. A few were actually reading, glaring into the pages as if they could absorb the knowledge fast, before they traded in the textbook for a fraction of what they'd paid for it.

He stood directly behind me in line and he was a nudger. He had his arms crossed over his chest and the same stony expression as everyone else. After half an hour, my arms got tired and then I, too, was a nudger.

The next time I turned to look at the line, he smiled faintly. "Too heavy?"

I nodded and looked down at his stack—a thick chemistry book on top—hoping something worth saying would come to me. Nothing did, so I turned back around.

A few minutes later he tapped me on the shoulder. "Hey, your *Psychology of Sex* book—can I look at it?"

I rolled my eyes and righted them before I turned. "It's not actually about sex. It's about sex differences in the brain."

He smiled. "I didn't expect it to be pornography. Can I see it anyway? It looks like a long wait."

I don't know why I hesitated. Maybe I was afraid he'd break the spine, tear a page, lessen the value of its practically pristine condition. "Look, I'll trade you for, um—how about *Intro to Soil Science?*" He waggled his eyebrows. "It's dirty."

I stood sideways so I could keep one eye on my textbook. He was wearing a U of M sweatshirt but he'd picked away the stitching that made the *of*, so his shirt just said UM.

He flipped pages like he was after something specific. When he noticed me noticing that, he said, "I'm sorry, do you want it back?"

"No! It's fine!" The words flew from my mouth like I'd been punched in the stomach. I clenched my jaw and focused on a calmer tone. "I'm Meriel. Are you looking for something specific?"

His head bobbled around like he wasn't sure. "I never heard any of this before, the stuff about men's and women's brains being different."

It was one chapter, some new findings, and just about everything else in the book refuted it. "Yeah, it's pretty interesting stuff."

"Like this part about the way men and women store memories. So that explains why a couple can't ever agree on what happened or whose fault it was."

"Kind of." Nothing as definitive as that was ever uttered in class. It was, in fact, the kind of unqualified statement that could get a student in a lot of trouble. But Mr. UM was looking at me intensely, the hair sticking up on one side of his head like he'd rushed straight from bed to be here just for this conversation. Like he needed his interpretation to be true.

I gave him what I could, what I dared. "How your brain

develops determines how you relate to the world. But it's hard to know what exactly has shaped your brain."

His eyes closed then for much longer than a normal blink. When they opened back up, he looked desperate. "So—is there or isn't there a difference in men's and women's brains?"

That was just it: after a whole semester, I still wasn't sure. The prof was always saying there were as many differences among the sexes as between them. But this guy seemed to need something definitive, and he seemed to need it from me. "Well there are hormones and physiology, and also socialization. There's so much happening to shape you starting even before you're born—" I realized the people standing around us were starting to listen so I shut up.

He picked up the thread. "So your brain gets shaped and then you just are who you are?"

"Yes!" It was so obvious, so eloquent. But then I looked at the book in his hand. "Well kind of."

We were almost at the front of the line. He handed me back my textbook. "You're a psych major?"

I nodded, and then I was. And it felt like absolutely the right choice.

"What did you say your name was? I'm Eric."

39.

ON THE LAST day of exams, I met Daneen at the bar upstairs in the student centre. The place was packed, the late afternoon sun blazing in through a wall of windows. We grabbed the last available table in the centre of the action. After we'd ordered, I looked around. The room buzzed with that kind of self-making festivity that teeters on the edge of frenzy. I was thinking that this could be the kind of evening where things careen dramatically off course. Then I spotted Eric. He was holding the brass railing and leaning into the room, searching so intensely it was as if he was willing someone to appear. When he saw me,

I kind of waved with my eyes—just "Hey, I recognize you"—and the next thing I knew he was standing beside me.

"Hi Meriel, how's your brain?"

"It's—" stalled. "Fine."

"Mind if I sit with you until my friends get here?"

I introduced him to Daneen and it all happened so fast. Eric and I were talking awkwardly about the effects of exams on our brains and Daneen leaned in. "You're a science boy? Do you know anything about kinetic energy? I need to understand it for something I'm writing."

It was like dropping antacid tablets in water, the fizz between them.

40.

WHEN THE CITY flooded in the fifties, Mom was sent away on a train. "My mother tucked five dollars in my hand and pushed me toward the ramp. I knew I wasn't allowed to cry." I heard the story so many times growing up that I could mouth the words—the river rising over its banks a block from the family bungalow, Doris too young to pile sandbags. "A foreign city, all by myself. And I was only eleven!" She always used the word *foreign* to describe her city of refuge, though she hadn't even left the province.

She'd written an essay about it, about the flood and how it made her understand sacrifice, and it won a national high-school writing competition. When she tutored students on composition at our dining-room table, she used that essay as her prime example of how to do it right. She even read the whole thing aloud for me once, and she made me include a copy of it in my junior-high project on floods.

Her retelling always ended with the same line as the essay: "That great flood put steel in my veins. It taught me to be independent, because self-reliance is the only kind that matters."

So naturally, I expected Mom to applaud my independence

when I told her over the phone I'd be living in the apartment all summer.

"Don't be ridiculous, Meriel-Claire. You girls can live with us again. There's plenty of room."

The idea of living in Calder again was like choking on dust. I opened up my throat and smiled, concentrated on making my voice sound like golden sweet honey. "Thanks, Mom, but we can't give up our apartment. You know how hard it is to find a good one."

"Your father and I are planning on putting in a pool in the backyard this summer. I thought you girls would enjoy spending afternoons relaxing around it."

"You're putting in a pool?"

"Yes we are. Very refreshing on hot afternoons."

She seemed to have forgotten that I'd be enjoying the air-conditioned dealership on most of those afternoons.

"I'll come by after work and visit a lot, Mom. I promise."

"And what about Daneen, stifling in that city apartment?"

Daneen had said no way was she spending the summer out there, not when she could spend it naked with Eric. "Daneen might get a job in the city this summer. It's just better—"

Mom changed tactics. "So you're going to waste money on rent and pay for all that gas to drive out here every day, and you think it's worth it just to keep that damn apartment?" A momentary pause as she gathered force. "Fine. I'll talk this over with your father."

She hung up.

Two days later, she called back to deliver the upshot of her conversation with Dad. I was cut off financially. "If you have enough to be that wasteful—" she tried to sound matter of fact, but a little smug slipped in—"then you can pay all your own expenses and your tuition."

I worked it out on paper, what the loss of their contribution meant. I'd need a part-time job year-round and probably a student loan, too—two things my parents had warned against for years, the famine and pestilence of the undergraduate burden dished up as my just desserts.

41.

DANEEN WANDERED INTO my room and stretched out diagonally across my unmade bed. She was fresh from a nap, wearing the black satin pajamas her new stepmother had sent for her birthday. Afternoon naps were a regular feature now that Daneen spent her nights with Eric. I was on my knees, heading into the closet to hunt for a pair of sandals that had worked their way into the deep recesses during the winter. Digging out the almost forgotten clothes of spring felt, every year, like finding a new wardrobe without spending a dime.

Behind me, satin slid and whispered as Daneen rearranged herself. "Oh Meriel, such serendipity, you taking my books to sell and finding Eric for me." She'd read an article called "The Magic of Serendipity" in *Glamour* and got stuck on the word. *Serendipity.* She loved its fusion of fate and luck, the way it suggested a special gift, how it played right into her hands. She said it sounded like it came from an exotic island, that it became a fragrant spice on her tongue.

Falling in love had made her complicated and deep again.

I crawled backwards out of the closet, clutching my sandals. "You make it sound like I fetched him and dragged him back to you."

"You're too literal, Meriel. You have to think of life like it's a string of pearls, one following another." She laid a satin arm across her forehead. The sheen of the pajamas and the sheen of her skin were the same. "And you—you're like the first pearl in the strand. If you hadn't gone to the bookstore and talked to Eric, I would never have met my beloved."

My beloved? I pretended to retch but already I'd started looking for serendipities of my own, for some small, destined moment that would build toward some blissful thing. I had, after all, delivered Eric to Daneen without protest or complaint, without ever saying dibs. I figured I must deserve a finder's fee, some kind of reward, some love as bright as the one they shared.

But nothing magical came my way. My life just kept to its straight, luck-free line, one that ran from our apartment to the dealership and back again along the same unswerving highway.

While I was driving that highway, Daneen bought a fine artist's paintbrush and a small jar of black ink from the bookstore where I'd become her first pearl. She trimmed the folded edges from a shoebox top, and on that white rectangle of cardboard she wrote *Serendipity* in her fluid hand with pencil—perfect the first time. Then she painted along the letters, thickening here and there for effect. When the paint was dry, she drove two nails through the top corners of the cardboard and into her bedroom door.

I worried about holes in that varnished oak, but she just shrugged. "There are holes everywhere in this dump. Who's gonna care?"

42.

WE KEPT ERIC a secret from my mother for most of the summer. He wasn't mine to tell and Daneen wasn't keen to share him. Anyway, Mom didn't exactly extend an olive branch though we showed up every Sunday, including the rainy ones, with our bathing suits. Once, I even tried to sweeten Mom up with pie. It was an old joke of my father's: "If your mother means to sweeten me up, there'd better be pie."

She'd accepted the pie—peach, for God's sake, fresh from a stand along the highway—and shared it around. She took a generous slice downstairs to Gord and even ate a sliver alongside us out by the new pool, which had turned out to be just a fiberglass oval perched on the grass. It looked refreshing, anyway, with its Mediterranean blue membrane. She asked Daneen what she was reading these days and spread sunscreen on both our sweaty backs, but still there was a stiffness about Mom, a chill that made me want to wrap my towel tight around my shoulders.

Finally Daneen served up Eric, plenty of details and heavy on the ardour. At first Mom gobbled it up, eyes and mouth wide and begging for more—but then her face closed, rigid again. She wanted to know why Daneen hadn't mentioned him before.

"I was afraid to jinx it, Doris." So much sincerity. "I wanted to be sure it was real before I talked about it."

"Of course." Doris broke into a big, lascivious grin. "And I guess I have to forgive you for barely coming around all summer."

After that, Mom went into overdrive trying to get Eric out to Calder, invitation after invitation until there was just no saying no to the annual Labour Day barbecue.

43.

IN MY LAST year of high school, I decided to donate a hundred dollars to Ethiopian famine relief. My mother objected vehemently. International aid was, in her opinion, a bungling misadventure at best—but more likely a swindle, a Christian scam. None of us, she said, should be taken in. But I knew the rules: my money, my choice. I just needed her to write me a cheque because I couldn't mail cash.

"Well, I will," Mom seized the upper hand, "but first, if you have money to throw away, Meriel-Claire, I guess you have enough to pay for your own graduation dress."

I considered not going to grad. Mom said that wasn't even an option, so I bought the cheapest dress that fit and I immediately started saving again. But by the time I'd accumulated enough to give, people with so much more had already saved the day. Live Aid's "We Are the World" wailed from the car radio for months. I was learning to drive a stick shift then, so the song became fused in my head with stalling, with grinding gears and getting nowhere.

The summer Daneen was lolling about in love with Eric while I toiled and saved and put off filling out a student loan application, I felt the same jaw-clenching frustration. But the last day of work before Labour Day, Dad brought my pay envelope, unsealed, to my office and then stood expectantly over my desk until I peeked in.

There was a second cheque.

"It's a bonus," he explained. "We've had a good summer and you've worked hard."

The fist in my belly unclenched for the first time in months. If I got a weekend job and kept close tabs on my spending, it would be enough to get me through without a student loan. I said thank you about three times.

Dad hesitated in the door. There was something else. "This is an employer-employee matter, Meriel-Claire. As such, I'd appreciate if you kept it between the two of us."

44.

THE LABOUR DAY decorations seemed more vigorous, the food more plentiful and my mother's dress more daring than ever before. The slit in it rose practically to her hip when Mom reached up to hug Eric as if he was an old friend, not someone she'd just that very instant met. And maybe it was because he hugged back that she took his hand in one of hers, Daneen's in the other, and led them into the fray. From the sidelines, I watched Mom introduce them to every single guest—all the old friends, all the dealership employees, even the otherwise-ignored cousins on Dad's side.

Daneen and Eric smiled and shook hands and with each encounter, they grew more iridescent. Moving from one group to another, Daneen leaned over to Eric and said something that made laughter rush up and burst out of him, his white teeth gleaming right across the yard. And then their faces composed into warmth again, like a royal couple visiting the colonies, making sure not to appear miserable in the midst of so much dulldom.

I filled my usual role, carrying plates of grilled hamburgers and oozing smokies from Dad's barbecue to the long tables Mom rented every year from the community hall. I wedged in alongside Eric with more burgers just in time to steer him away from the pale, chive-flecked potato salad to the superior version, the one with the mustard powder. Daneen reached around me for a taste from Eric's plate and said, "I'm hearing great stories. These people are fascinating!" She managed to hide any hint of sarcasm.

"I am so sorry, Daneen. You can go right after you eat."

"No way, I'm loving this!" Daneen plopped a dollop of the pale potato salad on her plate and looked at me as if I was an idiot. "I'm not kidding, Meriel, these people have the most astounding lives. And Jesus, they'll tell you anything if you ask."

I'd been around these people my whole life and I knew all their stories. I'd never heard anything that I would call astounding or even particularly interesting. But maybe when you hear stories incrementally, the steady day in, day out of them diminishes their worth, makes them just what you've come to expect and not much else.

The barbecue was turned off and the food nearly gone before Gord came out of the house. He was fresh from the shower and clean-shaven, but paler than usual and pudgy. He reminded me of dough, half-risen. Of course I hadn't seen him in months—he'd been keeping to himself, hiding in the basement, and I'd stopped making any effort to go down and say hello when I visited. I knew from Mom that he wasn't working, hadn't gone back to landscaping, but that's all I knew about him now.

He headed straight for the beer bucket. I caught Daneen watching him. My stomach tightened but she only smiled and took Eric by the wrist and led him to Gord.

An hour later, almost all the food and the guests were gone and Daneen and Eric were perched across from Gord at the picnic table furthest from the house. It was dusk but the patio lanterns strung around the yard cast just enough light that I could make out Eric's smile, Daneen's notebook. I started to gather up an armful of condiments but my mother said, "I'll get those. Go sit down and enjoy your friends."

I sidled onto the dark side of the picnic table next to Gord and tried to catch up to the conversation. Gord was talking about a swinger's club in Calder. "It was definitely going on in the seventies. Some of my friends remember walking in on big sex parties when they were little."

He took a swig of beer and I tried to get my head around these revelations.

I glanced toward the house. My parents, silhouetted behind the sliding glass doors, were kissing. Really kissing, not just the usual hello-goodbye peck. I looked away fast but it was too late. Gord had followed my gaze.

"It's probably still going on," he said. He looked hard at me. "I bet Mom and Dad are part of it. I bet they're swingers." Totally serious.

Daneen was writing furiously.

"Shut up, Gord. They are not."

"Fuck yes—I'm sure Mom and Dad are totally into that— or at least they were when they were younger."

On the way home, I told Daneen I was ninety-nine percent sure none of it was true, and one hundred percent sure my parents weren't involved, but that didn't stop her from using it later in that scene no one ever talked about, but I bet everyone dog-eared for future re-reading.

45.

"MY PERIOD'S LATE." Daneen's body ran like clockwork. It was another way we were different.

I stared at her for a minute. She stared back. "Do you think—?" I'm pretty sure I looked like I was watching a puppy run right out in front of a truck. I concentrated on relaxing my face. "You've been careful, right?"

She did that thing, that short burst of an exhale that signalled she didn't want to say anything then the long, slow breath in that meant she would anyway. "Condom broke."

"No silver bullet?"

"It's not funny." She got up fast like she was going somewhere, but she didn't. She just stood there, stuck. Behind her, the heart-shaped foil balloon that Eric had arrived with on Valentine's Day hovered near the floor, puckered from the loss of helium and unable to carry the weight of its shiny self and twirling ribbons even halfway to the ceiling.

"I know it's not. What should we do?" I was fast forwarding to tests, doctor's appointments.

"Well I'm not going to have it, obviously." Daneen picked up my open textbook from the coffee table, one of those heavy tomes with paper that feels like silk and smells like clay. When she slapped it shut, it made a deep whump. "Christ, it's like Eric came along just to keep me from getting anything done in my life."

My face must have registered disapproval, which she misunderstood. "Save it. I'm not throwing away my future for the shape of someone to come."

"If you need me to drive you somewhere—but I guess Eric—"

She lurched like I'd slapped her. "Don't you dare tell Eric. That's the last thing I need."

The next morning, I woke to Daneen's hallelujah shout of "Thank God!" from the bathroom. I thought everything would be okay then, but her false alarm changed things, as if someone had put lower wattage bulbs in all the sockets and nothing was quite as bright as before.

46.

DANEEN HAD STARTED work on a novel—one she'd abandon in favour of *Hidden Bargains*—and pieces of it covered every surface in the dining room. There were scribbled pages torn from a notebook and typed sheets, some she'd cut into strips and reorganized, stacking them in a new order on the windowsill without numbering anything. Outside the air was full of spring; inside it stayed still and dead because I didn't dare open a window and destroy the masterpiece she was accumulating.

One of her professors had told her, or maybe he'd told the whole class, that typewriters killed creativity. Too cumbersome, Daneen repeated to me, even less efficient than a pen. The only way to really go about writing and revising, adding and subtracting, was with a personal computer. She had to get one.

On a Saturday in May, I drove her to a squat building where I'd spotted a hand-drawn sign, *Computers for Sale*, in a storefront window. As we pulled in to park, I noted the sign had been replaced by a professionally printed banner: CUSTOMTECH COMPUTERS – WE HELP YOU KNOW WHAT YOU NEED. Inside, the *We* was just one man and he was busy talking to another customer, explaining the difference between hardware and software—the skull and the brain, he called them. I listened carefully as he described all the options. By the time he'd finished with that customer, I'd figured out exactly what Daneen should buy.

But since that configuration wasn't available just then, and since Daneen had to have a computer right away, that very day, she paid more for a deluxe floor model with a massive forty-megabyte hard drive. "Enough memory to last you a lifetime," the man told her while he rang up the sale. Then he asked how I knew so much about computers. I shrugged and said I didn't. I said I'd just eavesdropped on his earlier conversation.

He brought his hand to his face and tapped his chin, three fingers considering something and the tip of his middle finger typing it into his lower lip. "You want a job—ten to six, Tuesday to Saturday? I'll pay you eight bucks an hour."

I kind of laughed, but I couldn't think of a clever retort.

"Okay, how about nine bucks an hour?"

Daneen prodded my ankle with the side of her boot, the slightest rap intended to jar loose the needle that had obviously stuck in the soundtrack of my head. When I still didn't say anything, the man said, "So do you want the job?"

I just smiled harder at him, hoping the punch line would finally come into my reach.

Daneen nudged me again, using her elbow this time. "She sure does."

"Good, good. You can start on Tuesday." He extended his hand and we shook on it. "I'm Aubrey."

Even after Aubrey had carried Daneen's computer out to my car, he kept it up. When he said I should come early on Tuesday, before he opened, I finally understood that he really was offering me a job—one that paid half again as much as the dealership did.

Daneen lost her cool as soon as we were alone in the car. "Soooo, do you want a job?" She pursed her lips and tapped her chin in a poor impersonation. "God, he totally fell for you."

I flapped my hand. "Shut up, Daneen. This is awful. I already have a job."

"Jesus, Meriel, don't be an idiot. For once in your life take a leap."

47.

AUBREY STOOD WITH his hands on the hips of his faded corduroys, looking up into a jumble of metal and wire, monitors and keyboards on the shelves. His back arched so the elbow patches on his tan blazer pointed behind him. As usual, the muscle in his jaw was throbbing as if he was rhythmically clenching his teeth very quickly. The motion made the hair around the edges of his ears wiggle.

I could only look at Aubrey when he was looking somewhere else. When he was looking at me, talking to me, there was too much danger of getting sucked right into his face. His eyes were big and moist like a baby seal's, topped by shaggy eyebrows that were going for some kind of mobility record. It was easy to forget he was almost as old as my parents, to get drawn in by the excited kid who'd accidentally pulled on the wrong skin and a tweed jacket that morning.

"We'll have to order parts, Meriel. There's only enough here for two of those machines."

The principal of some junior high had just left the store, a copy of the invoice for one computer folded neatly and tucked in his suit pants' pocket. He was a friend of Aubrey's—a close friend once, maybe, but one Aubrey hadn't seen in a long time judging by all the hearty how-are-yas and upper arm slapping that accompanied their first handshake. Once they'd gotten down to business, I'd had a hard time following the order. Like usual, Aubrey was adding components and tossing out discounts. He pitched in the optional amber monitor at the end just to make the whole thing easier on the eyes. I couldn't keep up on the keyboard so I'd grabbed a pen even though Aubrey really wanted me to make the transition, to learn to listen and think and type the way I could already listen and think and write.

He wanted parts for more than two machines, but I'd only invoiced that principal for one. My stomach dropped. "How many is he buying?"

"Every school in the division is going to want one."

I flinched and said it fast. "The invoice I printed—I only charged him for one."

Aubrey nodded. "Uh huh, but once he sees what it can do, he'll be telling everyone to get one."

Aubrey started tapping his chin and lip. "I think they list all the schools in the phone book. You'll have to count them and order enough parts to build one computer for each." He tossed that last sentence over his shoulder as he headed toward the back storage area. A minute later he reappeared carrying two empty packing cartons, which he placed against the wall. "And add a few extra to that order—you know some people will want to have one at home."

He went to get more boxes. He was making room in the back for all the new machines he'd have to build. I got out the phone book.

I'd finished counting and typed up the order as Aubrey hoisted the last empty carton against the wall. He'd built a tower of improbable architecture, smaller boxes holding up larger boxes, the odd cardboard flap hanging like an indolent tongue. I wanted to ask if he was certain we should place the full order now for all those parts—expensive, non-returnable parts— before any of the orders actually came in, but behind Aubrey the tower trembled like it was about to topple. Without even looking back, he thrust his hand up and stabilized the whole conglomerate. I pushed *Enter* and the printhead began its back and forth tracking, line by noisy line.

Aubrey grinned wide. "This is going to be our best month ever!"

Our had started to slip in to his sentences the week before. It made me a little panicky, like I'd signed up for something more permanent than a summer job—but also flattered, like I'd been drawn into an inner circle, elevated above the level of assistant. Above Girl Friday, which is what my father had been calling me since I'd told him I wouldn't be working at the dealership anymore.

Dad had taken the news better than I'd expected. I'd braced for disappointment, for a tone that said I was leaving him in the lurch, that he'd been counting on me. I even had my defense ready—wouldn't it be better if I got some experience working outside the family business and anyway, could he match nine dollars an hour? I didn't need it, though. Dad had just said I'd make an excellent Girl Friday and that knowing about computers would be a real asset.

After we'd hung up, I felt deflated. I wondered if Dad had felt as stuck with me as I had with the dealership.

Aubrey expected me to know how to operate all the machines and all the programs. Every night I took home manuals and practiced formatting and merging and database construction on Daneen's computer whenever I got the chance. It was only pride that kept me from calling my father in the middle of the night to beg for my pencil and paper job back. Then I got my first paycheque and I was glad I'd stayed.

When the printer finished, I tore the order paper loose. Aubrey walked toward me as I started removing the perforated pinfeed strips. He kissed his fingers and pressed them to the top of my head.

I stopped moving, mid-rip.

He'd never done anything like that before and I had no idea what it meant so I held my breath. We both watched the thin ribbon of paper I'd torn dangle, half-free and quivering. Time dragged on. Finally I pulled off the last of the thin strip and handed him the order sheet, two pages still fan-folded together, my heart still hammering.

Aubrey checked it over and said, "Good to go," which meant I should fax the order to the supplier. Heading for the back room again, he called out, "Next month we'll both get a raise!"

And I believed him. I absolutely believed him.

48.

I ANSWERED THE phone on Friday night and Eric said, "Excellent, it's you." Then he asked me to meet him at the Pound

Sterling—right away, that night. I understood he wanted to get drunk and talk about Daneen, but that was at least a distraction from the ridiculous crush I'd developed on Aubrey, if crush was even the right word for a feeling so discomfiting. What I felt was more a thick, sloppy mix of sympathy and adulation, stewed together in the intimacy of working day after day in our little store, more and more now just the two of us without even the interruption of customers.

I told Daneen it was Aubrey on the phone, an emergency at the store. I couldn't tell her the truth. Daneen hadn't just broken up with Eric the month before, she'd severed all ties. If he called, she put the phone down as soon as she heard his voice. He'd been such a constant presence in our lives and I felt his absence profoundly, but I couldn't tell if she missed him at all. She'd cried just once, the day of, and then stopped like she'd slammed a dresser drawer and put its contents right out of her head. There'd been no discussion, no dissection—she wouldn't talk about it. It was all just over.

A week after she'd ended it, Eric had come to our door. I'd recognized his knock and started toward it.

"Don't you dare," Daneen's whispered rasp like a bolt sliding shut. Eric kept pounding, and after a while he'd called out—not to her but to me. When I took a step toward the door, Daneen had grabbed my arm. "You're supposed to be on my side. The rule is no contact—not for me, not for you. Not ever."

So when I agreed to meet him, I couldn't tell her. Instead, I wriggled into a skirt and re-applied my makeup in the car.

Eric lived across the highway from the Pound Sterling. We'd gone there with him a few times in the winter. It was like a secret club—you had to be tipped off to the small sign tucked around the side of the building, the entrance otherwise unmarked. Inside the heavy door, there was none of the rank desperation or thumping music of the dance clubs. There was just a thickly varnished L-shaped bar and tightly clustered tables, leather armchairs in the corner, memorabilia lining the walls. It was a crowded kind of cozy, a place for conversation, always the risk of an errant dart.

Eric sat with his back to the short end of the L. He'd been there long enough to drain at least one pint and he looked so glad to see me my insides shivered. But even though he bought me a gin and tonic and put his hand on the small of my back as we moved to a table, I knew this had nothing to do with me.

It didn't take him long to get to it, either. "I just don't understand. I thought things were fine."

That was a lie. I knew Daneen was irritated with him all the time, that she got angry easily. He'd mentioned it to me more than once. But I didn't remind him of that.

Eric gripped his pint glass. I could see he'd lost weight. He seemed smaller, fragile, and I wanted to give him some comforting rationale that his pride could accept, but all I could come up with were hazy explanations: nothing he'd done wrong, she just had different life goals.

She'd really said that, too—to him and to me. Life goals, and until then I hadn't known she had such firm plans or that anyone could see so clearly from this vantage point.

"I just want to talk to her, to get an explanation."

Once, when I'd pressed her, Daneen had given me an explanation, turning her words into fast-moving bullets. "He's boring, okay? He's fucking boring."

I couldn't tell Eric *boring*. It would be like sticking him with a serrated knife right in the middle of his favourite bar. Instead, I tried to explain what I'd finally figured out—that once the fervour had worn off, it was all too tame for Daneen. "Think of it like this, Eric—" I was near the bottom of my second drink— "Daneen's like a zipper. She needs a jagged set of teeth to pull herself along, not the easy action of a button hole."

He gaped at me like he was lost, or like I'd lost my mind. Then he looked to the door, hoping, maybe, for the diversion of a sudden entrance. Finally, he looked back at me. "So—so she's a zipper and I'm a button?"

Hole, I wanted to add. Button *hole*, but then I was laughing too hard. We were both laughing too hard, and every attempt at saying it only made it worse.

When we'd calmed down and emptied our glasses, Eric looked relaxed and even a little bit happy. He leaned toward me. His expression was so sweet. "Do you think it's because of her parents' divorce? Do I need to reassure her we won't turn out like them?"

I gave the bartender an emphatic, desperate two-finger wave. Then I laid my hands flat out on the table. "Look, it's none of the things you want to make it, Eric." I saw his pained expression resurfacing, but I didn't stop. "Daneen uses people. You were her favourite flavour for a while—now she's tired of you. That's it." I don't know if either of us fully believed that then, but it was the only course I could see.

"You're better off without her. Besides, she's done with you."

It was a mercy killing, my first, and I was absolutely certain of my motives, certain I just wanted to help him get over Daneen.

I was less certain three hours later, on my knees, Eric's cock in my mouth and his hands pressed on either side of my head. By then we were both past the shyness, past the surprise that it was us like this, naked and moaning and every so often opening our eyes and smiling like we were absolutely delighted to see each other.

49.

I GOT HOME at three in the morning, giddy and sticky and exhausted. I eased the front door closed but then I heard it, the sound of her typing. And she heard the floor creak and flew from the dining room right into my path.

"I knew it!" Her face a great big *aha* of a grin. "So is this brand new? Or have you been keeping it a secret for a while?"

Like a mouse caught on one of those sticky-paper traps, I could only squeak out, "New."

"I thought you had a thing for him." She put her hands on her hips and looked me up and down. "I totally get it—he has that disarming, muppety thing going on, mixed in with some distinguished mature-man charm."

My head bobbed beyond my control like a nodding confession.

"Women always end up sleeping with their bosses, Meriel. So come on, I want to hear the whole story."

"Can I tell you about this tomorrow?" I was so tired and so freaked out that I'd started to shake. "I have to work in the morning."

She smiled wider. "I don't think he's going to fire you if you come in a little late." She put a hand on my shoulder, wise old Auntie Daneen. "But okay—tell me all about it tomorrow."

I crawled into my bed knowing I couldn't possibly call in sick without her sniffing out the lie I technically hadn't told. Daneen sang out, "Sweet dreams!" from her room but I didn't dream—I didn't sleep. I just roiled around trying to figure out what to do. If Eric and I were a thing—were we a thing? I desperately wanted us to be more than a one-night mistake— then it was smart to let Daneen know, to let her get used to the idea before she saw us together.

But every scenario I played rushed headlong into disaster. She'd be furious because I was supposed to stay away from him, to keep the doors and windows barred and act like he was dead to us. Instead, I'd gone and let him back in, and how could this work?

I remembered her saying to me, the night she'd decided to end it with him, "I don't want him, but I never want to see him with anyone else." She'd be savage in her jealousy, and even if we got past that, Daneen was never going to play the third wheel like I had for the last year. I'd have to choose between them.

By sunrise I'd remade that scenario: Daneen's jealousy would make her think she wanted Eric back, and she'd fly at him so fast I'd be just a blurry memory—for both of them.

And then I realized that's exactly what Eric wanted. He was counting on it. He'd planned this whole thing and when I realized it, I got up and into the shower and tried to keep my sobbing quiet.

But by the time I was completely scrubbed of his sap, I'd started to question whether he could do that, whether Eric could ever be that cunning.

50.

ERIC CALLED ME at work in the afternoon and asked how I was, his voice soft and careful. The jittery parts of me rushed straight into euphoria, but I kept my voice soft and even, too, and prayed Aubrey would stay in the stockroom. Then Eric said, "We should probably talk," and it felt like my fingers had been slammed in a drawer, though I wasn't sure if it was the *should* or the *probably* that hurt, or maybe the *talk*.

At three in the afternoon I told Aubrey I felt like I was coming down with something. He studied me for a minute, concluded that I looked dreadful and told me to get some rest before those school orders came rolling in, because we were going to be busier than we'd ever been.

When I got to the Pound Sterling, Eric didn't look at all like *probably should*. He looked happier than that, and when my eyes adjusted to the dark of the bar, I could see he was flushed and jittery, too.

"Hi."

"Hi yourself."

"You look tired."

"So do you."

Weak laughter, both of us.

"Want a drink?" He didn't have one.

"I think I'd fall over. I wonder if they have any coffee—"

"Nope. Already asked."

Awkward silence. I sat down, braced the palms of my hands against the edge of my seat to keep me upright. Eric pointed out we probably shouldn't stay if we weren't ordering anything. "Want to go for a walk?"

"Yes." At least we wouldn't have to look across at each other, at least motion might make me a little less tired. We turned away from the highway, from Eric's apartment, and strolled down a residential side street. The sidewalk was cracked and pitted, dandelions wedging up bold as brass through the concrete. Our talk amounted to a handful of sentences.

"Did you tell her?"

"I didn't know what to say. She thinks—"

"What does she think?" He pulled away, moved further from me.

"She thinks I'm—" I couldn't find a better way to put it— "sleeping with my boss."

Eric laughed, sharp and loud. "Is that what you told her?"

I was too tired to be offended. "She assumed."

He considered that for a second, then shrugged. "It's none of her business anyway." He took my hand as we turned the corner, and he kept hold of it when we turned the next, heading back up another avenue, its sidewalk recently replaced. It was clean and even, brighter than any concrete I'd ever walked on before. Such a difference, just one block over, though the houses were all the same sort of post-war bungalows standing shoulder-to-shoulder, sensible in their vinyl siding, each with a picture window on one side and a flower bed lying hopefully beneath it.

"I think you're right. Let's not tell her anything."

I hadn't suggested that, but I didn't argue.

"Wait. Are you sleeping with your boss?"

It was cooler inside his apartment, and dim, and we were

just going to lie down and rest before I drove home. "Take a nap" is what he'd suggested and we both tried, or at least pretended to try, but then we were kissing and then we were naked and when we finally slept, both of us, it was like plunging off a cliff. I woke with a start to see it was almost eight thirty and I knew I had to call Daneen and tell her I'd be late, later—much later—maybe not home at all. And I knew I'd be non-specific and cryptic and let her assume whatever she wanted.

I waited until Eric woke up and went into the bathroom, then I dialed. At least one of us wouldn't have to hear this.

51.

ALL THROUGH JUNE, the components I'd ordered marched through the door: boxes of hard drives, CPUs and keyboards, crates of monitors swaddled in Styrofoam and bubble wrap. It was my job to figure out what to do with all the boxes. I started by putting the smaller inside the larger inside the largest like Russian dolls, but after just a few days the nesting cardboard threatened to choke out the last path through our little store. One afternoon a potential customer opened the door, looked around and backed out before I could say anything. We didn't get many customers; we couldn't afford to be scaring them away. I started flattening the boxes, then bound them with tape in stacks six inches deep and dragged them to the garbage bin behind the building.

Back in his workshop, Aubrey was starting to look like a crazed Giuseppe. His hair hadn't been cut all summer and it stuck out in a floppy fuzz around his ears. He was never without a small screwdriver, sometimes one in his hand and another poking up from his shirt pocket. And he hummed. He hummed all the time, a tuneless, keening kind of hum that wheedled in under my skin and made me want to cry. To drown him out and because there wasn't much else to do, I would pop bubble wrap between my fingers, working down one row and up another systematically until every single blister on the sheet was burst.

Aubrey built thirty computers in anticipation of the school orders, all identical. Once he realized there were no boxes left to put them in, and we'd put that awkward conversation behind us, I helped him line them up along the walls. He liked to turn the whole row of them on each day, to type in computer code on each system so the monitor screens all looked smart and busy. He thought it made the store livelier, the computers more intriguing.

All through June we waited, but none of the school orders came in. Not one. And then the schools closed.

In the first week of July, Aubrey stood right over my desk. He was curved like a lamp and looking at the floor instead of steadily into my eyes like he usually did. "Until we sell some of these, the store's a little short. So it can't pay you this week but it owes you." He said it all quickly, a douse of words. "Okay?"

An army of amber monitors blinked at me, daring me to say it wasn't.

52.

ERIC AND I met at the Pound Sterling a few times every week. Each time I expected we'd end our crazy fling, but we always left the bar fast, walked the block and then went to his place and tangled ourselves up deeper. If I'd just been honest with myself, at least I could have enjoyed it more.

We had only one rule: we wouldn't mention Daneen, not even in passing. It was Eric's suggestion—"So you don't get caught in the gears."

That might have meant he didn't want me tormented by divided loyalty, or it might have meant that up ahead, I'd be crushed. We were spooned together on his bed when he said it, our fingers interlaced across my waist. I couldn't look at him for clarification without untwining, so I just concurred. "If you're going to act like trailer-park sleaze, I guess it's best to stay out of tornado alley."

He laughed in the way that means it's funny because it's true.

Things rolled along that way all summer, twisting into a knot that held me fast. Sometimes I trembled and even my bones began to feel too fine, like they might snap if I moved suddenly. The only respite was inside Eric's apartment, where I could stomach food—even the Kraft Dinner and greasy tacos he fed me—and I could sleep deeply, as if guilt couldn't breach that concrete bunker.

It was the only pleasure I could afford. Every payday was the same: Aubrey told me there was a cash crunch, a big sale pending, that the money would be in long before I had to pay my tuition. And every time, he wrote me a promissory note so I knew he was good for the money. When I couldn't afford so much as a six-pack, I reminded myself that it was the world's best savings plan.

53.

DANEEN WAS BUSY with her first job, a summer apprenticeship at a journal. A professor had recommended her for it. It was supposed to be a chance to dip her toes into the literary world even if it was all admin work—stuffing envelopes, calling people whose subscriptions were about to expire. She didn't seem disappointed though, or care that it only paid minimum wage. What she cared about was impressing the journal's editor, Bryan DeCario. She talked about him incessantly using words like perspicacious, which I had to look up. Once, she said "beguiling," though she was really drunk when that slipped out. Every day she'd recount to me all the clever things he'd said and she'd flesh out the story with details of his wardrobe, which she intimated was just as smart as he was. She even told me the brand names of the shoes he wore. Until then, I hadn't known shoes had names that mattered.

I could have surmised that all her descriptions were just a complicated code for sexy, but Bryan was engaged and I didn't think Daneen would set herself up for that kind of disappointment. I figured she was just hanging around the hot-for-my-boss bandwagon she thought I was driving, hoping her divulgences would jar me out of my reticence.

She'd taken to catching me in the middle of something that made escape unlikely. I had my hands in a sink full of dishes when she leaned on the kitchen doorframe and said, "I just wish you'd tell me about it. I feel so left out. Why all the secrecy?"

I'd anticipated this one. "He asked me not to talk about it." I never said a name when I talked to her, so I couldn't be accused of outright lying. "We're trying to keep it just between us." I hoped this would appeal to Daneen's sense of romance, her appreciation of the delicate and the sacred.

"Oh my god, he's married, isn't he?"

"No. But—it's complicated."

"There's someone else and you're the other woman."

I nodded. That felt true.

"Interesting." She rolled this revelation around in her head while I slammed plates together in the sink. "Do you love him?"

The question took my breath away. I hadn't ever let the thought form. I stayed silent but my shoulders rose in a response that was half shrug, half self-defense. I turned to the dish rack so she wouldn't see the tears filling my eyes.

"Does he love you?"

It was like a blow from behind. I couldn't suppress the sudden intake of breath, somewhere between a gasp and a sob.

Daneen crossed the threshold and wrapped her arms around me from behind and I leaned back into her, despising myself for letting her comfort me. For letting her be the one to make me feel moored.

On Saturday, Daneen dropped by the store when she knew

she'd catch Aubrey and me both there. It wasn't like she was trying to catch us at something—it was more like she needed to quench her curiosity, to insert herself into my drama.

At least Aubrey had gone for a haircut the day before, so he looked a little more normal. When Daneen smiled and said, "Hello. How are you?" in a voice too eager and too familiar, he acted suitably weird, his response a combination of charm and fluster that made everything she believed seem true. I was afraid she'd say something cryptic or worse, something so direct he'd have no choice but to deny it. But she didn't. She slipped right into nonchalant—"Hey Meriel, just wondering if we can go get some groceries tonight, if you're not busy?" Not a wink, not a smile, not a quiver of tee-hee in her voice and no sign she discerned the neon billboard of my face, *DECEIT DECEIT DECEIT* strobing right across my forehead.

54.

ONCE WHEN WE were kids, Gord pinned my head under a leather stool after I beat him at the game where you match up pairs of face-down cards. I always won at that. It was so easy to remember where the cards were once you saw them the first time. We were sitting on the floor and I was shuffling—something I was also good at—and then Gord flipped the stool, pushed me over with it and piled on top. My head was wrenched sideways, one nostril and half my mouth squashed shut, trapping my screams.

Mom was a few feet away in the kitchen but she didn't come to my rescue. She didn't like to intervene in our fights. She thought we needed to learn to solve our own problems, to just get over things. When my panic lessened, I thought to switch from wordless cries to "Mommy, please!"

She used to say, "How can I know it's me you want help from, if you don't ask for me by name?"

After the stool was off my head and Gord had calmed down,

Mom said to him, "Winning a game of cards is all about luck, so there's no point in getting upset about it. Your sister can't help which cards turn up."

Later, while I was setting the table, she passed the sugar bowl to me and said, "Boys don't like to lose. You remember that."

I knew Calder was the last place I should go seeking comfort. Still, I woke up on my day off from the computer store and all I wanted was to be out there, far away from Daneen and Eric and the whole mess of my grown-up life. I thought if I could just sit by myself in my old room, I could sort something out. Or else I could sit downstairs with Gord and watch sports and pretend absolutely nothing was going on.

For months, I'd avoided contact with all of them. Gord's sulk had gone on for almost two years and it was hard to maintain any level of distress about it. My father's exasperation had at least shut down the special meal deliveries; now Gord came to the table, though he came offering nothing in the way of geniality. Mom, meanwhile, diverted her energy into buying him things—clothes and movies and, oddly, a banjo—anything to lure him out of his cave. I'd felt bad for a while about not making an effort, rarely even calling, but they were all so distantly located, so fixed in an orbit that seemed permanent.

When I arrived in Calder the house was buttoned up snug and I felt an acute sense of relief until my mother threw open the door. She was wearing her bathing suit and her pleasantly surprised face, and she hugged me like I was a long lost friend. Then she looked around me and asked about Daneen.

She insisted I put on one of her old suits and join her by the pool. When I did, she saw right away how the suit bagged around the missing bulk of me and started asking questions about how I'd managed it. I gave her vague answers, quelled the temptation to admit turmoil was my diet drug of choice. Her gaze travelled up and down me, practically rapturous. Then she suggested a snack—maybe some chips and dip, or some iced tea? I accepted the tea and asked if Gord was around.

"He's at work. They're both at work. I've given up hoping for a day when they're not."

"Gord's working at the dealership?"

Mom looked at me like I was an idiot. "Of course not. Your father had to hire a commerce student to do your job this summer." I knew that. Dad had told me when I'd called on Father's Day. "Gord's landscaping, same as always. Very long hours." She said it like this was a given, like it was inconsequential news.

"But when did he—" I was stuck for a phrase neutral enough.

Her eyebrows drew down and I braced. "They pick him up every morning. I'm sure I told you all this, Meriel-Claire."

I fiddled with a loose clasp on my earring, making sure it was done up. It was getting muggier, the temperature climbing into noon. A slight breeze that had been shimmering the poplars died away and the mosquitoes found us beside the pool.

My mother slapped her arm. "You know, I think his depression was chemical. Thank god he pulled himself out of it before we had to do—you know, Prozac or something." She swatted her leg and then she was up and heading for the water. "Come on, let's cool down."

I didn't get up. "I'm sorry I haven't been around much—I've been so busy with work."

The splash of my mother hitting the water drowned my last few words. I wasn't sure she'd heard until she came to the pool's edge and rested her chin on her forearm. "We knew you were having your own life, so we've tried not to bother you." Her legs floated up behind her, her calves surfacing. "Your father misses you at the dealership, but of course he understands about putting finances in front of family."

A mosquito flew right into my open mouth. I gagged,

lunged for my iced tea, drowned the bug and any defensive retort that may have been forming. Still, I had the sense of something stuck in my windpipe for a long time.

55.

ERIC AND I were propped on either side of the couch, our legs close but not touching in the sticky heat. Even with the windows and curtains shut, the inferno outside was seeping in.

It was Saturday. Aubrey had told me to leave early, giving me a whole found afternoon to spend with Eric. I hadn't even called first to see if I should come over—brash for me, practically a real girlfriend move—but when Eric had opened the door he hadn't look irritated, not even for a second. He'd just smiled so fast and bright I'd almost stepped backwards.

He'd been going through the university calendar, figuring out his final year, what he'd need to graduate. I also had to do that, but there was just one calendar, so I went to the kitchen for the only sharp knife he owned and I tried to sever the Arts section cleanly. It was pointless, the blade too dull against that cheap pulp paper. Finally I tore out the pages I needed, leaving a mess of ragged edges.

I found a pen on the floor but I couldn't concentrate. As soon as I circled a possible choice I thought about the cost, about how broke I was, though I knew Aubrey was close to signing a deal. He'd been meeting with a real estate company that wanted to bring its agents into the computer age. The day before, he'd even asked me to dust the display computers and he'd gone and bought a stack of boxes that it was my job to bend and fold and tape into secure cartons. He'd loaded each with a complete system so we'd be ready for the onslaught of sales.

The heat was making me queasy. Eric shifted on the couch and draped a leg over mine and I realized how impossible it would be to carry on a secret affair once classes began.

I almost said to Eric, "This is the closest we've ever come to discussing anything beyond tomorrow," only we weren't discussing anything. We were just sitting on opposite sides of an old couch, reading separate class descriptions to ourselves, not even out loud so they could hang in the air and reveal their worthiness. Choosing classes with Eric was boring. If I asked which course he thought sounded better, I knew he'd just give me a straight answer. And anyway, that wasn't even the problem. The problem was that it was too damn hot in his apartment.

I threw my ragged pages to the floor and got up. "Maybe we should go somewhere, Eric, like to an air-conditioned mall."

He lowered the calendar so I could see his mild surprise. "You're not worried someone will see us together?"

That infuriated me, though I'd been the one to insist on staying in before. "For your information, Daneen's out of town all day. I think we're safe."

Eric didn't call me on breaking the rule. He just sat up and circled an arm around my leg. "We're always safe here." He leaned to kiss the back of my thigh.

I pulled away and lurched toward the door. "Jesus, Eric, it's so fucking hot in here. I have to go."

He looked confused, like he found the billion degree heat completely acceptable. Like he couldn't see what might be bugging me.

Like he didn't care if I stayed or not.

56.

I TOOK A long cool shower and then I was sorry—sorry enough to call Eric and apologize, but I didn't get the chance. As I stepped from the bathroom, Daneen slammed through the front door. She planted her feet and glared at me. I stopped breathing, stood as still as if I'd been caught in amber, one hand clipping the towel closed at my chest. Finally a rolling shriek began at the back of her throat and emerged. "I can't fucking believe it!"

"What?" My voice low and level but my heart thumping.

"Alicia, the fiancée. She came along. I had to sit in the backseat like they were Mom and Dad. She hovered around us all day."

My legs went rubbery, the way they do after a close call with collision.

Bryan had picked Daneen up that morning for a festival an hour's drive north. She was supposed to sell subscriptions from a booth while he worked the room. The night before, she'd practiced clever things to say in the car, and it was my job to judge whether they sounded insightful. But I could feel the frustration arcing off her and I knew there'd been no opportunity at all for insight.

Daneen banged around in the kitchen while I pulled on clothes. When I emerged she was on the couch with a bottle of wine. She handed me a can of Coors Light from the pity pack she'd bought me when the heat wave had started. "Why doesn't he see what an airhead she is?"

I was sweating again. I held the can to my wrist, hoping to cool the blood passing underneath. "She must have something going for her if he wants to marry her."

Daneen moaned. "He can't marry Alicia." She always put a little knife twist through the centre of the name Alicia. It wasn't even really her name. Daneen had just slapped it on her the first time she'd seen her, before they were introduced. When introductions were finally made, Daneen didn't bother to listen to the real name.

She was shaking her head. "I just wanted to impress him so he'd know I wasn't just some admin assistant."

"You've worked there all summer, Daneen. I'm sure you've made an impression."

"He doesn't seem the least bit impressed." She poured herself more wine. "He knows a lot of important people—big names, a lot of writers. He talks about them all the time. But he never talks about her—real name Yolanda, if you can believe that."

"Well you've still got a few weeks left to make an impression."

She peered at me over her wine glass like I was the sunrise. Then she tipped her head. "Meriel, do you know you're missing an earring?"

It was nowhere. I scoured the apartment, looked in and under everything before I accepted that it might have escaped down the drain in the shower, or else it was at Eric's. My parents had given me those gold hoops—18 karat with a filigreed edge—for my seventeenth birthday and I'd worn them ever since. I unclasped the lone survivor and laid it on my dresser.

From the couch, Daneen called out, "I think I need some carnal pleasure. Maybe I should call Eric." Like she still had some claim to him. Like he was sitting by the phone, waiting for her summons. "It would be so nice to be adored for a night."

I gave up on the earring and went to stand behind the couch, where she couldn't see me. "Too complicated, Daneen, you'll regret it. Let's go to a club and you can shop around."

The noise and lights, the crush of strangers and the constant cigarettes between our fingers distracted us both from thoughts of Eric, and while Daneen didn't meet anyone worth the trouble that night she did come home with a brilliant idea for a story she'd scribbled—illegibly, it turned out—on a napkin.

The next morning she slept in and I got a clear shot at calling Eric. He sounded so glad to hear my voice. He asked if I was okay, and then he asked if we were okay, and just that *we* changed everything. After I hung up, I tipped over on the couch and grinned like an idiot.

57.

WHEN I GOT to work on Tuesday, Aubrey's car wasn't there. I

dug into my purse for the key I'd hardly ever used, since Aubrey was always first in. I was so busy jiggling the imperfect cut of that key in the lock that I didn't look through the glass into the store, so I didn't know the place had been cleared out until I stepped inside.

Robbed. Thieves had taken everything except a couple of stray power cords, some scattered papers and the clear packing tape I'd been using to seal up the boxes on Saturday morning. The tape sat on my desk, which they'd also left, though my chair and my files and even my stapler were gone. I looked in the back room, afraid I'd find Aubrey there, unconscious or worse, but it was also empty.

Since they'd taken my phone, I couldn't call the police; I could just walk in circles feeling sick, trying to fathom the extent of the loss. Finally my head cleared enough to think of the payphone at the 7-Eleven. I even locked up on my way out, though I did see the irony in that.

Though I suspected Aubrey was probably already at the police station, I called his home number, which I kept in my wallet. A recording answered. The number was not in service. I dialed again. Same recording. It was another humid day, the sky darkening as I walked slowly back to the store and peered once more through the unbroken—the utterly intact—storefront glass.

It wasn't until after I stepped into the mid-morning silence of my apartment that the gravity of it hit me. I had nothing to show for a whole summer of work, for weeks and weeks with no pay.

I looked up Aubrey's address in the phone book and I didn't even stop to think. I just got back in my car and I drove there, to a duplex, two front doors and a railing that divided A from B down the middle of the porch. The wind had picked up and the elm trees leaning out over the street were starting to fidget. I pounded on A first—it looked more dishevelled with its torn sheet hanging as a curtain in the front window. Very Aubrey.

No one answered, so I pounded some more and then I yelled, "Aubrey!"

I was suddenly so angry I wanted to kick the door in, and I might have tried except the door to B opened and a woman stuck her head out. "He's gone. Moved out on the weekend." She didn't know where but guessed it was far away since he'd rented one of those big U-Hauls, the kind that fit everything in one load.

I got back in my car and fought the urge to run straight to Eric. We had no precedent for real life.

As I drove slowly home, rain started to smack the windshield, sudden and hard as if the disparate forces of the universe—It's Not Fair and You Deserve This—had climbed into the backseat and called down the storm. It pummelled from all sides. The wipers raced to keep up, the windshield fogged. I opened all the windows and let the deluge in.

58.

DANEEN WAS MORE enraged than me because it affected her less. She wanted police involvement, charges pressed, a posse on horseback if we could manage one. She was sure there had to be some legal recourse, some sexual harassment tribunal I could charge him through. I shook my head emphatically, unable to speak, and she delivered a brief lecture on not being stupid, not letting my embarrassment get in the way of making him pay.

She was getting ready to go out, and she carried on the whole time about men and betrayal, about how they use us up and toss us away like old rags. I sat mute, sipping the beer she'd put in my hand, watching the sky outside try on various shades of gloomy until she stepped between me and the window.

"God, Meriel, you must be so hurt."

I started to cry then, not because I was hurt—though I was hurt—but because she was making it so much worse by going on like this, by pitying me and not for any of the right things. I choked "Please" from a constricted throat, "Can you just stop? I don't want to talk about this anymore—not ever. Can you just leave, please?"

"Fine." She walked around me, her heels clicking hard on the wood floor as she gathered up her things. "So what will you do for money now?"

That seemed unnecessarily cruel. It took a full minute for my throat to open enough to answer. "Drop out and find another job, I guess. Save up so I can go back next year."

She stood looking at me for a long minute, and then left without saying a word.

The next morning, Daneen stood in the doorway of my bedroom, staring at me until she knew I was awake. "Poor penniless waif is so boring. Here." She was holding a personal cheque out by its corner, waggling it like I was a dog and it was a treat.

"Daneen, don't. I can't take your money."

"I'm not about to watch you mope around all year."

"But I can't pay it back, not for a really long time."

"Just take it."

I could see the figure—three thousand dollars, almost as much as Aubrey would have owed me by the end of the summer—and I could see everything it represented. Right then I could have told her why she shouldn't be giving me a gift, but I didn't. I just took the cheque and promised to pay it back. I told her I'd write out a note.

Daneen was adamantly opposed to an IOU. "You can owe me a favour."

"No really, I will pay you back. I'll figure out something."

"I know you will." Not even the faintest hint of a smile. She began to turn from my doorway but turned back. "Oh, I almost

forgot—" She licked her lips in a way that bared all her teeth—
"I found your earring."

Daneen laid the little gold ring in the palm of my hand
beside the cheque and walked away, leaving me to consider how
all the zeroes lined up.

59.

IT TOOK ERIC four days to call me. I'd steeled myself for it but
at the sound of his voice my lungs emptied, lost all their
resiliency. He asked me to meet him at the Pound and I wanted
to so badly my throat tightened into a sob. When I could, I told
him no. I told him, "We can't keep doing this. I can't, anyway."

"I thought we had something here."

"What, Eric—what exactly do we have?" I wanted to hear
his response but my question sounded as impenetrable as a
concrete wall you'd bounce a ball off. I answered myself. "We
had a fun summer, that's all. It's over."

"You know what I think?" He was mad now, the sharp edges
of his voice all squared up and dancing, "I think we should just
tell Daneen and do what we want."

Of course his first thought was Daneen. Of course that's
what had him so riled up.

"Fuck you, Eric." There it was, the low steely tone I needed.
It lifted me to my feet. "You got what you wanted, avenged your
poor broken heart. You feel better now, right? Then I've done
my duty."

"That's not fair, Meriel."

"Life isn't fair, Eric—didn't anyone ever tell you that?" I
wanted to toss out something light, just so he wouldn't think I
was hemorrhaging internally. All I managed before I hung up
was, "See you around."

60.

ON LABOUR DAY, while I trudged through the ritual of polite

smiles and plastic forks in Calder, Daneen was making her big move, hammering out something on her computer that would elevate her above the level of admin assistant. At least that's what she'd told me, why she wasn't coming to Doris and Don's gala event. Standing on the lawn between the potato salad and the dealership gang, I had the sudden sensation that Daneen was hurtling forward while I was just milling about. Just keeping my eyes on the middle distance, which in this case fell on a row of poplars killed by whatever chemical soup the town spread on the roads to keep the gravel dust down.

The third time some relative asked about my friends, that lovely couple from last year's party, I killed Eric off. It was an accident. "A tragic accident. Awful. Oh, but she's fine, don't worry. She's completely over it now." Then I ducked inside before anyone could nail me on the particulars.

Within weeks, Daneen had exactly what she wanted— a short story to be published in the journal and Bryan's full attention. By then, I understood she was in love with him, though only because she overtly said so. "I love him and I deserve him" was exactly how she put it.

Bryan agreed, I guess, because he'd confessed all to Alicia-Yolanda, who'd spotted Daneen at the liquor store and stood, hands on her hips, blocking the path to the French wine. Daneen acted out the whole scene for me, moving in so close only a fist would fit between our noses, repeating what she'd said in that aisle.

"All's fair."

When I finally met him, Bryan wasn't at all what her descriptions had led me to expect. He was tall and thin, too hawkish to be handsome, a scruffy beard the only thing that mitigated his sharp features. At a glance, I certainly wouldn't have called him salubrious. And he wasn't as charming as she'd intimated, either, at least not to me. He started out with a hale handshake, then told me a great deal about himself and his aspirations, mentioned some names I didn't recognize and finally, when my attention was so obviously flagging, threw out a few questions that felt more like tests than conversation. I suppose I didn't pass, because he never made an effort again to say anything beyond basic pleasantries to me when he visited our apartment.

Soon, Daneen was spending most of her nights at Bryan's apartment, dropping by our place only for a change of clothes and a quick smoke. She'd quit, officially at least—smoking was, for Bryan, a deal breaker—and she'd developed a whole new lexicon: creative energy, wheat germ, chakra.

In December, on one of those rare mornings when she was at our apartment, she asked me if I could drive her to an exam. It was a chance for a few minutes alone together and I thought that might be nice.

"Hey, can we go through the drive-thru at McDonald's?" Daneen was eyelining into her compact mirror in the passenger seat. "I just want to eat some big corporate crap while he's not watching."

A kind of torpidity had settled over me and I knew my metabolism was preparing for a long, slow winter, so I didn't order anything for myself—a decision I regretted as soon as Daneen opened the bag and the smell of greasy goodness filled the car.

Oily spray-on snow blighted the windows of businesses all the way down our route, though there was no snow on the ground yet. I asked Daneen if she was coming out to Calder for Christmas. She shook her head, her jaw working on a mouthful of Egg McMuffin around which she said something about Bryan.

"You could bring Bryan. I'm sure Doris is dying to meet your new man."

Daneen put her ungloved hand to her throat as if she'd swallowed too much. "Didn't I tell you, Meriel? We were out in Calder for dinner last month. He was dying to meet her, too."

61.

CONVOCATION WAS A heavy word for a long, loaded ceremony, and there was little to do through the interminable speeches but worry about walking across that stage and try not to sweat under the nylon cap and gown. I couldn't even distract myself by looking around for Eric, since they'd split arts and sciences into separate ceremonies.

The last words I'd said to Eric had turned out to be untrue. I didn't see him around, not up close. Once, in the dark heart of winter, I was pretty sure I spotted him heading into the student centre. I wanted to run straight to him but it was windy, my hair a mess and my eyes tearing so I went in another door, stopped to smooth down and touch up, then walked past the coffee counter and the food court and up to the bar. But I couldn't find him. I stalked the whole building, top to bottom, side to side, my hard-heeled boots hammering the concrete floors. Eventually I gave up, figuring there'd be another chance, a perfect encounter. It never happened.

When my name was called to accept my degree, it was as if someone else walked across that stage. Afterward, dazed, my hands trembling as they clutched the folder to my pounding chest, I could barely recall any of it. I stared at the parchment, at the gold seal cut with pinking shears and above it my name. *Meriel Claire Elgin*. Drooling curlicues and no hyphen. I wasn't sure if that was the university's mistake or if I'd left it off the application to graduate. Beneath my name it said *Meritorious Degree*.

I'd hoped, when I saw the parchment, that I'd know what I was supposed to do next. I wanted to feel something—certainty, or satisfaction at least—but I didn't. I just felt sticky hot and weak once my stage fright had subsided. A long, long list of names followed mine, and each one called made my achievement seem smaller.

After the ceremony was over and we'd all filed out, our line turning to a mob, I saw my father coming toward me with a camera and a big smile. Tears welled up in his eyes after he took my picture and I knew exactly what I'd do. I knew I'd frame that degree and hang it over my desk at the dealership.

62.

DANEEN'S DEGREE CAME in the mail. She crammed it, the stiff envelope unopened, into the box she was packing. She'd skipped the ceremony, taken Bryan east for a week to meet, separately, her parents. I'd wanted to know about the reunion, hear all the gory details, but Daneen gave me almost nothing. She said it was fine, all fine, and it was as if there'd never been a dramatic, years-long rift at all. I thought it really must have healed, but a few days later, she announced that Bryan had a job in Vancouver and she was moving west with him. "I can't think of anything more perfect than living in a big, vibrant city so far from my parents," she told me.

And suddenly, we were packing her up. Daneen handed me a framed photo of the two of us hamming it up in Halloween costumes a few years earlier, a night I couldn't recall at all now. She was singing under her breath, a tune I didn't recognize. I chose a t-shirt from her worth-packing pile and wrapped it tight around the picture.

"You're just going to stay here, Meriel, banging around this old place? No other plans?"

"I'm not moving back to Calder, if that's what you mean." I wedged the wrapped photo along one side of an overstuffed box. Daneen was taking only what would fit in the trunk of Bryan's car. All the big stuff, all her furniture, would become mine. She was even leaving her computer, though she apologized for that, for leaving me the taint of Aubrey. I said it was fine to leave, that I was over him now. From the dining room, I could make out the sound of the printer whirring, its ball running side to side, spinning out her latest string of words.

Daneen picked up a pair of champagne flutes Eric had given

her. She held them out to me, one in each fist. I set them aside
to throw away later and told her, "My mother thinks Gord
should move in here."

Daneen didn't look up, which made it impossible to tell if
she already knew exactly what my mother thought. "At least you
wouldn't be alone."

Mom had said the same thing. The presumption stung more
coming from Daneen.

"If he actually pays his share, at least I'll be able to pay you
back faster." I always had every intention of paying her back. I
needed her to know that. "I've been thinking about a payment
schedule, starting right away—"

"Meriel, stop. I'm not worried about the money. It was a
gift. Besides, I know you'll do something for me if I ever need
your help."

I could tell there was no point arguing, and very soon after
that there was nothing left for us to talk about. There wasn't even
a short, poignant walk down memory lane. When Bryan called
to say he was on his way, Daneen folded shut the top on her one
box and we carried it together to the door. Then there was just
an awkward hug, the two of us reaching out over what so neatly
contained everything she wanted.

63.

GORD WAS SAILING through an expensive audio technician
course my parents were paying for. One of his teachers, some
studio bigshot, said he was a natural. Mom kept telling me that,
and every time, she added, "Gord's really found his groove."

And now wasn't it perfect that Gord needed a place in the
city just when I needed someone to help pay the rent?

I didn't need help, though I couldn't make Mom hear that.
I made enough as the official keeper of the dealership books,
the sole balancer. Everything payable and receivable now
flowed through me. Dad hiked my pay to match my new

responsibilities, then nudged it up a little further to recognize my meritoriousness. I figured it was his way of acknowledging that Gord might not be the most reliable of roommates.

On the last day of June, I moved my things into Daneen's larger room and opened the door to Gord without argument, like everyone knew I would. Mom, standing next to him, was huffing a bit from the stairs. She let Gord get the rest while she looked around assessing, I guess, how to rearrange things to better suit her boy. She looked into the bedroom I'd vacated. "I never realized that this one was so small. I hope Gord can fit all his things in here," she said.

She followed Gord downstairs for the final load. He came back alone, called out, "Honey, I'm home!" and dropped whatever he was carrying with a thud.

I continued to pry *Serendipity* off my bedroom door.

"MC, come tell me where to put my stuff and how much I have to pay."

Gord wrote me six post-dated cheques right then—neither of us could imagine this arrangement lasting longer than half a year—and handed them to me as if I was his landlord and not his little sister. As if, while he'd been sulking in our parents' basement, I'd zoomed right past him.

Later, I told him where he should set up his stereo and then we started, very carefully, getting to know each other again. Not right away, not at one overnight pajama party that made us best friends but slowly, as grown-ups who'd once known each other as kids.

It turned out to be easy, living with Gord. He was usually more cheerful and no messier than Daneen had been and not one single cheque bounced, not in that first batch of six and not in the next six, either.

64.

GORD WAS BALLED up on the couch, moaning. Faux moaning, really. "Why won't she stop calling me?"

"It's not that big a deal, Gord. C'mon, get changed or we'll be late." He'd promised to come with me to see *Reversal of Fortune*. I'd been waiting weeks for it to hit the cheap theatres and I didn't want to miss a minute. I figured if the director was doing his job, every bit of a movie mattered.

"What if she's crazy—I mean boil the bunny crazy?" Gord and I had gone to see *Fatal Attraction* the year before. I wondered if that movie put the fear of insane stalker bitches with crazy hair and crazier eyes into all men.

I looked Gord over. He was wearing an old blue sweatshirt that wasn't even dark enough to hide the ketchup stain from a previous night's dinner. I laughed out loud. "Because you're such hot stuff, and she can't live without you? I think she'll get over you, Gord."

He'd slept with Darla once. Only once, that's what he kept saying, *onccce*, hissing for emphasis. They met in the club where he was mixing sound for some half-baked band, which he did on the weekends to earn a little extra money. He'd gone back to her place for the night and had great sex—he'd made a point of telling me that the next day.

"I'm just not interested in her. For the long haul."

"Meaning you don't want to marry her, or you don't want to take her on a lengthy excursion?"

"Meaning I want her to stop calling. It's weird and it's scary."

Twice. She'd called *twice*—the first time about a week after the night that was, and this time, more than a month later. Only this time I'd taken the message, not the machine.

"You're overreacting, Gord. Twice is not scary. Twice is 'Hi, remember me? I like you.'" She hadn't actually sounded that upbeat on the phone. "Look, Gord, honestly, we don't all go rabid after a night of so-so sex. Now come on."

While we were at the movies, Darla left another message. "The rabbit," she said, "is dead. Call me." Then, like an afterthought, "Yes it's yours, asshole."

65.

SHE WAS KEEPING it. That was the upshot of their brief meeting at the mall, where Darla had taken a break from The Gap and met Gord at one of those cherry-red laminate tables in the food court. Gord told me she was already looking pudgy, that she'd made him buy her fries and a vanilla milkshake. Made him like it was his duty, the least he could do. That's how Gord told it, anyway.

Darla wanted to try, to see if they could fall in love and he did take her out a couple of times. "No way," he told me after the second date, "I'm just not interested."

For a few weeks afterward, Gord would talk to her when she called. To my ear, he was firm and clear but never unkind. But when the calls kept coming, he started to use the answering machine to screen them, refusing to pick up. He acted like he thought if he didn't talk to her, she'd go away and everything in his life would come together just fine.

And he was so close to that happening. Gord was the golden boy of his small class and he'd fallen hard for his final work placement, which had him making sound for local radio productions. He loved the work, even for next to no pay, and he was sure they were going to offer him a real job at the end of it. To graduate, he put on the brown suit my mother had bought him. He looked nonchalant and then cocky, and my parents beamed from the sidelines like they used to when he pitched a big game and no one but me seemed to notice calamity, warming up in the batter's box.

When we got home that night, there was one final, menacingly calm message from Darla. She wanted Gord to know she was going to squeeze him for every penny she could get. He erased the message and went to get undressed but came charging back, his unbuttoned shirt flapping behind him like a cape. "This is like being drafted into the army. It's a life sentence. How do I make this go away, MC?"

I didn't have a clue, didn't know what the options were for

a guy. He'd done nothing worse than I had half a dozen times, nothing more reckless than every girl I knew had done at some point. For the first time ever, I considered that being born male might have its pitfalls.

"It was one fucking night!" Gord yelled it twice then paced the room until he was calmer.

I asked him then when he planned to tell Mom and Dad. He froze in mid-pace and gradually thawed from the neck up. "They will freak out. They thought I finally had my shit together." He glared at me. "Promise me you'll never tell them, MC. *Never.*"

I promised, again and again, every time he asked me to.

66.

JUST INSIDE THE new year, Darla had a baby boy. As soon as he got the call, Gord grabbed his coat and headed to the hospital, leaving me on the couch, shaking and tearful, picturing a baby with Gord's cowlick. When he came home, the grim was gone from his face, the awful weight from his shoulders. He said he'd spent an hour just staring at that infant until he was certain he felt nothing—nothing huge or special at all. He thought it was a good sign, his lack of feeling. It was proof the kid wasn't his after all.

I didn't know how it worked, if there was some instinct that let you know a baby carried your genes, but a week later there was a blood test and then there was no doubt, just a letter from Darla's lawyer telling Gord to pay up. Gord's idea was just to ignore it, but I couldn't. I made an appointment with a lawyer and I took off Friday afternoon to make sure he got there. Mom and Dad had gone to visit friends who wintered in Texas, so no one questioned my absence.

As soon as we got home from the lawyer, Gord went to the kitchen and poured himself a rye and coke. "He said I don't have to help with the kid if I don't want to, right?"

"Right. He said you have to pay, but you don't have to parent."

Gord brought his drink into the living room but he didn't sit down. "Fucking unbelievable. How can a little baby cost three hundred dollars a month?"

At least three hundred, I wanted to remind him.

Gord looped the living room while I considered whether I should just get it over with, offer to pay more of our shared expenses. I knew it would come to that. When he headed back to the kitchen, his glass empty, I followed and joined him in a rye and coke, although I'd never developed a liking for hard liquor.

Halfway through my drink, I remembered the university job his studio teacher had called about. "Sounds boring as hell," Gord had said when he'd heard the message. "I'm not quitting a job I like for that."

I reminded him that this boring job paid half again as much and he'd been asked to apply.

"Why is it all on me? Why doesn't she have to get a job?"

"I don't know. I guess because she's looking after the baby."

"That's her choice. She's the one who wanted the baby, isn't she?"

He crossed back to the rye. I called after him, "You should get that application done. The deadline's Monday, right?"

His hand smacked the counter, hard. "Stop bossing me around, MC. One bitch ruining my life is enough."

My mouth hung open, stuffed full of silence. Maybe he saw the tears gathering because he took my glass and refilled it. I carried the drink to the couch and I concentrated on watching the carbonated fizz burst along the surface until one of us thought to turn on the TV.

The next morning I woke up early. I had heartburn and a dull ache behind my eyes that kept up even after two cups of coffee. Gord slept much later and when he got up he wasn't chipper, but at least he wasn't suffering.

He acted like nothing was wrong and I guess that's why I made him go.

I was supposed to check on the house in Calder every few days. Insurance, Dad had told me—someone had to make sure the furnace was on, the pipes weren't freezing. Someone had to water the plants every Friday, but with all the fuss of going to the lawyer, I hadn't been on Friday. And I was so sick of that highway, the monotony of it, the way it stretched just a little longer every day. So I told Gord it was his turn to go.

"What do you mean *my* turn? They asked you to do it."

"Christ, Gord, just this one time—just *once*—could you do something for me?"

67.

GORD HAD DISCOVERED the skateboard in Sears, propped against the back wall in the sporting goods section. My parents were shopping for a lawnmower and I suppose we were too young to be left at home, but old enough to wander around a department store without them.

Gord had no money saved up, of course, but he talked about the skateboard all the way home in the car and for days afterward—talked about it until I wanted that skateboard every bit as much as he did, until I counted out all my star-won allowance and I convinced my mother to take me back to the mall.

She didn't think that skateboard was right for me, couldn't even believe I wanted it. I could see, standing there in Sears, that she was completely blind to the grace of its curved black body, the terrifying beauty in its arc of orange flame.

It used up almost all my savings to buy it.

And it was worth every penny. Gord built obstacle courses and ramps, first on the driveway and then all summer in the empty school parking lot. They became more elaborate as he got better at manoeuvring, at landing still up on his feet. And even though I hardly ever got to ride my own skateboard and never quite got the hang of staying upright, I was so proud of what he could do that it felt like my own success.

I thought about that skateboard all the way to the hospital. I thought about how I couldn't remember ever seeing Gord fall.

68.

MY HAND SHOOK so hard I could barely get the quarter into the slot. I was down in the hospital lobby; there were phones closer to the ICU but I didn't know it yet. I'd noticed these ones on my way in, a kind of random observation as I hurtled toward the elevators, then backtracked to Information to find out where to go.

I had the operator on the line, but I couldn't remember the name of the town in Texas where my parents were staying with friends. Dad had written the number down on a small blue piece of paper and left it on the kitchen counter, the pen lying diagonally across it. That diagonal pen was code in our house for "Look—I just wrote this important thing down for you." But it was lying right across the number in my memory, obscuring all but the first few and the last few digits.

Directory Assistance needed the town's name to find the number. Dad had called it a snowbird nesting ground and at first I thought he meant there were a lot of birds to see. I offered that description but it didn't help the operator either, even after I explained about retirees flying south for the winter.

Doris and Don had gone down for a visit, just to have a look, to thaw out, but then they'd called to say they'd bought property. A deal, my dad called it, an investment for the future.

McAllen, Texas. That was it. I practically shouted it into the receiver. And when Dad came on the line, he didn't sound worried like people usually do when you call out of the blue. He sounded like he'd been waiting for a phone call all along and now here it was. Hello.

I remember the whole conversation, verbatim. My father said, "Hello," and I said, "You need to come home, right away."

And he asked why. Just "Why?" and I told him—and then my voice choked off and Dad asked if there was a fighting chance. I heard my mother's background moan, a noise like she already knew the answer, and my voice came back strong for the "No."

"What hospital?" And then, "We're on our way." I never, never asked about their trip, about how they got from that faraway town in Texas to the hospital, about the terrible hours in between.

I hung up and stared at the painted Jesus hung on the lobby wall, his hands clasped as if in prayer. I guess that's what he was doing—Jesus was praying to God his Father, which seemed an unlikely way for the two of them to communicate. For the first time in my life, I wished I knew more than the obvious things about Jesus and God, wished I'd been raised in some kind of faith, had some connection so I could holler up, ask, "Why are you doing this?" Yell, "Please don't," and maybe, "Let him be okay, let him be a miracle." So I could plead in the right way and believe someone might be listening, might reconsider. But I couldn't. I couldn't pray in front of that picture of Jesus, or walk into the chapel marked by its big cross just off the hospital lobby. I thought it would be cheating to start just because I suddenly had a big need. And anyway, the thought of praying made me feel like a Shop-Vac was hooked up right below my breastbone, between my ribs, pushed in and roaring, sucking my insides hollow.

What I really wanted was to drive my fist into that pious praying Jesus portrait, or to kick the bronze Virgin Mary a little further down, nearer the elevators. I wanted to kick her and kick her and kick her until my toes were broken and she got the point.

Instead, I flung the stairwell door open and stomped up to the ICU where there was nothing to do but lean against the concrete block wall, my back flat against the sheen of mint green paint. For who knows how long, I just stood, breathing in that pervasive hospital smell that isn't antiseptic and isn't sickness but is like some terrible, negotiated compromise between the two. I'd never been in a hospital before but already I was used to that smell and used to the hum and rasp of the machines, too.

If I took one step forward, I could have reached out and touched what was left of Gord, but I didn't. I stayed frozen against that wall, waiting for the next horrible part to come.

69.

THE POLICE TALKED to me, but I couldn't tell them much—just that Gord was on his way to water the plants, that it was supposed to be me but I'd made him go. They said it looked like he'd almost cleared the tracks, like maybe he'd just misjudged how much time he had. The train caught the back end of his car, flung it end over end down into the ditch.

The female officer got me some tissue from the nurse's desk and they waited until I calmed down. They were trying so hard to be nice but there were things they had to ask—things you'd expect: alcohol, drugs, mental state. I told them no, no way, he'd just gotten up that morning. I told them he sometimes played the radio really loud in the car.

I said I didn't know why he didn't stop. "I always stop at those tracks—I always look. Dad taught us that. You have to look, every time. I always do."

I told them again that he didn't want to go, that it was supposed to be me.

I started to apologize—sorry, sorry, sorry—but I stopped myself before the first feeble word escaped. I choked them all back right then, the million apologies rushing up in me. If I hadn't, I would have spent the rest of my life on them.

Much later, the doctor came to talk to me. First he looked around, asked if there was anyone else. I shook my head—there's just me—but that didn't stop him from looking around some more, as if someone else might suddenly appear. I could see I'd let him down by not drawing a crowd. I said I didn't know how long before my parents arrived. I told him again I was it, just me. Same last name, same address. I was next of kin and all the kin there was.

So he laid out for me what they wanted to do. And the way he told it, it was just a yes or no choice. It wasn't going to change anything, not for Gord, but it might give someone else a chance.

The doctor said Gord had signed the donor card on the back of his driver's license and he showed it to me and it was undoubtedly Gord's signature. Then he left me alone to think. I couldn't think, sitting there with all those machines humming their terrible hum, so I went for a walk, up and down all the corridors, floor after floor. I wanted to see this other family, the one waiting for my decision. I wanted it to be that obvious a transaction.

But I didn't see anyone. Later, when that doctor came back again, I said go ahead.

70.

FROM THE PAYPHONE right next to the ICU, I reached Daneen. I said something like, "Gord's dying. I mean, dead. I mean it's happening right now." They'd let me say goodbye, told me I could stay as long as I wanted. I'd held his hand, tried to think of things to say. I thought I would like to ruffle his goofy hair but his head was all wrapped up. Anyway, I knew someone else was waiting for pieces of Gord, and I knew I should let him go.

I have no idea what Daneen said when I told her, or how much I explained. I just remember, "I'm catching the next flight. Just hang on."

The relief of it—like I'd pulled off a small miracle, saved the day, undone everything. Like Daneen's coming could rewind some mystical clock.

As soon as I hung up, I ran back to Gord. I wanted to let him know Daneen was coming. I wanted to say, "Just hang on," and tell the doctors to stop.

But Gord wasn't there. Seeing me, a nurse headed over, the squeak of her rubber soles loud on the floor now that all the machines in the room had gone quiet. She said, "He's gone now," which was obvious. It was what I'd agreed to. There was no point in saying anything back. I forced my eyes from where the bed had been, found a place on the wall that was only white, and I stuck with it.

I thought maybe I could just stop breathing now, too, and maybe that would be fair. Or maybe I couldn't think anything so rational just then. Maybe that thought came later.

71.

MY MOTHER BARRELLED down the hallway, hair ragged and flying, her mouth wide open to drag in all the air. Fifteen feet behind her, my father lifted his legs with an effort that suggested he was having trouble adjusting to gravity. The sight of them like that, frantic and plodding, made it all seem like just a bad dream.

I hadn't expected them so soon—I thought it would take so much longer to come all the way from Texas. I'd only been sitting in a molded plastic chair in the hospital hallway for a few hours.

I barely managed to get to my feet before my mother got to me. "Where is he?"

I reached out my hand but only managed to connect with the purse hooked in the crook of her arm. "He's gone."

I hadn't even had time to practice what I'd say.

I watched it register—the sharp blow, and then the blur. She turned back to my father and buckled. My wrists caught her awkwardly under the armpits but I was sinking with her. It was Dad, suddenly there, who caught us both and hauled us all upright.

I nodded to Dad, confirmation of what he already knew.

Mom refocused. She was leaning into Dad but glaring straight at me. Crazed, a completely different woman than the one I'd expected. I guess I'd thought she'd enfold me. That's what I realized later—I was waiting to be gathered close.

I should never have said the next part. "They needed his organs, so I let them."

"You *let* them, before we even got here?"

"He was already—the doctors said there was no point." I shut my eyes against the terrible mistake I'd made.

"But we got here so fast." She backed away, her hands grabbing at the air like she needed a handhold to keep from falling. I wanted to tell her to give up, that there was nothing to hold onto.

"You can see him if you want. They're expecting that."

Finally an enfolding, my father's arms almost crushing me, the unfamiliar sound of his sobs.

72.

CALDER UNITED CHURCH almost burst at the seams. It wasn't just the whole town that turned up for the funeral—people from the farms came, and all the kids he'd gone to high school with, plus relatives from the city and my mother's sister from Alberta. It surprised me, so many people, but this was my first experience with sudden death, with young death, so I didn't know how the bright-white shock of it attracted.

After the funeral, they all streamed into our house. My mother had vetoed the church basement so I knew, under the ash of her face, beyond the slight tremor, that her true self was still there. I watched the door, watched everyone arrive carrying something—a tray, a covered casserole. The Wallaces from two doors down brought boxes of tissue and reams of toilet paper, essentials you might not think of until you ran out. But no one brought in a newborn baby. After an hour I relaxed and started noticing other things: the sunburn on my father's neck, his stooped shoulders pretending to be square in his navy suit. Daneen's bright salmon nailpolish peeling Saran Wrap off a tray of devilled eggs. She was saying, "People like to play a part in tragedy. It makes them feel important, like they're part of a drama."

"Or people might be here—" my indignation especially pungent because it was the first thing I'd felt all day—"because they actually cared about Gord."

Daneen lifted her hand and, for a split second, I imagined she would slap me. Instead she rested it on my upper arm, rubbed the slippery poly-satin paisley of the blouse I'd borrowed from Mom. "Of course. We're all here because we care. That's what I meant. These things make people realize what's important."

Daneen had come right away, just like she'd promised, and she'd let me tell her as much as I wanted to about the night Gord died, all the details I couldn't tell anyone else. She'd even brought cigarettes, which suddenly seemed so necessary, and we smoked them out back of the house late at night like we had years before.

I watched her carry the tray of eggs to the dining-room table, then move to hover beside my mother who was standing so straight and so unusually empty-handed. Daneen placed her hand on Mom's far shoulder so the whole of her forearm became a brace. Mom didn't flinch like she did when I tried to touch her. Instead, she leaned into the support.

Daneen belongs to us, I thought. She knows us better than we know ourselves.

73.

MY MOTHER LEFT to get groceries, but she didn't make it to the store. She lurched back into the driveway, stumbled through the front door and let out a high, keening scream that brought Dad and me running to the kitchen.

"Who would do it?" She was breathing hard. In a jagged voice she told us someone had pounded a white cross into the ditch beside the railroad track, right where Gord's car had finally come to rest. I remember thinking it was odd that she'd seen it at all, since the grocery store was in the absolute other direction.

"Go take it down—for God's sake, Donald, get it out of there."

My father tried to steer her into a chair, his hands firm on both her shoulders. "Doris, it's a memorial—it's meant to comfort." I couldn't tell if he already knew about the cross, if he'd had a hand in it.

"There's a headstone for that!" She writhed away from his hands like he was an electric eel.

We were alone, a week to the day after the funeral and everyone long gone, even Daneen. It surprised me, that people would think it was over as soon as Gord was in the ground, think they could just pack up and stand down. It wasn't over. It wasn't better and Gord was still dead and there was only me left to look after our parents.

So for me, that white cross in the ditch was at least some sign that everyone else in the world hadn't completely forgotten about Gord being dead.

"Maybe it's like a warning," I said, "to tell other people to watch out." It seemed like the right idea, and at first I wondered if it was something the town took care of, like a yield sign—a way to say, "Hey, pay attention. This is dangerous."

My parents were too focused on each other to even hear me.

"Someone must have thought it was important." Dad put his hands back on Mom's shoulders but he was shaking violently, and Mom's lips were parted as if she was panting. Finally she made a sound—a terrifying sound that made my father pull his hands away from her. The sound went with them, like he'd unplugged her.

The world was quiet until Mom said, "Every time I drive past there, I don't want to have to be reminded that my son is dead." She slapped her right hand against her chest. "Dead."

Dad fixed his eyes somewhere near the back of her skull. "Don't drive that way if you want so much to forget." I saw it then—Dad's face, the wreckage of it. The exhausted, unshaven, unslept, unhinged ruin of him. He shouted so loud I backed up. "As if we're ever going to forget that our son is dead!"

I'd been trying for so long not to cry in front of them, not to start anything, but it rose to my throat and my face buckled and I couldn't stop it and I couldn't get away, either. I was afraid to leave them.

Mom turned her attention to me then. "Why are you still here?"

"Doris—" All the rage had drained from my father's voice.

She ignored him, kept her gaze steady on me. "Go home and leave us alone."

74.

I DIDN'T TURN on a single light in the apartment. I just dropped everything—my purse, the clothes I'd crammed into plastic Foodway bags—and when I bumped into that big couch, I sat down. Then I lay down and I counted the cars driving past, the thrum of engines tearing the fragile air. I understood then, an off-to-the-side thought, why my mother was spending so much time in rooms with the lights out.

I'd expected the apartment to release me. I thought grief would rip out of me loud and long and awful, but that was still weeks away. That first night I lay still on the couch, pressed down by the heat rising from the rooms underneath, by the radiators knocking and the tires grinding on the snow-packed street. Eventually I slept, ten hours straight, and woke up with my shoes still on.

That was the worst of it, waking up into the bright of a

Sunday morning, the world holding its frozen breath. I walked through the silent rooms, ran a hand over all the still-there furniture: the rounded backs of the kitchen chairs, the flat, leathery arm of the couch, the surprisingly rough, cold surface of Gord's stereo equipment. And then I noticed it—the smell of him. Faint, but everywhere. It drew me to his bedroom and I fell face forward into his pillow, into that thick, sweet Gord smell. When I left the room a long time later, I closed the door to seal it in, to keep it from dissipating so I could visit him whenever I needed to.

Then I went down to check the mailbox. A week's worth of flyers and bills were pressed tight and encircled by a large, bent Benefact Life envelope.

75.

AT THE DEALERSHIP, everything remained predictable. Keep busy, that's what people said and Dad and I were both trying. But there isn't much busy going on at a car dealership in the dead of winter and anyway, everybody else was in overdrive trying to take care of things and keep the chatter down. Most days, when I walked past Dad's office on my way to the washroom, I'd see him staring at nothing. That's when I'd forget about columns of numbers and I'd remember about Gord, and for the rest of the day I'd get even less of the nothing done that there was to do.

I left Gord's life insurance papers in their envelope on the side table for more than a week. I didn't know how these things went, what was appropriate, how soon would be too soon to talk about money. Finally, when I couldn't stand it anymore, I went to my father's office and closed the door. "Gord had life insurance—"

My father nodded. "We all do, it's a group family plan. It covered the funeral expenses." His eyes focused. "If there are outstanding bills, it can cover them. Just bring them to me."

"No, this is from his work. An envelope came in the mail."

"Oh. Bring it in tomorrow, I'll take a look."

"Tomorrow's Sunday, Dad." I didn't admit I had it in the trunk of my car, that it had been riding with me for over a week.

"Right. Well bring it out to the house. Come for dinner. It would be good for your mother to see you."

I hadn't talked to Mom since she'd sent me away. Every day I asked about her, and Dad always said she was fine, but I knew she wasn't. I knew she was eviscerated by grief—eviscerated is what Daneen, who called us both every few days, had told me.

After dinner, I laid the envelope face down on the kitchen table so Dad wouldn't see the postmark. Next to him, Mom was looking out the window. She'd hugged me tight when I'd come through the door, smoothed the hair at my crown and asked how I was, and I'd clung to her hand for a long minute after that.

Dad slipped the papers out and scanned the first page. When he looked up, I couldn't tell if he was surprised. "It says you're the sole beneficiary, Meriel-Claire."

"I know, but I have to tell you something." For days I'd been weighing it, deciding whether to tell them about baby Justin. I'd been thinking about the balm he could be.

My mother sat back and fixed me with a stare. "Did you know about this? Is that why you were in such a hurry—"

My father said, "Doris" like a warning. If she heard it, she didn't blink.

Dad didn't read further. "Do you know how much you'll receive?"

I shook my head. "I haven't really read through it."

"It won't be much. He only worked there for a handful of months."

"I know, but there's something—" I wanted to ease into it, this news about Gord's son.

My mother jangled the ice cubes in her gin and tonic, then stilled them with a guzzle. She pushed back from the table.

"Gord obviously wanted you to have it. Now you do. I don't want to hear another word about it."

My father slid the papers toward me without turning a page. "Get in touch with them. It might be a nice little sum for doing something special. Think of it as—"

"My lucky break?" The words, my tone—a surprise to us all. I busied myself getting the papers back into their envelope while my parents wrapped themselves in necessary and unbearable silence. Finally we all agreed I should get home.

On the way, I stopped and bought a pack of cigarettes, but when I lit one in the parking lot, I could barely stand the bitter taste in my mouth. The suffocation of it.

Air didn't come fully back to my lungs until I heard Darla's voice on the answering machine. Darla, angry, berating Gord for not paying what he owed. In the background I could hear the baby, his single syllable complaints. Darla went on threatening a dead man until the baby began to wail.

I pulled the insurance papers out and read all the way through them for the first time. That's when I saw it: one hundred thousand dollars. The figure, all those zeroes, near the bottom of page two.

Here, finally, was something I could do right.

I spent almost a month talking to the insurance people, telling them the same things over and over, pointing them to police reports and filling out forms and going over it again until finally, they agreed Gord's death had been an accident. Then I went to a lawyer and I set up the trust—a hundred-thousand dollars set to pay out a little more each year until Justin turned eighteen. With interest, there'd be enough left over for his education.

It was easy to work out the money, much harder to compose the letter. I wanted it to say something about Gord, to capture some essential thing a little boy should know about his father, but all I had were facts—dates, hobbies, height. At the end of it, I wrote that Gord had wanted to be sure Justin was cared for. I included two pictures, one from when Gord was about four and one I'd taken in our apartment. He was laughing in both.

76.

THE INSURANCE PAYOUT was twice as much as I'd expected. Accidental death paid double and it was strange, the way I kept missing such crucial details.

Justin was already looked after by the intentional funds but the other half, this accidental half, belonged to no one. I opened a separate savings account and I buried it there.

I was twenty-four years old and it seemed like a fortune to me. I hadn't earned it, I hadn't asked for it and I couldn't spend it. But it was all I had left of Gord, this sum he'd entrusted to me, so I knew I had to make it count for something.

77.

HE ARRIVED IN a city cab while I was covering reception. Through the window, I watched the big man lumber out of the backseat and wait, hands in his pockets, while the cab driver hauled a big suitcase from the trunk. Baggage tags blew like an ensign in the wind. I thought it must have cost an astronomical amount to take a cab out to Calder from the airport.

I didn't recognize him and he didn't recognize me. He just asked if Don was available. Dad stepped out of his office and stopped dead, like he'd walked into a pole and stunned himself.

Even after the man clasped both hands on Dad's shoulders and said, "I came as soon as I heard. You know we've been in California for a few years. Jesus, Don, you could have got in touch," I didn't get who it was. It took an introduction, a moment of fog clearing, to understand why the façade of normal we'd been wearing for over a year, ever since we'd buried Gord, had melted right off my father.

Uncle Stewart was tall like Dad but much heavier. His stomach cascaded over his beltline; his round cheeks were scarlet. All that fat made it hard to see the family resemblance.

When I joined them in Calder for dinner the next night, Uncle Stewart's flesh was the only loose thing in the house. It seemed everything else, especially Doris and Don, had been tightly bound with plastic wrap. Even the air was taut, and though Stewart tried to break through with the bottle of expensive scotch he pulled from his suitcase, nothing and no one breathed easy.

While my mother cut a store-bought pie, Stewart poured himself another stiff drink and leaned back in his chair. "It's not getting better any time soon. You know that." I thought at first he was talking about Gord, but no, he meant the economy. Earlier, he'd explained what he was doing in California, how the company he worked for had closed its Canadian office after the free-trade deal was signed. "I've accepted that I won't be able to come back," he'd said. "The opportunity's all gone south."

With a mouthful of pie, he looked from Dad to Mom. "We've all got to accept things, sooner or later."

My mother put her fork down, her pie untouched. My father kept at his in silence, chewing in what seemed like deliberately slow motion. I regretted having said no to a piece. I needed something now to do with my hands, and I wasn't about to reach for the scotch Stewart had set in the centre of the table.

Stewart shook his head vigorously and a bit of flaky crust flew from his cheek. "Jesus, neither of us with a son now to even pass the business on to. Pop must be spinning in his grave." Mom and I stood simultaneously and started gathering the plates. Stewart said, "So I guess that's that then. It's done."

I thought he meant supper.

Two days later, Stewart came to the dealership on his way to the airport. This time he just walked straight into Dad's office, and after a few minutes my father got up and closed his door.

They were in there almost an hour, and when they came out they shook hands solemnly. Then Stewart asked me to call a cab and he waited outside. Dad went back to his office and shut the door again.

78.

DANEEN TOLD ME she was sending a copy of her book. I gave her the address for Elgin & Son, thinking it wouldn't fit in the small mailbox in the lobby of my apartment building. I was imagining the books my parents used to get from Reader's Digest in their fat cardboard cartons, but *Hidden Bargains* was surprisingly thin, its cover soft and sleek as I slid it from the manila envelope.

Daneen hadn't told me anything about it when she called to say it was off to print, only that some people were excited about it. She mentioned them all by name so I knew I should be impressed, that these were people who knew about such things. The next time I'd heard from Daneen was in a postcard: *Springtime in Paris—such a wonderful place to get married! Yesterday! Love D & B.* My parents got a different card with the exact same message penned across the back.

She'd changed her name, which surprised me. The wedding must have been planned because even the book cover said Daneen DeCario. And that's what she'd signed on the title page, too, the double-Ds oversized, the *o* trailing off into a little flourish.

I read the whole novel in one go, late into the night. *Hidden Bargains* was about a fucked-up family in a small prairie town and I don't know why I hadn't expected that. So much of it so familiar: the sunken living room, the landscape outside the windows, the way my mother wore her hair. And the favoured son—a drunk, always screwing up, losing his temper, falling into despair.

She'd painted my mother as sympathetic, of course, turning even her devotion to appearances into a fierce instinct to protect her home. But she'd depicted Dad as cold, stingy to the point of cruelty. The only glue holding the couple together in the pages of her book was their sexual insatiability. Orgies—it was completely ridiculous, the whole premise of that small town sex club. And worse, she'd created an all-seeing youngest daughter who peeped through broken vinyl blinds.

That young daughter, the narrator, was the only made-up person in the whole book. There was another character, a minor character, a silent middle daughter so much duller than the clever and captivating protagonist. She saw it all, that little sister, saw right through to the moral bankruptcy. The family's façade crumbled around that smart, serene narrator but her voice never wavered as she marched us toward the brother's death.

A suicide made to look like an accident—I doubled over, reading that part—and then the falling away of all the masks.

My heart was hammering but I couldn't stop reading. I needed to know what happened. I didn't get much relief. In the end, Daneen left us all wallowing in the shallow grave of our badly lived lives.

I went to bed with my blood still charging. I had to keep turning over, keep sucking breath into my too-tight chest.

79.

DANEEN ALSO SENT a copy to my mother. Some nasty thing in me found that exhilarating—that Mom would turn the pages and see so much revealed—but then dread took over. I knew I'd take the blame for not having protected the family from Daneen's savage pen, for letting her in the door in the first place.

But I couldn't avoid speaking to Mom forever. I was barely in the door on Father's Day when she launched, not even a hello. "I just loved Daneen's book!"

I decided to hang my jacket in the front closet. She followed me down the hall, something she only ever did when she was determined to make her point. "Didn't you?"

I half nodded, half shrugged, a time-tested manoeuvre to concede a point without seeming conciliatory. Doris both craved and despised conciliation.

"That girl has such talent, the way she takes you right inside a room, right inside people's heads." I agreed, this time unequivocally, but Mom stayed hot on my heels.

In the kitchen, she picked up a spatula like she had something to flip though nothing was cooking. She tapped it lightly against her palm. Finally: "I know her family has a lot of *issues*"—she turned the word down low so it took on extra weight—"and I'm sure some of it must be fictionalized, but I can't help wonder how her parents feel about being exposed like that."

80.

FOR MONTHS FOLLOWING Uncle Stewart's visit, Dad's office door was closed more than usual. One afternoon he opened his door, came across to my office and said, "Let's go for a drive."

It was late September, years since our last drive together and yet, after a few miles of bland talk about my work at the dealership and career stepping-stones, I relaxed. I was learning to ride along, to just be there, as pleasant and helpful as I could be. Dad turned off the highway and headed down along the Auberge River where the road narrowed and wound. The trees had changed to yellow; big cottonwood leaves drifted onto the banks.

Dad took a deep breath. "The dealership has been sold."

Not "I've sold" or "We've sold," just "has been," as if it was completely out of his control. "I'll tell the rest of the staff tomorrow. It changes hands at the end of the year."

I let my fingers and my face ask the questions I couldn't form on my tongue.

"Stewart wanted to cash out. I wasn't prepared to bury

myself in debt to buy him out."

"Dad, no—" I thought of Gord's money, sitting hidden, idle. "Is it too late?"

Dad slowed and studied me. "It's all done, yes. I've been thinking of this as an opportunity. For both of us."

He gave me a faint smile. "Of course your mother is thrilled. She's looking forward to a long retirement." He accelerated into a curve, added, "I'd like you to stay on until the end, if you can. But you'll need to start looking for something else."

I looked out my window at the shadows moving on the brown, riffling water, hoping he wouldn't see just how relieved I was.

81.

HIDDEN BARGAINS BECAME a kind of phenomenon, arcing its way onto bestseller lists and into newspaper and magazine articles that I kept coming across. The ones I didn't find, Doris showed me. She clipped and saved everything about Daneen in a big folder that sat smack in the middle of the kitchen counter. From Daneen, I heard only snippets—unfamiliar, exotic terms like royalties and foreign rights—but every conversation we had was just a glancing blow, a quick formality. I never asked for details, never even told her what I thought of the book, and she never gave me the opening.

I couldn't get over it, that a book about the dullest family ever had somehow mesmerized the world. Maybe it was all because of the made-up sexy bits. Still, it felt like being secretly famous. There was even talk about a movie, though Daneen told an interviewer she wouldn't accept any deal unless she had absolute control over the whole thing. "These characters are like my family. As their creator, I feel like a parent," was the exact quote.

Perhaps she could say things like that now that she was pregnant, which I'd learned three paragraphs earlier.

When I called her, Daneen dismissed the whole article,

made sure I knew she'd been taken out of context. Eventually, she got around to her pregnancy. "A baby, motherhood—it's such a big deal. Terrifying, really." She used her in-confidence tone and I felt gathered in, even though she'd told the reporter the exact same thing.

For a few weeks after that, we talked often about this impending, terrifying thing. Neither of us had a clue what to expect and our ignorance made for common ground, for an intimacy we hadn't shared in a long time. But as Daneen became more settled in her stretching skin, she disappeared again.

82.

THE CHRISTMAS PARTY doubled as the closing party for the dealership, and the false joviality and fake evergreen wreaths just intensified how crummy everybody felt. There were rumours some of the mechanics and sales staff would be hired by the new company, but I thought foreign cars might turn some people off. When I mentioned that to Dad, he said anybody who got an offer damn well better be happy, since the cars were superior and a job was a job.

Even Mom came to the party, and it was the first time I'd seen her at the dealership in years. She brought in plates of cookies from her trunk, but otherwise all the food came from the Prairie Peacock and the decorations were the standard lights and tinsel streamers, the big tree with the white and red balls that had occupied the same corner of the showroom every December of my life. Halfway through the party, Dad disappeared. He returned in a Santa suit, beard and all, and gave everyone who worked at Elgin & Son a new car from the dealer demo selection.

In the new year, after the dealership keys were handed over, my parents picked out a trailer—double wide, two bedrooms and an eat-in kitchen—from a show-home catalogue. By the time they got to Texas, it would be all hooked up, electricity and plumbing tethering it to the plot of land they'd bought the day before Gord had his accident.

They headed south on a savagely cold morning. I didn't watch them drive away, but I felt the vacuum of their leaving. Gord had been dead for two years and a day. When I knew for sure that they'd crossed the border, I started clearing his stuff out of my apartment.

I kept his speakers, threw out his toothbrush and stuffed everything else, his clothes and CDs and bedding, even his hairbrush, into garbage bags. They filled the passenger seat of my car and for a long time I sat next to Gord's belongings in the Salvation Army Thrift Store parking lot, thinking I could just take it all back home. But I didn't. I wrestled the bags from the car, cold plastic slipping from my mittened hands, and hoisted them into the bin marked *Donations* just inside the door. Then I walked around the store until my arms were full of other people's castoffs.

83.

DANEEN WAS SCHEDULED to appear on *The Shirley Show*. Someone tipped off my mother—maybe Daneen herself—and Mom called me from Texas, twice, to make sure my VCR was programmed. They didn't get Shirley down south.

The show's topic was super-functional children in dysfunctional families. There were three panellists: a psychiatrist, an expert through experience, and Daneen. Her very round belly was like an extra guest on that stage. She and Shirley bandied the word *fecundity* around for laughs, but I could see Daneen's condition gave weight to every word she uttered.

The show was pre-taped, of course. Daneen had given birth to a baby girl a month before it aired, three days before my parents had left town. In the week leading up to the birth, my mother had called Daneen every day and then, during labour, just about every hour. I'd half expected my mother to fly to

Vancouver, but then I heard her say she couldn't be away on the anniversary of Gord's death, like something about the date stuck her to Calder, like she had to be there when the train came through town. Maybe if Daneen had asked her to come—but I knew no such invitation had been extended.

I watched that *Shirley Show* episode three times, trying to decide if Daneen really was pretending to have grown up in the family she'd portrayed in *Hidden Bargains*—the family laid bare when Shirley read passages from the book to illustrate her guests' points. Daneen never actually said any of it was based on her own family, but she never corrected anyone who made that assumption, either. Instead, she stepped gingerly around questions that poked too close to her actual bones, and she garnered a lot of applause.

84.

WHILE DANEEN WAS flourishing, I was banging around that big apartment by myself, trying to figure out my next move. It turned out to be assessing tax returns for five months of the year—the kind of job you get by taking a proficiency test and keep by showing up on time and meeting a daily quota.

Tax returns were a seasonal affair, a sudden rush to get them in and turn them around. People hated waiting for refunds, so the government assembled a crack team of temps. We worked like mad from February to June and then we got extended a week or two before they laid us off—always with exactly enough weeks on the job to qualify for unemployment insurance. All we had to do to keep a little money rolling in while we waited for the call-back was to check the right boxes on the bi-weekly form.

Dad fumed about it. "Stealing from Peter to pay Paul," he called it. When I tried to explain the advantage of having a seasoned team on the bench, he only glared. I promised to look for something else but the truth was, I liked the job. The money was good and once I'd memorized the rules and the flowcharts, I could fly through returns. The pile with my four-digit identifier scribbled on the bottom grew faster than any of my co-workers' piles until one day my supervisor called me over—"You're 7919, right?"—and told me to slow it down, that I was driving up the unit quota.

Each afternoon, I joined a group of my co-workers on the front steps for a smoke break—my one indulgence, less than twenty cents a day for the chance to be sociable, to fit in somewhere.

It was a comfortable kind of cold storage, and it suited me fine.

85.

EVERY YEAR MY parents drove to Texas, leaving earlier each time, and all winter long I drove back and forth to Calder to check on things. Crossing the tracks, I took note of how that white cross still kept a place for Gord. It held its ground even after my mother's letter-writing campaign succeeded in getting warning lights installed at the crossing—just warning lights, not the big arm she'd demanded, the kind that blocks the path to obliteration.

The cross stood like a sentinel between the highway and the heart of Calder, naked to the elements until the grass and the twining vetch rose again in the spring to shelter it in their insensible embrace.

II.
RESTRICTED FUNDS

86.

BY THE BEGINNING of 1994, Gord's insurance payout was worth $136,782. I thought of it as six intermingling numbers—just that, numbers that swung each other around, shifting spots and changing partners. A digital do-si-do with no connection to any real-world value. Six intermingling numbers and the weight of a comma in the middle, like a pause on which to catch your breath.

I'd given care of the money over to Len, the same financial advisor my father used at the bank. I trusted Len, trusted that he'd keep the secret of that orphan account. He'd assured me of confidentiality right off the top, a rote pledge on his way to commending my parents for getting an early start on the transfer of wealth to the next generation.

I'd had to tell him no, he had the wrong idea about that—and he definitely had the wrong parents. Then I begged him not to mention the account, ever, not to anyone. I could have left it there but I worried he might think I was involved in something illegal or at least seamy, so I told him where the money had come from. His face relaxed immediately, then kept falling into the downturn of sympathy I'd grown inured to.

Once we'd settled all that, I opened a retirement fund of my own. I'd read that starting young was the key to saving enough. Len praised me so hard my face flamed as I handed over my paltry savings. After that, we met every February so I could write him a cheque and he could bring me up to speed on my very slow progress.

Len started this meeting like he had every meeting. "How are your parents?" He knew my father from Rotary Club; he'd been a regular at the Labour Day picnic for years.

"They're golfing up a storm in Texas, staying on a few extra weeks this spring." My parents called infrequently and when they did, they spoke incessantly about playing golf with their snowbird neighbours, like they couldn't believe their luck in finding a life that had absolutely nothing to do with the one from before.

"Good, good." Len squinted into his computer screen and punched at the keys with one finger. "Here you are." He followed that with plenty of staccato tapping and a slower, arrhythmic nod.

I laid my annual investment on the desk and wondered, as I did every year, if he just went along with having me as a client because he was fond of Doris and Don.

Len glanced at the tiny amount on my cheque and slid it off to the side. "Let's talk about your other account, the big one." He rattled off its current balance. "Interest rates have plunged. You won't be seeing the kind of growth you're used to. It's time to get aggressive in your investing."

I'd seen the fallout when my father's whole portfolio tumbled in the crash of '87, so I understood how investment could be a misnomer. I told Len I wasn't interested in aggression. He offered up a rare smile. "You're young and you're way ahead of the game, miles ahead of your peers."

I wanted to tell him that I didn't think of it as a game but if it was, I was pretty sure I wasn't winning. He didn't give me the opening. "Think long term—you have plenty of time to recover from hiccups in the market."

Then he considered me for a minute as if something had

just occurred to him. "I understand people your age are concerned about issues, the environment and what-not. Maybe we can find something that makes you feel good."

I resisted one option after another, reminded Len that I just wanted the money to be safe, that it wasn't really mine to spend. And then he hit me with biotechnology. "Burgeoning area—all kinds of disease research, cures for cancer. And people are always going to get sick, so I don't see how the industry can do anything but grow. Very, very worthwhile investment."

Worthwhile. Maybe that was it—if I could make the money do something good and still keep it safe, maybe Gord's death could have some meaning. And maybe I could be absolved.

The cure for cancer seemed a pretty good place to start, so I gave Len the nod.

87.

I'D BEEN PROMOTED to year-round employment, deciphering how tax accounts had gone awry. More money, less oversight and the occasional satisfaction of solving a complex mystery, all wrapped up in a cubicle built for two—a cubicle that came with a front-row seat to almost daily drama.

The revelations began every morning when Marvin slipped around the particleboard divide. He always asked, low and even, "Got a minute?" before he launched, though he didn't always wait for a response—not when he was in a hurry to get to the crying. I'd hear it start, his voice faltering, his fat fists swiping the tears in my peripheral vision. I'd peer at my computer screen harder, focus more intently on finding whatever misapplication of funds had kicked out the error code.

"I've tried to be patient like you told me, but I just want her back so much." Marvin's voice would break and the sack of his belly would shake and I'd try desperately to concentrate, terrified I'd fall behind or screw something up. My fear was so acute because Marvin was my supervisor—if he hauled me into his office to discuss my performance, I'd have to meet his eye. Every day I bit back the urge to tell him to be quieter, to remind him that beige fabric and particleboard made for poor sound-proofing. But I couldn't say anything. Marvin wasn't talking to me. He was talking to my cubicle mate, Carole.

Carole was widely believed to have the wisdom of the ages tucked beneath her loose, pastel clothing. She'd mastered innocuous—hair in a low ponytail and never a stitch of makeup to define her features. She was like someone photographed out of focus. I didn't get why a woman would choose to relinquish her power so readily. I knew I'd never be beautiful, but I'd figured out how to look attractive. I worked out and wore clothes that flattered my figure. I plucked and toned, highlighted and accessorized, and I got my share of spontaneous compliments, so the investment seemed worth it.

Carole was unfazed by Marvin's daily outbursts, just as she was by the steady parade of desperate colleagues who came to stand next to her chair and pour out their problems. She'd only occasionally glance at them, maybe nod a little at the whole sorry, unsavoury tale spewing onto her desk. Finally, she'd say something so banal it hardly qualified as advice.

"Love is a decision like any other," she told Marvin once. Another time, "Be patient and the right things will happen."

Stacy came asking how to push her teenage son to enroll in the pre-med program she'd picked. "We've talked about this since he was six years old!" she wailed.

"The future," Carole said, "has a way of finding itself." And Stacy didn't just accept that small fortune cookie missive, she thanked Carole profusely before she bounded away, gratitude in every step.

When Keith's wife just kept on flirting, despite his protests, Carole said, "Every time you rise to the bait, Keith, you risk getting caught on the hook." It was the closest she ever came to saying something substantial. Still, when Marvin's wife finally came home, he gave Carole full credit—"Just like you promised she would!"

It was like a trick and I was determined to figure out how it worked.

88.

AT THE RECEPTION after Gord's funeral, I overheard a neighbour tell Mom there was a reason for his death, that he'd been hand-picked by an angel. I recognized it, even then, as the kind of flimsy life raft people toss to the grief-stricken. My mother had grabbed hold. "I'm sure you're right," she'd said, dry eyed and cordial. "Gord was always so easygoing. And generous—always looking after his little sister, letting her tag along and play with his things. I remember he had this skateboard he'd bought—"

I'd snatched up a wayward fork and rushed it to the kitchen, but not fast enough to avoid hearing, "He was driving out here to look after our house," before her voice was swallowed by a roiling sea.

It wasn't until years later, watching Rwanda explode into carnage on the evening news, that I realized I'd believed in angels all along—that I, too, had wanted to pin wings on Gord, even if I sometimes envied the ease with which he'd earned them.

As the body count in Rwanda climbed until it was too unfathomable to even estimate, I sat transfixed in front of the television, thinking it was as if all the world's angels had made a sudden, hasty exit. As if there was no hand-picking to be done at all anymore. A sensation bubbled under my skin like I should do something, but I just sat watching, no plans, no company and the door locked as always.

At the end of June, Daneen left a message asking me, out of the blue, to come visit her. We talked so rarely that for months after her daughter Portia's birth, I thought the name printed on the birth announcement was pronounced *por-tee-a*. It didn't help that the few times we'd spoken, Daneen only referred to the baby as "the baby," so I remained oblivious to my mistake until my mother, affronted, corrected my pronunciation in her glossiest English teacher voice. When she did, Dad looked up from his newspaper. "Oh—" he said, "like the car."

A few weeks later, Daneen and Bryan had flown out with Portia to meet Bryan's parents—and mine, I suppose, all of us gathered in Calder. I held the baby just long enough that afternoon to gain the indelible imprint of her warm weight in my arms before Mom took her and, gazing into her sleeping face, wept so profoundly that Daneen announced they really couldn't stay.

I didn't hear from her again until she left that message while I was at work. She wanted me—no, *needed* me—to come. I shut off the machine, went back out the door, got in my car and drove with no particular destination in mind. At the edge of Calder, I saw Gord's cross had finally fallen, knocked down by heavy rains or maybe just rotted through at its base. I could barely make it out, swallowed as it was in the murky spring runoff.

I turned around, went home and called Daneen. Then I booked a plane ticket and a week off work.

89.

BRYAN LEFT HIS car—an old, sage-green Mustang that had belonged to Daneen's father—in the carpark at the airport. We'd pre-arranged it: how I'd find it, where he'd hide the keys. On the front seat, clipped to a city roadmap, was a sketch of how to get from the airport to their house, my route coerced by offhand arrows, the names of major arteries inked in blue and definitely not in Daneen's hand. It looked as if Bryan had scribbled it all down quickly, an afterthought that made me nervous. But when I found their street easily, his hasty cartography suddenly felt like an unsigned thank-you note. And why not? The alternative to my visit was coming home to Daneen after she'd spent a week alone with the one-and-a-half-year old she'd referred to as "a menace" on the phone.

The address was painted on the mailbox perched at the lip of their driveway. I missed it on the first pass, had to backtrack down that narrow road with its towering trees. From the outside, the house looked right out of a fairytale—a two-storey Tudor with leaded hatching that crisscrossed the windows, their diamond panes twinkling in the early afternoon sun. A wedding present from her father, that house—a big thank you, she'd told me, for not putting him through a wedding. He'd died not long after the newlyweds had moved in, though I didn't hear that until months afterward, the news delivered as a tearless fact. "Thank god everything with the house was signed off and paid for," Daneen had said almost in the same breath.

She didn't answer my knock but the door was unlocked. I crept in by careful, enquiring inches until I recognized a mirror that had once hung in our apartment. Still, I hovered in the foyer, daunted by its opulence, by dark wood and shadow and the way the whole house seemed to whisper hush. For a long moment, my heart was the only sound. Then I heard her voice. I checked my reflection in the mirror and headed toward the low and persistent murmuring.

Daneen was leaning over the kitchen table, a fierce expression on her face, talking in that low voice to a child bigger and more fully formed than I'd imagined she would be. Portia, arms crossed, had a fierceness of her own. On the table, an untouched sandwich; under her high chair, legs kicking furiously.

Shyness placed its firm hand over my mouth. The woman in that magazine-perfect kitchen was nothing at all like the cardboard cut-out I'd envisaged since Daneen had become, at least by my standards, famous.

I must have made some slight noise because she turned and, seeing me, shifted gears. "Hey, it's about time you got here!" She rushed to hug me. "Did you have any trouble finding the car?"

"No, everything was just where—"

"Great car, isn't it? It was Daddy's pride and joy, that Mustang. Of course he only took it out on perfect summer evenings. He'd hate it if he knew how we treated it." She pulled back and looked me over while she tucked a curl behind her ear. Her hair, bobbed to her chin, was shorter and smoother than I'd seen it. "My stepmom sent it out to us last year—a '67, same as me, I think that was the idea. Bryan loves it."

It was a strange greeting, that conversation, but maybe Daneen thought I'd developed an interest in cars during my long engagement with the dealership.

"What happened to the rest of your father's fleet?" I hadn't expected anything so muscular, so common. I always pictured her father's cars as sleek and foreign, shiny and racy and impossibly expensive.

"Fleet? Where'd you get that idea?" She turned back to Portia, who'd finally given in, unwatched, and was slowly chewing her sandwich. "Portia, this is your Auntie Meriel. She's going to play with you. Quietly."

I had no experience with small children, had only ever spent a few hours with toddlers as a teenage babysitter. But Daneen was so confident she spent just ten minutes showing me the ropes before saying she had a tight deadline and disappearing upstairs, leaving me to manage a small stranger who rampaged from one polished room to the next. There was little I could do to tame Portia, to keep her occupied and, above all, quiet, but that's why I'd been summoned. Daneen had been clear: what she needed from me was undisturbed time. And I meant to make sure she got it—she'd paid for my plane ticket in exchange for the help, after all. When a particularly bad tantrum threatened to disturb the peace, I gathered up the flailing girl and let her bruise and batter me all the way to the backyard.

On my second day, Daneen stayed upstairs into the evening. Only the occasional creak or scuff reminded me she was there at

all. After six, famished, I ransacked the kitchen to find something for dinner. Portia subsisted on grilled-cheese sandwiches
and apple wedges, so all I'd eaten during the day were her other
halves. In the pantry, there was a surfeit of lentils and organic
cornmeal. Since I had no idea what to do with that stuff, I kept
searching until I uncovered salmon steaks in the freezer.

By the time Daneen appeared, the salmon had thawed on
its blanket of foil and Portia was in her pajamas, clean and calm.
Then she was a hurtling flurry, whirling from my control to fling
herself at her mother's legs. Daneen scooped her up without
argument and waltzed her around the room, so I knew the day
had been successful enough.

She surveyed the tidy kitchen, the salad I'd already set on
the table, and started to ask something, but Portia tugged her
wrist and dragged her off to the toys. I pulled the foil snug
around the salmon and laid each piece under the broiler.
And then I realized I was, for the first time in a long time, quite
cheerful.

Later, Portia asleep and the dinner dishes done, Daneen and
I settled into the sofa. I waited for her to start some kind of
conversation and, when she didn't, I said, "It's a beautiful house."

"I like it. Bryan thinks it's too much upkeep. But he'll
only let me have the cleaning lady in once a week. He likes to
worry about how fast he thinks I'm running through Daddy's
money." I felt the familiar squeeze of envy tighten across my ribs.
"I guess he's right—there really is no more where that came
from. Between my mother and stepmother, they've picked dry
the bones."

"So you won't get any of his millions?"

Daneen expelled something close to *pfft*. "There weren't ever
millions. Honestly, Meriel, where did you get these ideas?"

I'd assumed millions. I'd always assumed millions. I'd
pictured mansions and a Rolls Royce, servants and pearls. But
I couldn't say exactly where those images had come from,

couldn't think of a single time Daneen had laid claim to that level of affluence.

I picked at a torn cuticle, studied it, bit into it. Waited. Finally, Daneen started talking about the book she was finishing. She called it part love story, part cautionary tale and offered me a quick synopsis. The protagonist—a brilliant businessman whose pursuit of wealth masks an emotional hunger—falls in love but must choose between his empire and his beloved mistress because his selfish, shallow, awful wife—Daneen turned awful into the drawn-out scrape of metal on asphalt—has the means to destroy him. She'd titled it *For Love or Money*. Surprisingly cliché, I thought, but since this was a world Daneen knew all about, I figured she was infusing it with vivid insight, rendering it new.

"So it's your family this time—" I ventured. For years, I'd waited for my chance to bring up *Hidden Bargains*, to elicit an apology, to let her know I didn't appreciate it.

Daneen cut me off before I could say any of it. "Not at all, not even close. My family is not that interesting."

I realized then how ridiculous it was, how wrong I'd been. All along it had been just a book, a fiction, her version of a story and in her spacious kitchen with its banks of white surfaces and sharp implements, my years-long umbrage dwindled to petty.

Daneen rested her jaw in her hand. "I'm nearly done, but I'm stuck on something. There's a scene where he impulsively pulls out his pocketknife and slices a portrait of his wife to ribbons. My editor thinks it's silly—out of character for an in-control man. But I really like that image. What do you think?"

I could picture it, a canvas coming undone, dropping in ribbons. I didn't know if I was expected to pretend that I'd never seen such a thing, so I tossed out the first safe thought that came to me. "Why is a businessman carrying a pocketknife?"

Daneen lifted her head from her hand but kept both cocked at the same angle. "Jesus, Meriel—" Her mouth stretched into a smile that said I was amazing. "You always see the essential problem."

She disappeared up the stairs then, provoked to put just the right blade in her hero's hand while I sat alone at the kitchen table as night deepened, marvelling that we'd crawled so fast, so easily back into our old skins.

90.

RAIN SETTLED IN overnight, trapping Portia and me inside those dark, moody rooms. She simpered and then she screamed. Once she bit me. Twice I lost my temper and three times Daneen clomped halfway down the stairs to tell us to be quiet, her tone less courteous with each descent. When the next day, my last, dawned every bit as wet and grim, Daneen drew me a map to the mall so at least I could take Portia out, wear her down by pumping quarter after quarter into those one-seater rides that loom in every mall entrance.

While Portia grinned her way through her third go on the big-eyed snail—a ride that was nothing more than a frenetic, side-to-side jiggle—I wondered how people stood it, looking after children day after day. After just a handful of days, I was longing for silence and stillness.

We stayed out as long as we could. By the time I drove back to Daneen's, the rain had stopped and the sun was doing its best to burn off the last of the grey. We came through the door just as Daneen was pounding down the stairs, a ream of paper held out in front of her like an offering. "It's done," she said, dropping it like a stone on the side table. "It's perfect. Let's go buy some wine."

Portia was particularly wound up, hard to get to sleep, and it was almost nine when Daneen opened the wine. Moments later, she lifted her near empty glass in a toast. "I hope that fucking kid stays asleep. This feels too good to stop."

The venom in *fucking kid* shocked me, though not nearly as

much as it might have a week earlier. I'd started to suspect that every mother ping-ponged from affection to antipathy, even if most glossed over it later, in the retelling. Maybe my mother's pendulum had just jammed at the exasperation extreme with me and, someday, it could make its way back to affection.

Daneen started in on her third glass and started in on me, too. "I can't believe you still live in that old dump."

"You'd be surprised how trendy the neighbourhood is now, Daneen."

"Uh huh. And your job—are taxes trendy now, too?"

I set my glass down hard, half hoping the stem would snap. "My job pays the rent in that big dump of an apartment that you chose."

"Meriel, you can't go through life just paying the rent." She sighed the way my mother did when she found me unfathomably disappointing. "You're taking the path of least resistance, standing still. You need to let go."

A flurry of words flew around inside my head, but I couldn't make enough order of them to set her straight. Anyway, I kept bumping up against Carole's dictum, against bait and hook, so I shut my mouth and watched her open another bottle. The cork made a deep thunk as she pulled it free, and that also sounded like an indictment.

Daneen changed the topic as she filled our glasses. "I'm sorry you have to leave tomorrow, before Bryan's even home. It's been so great having you here." I almost—almost—told her how much I'd miss her and Portia, but she didn't leave me an opening. "It's convinced me that we absolutely have to get a full-time nanny."

91.

DISEASE-BEATING BIOTECHNOLOGY had taken a turn for the worse. The whole sector was sick, stocks collapsing, a downturn so dire it made the national evening news. I called Len. He told me sure, Gord's net worth had just dropped by thirty percent, but I shouldn't worry. He made an eloquent argument on behalf of the long-term, pointed out the climb before the plunge. A temporary correction, he called it.

But I couldn't gamble away the only chance Gord had to live on.

I told Len to pull it all out, what was left, to put Gord's money somewhere safe. So much for saving lives.

92.

"WHY DON'T YOU know what you want?" The question hung in the cubicle until I realized Carole was talking to me. Her milky gaze was fixed on the *Real Estate Guide* I'd set on the corner of my desk.

After I'd come home from Daneen's house, I couldn't stand the confines of my apartment, so I'd spent the summer wandering open houses to see what I could afford. It wasn't much, but anything was better than climbing that dirty stairwell through the smell of everyone else's cooking just to arrive in a dump with crumbling plaster and cracked windowpanes.

"I just haven't found the right place," I told Carole. I didn't say a place that feels right, but that's what I meant. My real-estate agent Barry—Carole's brother-in-law—had a checklist that was all about closet space and nearby schools, but I was after something else, something I couldn't explain even to myself.

"There's no perfect house, you know," Carole said. "Maybe you have to lower your expectations. Or raise your budget."

Was it a message from Barry? When Carole had recommended him, she'd promised he wasn't one of those agents who try to force a client into a higher price range. I hadn't known anyone would do that—Dad had always tried to talk customers into less expensive purchases. I remember him shaking his head in disgust when a young man refused to settle for what he could comfortably afford.

"I never said I wanted a perfect house, Carole." I tried to keep the edge out my voice, to look as if I found the numbers on my screen riveting. I knew she was searching for a fissure, a way to crack me open and extract some personal revelation, but I was determined to stay shut. Despite a year in close proximity to her ears, I'd managed not to disclose anything. I wasn't even tempted, not once I'd deduced how she did it, how she compelled people to expose so much. It wasn't magic at all. She just listened—listened without argument or intrusion, without questioning a person's absolute certainty in their own point of view.

"Maybe you should make a decision, Meriel." Definitely a message from Barry. My heart sank. He'd seemed so supportive, showing me every possibility and never showing the slightest impatience.

Carole swivelled in her chair to face me. "It's just a house. It won't give you everything that's missing in your life."

I left our cubicle in search of a form I didn't even need.

93.

NOVEMBER OPENED WITH snow on the ground. I made an offer on a two bedroom with beige stucco, burgundy trim and that all-important new furnace. The offer was at the very top edge of my budget, though below asking price. When Barry called to say the seller had accepted—no counter offer, no chance to change my mind—all I could say was, "Oh no."

An amount that seemed a fortune to me was too paltry by banking standards to be worth any rigour. I had a slight skirmish with the loans officer over my downpayment—she thought twenty-seven percent was excessive. Her steel grey curls jumped as she suggested all kinds of other ways I might spend that money. I resisted, and resisted too her urging to pay the mortgage off over a longer period. Twenty years! I couldn't breathe at the thought of it.

My mouth felt full of grit, drier than the forced-air heat the bank kept on bust. Every time something was decided, she marked an X where my signature needed to be—each X like a screw pulling my muscles taut.

Finally, I let her win on the one-year term. "We wouldn't be encouraging shorter terms if we didn't expect the rate to go down," she said. And maybe she believed it. But a year later, I'd regret trusting her and I'd begrudge the bank the surprise renewal fee they charged me. I'd lock in then for five years— which would prove to be the wrong choice again.

After the mortgage was arranged, I had two weeks to wait before the house was mine—two weeks to panic over the deep chasm of debt into which I was spiralling. And what if something bad happened? What if the foundation crumbled, or the pipes burst, or I couldn't make the payments? What if I hated living there? There was no manner of calamity that seemed outside the realm of possibility in the middle of the night as I prowled the apartment, grateful I could navigate all of its sharp corners without having to turn on a single light.

On the eve of possession, long after midnight, I got dressed and drove to my new house. I parked along the opposite curb, turned off the engine and tried to imagine that this was coming home. Every house nearby was dark, the whole street shut up tight. The only illumination came from a streetlight down the block, its beam glinting on the brass house numbers: five-two-three.

Five-two-three. It came to me that it was a prime number comprised of prime numbers. And, there in the stillness of that street, it felt enough like serendipity to keep me breathing.

When I moved in, I made the decision to love my new house. And there were things to love—cove mouldings and veined plaster ceilings, pristine hardwood under the dingy shag. Upstairs, the bedrooms were small but their sloped ceilings were snug as an embrace. Outside, the elms lining the street held hands, a perfect arch all the way down the block.

But after I'd plastered the cracks and painted every room the colour of tea with milk, hung curtains from the linen bins at Value Village and configured that gargantuan furniture to fit the small rooms, I realized Carole was right. It was just a house. It was just one new thing in my same-old life.

And then, a month after I moved in, a week after I made my first mortgage payment, the notices came and I didn't have a job. Some of my colleagues celebrated our unexpected winter holiday, but they weren't paying enough attention. This was no short-term layoff, no reorganization of the endless give and take of the tax system—this had the feel of radical reform.

94.

OF ALL THE things not in my life, it was kissing I missed most. The longing would come at me suddenly, unpredictably, rushing through me, parting my lips and stealing my breath. If I was alone, I would close my eyes not against it but into it. I could take care of myself when I was horny, quietly and efficiently, but I couldn't satisfy this affliction, this longing for languorous kisses. It was so much more than sexual—the longing for a hand at the base of my skull, another one on the small of my back.

There wasn't anyone specific I wanted to kiss. I hadn't felt desire like that for someone in such a long time, and the one-night stand I'd had with a co-worker after the Christmas bowling tournament was like a snack of empty calories that just left me hungrier.

It wasn't sex, really, that I was after but something else. Something big and gothic and implausible. I wanted to be swept away.

The day after ABC announced it was cancelling *My So-Called Life*—just half a season in and already I'd wedged myself so deeply into that TV high-school clique—I cried for a solid day like I'd saved it up for years. I cried and wandered from room to room, thinking that I'd done all the things I was supposed to do, that I'd put all the scaffolding in place. That now I was ready for my real life to start.

95.

IN 1995, THE province opened its Debt Services Department, a kind of ride-along for a new era of fiscal constraint. When I saw the classified ad, it all added up. Everything I'd ever done had prepared me for just this unlikely calling: debt counsellor. On paper, I looked remarkably qualified—that's what the woman who greeted me said as she led me down the hall to the interview. Qualified on paper, and then revealed to be even more perfect because, after all—above all—I was virtually debt-free. They didn't ask about that, but I offered. I said that I paid every bill on time and never carried a balance on my credit card. That I had a diligent mortgage repayment plan. That I had mastered the art of living within my means.

I actually said that, and no one rolled their eyes. Both interviewers, in fact, nodded earnestly. Neither asked how being unacquainted with debt could possibly qualify me to advise those who were drowning in it. And I was so eager to share my moneywise skills, so focused on all the good I could do that I didn't see how preposterous it was, either. Like hiring someone to teach swimming who'd never even been wet.

In the three months before the Debt Services counselling centre officially opened, while the carpet was being laid and the paint was drying, I went for training. It turned out all the inter-personal manoeuvres I'd been trying to master had names and theoretical platforms: affirmative listening, cognitive reappraisal, conflict resolution. That last one made me think of Dad on the showroom floor, expertly defusing an irate customer whose new truck had turned defective right there in front of five other guys at the coffee shop. Dad nodding, suitably horrified, agreeing that it was absolutely unacceptable. Saying, "Let me tell you what we're going to do to make this right," a simple line that never failed to squelch a lit fuse, even though what Dad was prepared to do was always less than what the customer had initially demanded.

When I moved from role-play to real clients, it was the easiest thing in the world. Sitting behind my laminate desk, listening as strangers detailed their financial circumstances—the complicated details, the hard times, the excuses—was like watching talk-show TV, nodding at the right moments, leaning forward like a camera zooming in.

At first I feared my clients would see through the thin veneer of learned technique and false concern. They didn't, though, because it turned out my concern was real. I cared about them—all of them—all the exhausted single mothers who had a deficit of everything but desire; all the thick-fingered middle-aged men who'd believed their union jobs would last a lifetime; all the addicts and the compulsive shoppers who couldn't look me in the eye when they claimed they couldn't help it. I knew most of them would land, over and over again, in the column for doubtful accounts, but I still cared.

I even developed a fondness for the over-extended show-offs like Marko, whose gelled-stiff hair and gleaming teeth masked the soft underbelly of his fiscal stupidity. What finally broke him was a pyramid scheme, though Marko called it something else and still couldn't believe it wasn't a legitimate investment.

"So many people," he kept saying, incredulous, "so many guys I know doubled their money. And all I got was charged." Charged, fined, his huge investment lost, and now his wife certain to find out. Marko allowed that sure, maybe he should have known better, but could I please explain to him how this was so different from what the fellows on Wall Street did every day, swapping other people's money around and making a fortune for themselves?

I was only in my second week of appointments, so I didn't have an answer for that one.

96.

THE CRITICS TOOK no pains to spare Daneen's feelings. Her second novel, they agreed, was a big misstep, a book full of monied stereotypes in over-burdened scenes. A national newspaper review said, "She's written a soap opera. Unfortunately, she's used a vocabulary that's sure to put off those who gravitate toward such confectionary."

The next weekend, my local paper offered a big picture of Daneen's most beatific smile. The headline gave me a jolt, causing me to spill coffee right across her teeth: "Novelist strays too far from her prairie roots." The review was a little gentler, perhaps in deference to the author's local roots, but it wasn't positive, either. "Does anyone really need to be told that money isn't everything?" the reviewer asked before concluding, "Her first work succeeded because the author wrote about a world she understood. DeCario should stick closer to the life she knows."

97.

CHUCK TOLD ME just the day before that he wanted me to attend the Board of Trade dinner in his place. He didn't give any reason at all why he couldn't, so I knew he'd finally realized he was the boss and could just tell someone else to go to the dinner and listen to the federal finance minister talk about balancing the national budget.

"Special invitation," he said. "Someone from Debt Services has to be there, and it should be you, Meriel."

I'd never reattached the Claire to my name. Even the plate on my office door and the print in the corner of my cheques read Meriel Elgin. To everyone who met me as an adult, I was utterly unhyphenated.

Chuck handed me the envelope with his name on the front and a ticket for one tucked inside like he was handing me a dirty diaper. He may have thought going to hear Paul Martin speak was worse than a stick in the eye, but I was thrilled. Debt was, by this point, a national crisis. The size of the deficit had achieved a kind of celebrity status that had everyone talking. There was a vast and inescapable shortage of good fiscal news and now, finally, a finance minister willing to hand us the fistful of bitter pills we'd have to swallow for our own good.

I took the invitation to my office, then headed straight back to Chuck's. "What do you wear to something like this?" I'd never been to a gathering of the who's who outside of Calder. Chuck shrugged. "Blue suit, burgundy tie."

That evening, I walked the mall in search of the sweet spot between sophisticated sexy and seriously businesslike. What I found was a silk dress the colour of canned asparagus that fit like it was tailor made—but the price was twice what I'd come willing to pay. With little time left for rifling through racks, I was rushing to get out of the mall and over to the thrift store when the display in Coles Books stopped me cold. They were stacked in a pyramid, "From the Author of *Hidden Bargains*" emblazoned on every cover and across the display poster, too, and I guess reviews didn't matter all that much to book marketers.

I picked up a copy, flipped open to Daneen's black and white image. She was flawless, radiant, and it struck me that I was closing in on thirty years old and I didn't own a single decent thing to wear on a special occasion.

The next night, wrapped in that green silk dress, my make-up impeccable, I carried myself like someone who belonged in that expansive hotel dining room full of lavishly-set tables and well-dressed men. I found Chuck's place card near the back of the room. As I pulled out my chair, the man next to it looked up, then he looked me up and down.

"Hey, you're not Chuck." He picked up the place card and pointed it at me. "Are you Chuck?"

"No. Yes—" I stumbled like a kid caught in a lie. "Chuck couldn't come. But he thought it would be okay if I did."

"It's not okay. It's fantastic. We'd much rather have you than old Chuck." When he smiled, the creases beside his mouth spread all the way to his eyes like a stone thrown in a pond. "I'm Roger Hardy." A solid handshake, a navy suit with a burgundy tie.

When a bottle arrived at the table, Roger poured wine into every empty glass, even the ones at the unoccupied settings on either side of us. Then he got the introductions moving around the table. The four people across the table all worked for the Royal Bank. They were terse and complained about their back row seats, and after Roger referred to our table as the Hinterland Who's Who and I laughed, they lost interest in talking to either of us. But Roger was determined to turn the event into a proper party. He asked for another bottle of wine even before the main course and kept up a steady banter, though eventually he gave up on the bankers and turned all his attention on me.

He said he was a distributor for a big brewery, that he'd been roped into attending the dinner by a boss who didn't want to come. He said really, he didn't want to come either, he was a beer and pretzels kind of guy, but he was okay with playing the game. Then he asked about my work and when I told him "debt counsellor," he had about a million questions—what was the biggest debt I'd seen and could I really get people out of that kind of hole? I kept my answers light and vague and felt grateful for the distraction of chicken cordon bleu.

During the long introduction at the microphone, I spooned tiny domes of chocolate mousse into my mouth, but I had to set my spoon down to applaud when Paul Martin leapt, far more energetically than I'd anticipated, to the podium. He began by showing us where we were. Behind him, the national debt appeared and then appeared again, bigger, compounding, the gargantuan figure so much more alarming lit up on a big screen.

"No one can deny the stark arithmetic of compound interest," the Minister intoned. A bar graph climbed right off the top of the white screen, then reappeared to make the rapid, downhill descent of recent years. When we were sufficiently full of numbers, he moved on to the national psyche, talked about a willingness, finally, to endure the pain of restraint. "A zero deficit is of great symbolic significance, a benchmark that has been embraced by the public." The room erupted in applause.

Roger leaned over so our cheeks were almost touching. "Do you believe this guy?" The screen behind Martin changed to government program expenditures, another precipitous decline. "See, here's the real story—breaking the deficit over the little guy's back."

I met Roger's eye for a second, then turned back to the podium. Martin was saying, "Deep and necessary," and though I kept my hands clasped, my head bobbed in unison to the percussive approval of applause.

And I did approve. If Canada had walked into my office right then, sat down and unfolded its balance sheet, I would have recommended exactly the same thing. Tighten and tighter, I'd have said, and never mind whose fault it is. There's no point even talking about that now.

Roger nudged his chair closer to mine. "Jesus, you must see the tragedy of this all day long in your line of work."

I shifted into high alert, held his gaze. "The people I see have generally dug their own holes. It's the high interest rates that are killing them."

His eyebrows went up, which might have meant, "I stand corrected." Then he leaned back in his chair, away from me. Even his long leg, which had been so close to mine, withdrew.

Martin had turned the corner, was taking us toward a future unhampered by all that debt, but I'd stopped hearing him. I was formulating my next line and working up the nerve to deliver it. Finally I leaned over and whispered, "It's all about stealing from Peter to pay Paul Martin."

Roger's laugh was a fast, loud bark. The Royal Bankers glared. Roger moved in close again. "Let's get the hell out of here."

98.

CORINNE, THE RECEPTIONIST at Debt Services, was hurtling toward the Wal-Mart checkout, her cart loaded with paper and highlighters and notebooks of varying sorts and sizes. I was heading for the same short line unencumbered by a cart and carrying just a few items, but I stepped out of her way. We both knew it mattered more that she got back to the office on time. Besides, I didn't want to lay a box of condoms down in front of a co-worker.

Corinne was the only other woman on the Debt Services team in those early days and we'd tried, though not successfully, to be friends. She was a single mother with two kids and when she'd talked to me in the coffee room about her life—how she wasn't getting any support from her ex, financial or otherwise— I'd wanted to help, to point out all the avenues available to her. She'd only shot down my advice. When I'd suggested she get a court order for family maintenance payments, she'd told me she couldn't afford a lawyer. When I'd suggested Legal Aid, she'd smirked and said, "I'm not poor enough. I checked."

Frustrated, I'd suggested she at least give up smoking. I had no idea how much, exactly, she smoked but I knew she had a cigarette every day after lunch. The last time I'd splurged on a pack, they were up over five dollars. Corinne had stood up at that suggestion, smoothed her skirt and sighed. "You really don't have a clue, do you?"

In Wal-Mart, she waved a piece of paper at me like a half hello. "Back to school. It gets worse every year." Then she turned away and began unloading her cart, stacking and wedging and piling so the stuff all fit on the belt. When a price check at our till dragged on, she opened a package of markers, drew one out and started crossing off items on the mimeographed list. Then she crammed the marker back into its plastic pouch and pulled out her credit card, waving it as if to say, "Let's hurry this up."

I clutched my items to my chest, though Corinne kept her back to me as her purchases crawled forward on the conveyor belt. I thought she'd forgotten I was there, but handing over her Visa, she called over her shoulder, "Stand back, it might burst into flames."

I smiled, but I guess my eyes followed the card like they believed it could actually combust. Corinne pivoted to face me square on then. "I know what you're thinking—that I shouldn't be racking up the debt." She glared like I'd actually said it. "But the kids'll be in trouble if they show up at school without all this shit. What the hell else am I supposed to do?"

I shook my head and then I nodded because I wasn't sure which looked more like I was on her side. Then I turned over the box of granola bars I was using to shield the condoms and I scrutinized the label.

99.

I READ, IN some waiting room in a pricey woman's magazine I'd never buy, that the essential value of friendship is in being known. "Our girlfriends know our true selves in a way even our romantic partners can't, and our parents and children shouldn't." The article was accompanied by a photograph of four women leaning in at a café table, laughing, glasses of red wine glittering in front of them and their teeth uniformly white. The photographer had chosen a diverse racial mix to ensure we knew that intimacy and joy knew no boundaries, though of course all the women were exceedingly thin.

Maybe I didn't have enough experience with sustaining female friendships, but I knew that article was wrong. None of my girlfriends had ever known me as well, as deep down and absolutely, as Roger did.

From Roger I hid nothing. I stopped draping the sheet just right over me, stopped tightening my abs when he ran a hand anywhere near them. A few months in, I was barefaced as I moved on top of him, morning light falling over us and his gaze never wavering. His hands grasped my hips, pulled us tighter together. I was getting used to that full feeling under my ribcage every time our eyes met. I was learning not to be afraid.

"I know it's too soon to even talk about it," his voice deep and hoarse, "but I would love to spend my whole life with you, Meriel."

Roger was so certain of me, though he saw me naked and asleep and completely unguarded. I forgot to hide embarrassing things like how ragged some of my panties were, how I nibbled on raw potato chunks while I was slicing them, how I still listened to hokey soft rock from the early eighties. For the first time in my life, I understood what all those pop songs were saying.

On Gord's birthday, Roger helped me gather a bouquet of found flowers and deliver them. When I placed that funny little bunch down on Gord's grave and traced the name carved into the granite marker with my finger, Roger was right beside me. I didn't know how to explain about the ritual with the flowers, why it was important to pick them from the ditches rather than buy them, why any of it mattered. I knew Gord wasn't there, in that cemetery, hanging out hoping someone would drop by on his birthday. I knew it was pointless, but still, I needed to do it and Roger never questioned it.

Plus, my parents adored him. At his first Labour Day barbecue, Dad even asked him to take over at the grill for a spell. Later, the barbecue turned off and pushed aside and the early-out people drifting toward the driveway, Mom started to tell Roger about Daneen, calling her "my little writer" like she'd adopted her or maybe even invented her. Then she rushed off to get her folder full of clippings. It was thicker than ever. I wondered if the bad reviews of Daneen's second novel were in there, too—if Mom lived on the side of any-publicity-is-good-enough. From a safe distance, I watched Roger dutifully make his way through them, pausing to read often enough to seem interested.

When he finished with the folder and we finally got a minute alone, I apologized for my mother, for all of it, and thanked him for being so good and patient. He just laughed, took a gulp of beer and said, "Relax honey, I'm having a great time."

Roger saw all of me, and he kept on wanting me anyway.

100.

CHUCK CALLED A rare staff meeting to tell us the balancing act wasn't over, that government wages were still frozen and we'd be losing ten days pay again this year.

"Look, I'm supposed to sell this as a bonus—time to spend with your families, ten extra long weekends." He couldn't look at the five of us assembled around the little staffroom table. He just stared at the table's dusty-rose Formica like being the boss of bad tidings wasn't what he'd expected when he became the director of Debt Services. Chuck preferred arm's-length leadership, initialling his approval on our counselling reports and vacation requests but otherwise keeping his office door shut.

"I have to pay daycare for those days, whether or not I'm at work." Corinne said it like she was just stating fact, not picking a fight, so Chuck ignored the interruption.

"And I'm supposed to remind you it amounts to less than five percent of your annual salary, but it makes a big difference overall in our bottom line." Chuck was known to be a wizard with the departmental budget spreadsheet.

Corinne twirled a piece of her hair around and around two fingers. She had a perpetually anxious air about her, but it was cranked up to bust just now. "With all these program cuts, do you think they'll close us down, cut our jobs?"

Lars burst in with his mocking laugh, the one I worried he used with clients. "As long as we're helping collect back taxes, dear, I think we're safe."

Lars was the youngest person in our office, but he was a

master of the condescending *dear* and he dressed like a middle-aged man—golf shirts and a big gold watch. Already, he sported a little pouch of a belly that hung loosely over his belt. He'd come to Debt Services as a student intern during his commerce degree and Chuck had hired him outright when he'd graduated.

Lars turned to Chuck. "Not even cost-of-living?" He blew hard in disgust. "Don't expect me to be sympathetic the next time some retired guy complains about living on a fixed income."

Chuck gave his nothing-I-can-do shrug. "Look, I'm in the same boat as you, and it's low tide for all of us."

Since I'd taken this job, I'd never made the salary I signed up for. The mandated days-off without pay depleted my gross while rising deductions, the need to make up for decades of popular pension plan underfunding, diminished my net. Still, I didn't complain, not even to make a joke about it to Roger. I just turned down the heat and when Roger said he wasn't about to wear two pairs of socks to sleep in a meat locker for God and country, I lowered the thermostat even more and went to stay at his always-warm townhouse.

Small and necessary sacrifices, I said.

I guess Roger was impressed because he called me a foot soldier for fiscal holiness.

101.

A LOT OF people came in expecting a prescription, even a flat out cure for their financial problems. They brought along an envelope or sometimes a shoebox full of papers—bills, bank statements, letters from creditors—and they held it out as if I could rearrange the paper trail and bang, problem solved. Some other counsellors, especially the new ones, thought they had a magic formula, that money problems could be solved with mathematical equations. They offered some alchemy of amortization and consolidation and—presto!—manageable payments, no sacrifice required. I'd been like that in the beginning, but now I thought of such mathematical wizardry as just like painting over rotten wood.

Derrick and Michelle showed up with their shoebox on a brilliantly sunny Tuesday. They were lean and tall and attractive, obviously intelligent and very, very earnest. It was February. When I stood and reached to shake their hands, I was struck by how pale my skin seemed against theirs. As he took off his sunglasses, I noticed Derrick's nose was peeling. They settled into the two chairs facing my desk and Michelle perched the shoebox with its Nike logo on her lap carefully, as if it had sharp edges.

I started, as I always did, by asking them to tell me about themselves. The kind of answer people gave—though rarely the information itself—offered some insight. Most went straight to their debt problem, but others delivered a one-liner pulled from their income tax return: age, occupation, marital status and offspring. On occasion, I got the whole life story, from birth to here, complete with family details and best anecdotes. I'd listen without interrupting for a while, sometimes for twenty minutes, writing down random words just so the client would know I was paying attention. Most of it was irrelevant, a waste of my time, but I figured if someone needed to tell me so much they must be starved for the chance to talk.

Michelle and Derrick took the curriculum vitae route. She said she'd completed almost all of a history degree before she'd discovered bartending paid better, tips in, than anything she'd land after graduation. Five years later she was working in one of the busiest nightclubs in the city, making a good income and not sick of it yet. Derrick told me he was a journeyman electrician who'd just lost his job—the third job he'd lost in less than a year. Michelle interjected, calling it a run of bad luck. Derrick cut her off to insist it was the fault of all those asshole bosses who couldn't get their shit together. He tilted back his head so he was looking at me over his sunburnt nose. "I'm not too worried."

They both stared at me expectantly.

"So Michelle's income is the only money you have coming in?"

Derrick fiddled with his sunglasses. "That'll change."

Michelle smiled a little too confidently, swept the hair from her face with a long-handed, elegant gesture. For a split second, I was reminded of Daneen.

"And what's your debt situation like?"

"Not bad," Derrick said. Michelle's smile faded. Two years on this side of the desk had taught me that with couples, the trick was to watch the expression of the one who wasn't speaking. I kept my face absolutely neutral when I asked about their biggest financial challenge.

Michelle started to open the Pandora's Box on her lap, but I held my hand out flat to dissuade her. Real figures would muddy things—I wanted their impressions first.

"We only got into trouble because we bought furniture on one of those no-payments-no-interest-for-a-year rip-offs." Derrick's voice had lost its nonchalant quality, had descended into rancour. "We were in Cuba when they sent the letter telling us we had to pay by a certain date or else pay interest all the way back to the day we bought it. By the time we got around to opening the mail, the due date was past."

Michelle picked up the thread. "They don't tell you on the commercials that no interest means only if you pay it by a certain date."

Derrick rode right over top: "Now they want all the interest, plus fucking penalties, and we can't afford that—"

Michelle rose to his level of outrage. "We'd forgotten all about having to pay for the stuff after a year. And obviously we can't return it now—"

"So we went to get a loan from the bank but our credit rating was lousy, which is ridiculous." They were looking at each other, leaning inward, sharing their astonishment like two passengers in a plunging airplane.

I'd seen their credit rating and I knew it took more than one overdue debt to reach that level. But I also knew people were plagued by amnesia, oblivious to what they owed, sometimes able to overlook a teetering heap of debt even while it threatened to topple over and crush them.

"Can they do that, charge interest for the whole year in one giant lump, without warning?" Michelle's hands had turned to fists, and she held them on top of her shoebox as if the lid might blow right off.

I'd shifted my face from neutral to empathetic. I didn't want them to feel like idiots—at least not yet. "It was probably in the contract you signed, in the small print. A lot of people don't realize. Is there anywhere else you can turn for help?"

Michelle studied the top of her shoebox. "We've borrowed a lot from my parents in the past, but last time, they said they wouldn't—"

Derrick interjected. "They hate me."

"No they don't." She turned to face him, even leaned in a bit, her eyes beseeching. "Stop saying that."

He kept his eyes on me. "They do. They wish she'd break up with me."

"Derrick, they do not—"

I asked, sharply enough to break them out of their endless loop, "So just how deep is your debt?"

Numbers came from somewhere and flew from their mouths, his much lower than hers though I suspected both would prove to be wildly insufficient. I didn't wince. I didn't question their estimates. I just sent them home with their unopened shoebox, told them to figure out exactly what they had and what they owed and to come back in a few weeks with a clear picture.

They looked relieved, even grateful as they left.

Typing up my notes, I noticed a whiff of something sulfuric in the air and wondered if there was a problem with the building's heating system.

102.

ROGER MADE RESERVATIONS at one of the most expensive restaurants in the city for Valentine's Day. I tried not to anticipate what it might mean as I slipped into the green silk dress I'd worn the night we met. I started wishing I'd bought him something expensive, something more special than a greeting card I'd turned into a lewd voucher—*This entitles the bearer...*

Our meal was fabulous, five courses with wine and wait staff always hovering nearby. But that's all it was—a fabulous dinner, an expensive, romantic evening and I hated myself for having expected something else. Back at my place, I ramped up the lewd to show my appreciation; I even made a little more noise than came naturally to me.

Later, when I sunk back against Roger in the bathtub, he murmured, "You know, if we could bottle this feeling, we'd be rich. We could go around the world selling it." His words washed over me as I watched the water we'd splashed drift slowly across the old linoleum floor. I was imagining a new tile floor, Roger and I installing it from separate corners, coming together square by square.

I knew then, without a doubt, that Roger was the one—my one—and I knew he felt it, too. And it felt like sheer relief, as warm as his hand on my bent knee. I almost said it out loud but the phone rang and we both jumped, sending a fresh cascade over the tub's edge. It was too late at night not to expect bad news, so I grabbed a towel and rushed to answer the call.

Daneen's voice was thick and faint. "Bryan's left me." We hadn't spoken in months. I had no idea what precipitated his departure. I wondered if she'd dialed my number by mistake, if she'd meant to call a more recent confidante until she sobbed, "Meriel, you have to tell me what to do."

I wrapped the towel around me tighter, shivering until Roger brought me my robe.

103.

GORD'S MONEY, TUCKED into term deposits, had barely recovered from its disastrous excursion into life-saving technology. Even the biotech industry had made faster gains, just as Len said it would. But Len had retired; Glen was his replacement and the close-enough name wasn't going to fool anyone. This new guy brought a totally different spin to that black vinyl chair.

"If you'd invested this right, you'd have a quarter million dollars now," Glen had pronounced the first time we'd met. He'd leaned forward and dropped his voice. "Research tax credits—fast growing funds and worth a small fortune in tax deductions."

I told him then I wouldn't take the risk, that I had to keep the money safe but a year later, he was admonishing me again. "This is a very conservative portfolio, Meriel." His gold rings glinted as he positioned his hands like eagles landing on his big black keyboard. "You've got this large sum doing nothing for you."

He swivelled from the kitty-cornered screen to face me. He had a helmet of shiny grey hair—prematurely grey, I guessed, given his smooth skin and the age of everyone else in the Sears family portrait on his desk. Like a doctor about to deliver treatment options, he looked deadly serious. "If we look at your investor profile—" it materialized like magic—"you'll see you're rated for much higher risk."

We'd been through this before. "Risk-averse" I reminded him, pointing a finger at myself like it was a defining characteristic, a hyphenation that implied something innate the way bi-polar or well-endowed did. I figured a guy like Glen could appreciate a phrase like that.

"You have a lot of capital. But with prime dipping below six percent, interest is rock bottom low. So let's get more aggressive." He layered on some jargon designed to excite and maybe he thought I didn't understand what all the terms meant. I let him go on, nodding so he'd know he hadn't lost me, and as he wound down, I checked my watch and told him to roll Gord's money back into a term deposit. Then I asked him what he'd recommend for my own money.

Glen excelled at hawking whatever was in vogue. I always got the feeling he'd just finished reading some investors' newsletter and shoved it in his faux-wooden drawer as I came around the corner. Today's feature was the Narcissus Fund—"Local investment in innovation and hard work," he parroted, "Enthusiastically promoted by the provincial government. The tax incentives alone make this a great option. You'll get a good chunk of your money back in your refund right from the get-go." He handed me a pamphlet festooned with the fund's namesake, those hopeful yellow spring flowers, their sweet sunny faces promising years of growth.

I'd had a costly winter—major car repairs, a leaking roof— but caught up in all that enthusiasm, I wrote Glen a cheque for three thousand dollars, every penny I had to spare.

Glen clipped my cheque to the forms I'd signed. "This will keep your money working in the province, Meriel, and out of the hands of the government."

He said it completely without irony.

104.

"BE CAREFUL NOT to brush up against the walls, Roger." We were carrying an old table from the spare room, which I was desperate to transform into a suitable guest room for Daneen. I'd painted earlier and I wasn't sure it was dry. "I won't have time for touch-ups. I have too much to do."

"Sweetheart, she's coming to see you, not your house."

It was a nice thought, though I suspected Daneen wasn't coming to see me either—she was just escaping, just getting away from the pitying looks and the gossip hounds. "In a city this size you wouldn't think I'd constantly bump into the humiliation of it," she said the night she told me she'd booked a flight. "But the circle is so small—small like a noose."

By then I knew the whole story—that Bryan was seeing someone else, that he was making no effort whatsoever to reconcile. He'd rebuffed every overture, even after Daneen denied him access to Portia. That had lasted just a few weeks, just long enough for Daneen to realize that single parenting was too hard, even with a full-time nanny. She'd concocted a new scheme for keeping Bryan close, decreeing he could only see his daughter in the family home. "Stability," Daneen insisted. "A child needs the stability of one predictable home."

So Bryan would stay with Portia while Daneen came to stay with me. I might have been more enthused if I hadn't been anticipating Daneen in full crisis, all that high-octane emotion pent up in my shitty little house. And worse, her intensity coming up against Roger's irreverence, his happy-go-lucky impatience with drama.

Anxiety was like a force field around me. Roger didn't seem himself, either, but he'd gone along, scrubbing the built-up, burnt-on stains from around the stove's elements while I crawled along the walls to wash the baseboards. We'd been at it for hours but the more we did, the more I saw to do. Chipped paint, worn patches on the cheap brass cupboard handles, that hideous linoleum in the bathroom.

I looked around the spare room at all the crap I'd piled into it. "This whole place is a dump."

"Meriel, it isn't a dump. It's comfortable."

"Roger, try to understand—Daneen's got higher standards than you. She's got taste."

When he didn't come around to help me lift an old armchair, I turned to see him staring at me with an expression like he'd smelled something foul.

"Roger, what's wrong?"

"I think you just said I have no taste."

"Come on, that's not what I meant. I just meant Daneen is

used to serious luxury." He didn't budge. "Look, I just don't want her to think I live in a hovel, okay?"

"Jesus, Meriel, you're acting like your mother, trying so hard to impress this woman." A low blow and he knew it, but he didn't stop there. "If she's such a bigshot, do you really think she'll be impressed by anything you do around here?"

I wanted to punch back, but before I could think of anything beyond easy profanity, he'd stormed out of the house, leaving me with an armchair to haul downstairs and no help at all. I kicked it, and tried to lift it, and for the first time in years I wished I still had a pack of cigarettes wrapped in foil in the freezer. Tears of frustration boiled behind my eyes. I went halfway down the stairwell and then sat down, my head in my hands until it came to me that I could lay that chair flat on its back and slide it downstairs.

I hoped Roger would be impressed when he came back to apologize and saw the chair by the curb. Only he didn't come back—not that night and not the next day. Finally, I had to call him and say I was sorry, a calculated apology to erase our quarrel. I expected him to reciprocate. Instead he said, "Let's take a break, Meriel, until you're less stressed. I just can't take it."

I didn't want to take a break, but I went along. At least I wouldn't have to worry about how Roger and Daneen would clash.

The night before she arrived, I finally got around to the bathroom floor. I'd bought stick-down linoleum tiles, bluish-grey and textured like real slate, and I measured and peeled and placed them by myself. The tricky parts, like cutting around the toilet, took forever. I couldn't afford to screw up even one cut because I'd bought exactly the number of tiles I needed.

It was after midnight when I tacked the last of the base-boards back on. I stood in the doorway and surveyed my work, trying to see it as someone else would, trying not to focus on the imperfections.

105.

I SHOULD HAVE left for the airport earlier, but I couldn't stop fussing the house. By the time I put the key in the ignition, I was in a race. Right off the bat I got behind one of those old guys with reflexes too slow to handle the speed limit and a sense of entitlement too big to even consider pulling over and letting traffic pass. I swerved around him but hit so many red lights that, by the time I pulled up in front of the terminal, I knew Daneen was waiting in the airport, wondering where I was. There was no time to make the long hike from the short-term lot so I parked at the curb and sprinted inside.

Right away I spotted her blazing head beside the baggage carousel. When I touched her on the shoulder, Daneen turned and grabbed hold. "I thought you weren't coming!"

I pushed her away, told her to meet me out front and jogged back to my car. I'd been gone for two minutes. A parking ticket, sneering yellow, flapped against my windshield.

I snatched it out from under the wiper—forty-five fucking dollars!—and headed for the parking officer, easy to spot with his reflective orange X marking a target across his back. I watched him motion a car from the curb with a well-practiced gesture. I could see he was closer to sixty than thirty, and his age just made me madder, like he had no excuse—like he was a life-time bully who'd ascended to some kind of supreme parking monitor glory. Like he'd found his fistful of power and enjoyed throwing punches a little too much.

He saw me charging toward him, ticket in my hand, and he smirked but he didn't waste a word on me. He just pointed to a Loading Zone sign.

"I am loading. She's coming right now!"

"Lady, you leave the car parked here, you get a ticket." He was done with me, already tapping on the window of a pick-up truck, reprising his shove-off motion. The driver leaned to roll down his passenger window. "I'm waiting for my daughter. Can

I just leave my truck here for a sec and go find her?"

There was a lot of "No sir" and "Yes sir" before the defeated man rolled his window back up and started inching, as slowly as possible, along the empty curb. I stayed put, rigid with frustration. The bully turned back to me. "Get in your car and start driving before I write you another ticket." But I stood my ground and let it all roil up inside me.

I guess I'd forgotten what I'd told a young client just hours earlier about learning to play the game, about figuring out what the person with the power wants and giving it to them. That client had lost her job due to a lack of deference—that was her explanation, what she'd been told. But she wasn't interested in my good advice. She'd demanded to know if I'd give the same advice to a man and then stormed out of my office without even taking the budgeting tips brochure I held out to her.

I was inches from the parking guard, up on my toes and right in his face. "Fuck you, asshole!" His response was to lumber past me in the direction of my car, so I ran to beat him to it. I gunned the engine and pulled away. In the rearview mirror I could see where he'd stopped and crossed his arms, surveying his whole kingdom of precious curb. I had to drive the entire circuit then, out to the edge of the airport and back to the terminal entrance where Daneen now stood, smoking. I slid to a stop, popped the locks, rolled down the window and yelled for her to throw her suitcase in the back. She ditched the cigarette just before she closed the door.

The sharp tang of nicotine hanging on her smelled good. "I thought you quit."

"It's been a hell of a couple of months—"

The guard strolled past, his bulky frame bent into the wind and his reflective straps slapping against his impervious black jacket. I floored the accelerator, spun the wheels before they grabbed and we jerked away from the curb.

Daneen gaped at me. I hauled the yellow ticket from my

pocket and flung it toward her. "I just got a fucking parking ticket!"

"Just now, picking me up? Well I can pay for it."

"I didn't mean I can't pay it—I mean it's ridiculous!" Five minutes in town and she was already throwing her money around, pretending to be the serene one.

106.

I CALLED ROGER from work, hoping for a normal, friendly conversation. When he didn't answer, I left a voicemail, telling him I didn't know yet if he'd get to meet Daneen. I'd barely had a conversation with her, so I still didn't know if she needed careful handling.

When I got home, Roger's big white truck was parked outside my house. Inside, the two of them were sitting on opposite ends of the couch, talking in the too-loud, too-bright tones that strangers use. Wine glasses glittered in their hands, a near empty bottle was stationed nearby.

"Hello!" Daneen rolled herself to standing and came toward me, beaming. She appeared to have forgotten my surly welcome the night before. She hugged me hard and I hugged her back just as vigorously, holding on too long for Roger's benefit. He looked out the living-room window like he wasn't part of this particular scene.

Daneen was still beaming. "How was your day? Are you exhausted? Come and sit." I wanted to let her lead, to flop down next to her and dissolve into her but it was all wrong, her perched there on her old couch playing hostess in my house. So I stayed upright, aware that Roger was watching me, that his smile had vanished. I said, "I should get something out for dinner."

"Don't you dare. I'm taking us all out for dinner—Roger's already picked the place."

I looked straight at him then and my heart leapt absurdly, as if he'd just stepped from a train after a very long war.

"The new bathroom floor looks great, Meriel. It doesn't look like vinyl at all." Then, straight to Daneen, he said, "She wanted the house to look perfect for you, but of course she hates to spend a dime."

Daneen laughed—laughed and nodded like he was utterly charming, like they were soul mates. "You don't have to tell me. I lived with her for four years."

A pulsing started in my head again, a rush of blood that sounded like heavy traffic. I watched them grin at each other until the noise subsided. "Where are we going? Do I need to change?"

Roger barely glanced at me. "You're fine."

Daneen patted the cushion between them—"Sit, Meriel. Relax. I was just telling Roger about the reading I'm giving at a bookstore here on Thursday."

I took the smaller chair across from the couch instead, but I scooted it forward an inch to concede a little ground.

107.

I FAKED MY way through dinner that night but it kept coming back, that loud pulsing. The next evening we went to Calder, where at least nothing was expected of me. Dad and Mom filled the table with talk about Texas, then Doris and Daneen caught up while I sat mute on the couch, listening to the diesel engines in my head.

The noise lasted until Roger came over to my house bearing beer and an excuse about wanting to be sure we had an ample supply. He stayed to drink a few himself, the three of us standing in my kitchen. Daneen told funny stories about Portia while I worked at laughing naturally. I worried that she'd noticed how hands-off Roger and I were, but I needed some formal concession before I could relax. Finally Roger crossed the kitchen to set his empty bottle back in the case and stayed beside me, threading an arm around my waist and planting a soft kiss near my ear. My jaw unclenched and finally, that awful noise stopped.

I was in a fine mood the next day in the office, my load light and anchored by Michelle and Derrick's third appointment. For their second, they'd brought a raging hellfire of fury and panic, but no shoebox. They'd done the math, and then maybe they'd tossed recriminations back and forth at home—maybe they'd even buried that shoebox in their backyard and poured a ring of salt around the hole. But by the time I saw them, they were done blaming each other. In my office, they were on the offensive, unified against me, everything adding up to "How could you do this to us?" I'd let them rail on, let them name the beast they'd met in the numbers but I didn't promise to slay it. I just copied down the figures, handed a brief accounting back to them and promised that next time, we'd go beyond refinancing options to real solutions.

This appointment would be different. The third appointment always was. Flayed by their financial reality, they'd be wide open to any salve. For me, this was the payoff—time, finally, to focus on attitudes and habits, to affect some lasting change. The third appointment always ended with such palpable relief.

But while I was down the hall getting coffee, Michelle phoned and left a terse message. Derrick had found a new job, they'd consolidated their loans and they were no longer in trouble. Nothing even close to a thanks snuck in before her goodbye. I marked the file Potential Repeat and then I didn't have a single thing left on my calendar. I tackled a stack of subscription forms and surveys on my desk. When I'd whittled that pile away to nothing, I wiped down my computer screen and keyboard. I could have gone home to Daneen, but it was barely three o'clock so I reached for a back issue of *Psychology Today* and I read until anxiety completely took over and there was no point pretending to be productive.

I don't know why I got so nervous. I didn't have to stand at the microphone or feel embarrassed by a poor turnout, but the calmer Daneen acted in the days leading up to her event, the more agitated I'd become. She claimed not to care if anyone came to hear her read, said it was perfectly fine that Roger couldn't make it. It was such a small space, she said, a dozen would fill it. Besides, it was just part of the job; it didn't matter to her at all.

When we arrived at the bookstore, the alcove where she was to appear was nearly full. And people kept arriving in a stream, like ants following a sweet spill. The staff had to bring more folding chairs until no more would fit, until they had to move the podium so it faced out into the larger space. Daneen remained calm as glass.

My mother's book club came out in full force and all of them were clustered around the author, clutching copies of both her books and waiting to be introduced. My father, sitting next to me in the second row, whispered, "Who are all these people?"

I'd been wondering the same thing. When I turned in my seat, I recognized a face directly behind me, someone I was sure had lived in our dorm though I'd forgotten her name, if I ever knew it. Near the back of the room, I spotted an old guy who had been one of Daneen's English professors. And then it dawned on me. Eric might be in the crowd, too. I rearranged my face, flipped the light switch behind my eyes and tried to look casual about scanning the room but there wasn't time to find him. Daneen was being introduced and I was obliged to face forward.

I pulled my arms tight around me so Dad wouldn't sense that I'd started quaking. From the second Daneen opened her perfectly glossed mouth, it was clear she was impeccable at the podium. She read three short sections from *For Love or Money*, and said entertaining things when she moved from one to the next. She'd practiced it on me at home, the whole performance, so I didn't really listen. Instead I thought about the back of my head, wondering if the wave of my hair was right, if my collar was straight.

Afterward, Daneen signed books while vague young women with trays distributed plastic cups of wine. Someone uncovered a fruit and cheese plate in the corner. I stepped just far enough out of the fray to study the crowd, left to right, front to back. There was no Eric. Still I had a sense of him. I kept looking for some trace, like the trail jet fuel leaves behind.

Long after Dad had wandered back to Mom, Daneen was surrounded by admirers, her expression leaping over and over again to "How great to see you!" It struck me that just a stone's throw from my house, in the city where I'd stayed and she'd left, Daneen was somehow more at home than I could ever imagine being.

108.

ON SATURDAY, HER last day in town, Daneen wanted to check out the old neighbourhood. We walked over, the air thick and still when we started out but then the wind picked up and the temperature dropped so sharply we jackknifed into Murph's Place, a bar that hadn't changed in the decade since we'd last been in. And because it was exactly the same, we ordered exactly the same thing we always had: nachos and a pitcher of Caesars. When Daneen tipped back her head to take in a steaming clot of cheese and chips, time sheered like an elastic snapping and I was happy to go with it, to slip off the tenterhooks I'd been on since she'd called to say she was coming.

There hadn't been a single distraught moment in the past four days, so when she swallowed and said, "That waitress looks a lot like her—like Bryan's girlfriend," I didn't even tense. "Meriel, you wouldn't believe the vacuous thing he's replaced me with."

She'd told me all this on the phone. We'd been over and over the landscape of Bryan's leaving, which she'd taken as a temporary mid-life snit until he'd taken up with this friend of a friend, this unbelievably vacuous thing. I'd asked Daneen if she suspected the affair had begun before the separation. "What difference does five minutes make?" she'd responded. "He's still mine and she's still sleeping with him."

I couldn't tear my eyes from the waitress. I guess I was looking for whatever it was that made her more appealing than Daneen, because I hadn't realized yet that the equation was always more complicated than that.

Daneen picked at the green onions dotting the nachos platter and told me her lawyer said it could all play in her favour.

So there were lawyers already.

"Thank god for that pre-nuptial agreement."

"You had a pre-nup?"

She shrugged. "I didn't want one. Daddy insisted—a condition for buying us the house. It's all mine, at least. I won't have to sell or buy Bryan out." She looked out the window. Snow had begun to pelt down from the leaden April sky. "I realize he's not coming back, but I don't have to make it easy for him."

My mouth was opportunely full. I kept it that way until she changed the subject. "So tell me about you and Roger. Will you get married?"

I knew it was the sort of thing people asked, but it was the first time anyone had asked me. "He's talked about spending our lives together. I'm just waiting for him to ask me, officially."

The waitress laid our bill on the table and I lunged at the chance to say, "It's on me." Daneen ignored that.

"You could ask him—but I can see why you don't. Roger's one of those guys who wants things on his own terms, isn't he?" She nodded in answer to her own question and passed the waitress her credit card before my wallet had even made it to the table. After she'd signed the slip and slipped on her coat, she added, "He'd probably run away with the circus if you suggested a commitment."

I didn't know what Roger had done to make Daneen think so and I didn't ask; I just pulled my scarf tight around my face as we stepped out into a blizzard.

109.

WE WERE EXPECTED in Calder for Sunday brunch but that was off, the whole city shut down and muffled under thigh-high drifts, highways made impassable by blowing snow. It was only the cancellation of Daneen's flight, the possibility of rescheduling, that calmed my mother down. Daneen and I passed the morning in near silence as if we, too, were stifled under some heavy encumbrance, or else like we'd parcelled out all our conversation to fit within the allotted time and made no allowance for added hours.

When the wind died down, I pulled on my jacket and boots. Daneen laid down her book. "Doesn't Roger come over and shovel you out?" When I asked why he would, she laughed. "Because that's how it works, this boy-girl thing. Call him up and tell him to get over here and help."

I couldn't imagine making that call. As I forced the back door open against a drift, Daneen called out, "Men like to be heroes, Meriel!"

An hour later my arms ached but I'd shaken off my aggravation, stopped arguing with the shovel about heroics and who needed them. I'd cut paths in the front and the back and uncovered my car, but as I turned to go in I noticed the snow was packed tight to the top of my elderly neighbour's front door. I had to hold the shovel overhead to start on it. The woman watched from inside, and when the door was clear she pushed it open and held out a five dollar bill. She insisted nearly as ardently as I refused, and if I hadn't thought Daneen might be watching the whole ridiculous scene, I'd have given in and taken it.

I was in dry clothes making dinner when Daneen finally dialed Bryan. She opened with, "Hey, it's me," and I wondered just how long a person could claim the territory of "me" after a marriage ended.

"No flights. Nothing until tomorrow and that's iffy—" her voice warmer than her constricted face, a duplicity I'd never mastered. "Will you and Portia be okay if I don't come home for a few days?"

I was near enough, shredding cheese onto a tuna casserole, that I heard Bryan's response through the receiver. He was fine with her staying away. Portia was fine, the nanny was fine. Everything was just fine.

And that's what seemed to flip Daneen's switch—everything being just so fine. Her first shriek jolted me right out of my skin, sent the grater to the floor. I was stooped over picking up curled bits of cheese, so I didn't hear how Bryan responded to the sudden fury, if he was also stunned silent by the high-decibel litany of variations on what he was.

The weeping started as soon as she'd slammed down the receiver—started as fast and hard as the yelling had and kept up for a very long time. Some pipe full of misery had burst and the pump was running full tilt. This was what I'd dreaded: Daneen crumbling, my arms around her like an old habit. She kept saying "humiliating," but she didn't mean this drama in my kitchen—she meant Bryan, her real life, what all those people who mattered must think.

I kept saying, "shh shh" into the top of her head but I was thinking about the Saturday night a week earlier, Roger and I curled together on the couch watching TV, oblivious to the impossibility of enduring happiness.

110.

BEFORE WORK, I drove Daneen to Calder so she and Doris could have their time together and Mom could take her to the airport. But instead of catching the first available flight, Daneen extended her visit indefinitely, though I didn't find that out for several days, not until my mother called and invited me for dinner. "Your friend is a mess" was how she framed the invitation.

And Daneen was a mess, the red rims around her eyes turning them bottle-glass green and full of fractures. How much of her misery could be blamed on the ministrations of Doris I wasn't sure, but I found myself compelled to make the long trek to Calder every evening for two weeks while the warm spring air pushed its way north, filling the ditches with runoff from the fast-melting snow.

On the weekend, Roger asked to come along despite my warning about histrionics. We arrived in Calder to find sandbags piled in my parents' driveway and in the neighbours' driveways, too, so many that we had to park on the street with the rest of the cars. In the backyard, Dad was peering hard into the swollen river.

"The water's coming up fast. I've never seen it like this. We're building a dyke from there," he pointed in one direction, "to there." I wasn't sure where the end points were or who *we* entailed, but it was clear Roger and I had just enlisted. Neighbours were assembling along the banks and there was no time for hellos because wheelbarrows laden with sandbags were already barrelling toward us.

It was a weird kind of homecoming, standing shoulder to shoulder with people I hadn't spoken to in years, our human chain stretching the length of four big backyards. As I pivoted to pass a sandbag off to Roger, I let my hip roll into his. "Thanks for doing this."

In the space between the next bag he took my hand. "Tell me who all these people are," he said.

I looked down the line at the Wallaces, the Sheckmans, the Savoys. There were just as many faces I didn't know, but I could still string together a narrative—not just their names but how they fit. I knew who'd been mayor and who drank too much, whose parents had died in a house fire. When I got to the Peters, I explained about their grown son, standing between them earnest and clumsy and so dedicated to the work. I was afraid Roger would make a joke about the village idiot, but instead he said, "This is really a great community."

"I know." And for once I felt like I was a part of it, like I belonged someplace.

Even Daneen and Mom were working behind the scenes, keeping coffee thermoses filled. At lunch time, they brought out sandwiches and encouragement, distracted for a little while from the tragedy they'd been playing at all week.

Late in the day, when every jacket had been jettisoned and water had replaced coffee in our cups, we took a break. Harve Wallace thought we might stop, but Terry Savoy suggested another few rows before sunset. Dad seconded that and we took up the line again. Our dyke, high as my thigh, snaked for almost a thousand feet when we finally dispersed in the darkness, tired and exhilarated.

Roger and I were sent to sleep downstairs in the room still called Gord's. When I told Roger to take the first shower, he grabbed me by the wrist and pulled me along, barely giving me time to shed my clothes. He kissed me hard for a long time in that little stall, hot water coursing over our heads and down our sore arms, then he spun me around and bent me over, my head pressed to the acrylic wall. To keep from gasping while he drove into me, I had to concentrate on the gritty sand that washed off us and swirled slowly in the water.

The next morning the line resumed, this time with even more hands, and we fell into a steady rhythm that kept on until our sand ran out. Then there were hugs, handshakes, and a communal jubilation in the certainty our barricade could withstand whatever came. And it did, though as much through luck as by design.

Someone suggested taking a walk to look for low spots, for folks who needed our help closing the gap. I was ready for road duty but then I caught sight of Daneen across the yard, beckoning me with a fervent hand. "I have to show you something," she said as soon as I was near enough to hear. "Get in the car." Mom, I saw, was already idling in the driveway.

Roger had committed to the downstream march so I was alone in the backseat, sand still stuck to my sweaty parts, and neither Daneen nor my mother would give me a hint as the car swung along River Road to the older, higher part of town at the river bend. Finally, Mom stopped in a driveway and they both leapt out calling, "Come on!" in unison. I clambered from the car reluctantly.

Daneen pointed up the hill toward an old white house. "That's mine. I just bought it!"

Impossible. "Bought what?"

"The house! It's my perfect retreat." Barely visible through the scrub oak and the overgrown lilac bushes was one of the Calder originals, a town founder's old manse. "Or it will be. Come and see."

"You're moving to Calder?" I couldn't take a step.

Daneen was striding up the driveway but she turned to answer me. "Not right away. But once I have it restored, I can spend summers out here with Portia. Hide away."

Doris said something about safe haven, I think, but her gleefulness stopped up my ears so her words fell to the ground around me.

We stepped past the trees and the whole of it came into view. It was a tall house, its creaking bones held upright with a thick coat of new paint, and it perched on high ground where there was never any risk of flooding. Looking up, I could tell, when the sun angled in just right behind it, this house would really cast a shadow.

111.

IT WAS HAPPENING more often—a client would come into my office and I'd start to sneeze. Not right away, not until after the initial paperwork but long before we were done with the details. By the time the appointment was over, I'd be clogged solid, my throat swollen and my eyes watering. The first few times, I figured it must be the sudden onset of a cold yet my symptoms vanished as soon as I got outside. It happened every few weeks until I noticed a pattern: every time, the client had come looking for advice on declaring bankruptcy.

"I must be allergic to bankruptcy," I told Lars in the staffroom where he was putting his wallet in the safe. Although the code of conduct we signed every year made us promise not to give personal financial assistance to a client, Chuck insisted we lock away our wallets and chequebooks just to be sure we weren't tempted. "Look at me. I have this reaction every time."

Lars chuckled. "Meriel, Meriel." He closed the safe and turned to watch me open a new box of tissues. "You must have a perfume allergy."

"Lars, I'm not kidding. It only happens with bankruptcy."

He smiled the smile that knew it was smarter than me. "Exactly. People about to declare bankruptcy always ratchet up their credit cards on personal items like expensive perfume that can't be reclaimed. It's a known fact."

Lars made a habit of being certain about everything. When he'd first started—before he'd ever counselled a client of his own— he'd declared to Chuck and me that what people in financial trouble really needed was to get a clearer understanding about value. I'd nodded encouragingly. "That's right. It really is about values."

Both Lars and Chuck had looked at me strangely, and even though Chuck had tried to smooth things over by saying, "Well yes, values sometimes play a part," I'd left embarrassed.

Still, I figured Lars might be right about the perfume thing. Later, I asked Chuck if we could request that clients not wear scents, maybe post a few signs around the reception area. Chuck just looked confused, like he didn't quite get the joke I was trying to make. The next time it happened, once my sinuses had drained, I suggested to Chuck that he make Lars our bankruptcy specialist, because Lars had such a complete grasp on the complexities. Chuck liked that idea and I thought I'd pulled off a brilliant manoeuvre until I overheard him talking to Lars.

"I think bankruptcy offends her. You know how Meriel is— she'd just as soon see them all in debtor's prison."

112.

AFTER THE WATER had receded and the sandbags were cleared away, Dad started on a trench and a berm in the backyard, insurance against the next time.

Digging out there alone that summer, on land that had belonged to his family since it had belonged to anyone, Dad turned up an arrowhead. It was small and brown, about the size of his thumb and clearly honed by human hands. When he showed it to me, I imagined the sound of his shovel striking it, the unearthing, the wonder as the sun turned the sky brilliant orange around his silhouette. I don't know, really, if it was like that at all, but I know he was curious, hungry to know something about its origins. So curious he went to the library and when Calder Public couldn't answer his questions, he drove to the city on a Tuesday afternoon, picked me up at work and we went together to the big library at the university. I hadn't set foot on that campus in years but still I knew every turn. Dad talked to librarians and then to historians and finally to an anthropologist. He read original journals wearing white gloves and he scanned microfiche while I wandered the aisles. We were there for hours, but he never found out enough to fill up the hole that arrowhead had opened.

He donated his find to the prehistoric collection on campus and I thought it was done with, but driving me home he said, "Nothing is covered up that will not be revealed."

His voice had that Biblical intonation and I should have realized then that he'd looked too closely, too intently, that something had shifted. That some small pin in him had cracked.

113.

GLEN SENT ME things in the mail. Len had known better, but Glen was all about paper, or else about nudging me toward some greater commitment, some daring feat of investment. He started with quarterly statements, then newsletters about investment opportunities. In December, he sent me a birthday card that arrived right on the day. Soon it was photocopied newspaper clippings about local businesses that got their start-up funding from Narcissus. He guessed right that I'd like those stories, that the notion of investing in companies that mattered to people who might cross my path would matter to me. But I didn't need Glen to send them; I read the newspaper at work every day, too.

When I went to see Glen in February, I told him that. I told him to save his postage, but I suppose I muddied my message by handing him a hefty cheque to buy more Narcissus. My investment was bigger than usual—I'd emptied the savings account I kept for emergencies to round up the amount, reasoning I'd be able to restock it with my income tax refund.

Roger was delighted by that reasoning. He acted like it was some kind of breakthrough, a step in the right direction. "Sounds like you're finally borrowing a page from my financial planning strategy, honey."

Roger didn't have a financial planning strategy. He had a single chequing account and every dime he had went in and came out of that account. He didn't invest, he didn't put aside. He believed in spending it all while a person was still young enough to enjoy it and besides, he'd argue, old age is what your pension is for. Roger's only saving scheme was having too much tax deducted bi-weekly so in the spring, he'd get a big income tax refund to blow on something he wanted.

I tried a few times to explain why this was dumb, how he wasn't making any interest on that money, but he didn't care. "My friend Bill puts all his quarters, dimes and nickels—all of 'em—in a giant commercial pickle jar," he countered, "and Bill doesn't get any interest either. But every year he gets a trip to Vegas out of that pot. You can't say the same."

114.

WHEN MY MOTHER suggested Roger and I join them for Christmas in Texas, I stalled. I was sure Roger wouldn't want to; the flights were too expensive and the drive was too long and too treacherous, all that open road in winter.

But Roger said we should do it. Then he said he wouldn't consider not doing it. He loved the idea of a winter vacation, a getaway to somewhere warm and I remembered that he and his ex-girlfriend had travelled a lot, had taken a tropical vacation just about every year they were together. It wasn't that he talked about her often—I hadn't even known her name for months after we'd become a couple—but there were pictures of those trips propped all over his place, palm trees and surf and Aztec ruins, and naturally Tabitha found her way into some of the shots.

When I pointed out this trip wouldn't be like those—first of all, there was no way I could afford to fly and, secondly, the palm trees would be throwing their shadows across a retirees' trailer park—Roger said it would still be great, that his truck had four-wheel drive and plenty of room and we could camp outside once we got far enough south. He was excited, I think, for the excuse to buy some new camping gear.

I went to the auto association to get the best route and I brought home guidebooks for every state we'd traverse. I went through them, circling the cheapest motels in the northern states, the cheapest serviced campgrounds further south.

I was worried about everything—about blizzards and breakdowns, about getting lost even though the route they'd mapped for me looked pretty much like a straight line running north to south. Roger only worried that we might argue about what music to listen to. I suggested we pick up some books on tape, but he hated that idea. He wasn't much for reading and I think he imagined being trapped in a car with *Masterpiece Theatre* for twenty-eight hours. We agreed, finally, to alternate music choices: one of his, then one of mine. It was the hardest part of getting ready, selecting the music, making sure I chose things I'd want to hear in the middle of Nebraska that would neither embarrass me nor irritate him.

I left work at lunchtime. We planned to hit the road before two, put five or six hours of driving behind us. We could have done the drive in two long days but Roger wanted to maximize our road trip, to wake up on vacation as many days as possible, to poke around Topeka for no reason at all.

When he drove up to my house, I had everything ready to go: a reasonably small suitcase of clothing, a much smaller road-trip bag of essentials, an armload of gifts for my parents, four full grocery bags and a cooler of perishable food. I'd been up half the night making sandwiches and cheese cubes and carrot sticks, packing meals that would be easy to access as we drove. I'd washed fresh fruit, baked muffins, even assembled a collection of Roger's favourite junk foods.

"You're bringing all that?" He half-smiled like he thought I must be kidding.

"It's mostly food for the trip." I didn't want him to think I was some frivolous stereotype bringing fifteen pairs of shoes on vacation.

"We're driving through the U.S., not the Sahara Desert. There'll be plenty of places to stop and eat along the way."

"We can't eat in restaurants the whole time, Roger. It'll slow us down and cost a fortune."

"It's a vacation, Meriel, it's supposed to cost money." He picked up my suitcases. "Let's see what we can fit back there." I followed with the cooler.

When he opened the back hatch, I saw the cab was jammed full of camping gear and four cases of beer. He managed to wedge just my suitcase and my smaller pack in, and I almost stopped him, almost said, "That's the one I'll need for the drive," but I figured I could worry about that later.

In the end, we fit all the gifts in but had to leave behind the cooler with my carefully constructed meals and the bag of fruit. Roger knew I was unhappy about it because he threw his arm around me when he said, "We can truck stop all the way, baby. We won't starve." Then he peeled away from the curb too enthusiastically, AC/DC's "Highway to Hell" blasting from the stereo. I figured he'd made the effort to set it up that way, so I told him it was perfect.

Night dropped suddenly at the border as we explained ourselves to a customs officer who, thankfully, didn't search us to find all that beer in the back. After that, there was almost no traffic, the road a smooth ribbon drawing us along. Our headlights reflecting off the pavement seemed like the only light around for miles.

Roger said he was hungry and suggested we stop for the night, get some dinner. I told him no, insisted we drive another hour, explained that the motels got cheaper further south. I took over at the wheel and I drove us all the way to the Watertown Super 8 in South Dakota, happy because it was exactly where I'd planned for us to stop.

Roger picked up the tab for dinner and at every gas station diner along the way until the last day. Then I guess sleeping in a tent on the hard ground had made him cranky because at lunch, he looked at the face-down bill and said, "Are you getting this one?"

It would have been so easy to say yes.

"I bought food for the trip, remember? You're the one who wanted to eat in restaurants." I was half-joking, half wanting to remind him that I'd also been generous. He just got pissed off and even though I did buy lunch, we drove the last several hours in silence.

115.

ON CHRISTMAS EVE, my parents nipped over to a neighbours' annual Open Trailer, carrying a case of Roger's beer with them. Folks around here, they said, would be over the moon to see a case of Canadian come through the door. They acted like he'd brought them nectar of the gods, like he'd made some remarkably munificent sacrifice.

Their absence for an hour was a necessary and welcome respite after the McAllen crash-course—the who's who and what's what we'd endured since pulling up alongside their trailer. They'd even insisted on a driving tour of the whole of McAllen the day after we arrived, after we'd climbed out of our finally-stilled vehicle and remarked—out loud, both of us, directly to them—how good it was to stop moving, to be able to stand upright for hours at a time.

I was basking in the relief of being alone in that small trailer when Roger told me to sit on the couch. He held out his hand to me. A small box shimmered in silver paper in his palm. "I wanted to give you this while we were alone."

I took it from him carefully, trembling, amazed at how the body responds even before the mind has formed a coherent thought. I looked at my gift, at its thin red ribbon and then at him, his face lit with anticipation, all the tension of the drive gone. I didn't make a move to open the box.

"Would you rather wait and open it in front of your parents?"

I laughed, leaned over to kiss him and there was a nervousness about him, too. I swallowed hard and pulled the ribbon off without untying it. The paper was held in place by the barest bit of tape, and under that there was just a red velvet box. I didn't hesitate again. I lifted the hinged lid quickly.

Inside was a pair of opal earrings. Two studs, tiny diamonds twinkling at the bottom of each oval. Iridescent and lovely and I remembered that we'd walked past a jewelry store and I'd stopped to look at the opals on display, mentioned that I wished

I'd been born a few months earlier so they'd be my birthstone. I didn't think I was hinting, but maybe I was.

I'm sure I looked surprised. I smiled extra big so Roger would see how much I liked them, how grateful I was.

Doris and Don came in just then, worried that we were bothered by their absence. I showed my mother the earrings, still in the box, and she murmured, "Beautiful." Then she sighed. "But you can't wear those, Meriel-Claire, they aren't your birthstone. It's bad luck."

Roger looked from her to me and I made a face to show him I didn't believe in that stupid superstition. I put the earrings on right then. Then I picked the knot out of the red ribbon and I laid the paper flat and gingerly picked off the tape. It left barely a divot on one edge that could easily be trimmed off. My hand was halfway across the silvery expanse, smoothing out the wrinkles, when Roger reached over and yanked the paper from me, crumpling it into a tight ball.

"Hey!" One syllable of protest.

"You don't need to save the damn wrapping paper!"

He slammed the garbage can lid and strode to the bathroom, the whole trailer shaking under his hard heels, and I was left sitting in silence with my parents and my shiny ears and my embarrassment.

116.

I HAD NO interest in going golfing or even going along for the ride. I'd gone to the course a few times back home with Roger, and I'd found it alternately boring and frustrating. I could putt, could see the angle and speed a ball would need to reach the cup, but getting to the green was agonizing.

"I'm glad you're not coming," my mother said, untucking some hair and arranging it on her forehead beneath her sun visor. "I just feel better if someone's here when the housekeeper comes."

"You have a housekeeper?"

"Haven't I told you about Rachel? I share her with two other ladies. She comes two mornings a week."

I looked around. The trailer was done up nice enough, but it was half the size of their house in Calder and usually just had the two of them in it. "Since when?"

"Since I realized Daneen was right—people should spend their time doing the important things and leave the cleaning to someone else." My mother handed me three five dollar bills. "Give these to Rachel when she's done—but make sure she scrubs the kitchen sink. She missed it last time."

I couldn't believe my father had gone in for such a luxury. I asked him about it after Doris and Roger went to the car with their clubs. "She needs the work, Meriel-Claire. She has three kids and a family back in Mexico she sends money home to."

"Oh, it's charity!"

Dad looked at me strangely. "Well maybe there's an element, but I wouldn't call it charity. It's not something for nothing. It's a job."

I couldn't bear to sit by while someone else cleaned the toilet for us, so I went for a walk and then I leaned under the awning outside and tried to read a book. The vacuum made the walls of the trailer hum and I found I could follow its progress. When the sun drove around that side of the trailer, I finally went in out of the heat. The housekeeper, Raquel—she'd corrected me in a few careful words when I'd greeted her as Rachel—was mopping the kitchen floor, backing out of the room so the tiles would dry without footprints.

There was no way to check the sink. If she'd missed it, I'd have to clean it myself before Mom got home. As Raquel packed up her gear, I fished another bill from my wallet and handed her four five-dollar bills. She looked at them through tired eyes, then shook her head and passed one back. "No miss," she said, "just three." I was too embarrassed to insist.

117.

ROGER'S COMPANY FOUND out about our trip. Apparently there were rules about cross-border hauls—paperwork to complete, extra insurance, permissions. He claimed he hadn't known but they knew better. They let him go. Fired him. Two months later, his lease almost up and his finances strained, Roger suggested moving in with me.

I wanted to play it cool. I sat on my hands and asked if he wouldn't rather dip into his savings to bridge the gap until he found another position.

"What savings? My pension from the company's locked in." So yes, he was sure. He wanted to move in together and it was easy, since all he had to move was his a dresser and his leather recliner. Everything else—and how had I not known this?— everything else belonged to the furnished townhouse.

We'd always gotten along so well. I expected living together would just make everything easier, cut out the back and forth. But almost immediately, Roger and I were at odds. He hated the temperature I kept the house—it was too cold in April and then it was too hot in June. And he didn't like that I thought his recliner should go to the spare room so it didn't crowd the living room. He didn't even like how I folded his clothes or that I put them away in his drawers. I gave in on that one, left them perched on top of his dresser, though half the time he just dressed out of the stack until it all hit the laundry basket without ever having made a drawer's acquaintance.

I didn't like that he was dragging his feet on the job search, or that he always left dishes in the sink when there was a perfectly good, perfectly empty dishwasher next to it. But I did like having him there, knowing I'd go to sleep next to him every night and wake up next to him every morning. And some nights, we still made love with so much intensity that the bed moved away from the edge of the wall.

I could see the years unfurling before us, getting better and better. Some days I was so happy I wanted to paint the bedroom cornflower blue.

118.

I COULDN'T GET used to it, Daneen wanting to own a house in the centre of Calder. But as the legal battle with Bryan ramped up and the friends she thought were hers just wouldn't stop being his, her phone calls to me grew more frequent, more fervent until I got it. Her hideaway house had nothing to do with Calder. She could have chosen any of a thousand places, as long as they were far away from what she'd labelled the calamity of her life. Calder was just familiar and convenient.

The house needed extensive renovations. I'd entertained, briefly, daydreams of the two of us on ladders with paint rollers. I'd show Daneen how to cut mitered angles and demonstrate my growing mastery with caulking. But of course it wasn't like that. Daneen paid one quick visit to Calder a year after she bought the place and then there was an architect, a contractor, one team of journeymen after another—and Doris coordinating the whole operation.

I didn't like the idea of Mom on Daneen's payroll, and I liked even less that it turned out to be a volunteer effort, hours of her life given away. But Mom's enthusiasm was insufferable. Months went by during which she was so busy we didn't speak at all. For months after that, we spoke only about The Project, as she called it. One Saturday, she dropped by my house—an almost unprecedented occurrence. There were paint chips jutting out of her purse. Did I want to come with her to help choose a chandelier at a nearby lighting store? No, I didn't. "I'm doing my laundry," I told her.

In the middle of a raging heat wave, I picked Daneen and Portia up from the airport and drove them to Calder for the big unveiling. As we rounded the curve in the driveway, I saw the old house had been transformed, its wide verandah completely rebuilt. The front door had been stripped to bare wood and varnished to gleaming. Inside, the house was sparsely furnished, but every piece was perfect. Words came to me that I'm sure I'd never heard spoken, could only have known from books: davenport and sideboard and hutch.

Under a chandelier, my mother was polishing the dining room table as we came in. She dropped the cloth and watched, wide-eyed and flushed, for Daneen's first reaction. It didn't disappoint. I don't think I can recall another time when I'd seen Daneen struck speechless. She walked through the house, a slow syrup of *ohs* trickling out before the flurry of grateful hugs.

While Daneen and Portia took their luggage upstairs, I finished polishing the table on Mom's order, amazed at how the grain of old wood leapt out as the cloth moved over it. The fumes, a kind of lemony gasoline, made me dizzy.

Doris set four heavy chairs around the table and called up the staircase. "Okay my two gorgeous girls—come down here and eat something." She laid out sandwiches, cookies, and pickles on paper plates with plastic forks.

Daneen came down the stairs complaining. "It's an oven up there."

"I know," Mom said, pointing Portia to the chair next to hers. "You should have let me get window coverings if you won't have air conditioning."

Daneen tore an egg sandwich in half and handed the smaller portion to Portia.

"I've got measurements for all the windows. And of course we'll need to outfit the kitchen right away." Mom pulled a pack of photos from her purse. "But this is more interesting. I took photos in antique stores when I saw just the perfect thing."

Daneen was looking at me, the corners of her mouth twitching the code for can-you-believe-this? Mom fanned the photos out like a deck of cards but Daneen didn't look down. Instead, she looked up, formulating her response. "Doris,

I really appreciate all you've done, but I just want to keep it simple. I like how it feels now—like a clean slate, something I can invent slowly."

My mother crossed her arms. "You can't live like this. It's bare bones."

"Doris," an indulgent laugh, "you don't want me to wind up in Meriel's office, do you?"

Chuckles all around. Don't be ridiculous, I could see my mother thinking.

"I'm serious. Things are not good. Bryan's demanding an enormous settlement—alimony for years, plus plus plus. I'm just about tapped out. So I really can't spend a fortune in this house."

I'd never seen this financially-prudent side of Daneen. I guess she'd needed to show it before.

Mom was not impressed. She glumly nudged her photos back into one pile before speaking again. "But you have no cutlery, no dishes—you don't even have a toaster." The lack of a toaster, in particular, seemed to push her toward despair.

"So we won't eat toast." Daneen rubbed her forehead until she was ready to concede a small point. "Okay, a few necessities for the kitchen, but that's it. You have to stop."

Portia tugged on my mother's arm. "Grandma Doris, will you read to me?"

Daneen put a hand on the little girl's head and turned her toward the stairs. "Not now, I'm talking to Grandma Doris. Go read to yourself." Portia went without a fuss.

Daneen turned back to us. "Do you know anyone around here who's from Czechoslovakia?" It came right out of left field. It would be years before the question's import crystallized.

My mother brightened. "Yes—my grandfather came from Prague in 1918, why?"

"Not recent enough." Daneen brushed away the useless information with a flick of her hand. I saw the current of air it made swell and wash over Doris, saw her eyes fill with the shock of that dismissal. Daneen didn't notice at all. She just gave her head a vague shake and said, "Doesn't matter—something I'm working on."

Working was how Daneen spent the summer in that big house on the hill. After they'd outfitted the kitchen and dressed the windows appropriately, she put Portia in day camp—other children are important to a six year old, Daneen insisted—and poor Doris, who'd anticipated a summer of lounging by the pool with her two gorgeous girls, was shuffled off.

Word went out: Daneen was not to be disturbed. To underline the point, she refused to have a phone installed. To drop by would be to risk interrupting the creation of some great thing, so Doris and I kept our distance.

119.

I CAME HOME on a dreary fall day to an envelope from Glen. Inside, a handwritten note was stapled to the front of my quarterly statement. Glen had written his message in block letters, all capitals with the true caps slightly larger than the rest— MERIEL, YOUR MYSTERY FUND HASN'T EVEN DOUBLED, BUT IT COULD HAVE TRIPLED! CALL ME TO TALK ABOUT MAKING IT GROW FASTER, TAX FREE!!

I could picture him slathering over the figures, furtively calculating exactly how many more days, hours, minutes would pass before I came swishing into his office and jacked up his commission. He'd underlined FASTER and double-underlined TRIPLED and TAX FREE, like this was play money, some flimsy lottery win that could be made to sing and dance.

I was so angry I dialed without even rehearsing what I'd say, but it was too late in the day to catch Glen in the office. I slapped the statement face down on the counter and went to take a shower.

The sound of the bathroom door opening startled me. Then Roger's voice. "Meriel, what the hell?"

"Hey, I wasn't expecting you home so early—I thought you had an interview at four."

"It was over in fifteen minutes, which is when I said no thanks. Are you going to tell me about your huge, secret stash of cash?"

Oh God. My mouth opened and closed under the stream of water like a carp's. "It's not a secret stash—it's not even mine." I said it lightly but my hands mimed the strangling of Glen. "I'll explain later."

Roger didn't say anything else, so I did. "Hey—why don't you come in here with me?" It seemed like a very long time since the last time.

I tipped my head back to rinse the shampoo, stretched myself out and let the suds run down over my breasts while I waited for him to step out of his clothes and into the heat. He took a long time, and then longer. Finally I peeped around the curtain. Roger was gone.

I found him waiting in the kitchen, leaning on the counter instead of reclining in his favourite chair like he usually did. He was clutching the note from Glen. "So whose money is it then, and why is it in your name?" His voice was neutral but his eyes hooded, ready.

"It's Gord's."

He looked at the numbers and then back at me. "Dead people don't generally have this much money. I'm sure you've heard you can't take it with you."

Suddenly I didn't want to explain anything. "Why is this any of your business, Roger? We keep our finances separate, remember? We're not married—we don't even have a joint account."

I'd mentioned a joint account when he'd first moved in but he'd shrugged it off, promising he'd buy groceries or pay any bill I asked him to. I still bought most of the groceries, and he'd never paid a bill. He'd just stocked the fridge with beer and signed us up for a deluxe cable package. The last time I'd brought up the imbalance in our fiscal life, he'd said, "I didn't know you were keeping score, Meriel. Maybe you could wait until I find a job before sticking your hand out again."

Roger dropped Glen's note on the counter, face up, and favoured me with a thin, unfriendly smile. "Is that when you planned to tell me your I'm-so-poor act was a sham—after I married you? Maybe you could mention it on our honeymoon— the honeymoon I'll have paid for, since you never have money for anything fun."

An electric current zapped my breath, made me feel like I was lit up hot and bright. I wanted to shout but I was afraid— afraid that the haze around my head kept me from seeing that I'd done something wrong, that I should be apologizing instead of attacking. I turned around so I wouldn't have to look at Roger and braced myself, hands and forehead against the refrigerator until my breathing evened out. Then I tried to explain, this time right from the beginning, about the insurance settlement, my parent's insistence that I take it because Gord had left it to me. I almost told him about Justin, too, but it seemed like my story was already too convoluted.

"So it is your money."

I turned to face his crossed arms, his stony face. "It's not my money, Roger. It's Gord's legacy. It's for doing something with a purpose. What I mean is, it's supposed to do something worthwhile."

"Like what?"

It was terrible, the way he thought I should know.

"I can't talk about this anymore. Please." My throat tightened even though I was telling myself not to cry. "Please, can we just stop?"

Maybe it was the sight of me struggling for air, or some sudden understanding that came over Roger, but his furious face dissolved. "Okay, let's make a deal. You promise you'll loosen up and stop being so tight-fisted, and I won't mention this again. We can pretend I never found out about it."

The voltage drained like he'd killed the switch. I couldn't stop promising, couldn't stop thanking him for wrenching me free from that terrible current.

120.

WHATEVER SONIA REYES did when she found our reception desk unattended, it was enough to bring Chuck out of his office. Chuck hated interruptions, drop-ins, disorder. He kept his door closed and he ignored everything that happened outside of it. But I guess he'd glimpsed Sonia, her soap-opera femme-fatale good looks, and decided he should pause the computer game he pretended not to play all afternoon.

I came back from a haircut to find Chuck leaning casually on the reception desk, explaining the need for an appointment and trying, I think, to look younger and more engaging than he actually was. Sonia was ignoring his words and paying attention to the way the angle of his body said, "Stick around."

I looked at my watch. It was just five to one. "Sonia, do we have an appointment?" If we had, she was uncharacteristically early. She'd always been late before, rushing in flustered, out of breath and ripping the gloves off her hands as if they were on fire. By the third re-enactment, I understood Sonia liked the adrenaline kick of urgency, the way rushing made her feel important.

But she was different this time, icily calm when she turned her attention from Chuck to me. "I have to talk to you."

I let her follow me back to my office. I had a little free time, and certainly time for Sonia. She was a star pupil. Months earlier, she'd been staggering under a mountain of debt, using her line of credit to make the minimum payments on her credit cards, everything ratcheted up to the hilt. Bankruptcy had seemed a possibility, but she was so self-effacing, so willing to do whatever it took that I couldn't bear to turn her over to Lars.

On the surface, her level of debt was puzzling. Her salary was decent, her rent wasn't outrageous and her car, while new, wasn't deluxe. She had no dependants, no family maintenance payments and she insisted she took no drugs, not even aspirin. On paper, her only financial risk factor was "single female"— significant, but not deadly.

I asked first for a year's worth of statements, receipts, whatever she had. When she'd returned with just a handful, I wasn't surprised. Disorganization was a regular companion of runaway debt.

Anyway, it turned out I didn't need a paper trail. Sonia named her problem soon enough: everybody. Everybody has one. Everybody buys that brand. Everybody at work wears nice clothes. When I'd asked about eating lunch in a restaurant every day, she'd combed her over-accessorized fingers through her glossy dark hair. "Of course. Everybody goes out for lunch."

Sonia was a social spender, and they don't have spending habits—they have tribal customs. I'd done a workshop on it once for the rest of the team.

Social spenders buy to belong, and since Sonia was extremely gregarious, she was tangled up in a whole lot of expensive relationships. But she was prepared to change. She even came to her third appointment with a set of solutions written in a list headed *Sonia's New Life Plan*. I hadn't asked her to do that—I'd been treading lightly, aware too much could tip the balance, lead to resentment and then rebellion. But Sonia needed my applause, so she got it. She was especially thrilled when I asked if could tell my colleagues about her most ingenious ideas.

Sometimes, I thought I did some good in my work, that a client left my office a little bit better off, at least temporarily. But there were very few people whose lives I absolutely knew I'd improved. Sonia was one of the big successes.

So it was a surprise, the way she was slumped in her chair, glowering at me across the desk. A lock of her black hair had broken away from the artfully-styled swoop across her forehead, and that loose piece arced forward like water from a hose. More than anything, I wanted her to paste that hair back into place.

"I did all the things you told me to," she said finally. "I made a budget and stopped buying stuff just because someone else did." Her top lip pulled up until it was almost snarling.

"Are you finding it tough?" I could feel the blunt-cut edges of my own hair grazing my neck. "Are other people trying to sabotage you?"

"There's a poster in your lobby, a gambling poster." She pointed behind her. "It talks about the odds of winning and the odds of losing everything." I knew the one she meant. "I saw it last time I was here, so I decided to stop putting five dollars a week into the office 6/49 pool."

I couldn't remember ever talking to Sonia about gambling, and I certainly would never target anything as insignificant as five dollars, but I nodded my approval. It was the principal in practice.

"You know how it works, right? You put in your money and they buy a bunch of tickets and everybody shares the winnings."

I could see it coming then.

"I stopped playing last month. Like you told me to."

Hurtling toward me like a meteorite, barely enough time to wonder "What are the odds?"

"Sonia, I didn't tell you to—"

"Well they won. They won and they split it thirteen ways. And now they're all so happy, and everybody keeps saying 'It's too bad you didn't have faith.' And then they all go to lunch and celebrate."

I didn't have a script for this, for comforting a client who'd been bitten by fiscal prudence. I could have told her that many lottery winners end up deeper in debt a few years down the line, but that seemed like small comfort in the face of so much loss.

Sonia sat up straight, her frown deepening. "They each got four thousand dollars."

I let that sink in, pictured the number in my head. I'd been expecting plenty more zeroes, a life-changing figure. Relief surged through me until Sonia turned off its tap.

"Do you know what that money would have meant to me? I could have paid off my car, stopped eating lunch alone at my desk." Her face crumpled like a little kid's. She turned her hands up and out toward me like she expected me to place something solid in them. "It would have changed my life."

I wanted to tell her that it wouldn't—that windfalls weren't a magic bullet. That they were just one more thing to worry about. Instead, I pulled all the points of my face down to mirror hers and I said, "Oh Sonia, that sucks."

121.

ROGER THOUGHT WE needed a new vehicle. He'd lost his pick-up along with his beer job, of course. I was perfectly happy with the old sedan I'd driven since the dealership closed, and perfectly happy to let Roger use it whenever he wanted. I liked walking to work anyway. I'd devised a nearly straight line of diagonal crossings. Moving briskly, I could make it in twenty-four minutes. I calculated the average time it took me to drive— from clearing the windshield to locking up the car—and then figured out I was getting forty-eight minutes of exercise for the bargain price of just thirty-four minutes extra out of my day. I invested in a pair of boots that were guaranteed good to minus thirty and cancelled my gym membership. Plus I was saving a fortune on gas. I'd even added, "Walk instead of taking the car or a bus—the savings really add up!" to the sheet of money-saving tips I handed to clients.

But none of that mattered to Roger. He was embarrassed by my car, its dated styling and faded dash, the thumbprints of rust pressing in around the fuel door and the wheel wells.

Besides, he wanted a sport utility vehicle, something with enough room to move a dresser, he said. That was his example, moving a dresser, even though we'd already moved his into my house and we had no plans to buy another.

Over and over, I told Roger that buying a brand new car was a terrible investment. Dad used to say the value blew off them like confetti when they left the lot. "Two turns around the block and she's as good as old." They had a book at the dealership that suggested prices for used models. I offered to get one for Roger, but he wasn't interested. He already knew just what he wanted: a scarlet Honda with a sunroof, a colour so tangy I felt it on the back of my tongue. Still, he went along when I said we should test drive different makes. They all seemed pretty much the same to me, the size of them, the way they handled, but each test drive only solidified in Roger's mind the supremacy of that most expensive vehicle.

At least he let me negotiate the purchase and was suitably impressed with the trade-in amount I got for a car he'd been calling a beater for years. Still, the new vehicle was expensive and the loan we needed substantial.

"Our first big purchase together," Roger said. If he hoped that would sweeten the deal for me, he was right. I was practically giddy about it, seeing our two names come together, officially, on all that paperwork. When the loans officer left to make photocopies, I got up from my chair and leaned over Roger to seriously kiss him.

122.

DAD ASSEMBLED THE plastic spruce in the living room. It was the first time in years it had emerged from the basement, the first time in years my parents had stayed in Calder all winter. "The problem with retiring early," Dad had said when he told me about their decision, "is that you have to make the money last a long time."

Roger had helped Dad with the outside lights earlier in the afternoon, had held the ladder and flicked switches, but he'd since left for his standing Sunday night hockey game, leaving the three of us to trim the tree. I was unwrapping ornaments, trying not to get swamped with Christmas memories of Gord. My mother was untangling a string of lights.

"So, when are you and Roger going to get married?"

She laid the lights down and looked at me expectantly.

"It hasn't come up."

"It's been—what, close to four years already?" She'd asked me the same thing a few months before, so I knew we were heading down the road toward the man who won't buy the cow if it gives him the milk for free.

"Four and a half. And we're happy with the way things are right now." I jabbed my finger with the hook I was threading through the silver loop of an ornament. When I checked, there was just a pinprick of blood.

"Well maybe I should mention to him that Christmas is a good time for a ring. Frankly, I don't believe you wouldn't be thrilled to be Mrs. Hardy."

I was about to remind her that women didn't have to change their names anymore when my father tipped his head out from under the lower branches where he was adjusting the tree stand. "It's none of my business—" This was a favourite new phrase of Dad's, a way of warning us that he had an opinion and it wasn't going to be popular. "But if a man's ready to marry someone, he'll ask without prompting."

"She's not getting any younger, Don." Mom was cradling an untangled string of lights. "You're not getting any younger, Meriel-Claire. Your body won't wait forever to have a baby."

I knew how old I was, so I didn't respond.

I watched my father take the lights from her and begin to drape them in sloping rings from the top of the tree. When he was almost finished, my mother said, "It's better to plug them in first and start at the bottom, so you can see how they look as you go along."

Dad stood still for a minute before he started unwinding.

When Roger came back in the evening, I steeled myself for what Mom might say, but he arrived brandishing a fat book of 50-50 tickets, a fundraiser for his hockey team—three dollars apiece, five for ten dollars—and she was too busy writing her name on twenty tickets to mention anything about marriage.

Roger held the book out to me, but I refused it. "I don't have any money on me. Anyway, what would I do with a motorbike if I won it?"

My mother placed her palm against Roger's back and shook her head. "Don't bother with that one. She's as tight as a miser's fist."

As soon as we'd backed out of the driveway, I said, "I don't know why she has to say things like that."

Roger exhaled hard, his breath making a small circle of steam on the windshield. He shoved the stick into drive. "Christ, Meriel, can't we ever leave here without you being upset about something?"

123.

DANEEN CALLED FROM Vancouver on the cusp of the brand new year, just after Y2K had failed to dismantle civilization on the eastern half of the continent. I'd had just enough time to feel relieved, and then foolish about the twenty-dollar bills I'd been withdrawing in little bundles all week. I was looking forward to the champagne cork Roger and I would pop.

Daneen was celebrating alone—there'd briefly been a man in the fall, but he was a flash and gone—and it sounded like she'd been celebrating for hours. She'd called to share her resolutions, what she'd resolved to do to Bryan, how she planned to skewer him anew.

I knew every version of this story and I knew all the angles were sharp. The constant parade through my office of the divorced and aggrieved was all the proof I needed that there was no fifty-fifty split at the end of love. I had file drawers full of vengeful exes—the ones who paid nothing and the ones who took all they could and kept coming back for more because they felt justified, because poverty was a fit punishment for the villain who'd failed to keep loving them.

The takers were at least honest and self-directed. For me, the givers were harder to take.

I almost couldn't bear those wretches who sat across from me, broke and rubbing together the hands they'd held up in surrender: "Take it all, whatever you want." Every one of them spoke about the price of freedom like they'd invented the phrase, but I knew they were all trying to buy the same thing: a thank you, a hero's medal, some ultimate approbation for their sacrifice. And it was my sorry job to tell them they'd never get it, that they might as well just grab their fair share.

Daneen, however, needed no such advice. She was certain of what she deserved in the divorce equation and anyway, she wasn't my client. There was no need for me to weigh in beyond the occasional "Mmm," just so she'd know I was still on the line.

"He's the one with a regular income. He should be paying me." Daneen was starting to slur. "Anyway, he left so he doesn't deserve a damn thing."

I checked my hair in the front-hall mirror, fiddled with the straps on my black satin dress, offered another "uh huh."

It was almost midnight before I hung up and rejoined Roger. He didn't look like he felt festive. "You never actually say anything when you talk to her you know."

I laughed and cozied up to him on the couch. "She doesn't really give me a chance. Anyway, she wouldn't like what I might say."

"So you punish her with silence? Nice." He'd just finished another beer. The champagne was still in the fridge.

"I'm not punishing her, Roger. I listened, I gave her words—"

"Syllables. That's all you ever give her. Jesus. And wasn't she the one who supported you through university?"

I bolted upright, turning to face him but putting a little distance between us. "Who told you that?"

"I guess you've got some big scorecard for her, too, so you know exactly how many syllables you owe her. You wouldn't want to be too generous with your so-called best friend on New Year's Eve at the start of a new millennium—"

"Stop saying that, Roger." He knew how much I hated it. "It's not the new millennium. There was no year zero!" I'd explained it to him a thousand times, that this was just the last year of the old millennium. But he kept saying it anyway like he'd rather be in the camp of the mathematically illiterate.

We retreated into silence, arms crossed. Then it struck me. "Shit. Roger, what time is it?"

He checked his new watch. "Two minutes after twelve."

124.

LARS WAS LEAVING Debt Services. He'd landed a managerial job at an insurance firm. Chuck booked a tony downtown steakhouse and issued an invitation to the whole staff that sounded more like a command. At the restaurant, he ordered wine— three bottles for seven of us—and a selection of appetizers, and then he made us all toast the incredible future stretching out in front of Lars.

"Double the pay," Lars told us again from his perch at one end of the table. Chuck refilled our glasses. "Seriously—double. Plus a secretary. And the best part? Absolutely no dealings with the public."

"We sure can't compete with that!" There was an undercurrent in Chuck's voice that sounded like "Tell us that tale again!" but the entrées had finally arrived.

Corinne asked me for the time, and then she asked the

waiter to package her untouched lunch to go. When we'd left the office, Corinne and I both hitching a ride with Chuck, she'd taped a hand-printed sign on the door: *Back at 1:30*. Everyone else could be late, but she had to reopen the doors.

"There must be a million buses that come by here," Chuck told Corinne when she asked him for cab fare. Maybe it was the disbelief on her face and the brutal cold outside, or maybe Chuck just didn't want a scene in the middle of his special lunch, but he capitulated. "Just make sure you get a receipt from the driver."

The rest of us lingered over our lunches and that last glass of wine. By the time we got back to the office, my two o'clock had been waiting for ten minutes. Corinne thrust the file at me like a reprimand and I felt my flushed face grow even warmer. I prepared an apology before I stepped around the divider into the waiting room, but only got as far as "I'm so sorry—"

Ugly. There was no other word for her. Addie Sullivan had a frizz of mouse-coloured hair and a beak for a nose. Perched on that beak were round, thick eyeglasses in a rose-pink frame that was too big for her face, though not big enough to conceal the full mass of her eyebrows. Early fifties, I guessed, though it was hard to tell. When she stood up, I noticed she wore a man's blue flannel shirt that billowed out to conceal any shape she might have had.

We introduced ourselves. Her handshake was limp. I formed the impression that she was made of uncooked dough.

I tucked my purse up under my arm and led Addie to my office, concentrating on keeping my heavy limbs in line. I hoped she couldn't smell the wine underneath the peppermint I'd sucked in the car.

While she dug a small spiral notebook and pen from her plastic bag, I glanced at the client sheet in her file. There was nothing on it but her name, her address and *Owes social assistance $320*. The file wasn't tagged yellow, our code for court-ordered, but that note suggested this wasn't a voluntary visit. I braced myself. Involuntary clients tended toward sullen, toward always blaming someone or something else for their problems.

I leaned forward like I always did, then remembered the wine and leaned back. "What brings you in?" Too abrupt for an opening gambit. I needed to find my balance.

"My social worker thought you might be able to help." She had two black, raised moles on her left cheek. Both sprouted hairs. The sunlight streaming through the window behind me reflected off her thick lenses. I readjusted the angle of my head so I could make eye contact, but the light was reflecting off her dark eyes, too, and they were twinkling. Merrily. It was unnerving.

I moved my gaze back to the moles and asked her to tell me the whole story.

The whole story wasn't quite what I meant, but that's what I got—a long-winded tragedy that would have given Job a run for his money. A hardscrabble upbringing on the east coast, a violent marriage, two children taken away and never returned. Addie, abandoned and far from home without a cent to her name. Then high blood pressure, thyroid trouble, cavities. Addie's features dissolved and reassembled constantly as she spoke. And through it all, through the whole damn monologue, her eyes twinkled. Twinkled and sparkled and beamed until finally we arrived at recent history, at the part where Addie was beaten by a gang of young men outside her apartment building.

"For weeks I stayed inside." She looked down at her hands and though I couldn't see for sure, I thought the twinkle had vanished. "I've been hit a lot in my life, but not like that— not by strangers. I think it was the randomness that made me so afraid."

At a moment like this, or long before, Lars would have stopped her and said something like, "We're here to talk about your finances, not your miserable life." To make his point crystal clear, he'd place a hand on the adding machine he kept on his desk and say, "If I can't punch it in there, you shouldn't bother telling me about it."

Lars was devoted to the quantifiable. I guess that's why he was moving on, moving up, making it in the world. Before lunch, he'd sauntered in and given me his adding machine. "You need something weightier than your little calculator. People respect what you say when you put a printed column of numbers right into their hands." I'd put the machine in a drawer and said good riddance in my head, but listening to Addie's chronicle, I wished I'd kept it handy.

Addie was saying she'd run out of her thyroid medication. She'd also run out of food. Still, she couldn't bring herself to step outside.

"I just stayed in bed, re-reading my old favourites." A lattice of laugh lines blossomed on her face when she smiled. "*The Mill on the Floss*—have you read it?"

I shook my head. Jesus, now we were talking about books.

"Oh, you should. It seems like it's all about family dynamics and thwarted dreams, but it's really about whether people have individual choice or if everything's predetermined. George Eliot wrote it—she was a woman, you know, back when a woman had to use a man's name to get taken seriously." Addie's twinkle was back, full force, and I knew the conversation was careering all over but I couldn't figure out how to steer. My usual reflexes were out cold.

"I can lend it to you if you like. But I'll warn you, it takes a lot of patience. It does go on and on. It was written when books came out in installments. I guess they were the soap operas of the last century." She grinned wide, revealing a mouth full of crowded teeth. "I mean the century before the last century."

I wasn't so much nodding as bobbing, only half listening, but I heard that loud and clear. It might not be a new millennium, but it sure as hell was a new century, a time to make some changes. Maybe Roger was right. Maybe I was too busy counting things up and keeping score. Maybe I could be less uptight, more generous.

The word *miracle* snapped me back to Addie. Her story had veered somewhere else. "She just happened to notice I hadn't been cashing my cheques, so this angel from heaven showed up to save me."

I blinked rapidly. "Who?"

"My social worker. She found me half-starved and out of meds and right away she took me to the bank and the pharmacy and the grocery store. She even helped me find a new place to live." Addie's eyebrows waggled up and down, wiry hairs pointing in every direction. I picked up my pen and wrote the date and the time on her client sheet. I was going to write something else but I was distracted by the sight of my purse, sitting where it was never supposed to be.

Addie was saying, "I love my new apartment, and I have friends in the building and I feel safe. I'm lucky like that— someone always helps me. I'm the luckiest person in the world."

I resisted the urge to write *luckiest person* and tried to concentrate on gathering a question into my mouth. "So you owe money to pay back your social worker for her help?"

Addie recoiled, hand to her chin like I'd socked her in the jaw. "No! I mean I tried to pay her back for her gas, but she wouldn't take it—said she couldn't take any money from me."

"Okay, let's focus, Addie. I need you to tell me why you owe money to social services."

"They didn't tell you?"

I lifted the single piece of paper in her file in case I'd missed something. "Who didn't tell me?"

"The welfare police. I thought it would be on your computers."

I suppressed a smile. "Coordination between government departments isn't always—we don't share that kind of infor-mation."

I neglected to ask a follow-up question. Addie started the next chapter.

"I decided to sell some of my books—I had too many of them anyway. That was obvious when I started moving. So I sold them, twenty-five cents each, fifty for hardcover. I just wanted a couple of extra dollars so I could feed the cat I'd adopted. Sweetest little thing. I never expected it to turn into a business."

"A business?"

"People saw me selling my books and they started bringing me theirs to get rid of them. And we'd get talking and then they'd buy something to take away." She was starting to fidget like a kid in the principal's office. I thought we must be getting close to something meaningful. "After a while, I had so many books I had to move them around in a shopping cart." Her eyes widened. "Oh, I didn't steal it. Honestly. I just found it—it was already stolen!"

"It's okay, I don't work with the cart police."

She half rose and resettled herself more comfortably in her chair. "Anyway, I started taking my cart to the city park and setting up near the fountain." I could picture it, Addie sitting on a red blanket with books fanned out all around her, the fountain spraying up behind while people kneeled to get a closer look. The image was so clear I realized I'd seen her there.

She was leaning forward now. "I used to try to read them all, when there weren't so many, so I could recommend things. People like that, you know, and you don't get that at a bookstore anymore—or even at the library most of the time."

"Addie, we need to focus on the money. How much are you earning and what do you owe?"

I noticed a hole in the thigh of her sweatpants. It was just a cigarette-sized hole now, but I could see the fabric at the edges was starting to unravel. I knew the slightest pressure would cause that little breach to widen.

"Actually, I make good money." Addie laughed, a deep throaty chuckle like she couldn't quite believe it herself. "Six or seven dollars most days!"

I wrote $6-7/day on her client sheet, and put my pen down before I could write anything sarcastic. "And you're out there every day?"

"Except when it rains, and Sundays. I have to close up for winter, of course, but I'd saved up enough to feed the cat all year. Or I thought I had anyway, before they caught me."

Before they caught me. Of course—none of this was legal. No business license, no permission to be selling anything. "What happened?"

"Someone must have told the welfare police I was making extra money." She took off her glasses to clean a lens on her shirt tail, and her right eye wandered off toward the wall. She slipped the frames back on and looked straight at me again. "I never meant it as a fraud, I swear."

There'd been a lot of talk about stopping welfare fraud—about new resources, investigations, enforcement. All along, I'd imagined men with gold jewelry and greasy hair cranking out fake ID in their basements, rows of post-office boxes filling with cheques for phony recipients. I had never pictured this woman with her sweatpants and twinkly eyes and her too-many teeth selling a couple of bucks' worth of books in the park.

"A man asked me some questions one day—questions like you're asking. I remember him because he didn't seem interested in the books, but I answered anyway. I was hoping he'd buy something." She took off her glasses and cleaned the other lens. "Then I got a letter saying my undeclared income constituted fraud—that's a quote—and I had to pay it back. The letter said they'd get it back by reducing my cheques."

"So that's the three hundred and twenty dollars?"

She nodded. "My social worker talked them into spreading it out over four months, so I wouldn't starve. I need you to help me make a budget." Finally.

She handed me her notebook, opened to a detailed list of every expense, down to the penny. It was hard to imagine anyone more meticulous. I went through the numbers, took out my calculator, and went through them again. An increase in income would trigger a drop in her welfare cheque, so cutting expenses was the only option. But there was no obvious way to whittle it. Even her few luxuries—cat food being the biggest—didn't come close to covering what was being deducted. The more I crunched, the more impossible the numbers seemed. When I surrendered and looked up, the light went out of her eyes.

"I have to give up my cat, don't I?"

I almost said, "And you have to move," but Corinne tapped at the door and peered in through the narrow strip of glass along the side. I gave her my five-more-minutes hand.

"Do you plan to keep selling books, Addie?"

She considered me from the bottom of her thick lenses. "I'd like to, but you're all watching me now. Maybe I should just give the books away—I can do that without getting in trouble, right?" She crossed her arms, pulling the shirt tight enough to define a pair of mammoth breasts. All the ugly had come back to her face.

I was writing the cheque before I even considered doing it. Three hundred dollars—just enough to untangle her immediate problem.

"You can just do that?" she asked.

I bounced the pen on the desk and tried to look mischievous. "You can't ever tell anyone I gave this to you. If they ask where the money came from, tell them it's what you saved from the book sales."

Addie looked uncertain, and then she looked afraid.

"Listen, Addie, they'll have to believe it. They claim you get enough to live on, right? So they have to at least pretend to think you had all this money left over, that you were hiding it away." I signed the cheque *MC Elgin*, more of a scrawl than usual, and handed it to her.

I told her from now on, she should declare some portion of

her book sales every week. She let that soak in, then grinned. "But not all of it, right?"

"Well I can't tell you to do that." I could feel myself grinning back at her like a crazy person.

She looked at the cheque, looked I guess at my signature, not the grown-up name printed in the top corner. "Thanks, MC, you saved my life."

After she'd gone, the adrenaline leaked out of me, replaced by a heaviness that started in my legs and dragged itself up into my chest. I knew better, knew that giving money to a client was unethical in a hundred different ways. I'd be in serious trouble if Addie told a soul. Worse, I'd just made things tougher for her. She'd arrived in a precarious position and I'd handed her a permission slip to dance a little closer to the edge. Maybe next, they'd charge her for operating without a business license, take all the money and all the books. Maybe they'd throw her in jail.

I thought about going after her, and then about marching into Chuck's office and confessing. I considered writing a letter of resignation and slipping out the back door. But I did none of those things. Torpor pinned me to my chair. Finally I wrote *Helped client work out payment plan* on her file, slid it to the middle of my stack and buzzed Corinne so she'd know I was ready for the next one.

125.

A THUDDING CRAWLED into my head and struck up a marching band beneath my skull. It was all that wine at lunch. I needed a painkiller and a dark, quiet place to lie down. But first, I had to tell Roger what I'd done. To confess. Trudging home, that's what I told myself it would be—confession, contrition—but as soon as I stepped through the door and called out his name, I saw the truth. I wanted to brag. I wanted Roger to know I'd broken the rules and written a cheque to a total stranger. It was just the sort of free-spending impulse he'd love.

He came down the stairs in a rush like a dog whose master was finally home—a well-dressed dog wearing a blue suit, his only suit, and a face that said having me home was the best thing ever.

For a second, I forgot my headache.

"You are looking at—" Roger threw his arms open wide. I'd have flung myself right into them if I wasn't just then wrestling off my heavy winter coat. "—the new district corporate sales guy for Future Buy!"

I searched my blistered brain for some previous conversation about this job. "You got a job at an electronics store? When did this happen?"

"I went in for a second interview this morning. They just called." He looked so self-satisfied, standing there in his suit and tie. "And I'm not some snot-nosed clerk on the store floor. I'll be selling directly to businesses."

When I bent over to unlace my boots, my head almost burst. I straightened up fast, boots still laced tight. "You don't know anything about computers, Roger."

"I don't have to—I know how to sell. And it's not just computers, it's all the doodads that go with them, printers and stuff. That's where the real money is anyway."

"Is the money good?" The pounding in my head wanted to tell him no matter what they promised, he'd never see a dime. But I wasn't up to telling him the whole story to back that up.

"It can be as good as I want it to be. It's commission sales—a good percentage. And this whole industry is about to explode." When I didn't say anything, the last wag went out of his tail. "I thought you'd be happier."

I needed to sit down. "I just think commission sales, you know, it's not a reliable income. And believe me, selling computers can be impossible."

"That's it—that's what you have to say to me?" He was out the door before anything that sounded like congratulations could even take shape in my throbbing head.

126.

DAD WAS IN the middle of renovating the basement when he hurt himself. He'd taken down the walls that once contained Gord, ripped out the old bathroom and dragged everything upstairs by himself, even the old shower stall. He was empty-handed, heading back down, when he misjudged a step, grabbed the railing with his right hand and tore something deep inside.

I didn't know anything about it until my mother called and told me to come out. "Your father's really glum. I can't do a thing with him." Not a word about his injury, the sling a complete surprise when I came through the door.

And he was glum—glummer than I'd ever seen him, frustrated because his basement reno was unfinished and everything was a struggle now—brushing his teeth, cutting his meat, buttoning his shirt.

"Age catches up to all of us," he told me. "And I guess it's always a shock when it does."

I figured that he was just bored, nothing to keep him busy and stuck in all winter now that they'd sold their trailer in Texas. He couldn't even drive. He was completely dependent on Mom to get around.

And Mom wasn't helping. She was also bored, I guess, but also rancorous. Over dinner, she railed against the government for letting our dollar sink so low against the American dollar. A national disgrace, she called it. "They don't give a damn about decent people who worked all their lives and want to enjoy some warmth in their golden years."

Mom used to get away with saying things like that, but Dad made no effort to hide his exasperation. "Doris, it's not the government's job to help us spend our money outside the country."

That evening, I think I heard them argue more than I had during my entire childhood.

127.

A MONTH INTO his new job, Roger really was making pretty good money. I had to hand it to him, he knew how to sell, and he'd figured out the whole computer thing pretty fast. He even brought one home, though I couldn't see any reason why we needed a computer.

"Everyone needs one," he told me. "You won't believe what these things make possible."

"Roger, I work on a computer all day at the office. I have for years. I know what they do."

"Work's one thing, Meriel. I bet you don't know how to have any fun with it." He had the whole system set up and connected in an hour and after that, I watched TV alone every night while he played games on the computer.

When Roger nailed down a major contract—one that came with a huge commission—he told me it was the job he was born to do. There was a kick in his step I hadn't even realized I'd missed. I offered to take him out for dinner, my treat, and let him pick the restaurant. I was hoping a celebration, finally, would unsay what I'd said when he'd landed the job. I wanted to atone for my bad first reaction.

Roger picked Tony Roma's. We had drinks and wine with dinner and I asked all kinds of questions about his job and I didn't say anything wrong. It was perfect, and our fingers were sticky with rib sauce and we'd both dropped our shoulders.

After our plates were clean and the wine bottle empty, Roger mentioned a couple who'd invited us to their Jamaican beach wedding. When the invitation had come, I'd told him I thought it was unfair, expecting guests to spring for plane tickets. But now that Roger had some money, he wanted to go. He said he could probably get a few days off and he was looking at me with his head cocked and his eyes big and hopeful.

I wanted to say yes to the whole crazy idea. Instead, what came out of my mouth was, "If we go, we should get married too, to justify the cost."

Roger didn't say anything. He just blinked and then turned all his attention to the waitress, looking at her with such intensity that she stopped on the spot, a tray full of drinks held high, and asked if he needed something.

Coffee. He needed coffee. She was gone before I could ask for another glass of wine.

128.

I WAS UNDER orders to order blinds. There were no privacy issues up on the third floor, but Debt Services had too much money in its budget and just a week to spend it before the fiscal year ended. "Spend it or lose it, and maybe they'll think we don't need so much next year," Chuck had warned when he'd tossed around the office furniture catalogues on Tuesday.

Deficit was now a dim memory; leniency had replaced stringency. There was a new microwave and a mini-fridge in the staffroom; all our posters and pamphlets had been redesigned.

When Dad called, I didn't tell him I was standing on a chair, measuring my office window for unnecessary blinds. I just told him I wasn't too busy for the rest of the afternoon and sure, I could come get him.

He was waiting for me outside the physiotherapy clinic, his jacket undone and draped over his sling. Mom had dropped him off at noon for his appointment and promised to come back in an hour. It was three thirty when he climbed into my car and there was still no sign of her. She wasn't answering the car phone, something she'd had to have, and she wasn't at home.

I asked Dad if he'd called the police. He shook his head. "I didn't mean to alarm you, sweetheart—she's fine. She does this sometimes, forgets to show up when she said she would."

"But where does she go?"

"She can't say, exactly. She says she just likes to wander and she doesn't need me keeping tabs on her. So I don't." His voice said to leave it alone.

Oh my God, my mother was not dead in a ditch. My mother was having an affair. But who the hell would have an affair with Mom? I flicked the thought away and asked Dad if he expected his shoulder would heal before golf season.

"Meriel-Claire, I don't care if I ever play another game of golf for as long as I live."

"I thought you loved it?"

"In the beginning I liked the challenge. But more and more it just feels..." he held out his left hand as if it contained a selection of words he might choose. "Frivolous, I guess."

This surprised me less than his passion for the game had in the first place. Mounting the overpass, I realized I hadn't been alone with Dad for more than just a few minutes in years.

"I think I've wasted enough time." He said it quietly, like he wasn't exactly saying it to me, so I let it hang in the air. Further down the highway, he said, "I've been reading your friend's book—Daneen's book."

"Which one?"

"The first one, *Hidden Bargains*." He was turned away, watching a pickup truck jounce down a gravel side road. Its back end fishtailed as it picked up speed. I was grateful for the distraction, glad Dad wasn't taking in my wide-eyed distress. "I can't do much else but read with this shoulder."

Five minutes later, when the iron grip on my ribcage had relaxed, he said, "I think it's about us, don't you? I mean not precisely, but I think she based that book on our family."

I waited a long time before I said, "I think so, too." I wanted to say more, to tell him he was nothing like the cold, stingy father in Daneen's book, but I decided abruptly, belatedly, to follow the unpaved road into Calder. I took the turn too sharp and flung Dad, injury first, into the car door. "Sorry," I said instead. "Sorry, Dad."

He looked at me then. "It's a rare opportunity, isn't it? I mean to see yourself from the outside, from someone else's perspective. It makes you want to be better." The road was rutted and it took all my concentration to hold the line. "I wish I'd read it a long time ago."

129.

ROGER TOOK A phone call one Saturday morning and then he left for the gym, but he forgot his gym gear. I noticed his duffel bag stuffed full and hunkered down by the back door when I went to move the laundry to the dryer. By the time Roger came back, I was folding the clean towels.

"Hey, you forgot your stuff."

He put his hands in his pants pockets and studied the floor. "Roger?"

He glanced up and back down quickly. "Look, Meriel," he said. "We both know it's not working." There was a long stretch of seconds while I tried to figure out what, exactly, was broken. "I've found an apartment."

I dropped an unfolded facecloth back into the basket. "You don't want to live with me anymore?"

"I don't want to *be* with you anymore, Meriel."

I don't remember what he said after that—what either of us said. I do remember him packing clothes into a suitcase, and I remember noticing that his drawers seemed emptier than usual even before he started, as if they'd had a slow leak. I remember thinking, "He's not going to change his mind."

And then I got worried. Did he want half the house? He'd lived here for more than a year, which made things official. But when I asked about it, he got angry. "For Christ's sake, the house is yours. I know that. I'll take the vehicle and we'll call it square."

Tears welled up in my eyes but I turned fast—I wasn't about to cry in front of him. I got a plastic grocery bag and I went to the bookshelf and grabbed the few things that were his, and then I got another bag and did the same at the CD rack—yanking out every CD he'd brought and also every one we'd bought together. I didn't want him to feel like he'd left without his fair share.

I certainly didn't want him to ever have the right to say I'd made it hard to leave.

When I got back to the bedroom, his suitcase was zipped.

"What about the bed?" I asked. "You'll need a place to sleep." We'd bought a serious sleep set two months earlier. My old mattress hurt his back, though now I wished we hadn't put it out by the curb and let the city take it away. *Waste not* went through my head.

"Keep it. I'll go buy a bed this afternoon."

"And the computer?"

"I can get another one."

"You have to take your chair." I said it so calmly. The trick was to stay rational.

While he wrestled that leather recliner into the back of the SUV, I thought of the bathroom. I thought of deodorant first but there was much more, a surprising amount of toiletries— enough to fill another plastic bag. As he stepped through the door, I handed it to him. "I think this is the last of it, but you might want to look around so you don't have to come back for anything."

He looked hard at me for a minute. "That's all I want—if there's anything else, just throw it away."

I wanted to say something expansive and mean then, something about throwing away five years, but Roger suddenly looked so sad, standing in front of the door. I guess he hadn't rehearsed this part, how he'd make a graceful exit.

"It's fine, Roger. Just go." I wanted to help him get past the awkward part. Besides, I'd fallen into a deep calm, like all along I'd been waiting for this and it was no worse than diving into a cold lake—shocking for the first few seconds but easy to get used to as long as I stayed underwater.

"I'm really sorry, Meriel." He was staring at his hand on the doorknob like he was unsure how it worked. I remembered his beer in the fridge.

"Wait—your beer." I started toward the kitchen.

"Oh Meriel, don't be a bitch."

The door closed firmly behind him. In the window, I watched as Roger swung the bag full of his shit all the way to his shiny red vehicle. He drove away and left me stranded.

130.

FOR A LONG time I stayed underwater where everything was murky and monochrome, and I didn't care. And then I kind of did care, and I started looking around but even the most obvious things—leaves bursting on the dark elms, grass greening and daffodils waving their yellow heads about—even those things seemed colourless. On Gord's birthday I rented a car and picked a wild bouquet. I drove to the graveyard and talked to the headstone like always. I told it why Roger wasn't there with me. The flowers I'd picked looked pale and weedy and ridiculous beneath the immutability of Gord's full name, the years of his life carved forever into black granite.

When I went to my parents' house for dinner, my mother brought up the break-up and I don't know why I was surprised. It was the reason I'd avoided visiting, even after the risk of bursting into tears had passed. "We don't have to talk about this, I'm okay," I insisted.

She kept at it though, kept at it until Dad came to my rescue. "Doris, she doesn't want to talk about this—she said she's okay."

"Of course she's not okay—she's heartbroken, you idiot."

I had to yell, "I'm fine. Really, I'm fine!" to make it stop. I couldn't bear them getting into some stupid fight right in the middle of Gord's birthday party. My mother shook her head in exasperation, but she dropped it.

131.

"I NEVER LIKED him." I didn't think that was true, but I appreciated Daneen saying so. She was driving me to pick up my new car—I'd grown sick of walking to work in the rain—and it was the first time she'd ever driven me anywhere. She'd only gotten her license in the last year so she wouldn't be trapped in Calder, so she wouldn't have to rely on Doris to get around.

Portia was belted in the backseat of their rental car with their luggage strapped in next to her. They were flying home that afternoon, just two weeks after arriving in Calder. Daneen had finished the last edits to *Desperate and Bliss* and wanted to get back to real life before August was over. I turned around to see Portia staring out the window, her eyes already far away. When she noticed me looking, she offered a gratuitous smile, which I understood to be all the ammunition a nine year old carries. There was a complacency about her that I recognized, an acceptance of being powerless. I hoped hers wouldn't last much longer.

"So what did you buy? Something impractical I hope." Daneen's question brought me back to the front seat, to the point of this expensive errand.

"Nope, very practical, but it seems like a good buy."

"Too bad you didn't get it sooner. You could have come out to visit me while I was here."

"Or you could have come to see me." I held my breath as she changed lanes without signalling. "Besides, I came to see you read at the gallery. I came on the bus. That should count for something."

Daneen gave me a quizzical look. I wished she'd keep her eyes on the road. "Don't be testy, Meriel. So what did you think of the reading?"

"I thought it was great. I can't wait to read the whole book. And I am not testy."

But I was testy—upset that she was leaving and I hadn't had the chance to pour my heart out, to collect the consolation I felt I was owed. I'd waited for Daneen to call, to say she was coming over. I was sure that she could deliver some kind of salve. But all I got was this ten minute ferry to get my new car—a car I'd had to take out a loan to buy—and the half-pack of cigarettes she left me with because she didn't smoke anymore, back in her real life.

Testy and then, after Daneen dropped me off, completely drained, devoid of enthusiasm for my new car with its faux suede seats. I just climbed in, perched the plate in the back window, shoved the key in the ignition and headed home.

And that's when I spotted Aubrey strolling down the sidewalk.

I was sure it was him—the sandy hair, the shuffling gait, the hands in his pockets. I did a U-turn and parked along the street. I had to run to catch up to him, slowing as I neared so I wouldn't chase him off. In my head, I rehearsed what I'd say when he recognized me: "I think you might owe me something."

I caught up to him while he waited for a Do Not Walk to change. I marched right up alongside and stared into his face.

It wasn't Aubrey at all.

Of course it wasn't Aubrey—it was just some stranger with his hands in his pockets, and my disappointment was the same lacklustre shade as everything else.

132.

MY STAPLER WAS empty and my bladder was full and I had four minutes between clients to finish writing up a file and get to the bathroom. The strain of not scrawling *IDIOT* in big black letters across the file had me tense. I guess I'd finally lost patience with the lopsided, malevolent unfairness of everything. Every morning the vulture of iniquity flew into my office and hunched over my desk while I went through the meagre motions of shooing it away. It wasn't so bad when the clients sitting opposite me were there because of their own irresponsibility or greed, but just as many of them were blameless, were victims of bad luck or bad people.

Of course in this optimistic, all-things-being-equal new millennium, we weren't supposed to use the V word. I'd learned, in a professional development seminar, that *victim* stripped power, suggested someone had no control over their own fortune—which wasn't supposed to be true, even when it was.

I was whamming on the stapler with my fist, trying to fasten something together, when Corinne knocked on the door jamb to get my attention.

"What?" I folded my hands placidly on my desk and punched with my voice instead.

She held out an envelope in reply. "I found this on the floor inside the doors this morning."

Ms. Elgin was written on the front in elegant cursive. There'd been three others just like it in the past few months. I knew this one would contain a little cash and nothing else, no indication what the money was about. I kept them all, cash intact, in my desk drawer.

I dropped the envelope into my lap and told Corinne to hold my appointment so I could get to the bathroom. I didn't mention I was nipping out for a cigarette—she was all judgment about that since she'd quit. I'd seen the tsk tsk on her face when she'd caught sight of me smoking in the parking lot the week before. I'd been doing it for months and every day I told myself I'd knock it off. When I got close to the end of a pack I said, "That's it," but I always went and bought another. I figured a few cigarettes every day was a pretty small indulgence, my only indulgence, and the only thing that made me feel a little lifted.

Corinne reached for my stapler. "I'll go fill this for you."

"I can get my own damn staples, thanks. Just go."

Corinne didn't flinch and she didn't look hurt, but she didn't leave either. Instead, she set the stapler down gently, exactly where it had been, and leaned into the hands she'd placed on the edge of my desk. "I think you better start getting more exercise or something, Meriel, because you're acting like a total bitch lately."

I was too taken aback to say anything right then, but after my last appointment I told Corinne I was leaving work early to go walking. I wanted her to know that I'd heard her, that I was following her advice.

The wind was sharp and cold, stripping the last of the leaves from the trees, but I didn't care. I left my house and headed south and I just kept moving, cutting diagonally through neighbourhoods and over the tracks, skirting the highway and not thinking about anything until I ended up right in front of Eric's old apartment building. All these years later, everything about that concrete block looked exactly the same except the banner strung across the side of the building: UNITS FOR LEASE.

I crossed the highway, over to where the Pound Sterling had been. It was a Chinese restaurant now, *Dine In or Take Out* sprayed across the window and a greasy tang emanating from a vent. I ventured a little ways down the side street where Eric and I used to walk. All the houses still stood shoulder to shoulder, their siding as beige as ever but the short grass was faded now, prepared for a long, dull winter.

133.

IN EARLY MARCH, I cancelled my annual appointment with Glen at the bank. I didn't have much to invest and I had all the usual excuses—car payments, inflation—but in truth, I'd never forgiven him for that note he'd sent, for revealing me to Roger as untrustworthy. Unlovable. I enjoyed punishing Glen by ignoring his bleats, by letting Gord's money fester in its low-performing, low-interest safe place.

I was feeling particularly bleak the day of the appointment, anyway. The night before, I'd sat down to read *Desperate and*

Bliss, which I'd just bought when Daneen passed through on her whirlwind tour. Her publisher had planned book launches out west, in Toronto, and here in the mucky middle—all three places claiming Daneen as their own.

Right from the novel's first page, I felt it. There was something about the narrator's voice—something so unfamiliar it unsettled me. I told myself it was because she was writing from a foreign perspective. Then I told myself it was just a sign of the way life changes us. Then I put the book down, two dozen pages in, because the strangeness of it made me unsteady, like the world had shifted on its axis and nothing would ever sit straight again.

134.

I STAYED IN the office between work and the monthly Good Cents Association board meeting at seven, so I had plenty of time to prepare. After four meetings, I'd established some pretty high expectations: eight copies of the agenda and minutes from the last meeting collated, stapled and arranged around the table. Coffee on, a selection of cold canned drinks handy. At my first meeting—Chuck's last as chairperson—he'd nominated me for board secretary to unanimous approval. I was flattered then, but later I wondered if it was just the continuity of office space and my willingness to photocopy that had secured my spot on the executive.

Good Cents taught kids employment and money management skills. We printed pamphlets explaining things like interest rates and interview techniques, all in what our mission statement promised was "age-appropriate language." My favourite was a primer that used frogs and toads to illustrate the difference between needs and wants. The frogs, of course, were the sleek and righteous needs, snapping flies from the air only when truly hungry. The warty brown toads were bloated with their unseemly wants, grotesque in their greed for more when they already had too much. In the end, of course, the frogs triumphed, hopping on to another pond when the fly population collapsed, leaving the corpulent toads stuck in the mud to starve, victims of their own gluttony. At the last meeting, we'd decided to reprint the booklet on better quality paper.

I was on my way to the meeting room, my stapled stack of papers in hand, when an envelope slipped through the thin space between the locked entrance doors. I saw it peripherally as it plunged in. It landed face up. *Ms. Elgin* was penned across it.

I rushed the door, turned the bolt and pulled with the same hand. She was just steps away but she turned in surprise and, seeing me, smiled her twinkle-eyed, crowded-tooth grin. It took me a second to remember who she was.

I pointed to the envelope at my feet but she hurried into an apology. "I'm sorry. I know it's taking me a long time to pay it all back. I'll pay interest, I promise."

I was still catching up, could only say, "It's you!" Behind me, the alarm chirped down toward full siren. "Come in here quick, and shut the door." I clutched the Good Cents agendas to my chest like top secret documents and pressed my code into the alarm box. The noise ceased, the blinking red light turned solid green.

"It's Addie—your name, right?" She nodded without taking her eyes off the security alarm. "I had no idea who'd been leaving those envelopes."

"I didn't want to get you in trouble. I saw it was a personal cheque you gave me, so I figured it was a side deal and maybe it wasn't allowed."

"It wasn't. Allowed, I mean." We sized each other up. "I didn't expect you to pay it back—I just gave you the money as—"

Her face darkened. "Charity? You were hoping to buy your way into heaven?"

"No—" I scrambled to recall why I'd given her the money in the first place. Whatever my intent, hazy as it seemed now, I was pretty sure I hadn't called it a loan. "It was a gift." Her steady gaze had me feeling like I was on slippery ground. "Look, it was just an impulse. It was—what's the phrase, a random kindness?"

"A random act of kindness." Each word flat and deliberate.

"Yes, that's it."

She considered me from behind her thick lenses. I looked down at the papers I was cradling, self-conscious.

"I thought it was a loan, that you trusted me to pay you back. That it was microfinance."

I couldn't rearrange my face fast enough to shed my surprise. She began to explain about small loans for small businesses. "It's a global trend—"

I said I knew what microfinancing was, but she was unstoppable. "It gets people on their feet. And then they pay it back. That's why it works." She bent down awkwardly to pick up the envelope that still lay between us.

"Addie, you don't have to worry about it."

She leaned toward me, her eyes bright and fierce, and poked the envelope right into my ribcage. "I want to worry about it. Don't take that away from me."

I shuffled nervously, and then her face changed and all at once she was laughing. "My mother always said some people get their kicks from giving and some from taking—that's what keeps the world in balance. I guess one of us better give in or the whole world's going to falter."

I rolled that through my head. I was thinking how I might use it with my clients.

"So think of it this way," Addie was holding the envelope out to me again, "you're giving me something by letting me pay you back—and you're saving the world."

"Okay." I took the envelope from her. "Okay."

135.

WHEN MY MOTHER summoned me to Calder on a Saturday morning, she said it was an emergency. She must have heard my panic then because she backed off a bit. "It's not that kind of emergency, Meriel-Claire. It's just that your father's lost his mind."

She wouldn't tell me more over the phone so I left in a hurry, no makeup and a travel mug dribbling coffee down the front of my coat. Winter had come early, a week before Halloween, and there was ice on the highway where snow had blown across it and been polished by wheel after turning wheel. On one patch, my back tires slid over the centre line. I managed to steer out of the impending spin. I slowed down then, but after a few minutes the speedometer crept up again.

Mom was sitting at the kitchen table with her arms crossed when I arrived, glaring into a cup of coffee. It was the mug she'd bought for Daneen that first summer she'd lived with us in Calder. The red and yellow flowers were faded from the dishwasher but you could still read the cup's cursive message: *Friends are the family you give yourself.*

"Your father," Mom said even before I had my coat off, "has joined the Jehovah's Witnesses."

I let my coat drop to the floor.

"I guess that sneaky Christian streak in him finally came to the fore. Or else it's dementia."

I'd spoken to him a week before. There'd been no sign of confusion or psychic break. No mention of the Jehovah's, either. "Mom, he's only sixty-three. I don't think he's senile."

"He's sixty-four, and he's out there with them now, knocking on doors like some old fool." She shook a bent, angry finger at the kitchen window.

Out that window, what had once been an open vista of fields beyond our back yard and across the river was blocked now with big houses, their hulking shapes pressed together. Subdivided land was the cash crop of the day, wheat and barley replaced by stucco and high fences. The shift to a bedroom community had been so all-consuming that it was hard to remember how Calder looked back when there was only one grocery store.

"Oh stop looking, you won't see him out there." My mother slammed her coffee cup onto the table. "He's in the city, where at least people won't recognize him."

She'd cut her hair really short, dyed it a bright copper. I wondered who'd convinced her the style would be flattering.

I asked her to start from the beginning. Two weeks earlier, she'd come home to find Dad sitting at the table with two women, one elderly with a red felt fedora and another, much younger woman with dark blue-black skin and an accent my mother called African. The younger woman had also worn a hat, and the fact that both women were wearing hats on a cold day seemed an important detail to Mom, who wore earmuffs in January but never, ever covered her whole head.

"They were sitting on one side of the table, your father on the other. He'd made them tea, for God's sake. He had his Bible laid open on the table so they could compare passages. Even after I came in and started making my lunch, they stayed for almost an hour." Mom held her empty mug out to me. "It's strange, how fast they recruited him. I mean, he went to church every Sunday in Texas but—"

"He did?" I refilled my mother's mug and got out one for myself.

"It was a little United Church they'd set up for the Canadians. I thought he was just being sociable." She scooped a teaspoon of sugar into her mug and stirred with the sugar spoon. "When I asked him why he bothered, he said, 'It's all I can think to do.'"

"Are you sure that's where he is now, knocking on doors?"

"They've been back three days in a row, leaving copies of *The Watchtower* and that other one." Mom pointed to a small pamphlet called *Awake!* on the counter. I started to reach for it but she cried, "Don't touch it! They might put something on it, some chemical that brainwashes people!"

I actually froze for a split second before thinking that

through. "They're not using chemicals, Mom." I picked it up and flipped to a page about providing homes for victims of flooding down south. Dad or someone had underlined a passage at the bottom: *What the Bible Says About Helping Others.*

"Did Dad say why he was suddenly into this?"

"Just vague things—that it's all so interesting. He tried to tell me there's a lot of truth in what the Bible says is happening in our world." She ran a hand through her spiky flames of hair. "A few days ago, he actually tried to read me one of those doom and gloom prophecies."

I imagined Dad doing that, imagined his isn't-this-worth-thinking-about expression running right into the slammed door of Doris's animosity. Then I thought of telling her what Dad had said in the car the previous spring about not wasting more time, but the Jehovah's Witnesses seemed a million miles from where we'd been that day. I went back to the pamphlet, looking for clues. It turned out to be what I expected but better written, the tone so warm I wanted to keep reading.

When I looked up, Mom was glaring, her mouth turned down more than usual. "I told him to keep his new pals and his Judgment Day out of my house—so I guess that's what he's doing now."

She went to get dressed, but a minute later she charged back into the kitchen still in her robe, an *aha* expression on her face. "Maybe this is all some weird reaction to terrorism."

I gaped at her.

"September eleventh, Meriel-Claire. That's when he started acting funny, when we were watching it happen. Maybe this is some kind of post-traumatic thing."

She left me to think about that. I couldn't imagine my father traumatized by something so far away, though I knew lots of people were. Chuck, for instance. The morning the twin towers came down, he'd stood open-mouthed in the staffroom, pointing at the television and shouting, "I've been there. Right there—right in front of those buildings. Just a few years ago. I was right there!" Shaking, looking to the assembled staff for support like this was his own personal tragedy. "And I remember there was this crazy girl sitting on the sidewalk out front, wearing a sign that said *Kick Me, Only a Dollar*."

He turned back to the television then. "Jesus Christ, look at that!"

I watched for a while, shocked like everyone I guess, and then I went back to work. I didn't linger in front of the TV, not then and not after. I didn't watch the fiery footage over and over, and I avoided listening to the recordings of desperate last phone calls that played on the radio. But Chuck grew ragged from nights pinned to CNN, and Corinne was weak from soaking tissues. Maybe I really had become heartless, but I couldn't see how it helped, getting worked up into such a frenzy. The only image that lingered for me was that girl, the one Chuck had seen years earlier. I wanted to know what her sign was all about and whether she'd still been there, soliciting bruises and dollars while everything fell down around her.

I couldn't see Dad jumping on the bandwagon of tumultuous emotion. Mom, however, was clinging to the notion. She came back into the kitchen buttoning one of the denim-look blouses she'd bought in Texas.

"When they showed that man falling—the man who jumped, you know—" I nodded. I'd never seen it, but I'd heard. "We were crying. Even your father was crying. And after a minute he wiped his face and said, 'Well there it is. A metaphor for all our lives.' Then he got up and walked to the bathroom like nothing at all. I should have taken him to the doctor right then."

Mom reached for her coat and when I asked where she was going, she just said, "I'm not sitting here all day by myself. You can deal with him when he comes home." Then as she pulled on her gloves, she asked if I had any cash with me.

I'd heard there was a moment when the balance shifts between parent and child, when the child becomes the adult in charge. I just hadn't expected it to happen so abruptly or to be so disconcerting. It was like trying to go up the down escalator. I was dizzy from the way the world was moving under me.

Mom held out one black-leathered hand. I reached for my purse.

136.

MY MOTHER BELIEVED religion, all religion, was a sham. And because her beliefs were stronger—or at least louder—than Dad's, faith was never discussed in our house. We never went to church unless there was a wedding, a funeral or a bake sale.

When I was nine, I read Hans Christian Andersen's story *The Little Mermaid*—one of my mother's choices from the library. Nothing in my life, nothing in my understanding of love and sacrifice and the proper direction for stories, prepared me for the cruelty of that book's ending. The little mermaid gave up her voice and her home, accepted the excruciating pain of walking on hard ground in exchange for true love—and then she died anyway, alone and unloved. Once I'd finished crying, I shoved that book in the returns slot at the Calder Public Library so hard it clanged against the far side of the chute. But the ending, the way the mermaid's spirit had turned into sea foam, sentient and freed, stuck with me. Whenever I saw foamy flecks on the edge of the river, I felt like they were looking back at me.

That was the closest I'd ever come to a conscious spiritual belief, so I was both alarmed and fascinated by the idea of my father's new religious fervour. In the weeks after my mother set off the sirens, I desperately wanted to discuss it with him but I had no idea where to start. My chance finally came when Mom went to visit her sister. She and her sister weren't close at all, so I thought she must be really fed up.

I offered to bring Dad dinner one evening. He wanted pepperoni pizza, which was just about as unexpected as everything else but easy, at least, to get right. I bought it with a twenty dollar bill from the last envelope that Addie had slid between the locked reception doors in the fall, before her selling season had ended. I'd made up my mind to treat her small deposits as mad money, to never spend it on a necessity and never let it near a bank.

Over pizza, I prodded gingerly but my questions of the so-what's-new-with-you sort failed to elicit anything even remotely connected to religion. Dad didn't seem alien or lost or confused—he seemed the same as ever. He wanted, as usual, to hear about my clients, about the weird ones and their whopping debts. When I'd been new at the job and was uncertain about the best course of action, I had occasionally called to ask his advice. I hadn't needed to do that for years, but I always tucked away a few stand-out stories I thought he'd enjoy. He always asked what I'd advised, and he always nodded his approval.

After the pizza was gone, the box flattened and the plates loaded into the dishwasher, Dad went to sit in the living room. He was watching *Wheel of Fortune* from his favourite chair when I plunked down on the couch opposite. I'd picked up an issue of *The Watchtower* in the kitchen and carried it to the living room casually, like a reminder of this thing that hadn't been on my mind at all.

Mom's copy of *Desperate and Bliss* was on the coffee table. There was a bookmark poking out, about three quarters of the way through.

I pointed. "Does Mom like the new book?"

"I don't know if she's read it. She's never said. That's my bookmark. It's quite remarkable, isn't it?"

"I haven't had a chance yet." I set *The Watchtower* down over top of that blurred woman sitting alone on a front stoop, staring out from the cover of Daneen's masterpiece. Dad pretended not to notice.

"I'll be interested to talk about the novel when you've read it. To tell you the truth, Meriel-Claire, it surprised me. I guess you know I've always had misgivings about—" he paused, and I knew he was looking for something inoffensive—"about Daneen's influence in this house." I knew Dad's use of *in this house* included me, though I'd lived away from it for so much longer than I'd lived in it. "But this book has such moral resonance, such empathy. Perhaps influence is a two-way street."

Dad finally let himself see *The Watchtower*. "So what's on your mind?"

"Mom tells me you've been hanging out with the Jehovah's Witnesses."

"Ah, that's what this visit is about."

"Of course not, Dad. I wanted to see you." I could see he wasn't buying it. "But I am curious."

Dad muted the television just as a contestant solved "Run for your life!" at the top of her lungs. He studied me for a moment to assess, maybe, how much scorn I might be wielding. I turned my palms up to receive whatever he said.

"The Jehovah's Witnesses knocked on the door. We got into an interesting discussion, which opened some questions I wanted to pursue. I don't know what your mother told you, but I haven't joined a cult or been brainwashed."

I concentrated on radiating "Yes, I believe you" without interrupting him. He was defensive enough.

"I've just been trying to figure something out."

The next pause extended until it was unbearable. Finally I asked, softly, "What?"

He kept his focus on the silent TV, but he was lowering his guard in small degrees. "It's a very interesting religion, you know. Rigorous in its belief system, nothing loosy-goosy about it."

I imagined loosy-goosy was my mother's damning indictment.

"And I appreciate that foundation. I like looking at all the connections." This all seemed like scaffolding for whatever he was going to tell me next. He picked up *The Watchtower* and started paging through it. "But whether or not I embrace all the tenets—well, I'm not in the truth, as they say. I wanted to know if there was comfort in such certainty, but it doesn't really suit me."

I couldn't tell whether my relief was for him, or me, or just because now my mother might calm down.

Dad stood up, then sat back down. "When your brother died, after the shock and the pain eased a little, I started wondering what God wants from me." Dad's voice turned gruff and he cleared his throat.

"Have you figured it out?" I managed barely a whisper. I didn't have any connection to that God. I just had my half-formed notion of Gord as a fleck of foam.

"I don't know. I thought maybe it was to serve, to minister." He half laughed. "These past few weekends, out there in the cold watching people shake their heads and slam their doors and go back to doing whatever it was they wanted to be doing, I realized maybe I'd been asking the wrong question. Maybe the question is 'What do I want to do?'"

"And?"

"I haven't known my whole life. I've just always done what I thought I should." Another very long pause. "But there's nothing I've done in a long time, Meriel-Claire, that I can say I'm proud of." He rolled his eyes, made a faux-sheepish smirk. "So there you go. Your dad's having a late-life crisis."

I stood then. "I think I'll have a drink. Would you like something?" Dad shook his head. When I returned, he was flicking through the channels with the volume still off.

"Mom's really upset about this, you know. She wants you to see a doctor."

"Well we always know what your mother wants. That's never a mystery, is it?"

137.

WHEN DANEEN WON the Turncott Prize, she called me at four in the morning. "Hey, guess what—I won." The connection so crisp it was like she was in the next room. "I really won!"

I was still surfacing, so it took a few beats to understand what we were talking about. I did try to rise to the moment, to say the right things. Some part of me was happy that she'd wanted to tell me, even then, even at that hour. She hadn't responded to my emails since the shortlist had come out, but I'd assumed she wasn't responding to anyone, that she was afraid just talking about it would make it come untrue.

My groggy congratulations sounded halfhearted, even to my own ear. After a brief silence, Daneen switched gears in that way she always could. "So what's new with you?"

What could be new? It was the middle of the night, colder than it should be at the end of March. I swung my legs over the side of the bed and stood up, hoping that would jog me into coming up with just one interesting thing to say but Daneen was already promising to call when she got home, when things died down.

I mustered another congratulations, stronger this time, but she'd already hung up.

I couldn't get back to sleep. The room was cold and a patch of eczema behind my knee had started to itch, so I got up. Then I got anxious. Maybe I should phone my mother and let her know. But it was Daneen's news to tell, I told myself, and I got dressed.

In my office, dawn just starting to colour the sky, I looked for news on the Internet. "The Turncott Award is one of the most lucrative writing prizes in the English language," I read, but then I couldn't find the dollar figure, as if there was some squeamishness about cheapening the honour.

Later in the day, when I went out to buy a pack of cigarettes at 7-Eleven, Daneen's face grinned up at me from the newspaper rack—"Local writer wins international prize"—and I realized, acutely, that I didn't care about the dollar figure anyway, that it wasn't the money I envied. It was how self-assured she looked on the world stage, how valuable she'd become.

Exhaustion fell over me like a lead apron. During my last appointment I could barely hold a pen. There was nothing worth writing down anyway.

"You have to live small," I heard myself say. "Accept what you've got. Stop trying so hard."

138.

DAD AND I met every Sunday, at whatever restaurant was closest to the church he'd just attended. He'd stopped going around with the Jehovah's Witnesses as fast as he'd started and was knocking on different doors now. He'd spent several Sundays sitting in a back pew at Catholic ceremonies, first Roman tradition then Eastern orthodox. He wasn't looking to convert, he told me—he just wanted to start at the beginning. I asked why he hadn't started with Judaism then. I was kidding, but for an entire month, lunch shifted to Saturday after synagogue.

As far as I know, I was the only one Dad talked to about his search. I understood he wasn't browsing and he wasn't bargain hunting—he was shopping for meaning like other people shop for a major purchase. He was balancing the options, looking for quality and durability.

Dad carried a small black notebook in his breast pocket with an elastic strap, and in it he wrote down lines of scripture and hymns and things he'd heard people say. Sometimes while we waited for our food, he'd take that notebook out and read me the latest tidbits.

"Two things today." He'd just come from a Methodist service. "The lady sitting next to me said, 'Lord, let him be mercifully quick today, this hard pew is murder on my hemorrhoids.'"

I nearly choked on my coffee. "She said that to you?"

"I think she was talking to Jesus. I just happened to be within earshot." He flipped the page. "The sermon today was about the ministry of the open hand. 'God loves a cheerful giver.'" Dad closed his notebook and smiled. "My father always said that. Of course he usually said it about a customer who'd just paid too much."

The waitress set a filet mignon and fries down in front of Dad. His mountain of food looked so much more substantial, so much more fulfilling than my grilled-chicken Caesar with its bacon bits and big, oily croutons. It had become a joke between us, how much we both packed away at our lunches, how ravenous we were. My clothes were getting too snug and the shape I'd worked so hard to maintain for years was softening, was getting buried under buttered bread and creamy dressings. But for the first time in my life, I didn't care. These lunches were the best part of my week, the only time when I wasn't lonely.

I picked up a fork and ploughed in, asking just ahead of the first mouthful, "Was Granddad a religious man?"

Dad squeezed a pool of ketchup onto his plate while he thought about my question. "He was a church-goer, never missed a Sunday—but I think that was a community expectation. He quoted scripture when it suited him, but really, he was too practical, too much a businessman for spiritual matters." Dad daubed a fry in his ketchup and looked at it thoughtfully. Finally, he chuckled. "He sure wasn't pleased when I told him I wanted to study theology."

I froze, crouton poised. "Theology?"

"That was my plan. But then Stewart left Calder, and one of us had to take over the dealership—my father had already changed the sign to Elgin & Son." Dad cut the last of his filet mignon into three chunks and indicated with his fork that I should take one. I reached over, speared one, and asked why Stewart had left.

"Stewart was always all about Stewart. A lousy salesman—too interested in what he could get from a customer to care what the customer needed. One day he just said it wasn't for him, and he took off." Dad was pushing the last two chunks around on his plate. "Then I was it, the only son."

He filled his mouth and chewed slowly. I laid my fork in my empty salad bowl and tried to digest it all. "Did you resent it? Especially since Stewart got half the business anyway?"

Dad focused on his fries for a while. Finally, "I suppose, at first. But then I realized resentment is like a slow poison. It just eats you up. Besides, I met your mother, and settling down with her seemed like the best kind of spiritual life." He noted my disbelief and smiled. "She was a beautiful woman, your mother. Very confident, very sure of her place in the world. And fun—she was all the fun I wasn't having."

Mom never joined us for lunch. I thought it was because she couldn't bear to hear about Dad's church experiences, but he said she went out every Sunday—with friends or else shopping, he wasn't sure, but she was gone all day. And it wasn't just Sundays—she disappeared sometimes during the week, as she'd been doing for a few years now. I'd suggested she might be having an affair. I didn't want to hurt Dad, but I thought he should at least consider the possibility.

Dad had thrown his head back and laughed. "Of all the things I worry about in this lifetime, that's not one of them, Meriel-Claire."

I don't know what made him so certain, but I was prepared to agree—Mom with a lover was preposterous. Still, her mysterious disappearances bothered me, though at least she wasn't home sulking all summer because Daneen wasn't coming at all. "Too many other places to be," Daneen had said, forcing my mother to abandon plans for a big celebration in the great author's honour. Instead, Mom had spent the spring getting Daneen's Calder house ready to rent to some playwright from Toronto.

The waitress cleared away our dishes and Dad told me more about the morning service. "It was a good sermon—'Give generously and without a grudging heart.'" He reached across the table to place his hand over mine, such an uncharacteristic gesture. "You are certainly generous to listen to all this, Meriel-Claire. Let me get lunch today."

I could have said a million things. I could have told him how much the time we spent together meant to me. Instead, I said, "Well I find it very interesting. And we should split the bill." The words came out in my work voice, cordial and sincere. I tried to think of something else to say, some way to reverse that, but Dad had already picked up the tab and was moving away.

139.

MOM GAVE THE police officer my name and work number. She had no other choice. Dad was both out of the question and out of the country, and Doris wanted to keep the whole sticky mess from leaking outside the careful confines of family. When I got to the hospital that afternoon, they were taking her to put a cast on her hand and arm. They'd already given her something for the pain, I guess, because she was happy to see me in a lopsided way, half grin and half contrite. I stayed back to talk with the officer.

There wouldn't be any charges this time, he told me. Mom hadn't actually done any damage, since slot machines were tougher than the bones of the human hand. But she had been banned from the casino, her player's card confiscated.

Banned. From the casino. The words added up slowly.

Mom's forearm was pinned tight to her chest by a sling that kept the injury stable. It looked like a forced pledge, hand placed over her heart and bound there. She wouldn't abide the shoulder strap of her seatbelt so I tucked it in behind her. She told me—again—that I'd have to rescue her car from the casino parking lot, then she closed her eyes and I couldn't tell if she'd dozed off or just wanted me to believe she had. We were almost in Calder before she spoke again.

"Don't you dare tell your father about this." Her voice was sharper, less drug-smudged.

I reminded her that I didn't even know how to get in touch with Dad and she lapsed into silence again.

For weeks, my father had been in Malawi working on a project with the Salvation Army. The Salvation Army—Christianity with its sleeves rolled up, they called it—had turned out to be the right fit for Dad, and it seemed so obvious I sometimes wondered why Dad hadn't just gone straight to it.

But for my mother, the potential for humiliation was every bit as acute as it had been with the Jehovah's. At Christmas dinner, just the three of us, she'd extracted a promise—and not for the first time, I sensed—that Dad wouldn't wear the uniform, that he'd never ring the bell or man the donation kettle in front of the Calder Foodway. Dad had agreed to that, readily and even cheerfully, but two days later he'd accepted the mission overseas without even consulting my mother. It all happened in a blur. One minute he was volunteering at the local thrift store and then word of his managerial and logistical skill got out and right away he was picking up malaria pills.

When I got Mom home, she refused to get into bed so I settled her in the big recliner and brought her a glass of orange juice. "Never mind juice," she growled, "go get my car."

"Let's figure that out tomorrow, Mom. I can't drive two cars at once."

She tried to shift her weight, putting pressure on her cast, and winced. "For heaven's sake, Meriel-Claire, I have a broken hand. Can't you just go do this for me?"

I drove to my house to drop my car, called a cab and then called work to say I'd have to take a few family-leave days. Corinne asked if everything was okay. I knew she was just making small talk while she pulled my attendance record, and soon enough she had it. "You already used a half day, so you only have two and a half left for the year. I hope that's enough."

At the casino, the taxi dropped me between two massive, pale pink pillars that flanked the entrance. I'd never seen the place before—it was well beyond my regular route—and the opulence of its entrance surprised me. Instead of heading straight to the parking lot to find my mother's car, I followed the blood red carpet past the topiary guarding the front doors and kept walking toward the noise.

The building was as big as a shopping mall, with ornate chandeliers and pools of light and dim. I smelled expensive roast beef but when I got closer to the rows of slot machines, I couldn't smell anything. My senses were overwhelmed by the cacophony of ringing and pinging and high-pitched bleating. Above each machine there were lit-up pictures of pyramids, sparkling jewels and gleeful-looking mythical creatures. But no one was looking up at those creatures. The players were all slouched, staring down at the fast-moving numbers, the blinking lights, every mouth set in grim determination, each with a hand poised above a button.

It was five o'clock on a Thursday afternoon. The place was only half full, but that still meant hundreds of people were feeding their money into machines with names like Diamond Mine and Lucky Monkey. Since gambling had been sanctioned as a cash cow in the province, I'd met my share of people who'd lost big. If they were still at it, I didn't counsel them. There were specialists for problem gamblers—hotlines and rehab services paid for directly out of the government's gambling revenue. Instead, I counselled the families left in the lurch, the parents who never saw child support, the suicide widows who couldn't pay the outstanding taxes.

In a distant corner, a siren sounded. I could make out a flashing yellow strobe on the ceiling and I wondered if that meant there was an emergency—if someone else had gone berserk and started punching a machine.

"Big winner over there," a woman said to the man on her left, and then I understood the siren.

At the end of a row, I stopped behind an elderly woman, her white hair twisted into a complicated bun fastened with scores of bobby pins. Her knuckles were the size of nickels on the hand that hovered over the button. No one sat on either side of her and she'd put her grey purse, a stiff rectangle with all its compartments gaping open, on an empty seat. I wondered if that was a breach of casino protocol or just a stupid risk. It would be so easy for me to lift it up and stroll out while all her attention was focused on the screen in front of her. Then I remembered the guards, the cameras that were probably everywhere.

I looked down the aisle at the two rows of players sitting back to back, at the preponderance of grey hair, creased necks and curved spines. Canes leaned against the swivel chairs and I saw what I'd missed all along about the government's foray into gambling: the machines could take from a wealthy generation what no politician would dare to tax.

The woman in front of me reached into her purse and fished out a twenty dollar bill without taking her eyes off her machine. She fed the bill into a slot. The red display of points spasmed and spiralled upwards. Watching, I tried to get the gist of Poseidon's Treasure, to figure out the plus and minus of it but it all moved too fast. Nine spinning squares would stop, pictures would flash and the woman would tap the button with a hard, pink fingernail that made a click audible even over all the noise. Her points declined, then jumped higher then plunged again. In just a few minutes they'd dropped from over twenty thousand to under six.

I'd read some of the science, the way the light and motion was designed to affect the brain's pleasure centre, but I seemed to be wired wrong. All the flickering just made me agitated.

Click. The woman reached again for her purse, her expression never changing.

140.

"DON'T THROW THAT away." My mother was sitting in the chair she'd pulled around to the end of the counter, looking at the olive-green coffee mug in my hand. I'd just plucked it from the back corner of the top cupboard. The mug had two plaster stumps where its handle should have been. The handle was tucked inside, but it hadn't made a sound when I'd tipped the cup—it was stuck fast by that mix of aerated fat and dust that gathers in kitchens, coating anything that doesn't get at least occasional attention.

"It's broken, Mom. Why would you save it?" I stepped down off the chair.

"I like it."

Behind her, tacked to the refrigerator, was the *National Post*'s coverage of Daneen's big Turncott win. A picture from the awards gala—full colour, taking almost the entire front page of the review section. In it, Daneen's wearing a buttercup yellow dress, lots of froth spilling out below the fold. The picture runs from her smiling face all the way to the heels of her high black boots, with the first part of the article printed right across the ruffle of her skirt. I knew that newspaper clipping would eventually get so discoloured that it would have to be thrown out, but I also knew that Mom had another copy carefully folded and slid into a transparent sleeve for safekeeping. She was meticulous about some things.

"That was my favourite cup. It reminds me of better times."

I wished again that I'd started this after she'd gone to bed, or at least when she was distracted by one of her soap operas. "Mom, no one has laid eyes on this cup for years."

"Well I know it's up there, and I want it to stay there."

I acquiesced, setting the mug inside the sink full of soapy water, hoping I'd remember it before I cut myself on the broken edges.

I'd started cleaning kitchen cupboards and drawers out of

boredom, more than anything. Nearly a week in Calder with my mother had used up all my family leave days, eaten into my annual vacation time and drained my patience. But I couldn't leave her alone, not as long as she was on the painkillers and still trying to sneak out to the casino. The first time she'd tried it right in front of me, easing her coat over the cast and putting on her boots with just her left hand. I kept asking where she was headed and she kept saying, "Outside." But when she gathered up her car keys and purse, I reached for my own coat.

"I'm just going shopping. I need to get some things."

She insisted she could go by herself. I imagined her reaching her left hand across her body to put the car into gear. "Mom, you can't drive. I'll take you."

She'd stared at me for a moment, then muttered, "Never mind," dropped her purse, flung her keys to the floor and stomped off to her bedroom still wearing her boots.

The second time, Mom had tried to sneak out after we'd gone to bed. I'd only caught her because I snuck out for a cigarette. She was scraping her frost-coated windshield using her left hand, but she wasn't very good at it. She ignored me for a long time—long enough for my hands to go numb even inside my pockets. Finally, I had to remind her that there was no point, that she was barred from the casino. I took her car keys and her purse, and when she wasn't looking I locked them in the trunk of my car. Then I hid the keys to my car and Dad's car, too.

She'd been frosty since that midnight escapade but she'd come running when she heard me start in on her cupboards. She didn't want to help, she just wanted to make sure I didn't do any damage, throw away anything important. And everything was important. It was as if every single broken dish and years-old jar of rock solid onion flakes held a rare and specific meaning—a memory, or else a fragment of a heart that could be pieced back together someday as long as none of the pieces went missing.

In normal circumstances, I wouldn't have dreamed of mucking about in her cupboards. I wouldn't think she'd want me to. But every day, Mom had made some comment about how she'd been left alone to fend, how no one lifted a finger to help her. When I asked about the gambling, how long she'd been at it, she said, "Your father's run off with God and you're nowhere to be found. What did you expect me to do all day after everyone abandoned me—sit here and wait to die alone?"

It was hard to believe my mother, so much in charge, so self-contained, could feel so adrift. I assumed it was the painkillers talking. It was harder to be sympathetic after she'd been churlish on the phone with Dad. She didn't tell him a thing, not even that I was standing right there, and she didn't ask him anything either—not how he was, if he was healthy and safe, or what it was like in Malawi. Nothing. She was all one-word answers and no warmth, and after she hung up and I asked if she was happy to hear from him, she just shrugged. "He calls every Sunday."

From the cupboard, I pulled a pack of Styrofoam plates. They were misshapen from the crush of things pressing against them.

"Those can go in the garbage. We certainly won't be having any more barbecues." Two years had passed since the last Labour Day party, which had been a lacklustre affair with few people. Some of the regulars were in bad health—cancers, strokes, emphysema—and others had retired and left Calder, gone to the city or much further away. The next year, my parents hadn't bothered to send out invitations but they were ready for some folks to show up. It poured all day, and no one did. It was as if there'd been a general agreement in town that the time for parties was past.

I tossed the Styrofoam plates in the garbage, then followed them with plastic containers, a cracked bowl and a box of toothpicks that had opened and spilled. In the next cupboard,

I found mystery items wrapped in clouded Saran. Gingerly, I unwrapped the first—it was a wedding cake topper, a perfect plastic bride and groom, creamy white with gold painted highlights. Mom reached out for it, and stared happily at it while I uncovered a cake cutter with a plastic pearl handle.

"We were so happy that day." She let a long sigh travel the distance between us, and then handed back the little bride and groom. "I miss him so much."

I saw the tears gathering in her eyes and I was moved to go to her, to lay a hand on her shoulder and my cheek against her thinning crown. She let me, even leaned into me until I said, "He'll be back in a few weeks—"

She shifted away. "That's not what I mean."

I returned to where I'd piled the wrapped treasures, peeled back more layers, discovered a crystal sugar and cream, an heirloom from my father's side. Mom said I could have it if I wanted it, and I did. Next I revealed a ceramic bowl and cup with wistful-looking Beatrix Potter characters frolicking along the edges.

"Gord's first cup and saucer." Mom was smiling again. "It was a gift from my mother. I was saving it for grandchildren."

I pushed the set down the counter toward her. She picked it up. "It's too bad we didn't know about Justin when he was still a baby. I guess that was my only chance."

I have no idea how long the silence extended. It seemed to stretch thinner and thinner until, sure it would snap and knock us both flat, I repeated, "Justin?" to make sure I'd heard right.

"Oh—I forgot. You don't know."

"Know what?" I stepped carefully, the tightrope under me so very thin.

Mom breathed heavily through her nose and I considered getting Peter Rabbit and the rest of the gang wrapped up quickly, before anything else escaped. But I would have had to pry the cup from her hands, from the fingers sticking slyly out of her cast.

"I shouldn't tell you. We decided we wouldn't. But I guess you might as well know." She was turning that two handled cup around and around. "Your brother got a girl pregnant before he died. There was a baby boy."

She paused and let that sink in, watching me closely. If she was looking for signs of shock, she saw them. "A year ago or more, we got a letter from that boy. He's eleven now. His name is Justin. He lives in Calgary, that's all we know. The letter was from a lawyer's office." Joy had transformed her face. "He sent a picture and it was obviously true—Gord's smile, Gord's cowlick. And he needed some money so he could play hockey, just like Gord."

She smiled. "It was like this miracle had come into our lives. We sent the money right away, of course, and we asked to meet him. We were ready to fly out there immediately." Her mouth resumed its usual tight, downward crescent. "Then we got a letter from a lawyer, forbidding us to contact him again."

She lifted the Peter Rabbit plate from her lap and handed it back to me. "The mother's name is Darla—does that mean anything to you?"

I shook my head so slightly it couldn't really be called a lie.

"Your father told me to leave it alone, to just forget it, but I couldn't pretend my grandson didn't exist. That's why I went to Calgary last year, to find him."

"When you went to visit your sister." All of it adding up slowly.

"Yes. The only address we had was the lawyer's, but he wouldn't tell me anything. So I parked outside schools and I watched for a boy who looked like Gord. I thought I saw him once, but there was no way I could be sure."

I pictured her sunk low in a car, peering at every boy on the schoolyard at recess, trying to catch just a glimpse. The thought of it almost unbearable.

"I sent more money, hoping she'd change her mind but they've never even acknowledged it."

I wanted to tell Mom to stop sending money, that Darla was greedy and mean and Gord had already provided. Instead, I pulled out a tall pepper grinder, the crank dotted with rust, the wood tacky against my fingers.

"You can have that." Mom's eyes met mine. "Imagine, Gord never even knew he had a child."

141.

IT TOOK ME well into the evening to get the cupboards cleared out and washed and everything that needed to be under wraps wrapped up again. I tried to stay focused on order, on adding clarity with masking tape and a marker. Mom, at least, had quit watching, which allowed me to nearly fill the garbage bag and the box marked THRIFT STORE.

I wanted to get everything put away, shut up tight in the dark recesses like before, but I knew the cupboards needed to dry, doors gaping open overnight.

The next morning, I called Mom into the kitchen to show her how it looked, where everything was. She came in talking. "If you're angry because I didn't tell you about Justin, blame your father. He was the one who thought you'd been through enough. It was his decision."

"Dad wanted to keep this a secret from me?" It seemed impossible.

"You were such a mess when Gord died, you handled it so badly. And Roger had just left you. Even Daneen agreed it would be wrong to tell you."

The phone started to ring.

"Daneen knows about this?"

My mother looked like this was an inconsequential detail and answered the phone, switching automatically to her polite stranger voice. I went outside. When I came back, she was sorting the mail that had taken over the counter, pushing what looked like junk off to the floor and making a neat stack of the envelopes that looked like business.

"That was the bank. Something's wrong with our chequing account." She passed the stack to me. "Open these so we can figure out what's going on. Goddamn it, your father's left me holding the bag on everything."

Mom obviously hadn't opened an envelope since he'd left. It took us over an hour just to organize all the bills and statements and letters by date. The problem with the chequing account turned out to be a simple one: all the money had been withdrawn. In fact the account was seriously overdrawn, beyond, even, the thousand dollar overdraft. Withdrawal after withdrawal, the rapid decline of a healthy balance. Near the end, a big cheque to Darla had bounced. Automatic bill payments, too, had fizzled on the line and it was unpaid utility bills that had finally spurred the bank to call.

"It looks like someone's completely drained your account."

My mother took the statement, her eyes widening as they moved through it. But she didn't speak, didn't say a word that might derail my thoughts so I arrived faster at a conclusion than I otherwise might have.

Banned. From the casino.

I focused on the mathematics, on staying rational right up until Mom tried blaming Dad again, saying he must have cleaned out the account on his way out of town. She'd evidently forgotten how familiar I was with this territory, how well I understood the rise and fall of numbers. I slapped a statement down in front of her so hard she flinched. Then I let my index finger walk her from Dad's departure date down through the debit column. Forty dollars, forty dollars, sixty dollars— sometimes five or six in an hour. She'd gambled it away to nothing.

That was only a start. Joint chequing, it turned out, had been her last refuge. For a long time, two years at least, she'd been pulling cash off her credit cards and getting the limits jacked up. She'd maxed them all—a combined credit-card debt of well over thirty thousand dollars. I made her get me everything then, every statement from every account and investment. She hesitated and she argued, and I had to put the calculator down between us and speak to her in a tone I recognized as hers, as the low, menacing voice she'd used on Gord and me when we were kids and she meant business.

It was worse than I could have imagined. She'd gambled away everything she could easily get her hands on. After I'd totalled it all up and paper-clipped the separate stacks in order, we sat in silence. I was safe inside my professional skin, able to see just the tidy row of figures I'd compiled, the fullness of the zeroes, the slope and tangle in the sevens and the twos.

Finally, my mother said what everyone says, punctuated the way everyone punctuates it. "What. Am I going. To do?"

I anticipated what came next, the usual head-shaking amazement, the earnest promises to get back on the straight and solvent. But Mom headed in a different direction.

"This will tear your father apart. It will be the end of us, of our marriage."

"Mom, I think we have to remember—"

"Remember what—that your father's joined the Salvation Army? Gambling is a big sin for those people, Meriel-Claire. They'll take him away from me."

Would they? Was that how it worked?

"All our other money is invested and he handles all that. I can't take anything out of those funds to cover it up—"

I couldn't look at her, couldn't let her see how the skin of my certainty was peeling away.

"Meriel-Claire, please, you have to help me fix this. You can't tear us apart like this."

I thought of Dad at the dealership checking my work, the wooden ruler he used to keep the columns straight. "Mom, he's going to find out. It's too big to hide."

She looked at me, round-eyed, clear-focused and desperate, as if the fog of painkillers she'd stopped taking just the day before had finally lifted. "I've never asked you for anything before. But I'm asking you now. I'll do whatever it takes."

"Own up to it" was on the tip of my tongue, but she'd started to cry. I put my arm around her and let her bury her face in my neck, let the sharp words pile up on my tongue like splinters, their taste bitter but reassuring.

142.

MOM SAID NOTHING except to complain of the pain in her wrist for the rest of the day. I braced when she poured herself a drink after dinner, but she left it half-finished and headed to bed early. I drank the rest of it, then made myself another and went back over the numbers, disbelief still obscuring the enormity of what she'd done. Nothing in my professional experience had prepared me for the shock of being inside a calamity like this. I was like the preacher trying to comprehend his teenage daughter's promiscuity.

In the morning, Mom was up early, bright-eyed and pain-free. She made us an omelet to show off her one-handed egg breaking technique, and she made a point of thanking me for cleaning out the cupboards. After breakfast, I tried again to get her thinking about how she was going to tell Dad about the gambling. She became defensive, of course, but I'd anticipated that. I was ready with a speech about doing the right thing and no other option, about addiction and admitting the problem. About my willingness to stand beside her while she confessed.

"If you want to stand beside me, help me fix this so your father doesn't find out." When I refused, she came back with bitter recriminations. I reminded her that it was her responsibility and I looked at her steadily, respectfully, just as I would any client in my office.

She stormed off to her bedroom and slammed the door.

We went around like that again as I heated soup for lunch. She came to the table calm, even borderline cheerful. She swallowed a spoonful of Scotch broth, then laid her spoon down and said, "You haven't changed since the day you were born, Meriel-Claire." I steeled myself for what savagery might come next. "My god you were a beautiful baby. Gorgeous—but impossible."

I'd heard this before, what a terrible trial I'd been as a colicky infant.

"I cried when I found out I was pregnant with you, Gord just learning to crawl and another baby expected before he'd ever have a chance to get steady on his feet." Between sentences, Mom lifted spoonfuls of soup to her mouth. She seemed determined to tell me the whole tale—how my screaming had sent Gord into fits, how she'd hand me over to my father as soon as he came through the door and he'd put my bassinet in the backseat of his car and drive around, sometimes for hours, motion the only thing that kept me quiet. I knew they'd gone through countless gallons of gasoline before they thought to strap my bassinet to the top of a running dryer, but this was the only detail Mom left out in her retelling.

Mom pushed her empty bowl away. "You were so demanding. Your poor brother didn't stand a chance." She stood up from the table. "I didn't either. The only person you were ever agreeable for was your father."

I gathered up the bowls. Mom followed me to the sink, stood behind me with her hands on my shoulders. "Help me, Meriel-Claire. It's the least you can do." I could feel her breath on my neck. "You know if Gord was alive instead, he would help me."

Instead.

"He'd give me every penny he had."

I grabbed the faucet to steady myself. Would he?

Would he?

I looked out the window at all the big houses that hadn't been there when Gord had been, at how changed the view, how different the world. Maybe he'd be different now, too. Maybe Gord would have grown into moments of surprising generosity.

143.

I GOT TO the bank just as it opened, hoping for a small hole in Glen's schedule. At the customer service counter, a woman told me Glen had left—just left, no longer working there, no explanation. My chest tightened with disappointment. I'd been looking forward to watching Glen's face as I gutted that big, fat, low-performing fund he loved so much.

Someone named Dylan had taken over for Glen. A phone call was made. Luckily, very luckily, Dylan was available and another woman led me to his lair. For a long stretch of seconds, Dylan pattered away on his computer while I considered him from just inside the door. He was still young enough to have a pimpled neck, red and angry from his morning shave. When he finally stood and reached to shake my hand, I saw he was gangly, like he hadn't grown into his extremities yet.

He had my portfolio onscreen and worked himself into a lather before I'd even unbuttoned my coat. "I have some very definite ideas about how to make this money work harder for you. Have a seat, let's take a look at how much better off you could be."

I knew all about the power dynamics of this room, about sitting behind the desk versus sitting in the angled chair with all your limbs exposed. I changed my mind about undoing my coat.

"I'm only here to withdraw money. How much is in that account?"

He turned his computer screen so I could see it, though I was still obliged to lean over the desk to make out the figure he pointed to with the end of his pen. $167,675 and change.

My mother had blown every bit of interest Gord's fund had accumulated in over a decade.

Dylan's expression adjusted when I told him how much I needed. "Is there something we can do to keep that money working for you here?" There was a definite squeak at the end of his voice. "We could move it to a higher yield fund. You can take out a loan to cover whatever purchase—"

"No. I need seventy-two thousand dollars. Now."

Dylan looked grave, but he gave up easier than Glen ever would have and pulled out the forms. While he was writing in the little boxes, I decided to take another twenty thousand. I could fill up the savings account I'd emptied to pay the most urgent of Mom's bills, and give myself a little mad money besides—money for going mad, or getting mad maybe, if I discovered Mom had gambled away even more than I knew about.

Dylan wrote down the new number, then started prattling on again about hot equities, about how unnecessarily high my tax burden was. "If you leave this money here, with the market as strong as it is, in six or seven years we could turn this into half a million dollars."

I wondered if they taught all these investment guys to talk in fractions of a more grandiose number. While I signed papers, he pulled up graphs of high-performing funds on his computer, used phrases like "maximize the remainder." His verbs grew more intense until I couldn't take it anymore.

"Look, Dylan, I have to go. I don't care—take another, I don't know, twelve grand and put it somewhere." I'd pulled the number out of air. "You know what, put it in the Narcissus Fund." I wasn't interested anymore in whatever good that fund might be doing. The optimism that had once propelled me had vanished, and the affection I'd felt for strangers had dried up. I just wanted the biggest break I could get on my taxes.

Dylan nodded enthusiastically. "Awesome choice!"

I guess rumours about the fund's imminent collapse hadn't

started to swirl or, if they had, they hadn't reached young Dylan's shiny ears. I'd learn months later from the evening news that Narcissus had gone into receivership, and I'd get all the legal details in the correspondence from the fund's trustee. But I would never hear a word about the whole sticky mess from any of the guys who advised me to invest in that fund and collected their commissions when I did.

I suppose it wasn't a lot by some people's standards, what I lost in that doomed fund, but it was almost half of what I'd invested for my retirement.

None of that mattered yet. I walked out of the bank that morning with a fat cashier's cheque made out to my mother in my purse, and a healthy sum in my own bank account. I'd done the thing I'd said I never would—gouged deep into Gord's money without any higher purpose, but as I walked out into brilliant sunshine, I was light as the air. For once, probably forever now, I knew my mother was going to value me.

144.

BEFORE I AGREED to give Mom the money, I extracted a promise—no more casino, not ever, plus she'd see a counsellor about her gambling addiction.

"I don't have an addiction, Meriel-Claire, that's ridiculous." But when I started to pull the evidence from my purse—the stack of financial statements and overdue bills she'd given me to shred—she gave in.

A week later, I took the afternoon off work to drive her to that counselling session. I had to lie to Corinne, pretend I was sick myself because I'd used every scrap of family leave and all my accumulated vacation. Mom churned all the way to the city, silent and tugging on her seatbelt, but she metamorphosed into someone gracious as soon as she stepped up to that reception desk.

In the tranquility of the waiting room, I paged through thick, glossy decorator magazines and imagined refurnishing my house. There was a tear in the back of the couch that I had to cover with an afghan, and it was long past time to start anew.

Near the end of her hour, Mom emerged with the counsellor, a woman about her age. Mom pointed at me. I would have smiled if her counsellor hadn't looked so stern when she asked to speak to me alone.

In her office, she motioned to a chair but neither of us sat. I girded for a grim prognosis.

"Your mother has been quite forthcoming this afternoon, more than most people, so I'm comfortable saying right now that I don't think this is really a gambling problem."

I laughed. "Did she tell you how much money she'd gone through at the casino?"

She held her palms toward me, flat like a traffic cop. That's against the rules, I thought.

"When people are depressed, they often go to extremes to get attention. Especially if they're feeling abandoned."

"She hasn't been abandoned. My father's on a relief mission helping people who are desperately in need. He calls her every Sunday. He'll be home in a few weeks." His few weeks had been extended a few weeks, but I didn't mention that.

She'd turned her back to gather up her notes while I spoke. That's also against the rules, I wanted to say.

"Your mother says she hasn't been to the casino in weeks. Do you believe that?"

"Yes, but—"

"She says there's no financial distress, no outstanding debt—" She laid down the notebook. I slipped over the edge while she wasn't watching.

"That's because I paid her debts! Did she tell you that? Did she tell you how much money I gave her?"

The palms again, this time with fingers splayed. "This is not about you, or what you did or didn't do. But yes, she told me you gave her some money. She also told me there were conditions."

"Conditions?"

"Strings attached. And I'll ask you not to raise your voice again."

I couldn't anyway, not after that punch in the gut.

"It's fairly clear to me that in exchange for your 'donation'—" she clawed the air with her fingers to suggest quotation marks— "you expected your mother to be subservient. When someone's been going along for years, we come to expect it, don't we?"

My head raged, though I knew better than to show any outward sign of resistance. The counsellor was sneering now, though she wouldn't have believed it if I'd called her on it. "If you want your mother to stop feeling that she has to do destructive things to get your attention, then give her the respect and attention she deserves."

She wanted to say more—I could see she was itching to— but she let it go at that.

In the car, Mom said, "Satisfied?" The pucker lines around her mouth had softened to feathery. Neither of us spoke again until I pulled into the driveway in Calder and she asked if I could gather up the garbage and take it to the curb.

She watched while I tied up the kitchen garbage bag. "I know you don't care for me, Meriel-Claire. If you had children, you'd know how painful that is." I dropped the bag on the floor and stared at her. She just kept talking. "If your brother was still alive—"

Inside me, a rending, like Velcro fasteners that held my internal self to my outer shell were tearing loose. It was so loud I was sure Mom could hear it, could see how unfastened I'd become, but she gave no indication. "Gord would be happy to help me out."

"Well Gord isn't here, is he?" I picked up the garbage and hurried to the front door to get my coat. Words were coming out of me without even asking permission. "And since Gord never learned how to look both ways, I'm not sure how much help he'd actually be."

That shut her up. She stood in the kitchen doorway pretending to look at me but she couldn't quite do it, she could only look past my head at the doorframe. While I pulled on my boots, I focused on the laminate flooring they'd installed two years ago and I longed for the old silver-blue shag carpet with the trails of our footsteps still crushed into it.

145.

I'D SPENT AN hour trying to convince a client that failing to make his child support payments wasn't the best way to prove he was the good guy, so I was beleaguered even before Jeffrey Semple ambled into my office. Right away I saw he was too old and too affluent to be there. His clothes had that effortless way of hanging that suggests extra density has been infused into every fiber. Before he sat, he considered the fabric covering the client chair as if he expected to find evidence of the leaking scourge who'd come before him. The patterned fabric hid its secrets well, I guess, because he finally settled in.

"Mr. Semple, how can I help you?"

"I'm here because I was ordered by a judge to be here, so let's cut the crap."

I opened the folder and skimmed his file. It suggested what his attitude did, that he was some kind of big deal, someone used to running the show.

"You owe a lot of income tax but you refuse to pay it?" My voice was clumsy, my phrasing blunt. Semple's tax arrears were, in fact, more than triple my annual salary—but that wasn't the source of my surprise. I couldn't figure out what the hell this guy was doing here. Men like this didn't get referred to us by judges. Judges were their peers, sometimes even their pals—and if the boys had a falling out, well that's what a cache of lawyers was standing by to sort out.

"So you're here to get help with a payment plan?"

He snorted, actually snorted. "No, I'm certainly not. I'm

not paying another dime so the goddamned government can waste my money."

"You understand you are legally mandated to pay your taxes." Plain fact. I wanted to threaten him with a lengthy jail term, but we both knew wealthy tax evaders weren't put in prisons in this country, they were put on installment payments.

"Listen, honey, I know lackeys like you need men like me to pay up so you get your salary—" Even supercilious scorn failed to reveal the lines in his face. Lucky genes, I wondered, or chemical intervention? "I've worked hard my whole life and earned my money. And I'm sick and tired of the rest of you lining up to take away what men like me have built."

"What, exactly, did you build?"

Idle curiosity, completely neutral. It infuriated him.

Two fingers pounded out the rhythm of his answer. "A whole lot of houses for a whole lot of people. Semple Heights— that's what I built." So I'd failed to recognize his name, to connect it to the huge subdivision on the city's south end. "That land's been in my family since my grandparents settled it in 1892."

He didn't tell a particularly intriguing story, neither vivid nor subtle, and in his rush to offer me a history lesson he seemed to forget his newfound hardship. I did my best to look inter- ested while the land passed from father to son, morphed from hardscrabble homestead into tony neighbourhood.

"I see, Mr. Semple. So you are financially able to make the payments but you choose not to?"

He rolled his eyes. "No, I am not financially able to make these payments."

I looked back in his file, turned to the detailed financial statements he'd given the court. His vehicle costs, his personal grooming costs, his weekly food budget—all astronomical. If I could have mustered the energy, I'd have gone to the window to look for the luxury sedan he'd probably parked across two spaces. "Your expenses are quite high."

"They're perfectly reasonable. Most of the people I know couldn't get by on half of what I'm living on."

I flipped a page with some effort, as if the paper was made of lead. "Your income seems quite low for your standard of living."

"It's been a slow year." He smirked like this was a great triumph.

I turned another page and noticed something else. His assets were negligible, his bank balances lower than my own. "Where's all your money, Mr. Semple?" I realized then that I'd slumped sideways in my chair, that my face was leaning against my fist.

"That's the thing, honey, I don't have any money." He made a point of overtly checking his platinum watch. "So maybe you can tell that lady judge that there's no blood to squeeze from this stone."

Suddenly, I was exhausted. I was so drained it might have been four in the morning and I might have been sitting across from Jeffrey Semple for the last twelve consecutive hours. I might have run a marathon on an empty stomach and come straight to work for this twelve-hour appointment. That's how fatigued I was, sitting across from his superb haircut and his weighty V-neck sweater.

"Just tell me what I have to do to get a discharge, or whatever it is you give me, and we'll let the lawyers take care of the rest."

I sat up straight, put down my pen, closed his file, and knit my hands together as if I was about to make the steeple. "Thank you for coming in, Mr. Semple. I'll just make a note on your file about your reasons for not paying."

Amazement replaced his arrogance. "That's it? That's all that happens here? I'm free to go?"

"Of course. This isn't a locked facility. We can't force you to do anything." I wanted to smile, but the effort was too much. "If there's nothing you can change, then there's nothing I can do."

"What a bunch of bullshit this is." He looked extremely pleased as he got to his feet. "What a goddamned waste of time and tax dollars."

I followed him to the door and slammed it once he'd gone. The reverberation felt like a sharp intake of necessary air. After I'd scribbled a note on his client form, I laid my forehead on my crossed arms and stayed that way until it was time to go home.

146.

I HAD A light load the next morning. I should have been finishing reports or reading new research or filing and shredding, but I was just staring out the window when Chuck called me into his office.

"The Jeffrey Semple file—"

"Uh huh." I didn't pretend to gag, or make a face or anything.

"I think you forgot to write a report."

"You're holding my report."

Chuck closed the file and looked at me. A questioning half smile flickered around his face, like he might be missing the joke. "I can't sign this."

I shrugged. "Whatever." The sullen teenager in my voice surprised me.

Chuck sat back and studied me for a minute. Then he got up, walked a big circle around me and closed his office door. "Have a seat, Meriel. How long have you worked here?"

I stayed on my feet. "Seven years, Chuck. Just like you. We started on the same day—remember?" My hands did something that seemed to indicate the size of his office, though I hadn't told them to.

"So what's going on here, Meriel? Do you think it's time for a change?"

I peered at him like I'd never seen him before, and maybe I

hadn't. "Are you firing me, Chuck?" I said it with a laugh, because it was absurd. Because he'd have to be nuts.

"Of course not, but I don't like the way you're acting. You seem a bit—unhinged lately. Corinne says she avoids you because of your hostility. Whatever's going on, it's starting to affect your work."

"I'm fine, Chuck. I've had a few bad days. What the hell do you care?"

"It's not just a few days." He folded his hands on his desk. "Your reports are sloppy, and clients are starting to complain."

"My clients have complained?"

"I've had a few calls." I wanted to ask who, wanted to know which loser had called to complain behind my back, but Chuck dismissed that line of enquiry with a wave of his hand. "I'm not worried about that. I'm worried about you—you look like hell, Meriel."

"Well, Chuck, I—"

He pushed himself back from his desk with one hand, the other held up as a shield. "I don't want you to tell me about your personal problems."

I'd been about to tell him what I thought of how he looked—his puffy eyes and double chin and the hair he didn't seem to realize was sprouting from his ears—but he wasn't going to give me the opening.

"I think you need a vacation, Meriel. Why don't you take some time off."

"I don't have any vacation time left Chuck. We determined that last month, remember?" Was I shouting? My voice was reverberating inside my head so maybe I was. Chuck wasn't flinching though, and he wasn't telling me to pipe down. He was just looking at me with big, flat eyes.

No, they were sad eyes. God, I'd never seen such sad eyes. If there had been a tear left inside me, I'd have started to weep over Chuck's sad eyes.

"I'm talking about a leave of absence. A stress leave. I've set you up an appointment with employee assistance. Right now. You're going up there to talk to them."

Chuck was really starting to piss me off with his sad eyes and his condescending voice. It was outrageous, after all the years I'd carried his sorry ass, doing the real work while he signed off on it and fiddled with paper clips and took home nearly twice the pay. But Chuck was already ushering me to the elevator. I let him push the button, and then I said I'd take the stairs.

The EAP counsellors were conveniently located just a floor above us. Above them, on the top floor, was a law office that specialized in pardons. Our whole building was a layer cake made for fuck-ups.

Chuck had obviously called ahead because I didn't even have to wait to see someone—they sent me straight in to see the top gun, a big guy in a leather-look chair. Not just a counsellor but the overseeing psychologist, *Dr.* stenciled in front of his name. He asked me a series of standard questions about drugs and alcohol and sexual abuse, and then he threw out a few testers to see if I was psychotic. I recognized those, and I answered them carefully.

Satisfied, he asked about my life. I told him there was nothing to tell. I said, "This job is my life. The rest of my life is in a coma. It's on life support."

I meant it to be flippant but as soon as I said it I thought about Gord, about how I'd let them take him off life support, and then I thought about how fucked up my family was, how maybe we were all chemically unbalanced. Then it occurred to me there might be something in the groundwater in Calder that made us all crazy.

I don't think I said any of that out loud.

"What's been going on in your life—the rest of your life—lately?"

"Not much. My father left my mother for Jesus, so she

gambled away all their money and got arrested. And I had to fix it because that was also my fault."

"Why was it your fault?"

I didn't answer. Instead, I concentrated on holding very still.

"What else is your fault, Meriel?"

I could see it was a trap and if I fell in, I might just keep falling forever so I kept my mouth shut. I'd already said far more than I'd intended to.

"How about work? Tell me about your job." His sudden sharp turn away from family was a surprise. I relaxed my grip on the chair.

"My job is fine. I mean it's stupid, and most of my clients are hopeless idiots, and nothing good ever comes of it, but I'm used to that." Too much. I'd meant to stop at fine.

The doctor put his hand to his chin and considered me, nodding. His big chair wobbled. "Do you think you need some time away from other people's problems?"

"No—"

He leaned forward a little, reached for a notepad without taking his eyes off me. It made me feel like he thought I was about to lunge, and that made me want to do something extravagant, something shocking. It made me want to pull a pistol from a holster under my skirt and take control of this conversation.

"Because I do. I think you need a much deserved break while you sort some things out, Meriel."

"I can't afford to be off work." I sounded desperate, wheedling.

He put both hands on his desk, his fingers splayed so only some of them were pointing at me. "As a counsellor, you know you cannot be of any assistance to anyone—" Assistance. *Assistance.* In the rarified fourth-floor sunshine, I saw the word spray from his mouth. "—if you're resentful and exhausted."

"I need my fucking job!" I'd yelled for sure that time.

"I'm going to recommend you take at least a short-term medical leave."

Medical leave. Stress leave is what he meant, the refuge of the weak and the lazy. I shook my head. "You don't understand, I need to work. And they need me here. I'm the only one—"

I realized then that I was crying. I had no idea how long that had been going on.

"You're certainly not the only one. I'm also going to recommend you come in for some regular counselling, and that you don't return to work until you've been reassessed." He had a smug, for-your-own-good tone. Nothing I said was going to make any difference so I swiped my tears on the back of my hand and buried them under my crossed arms, then composed my face so I knew he couldn't see through my skin, could only see what was sitting right in front of him.

He held his pen like he was choking it and it scritched across the notepad. "You can make an appointment on your way out."

He had terrible handwriting.

To Chuck, I said, "They suggested I take some time off when I can. Maybe in a few weeks." Chuck asked for the note he already knew about, like they had some fucking hotline between the floors. I made him ask twice. When I handed it over he barely glanced at it, and then he laughed. "You're on stress leave, starting now, and you're going home immediately. Give me your keys so you're not even tempted to come back."

"Fuck off, Chuck. I have work to do."

I started to leave but Chuck repeated "Now." He held out his hand and there was no room in his tone for negotiation so I pulled the keys from my pocket and tossed them onto his desk. They slid over the edge, fell to the floor. He didn't bend down to retrieve them. Instead, he held up a folder. "Just one thing before you go. Jeffrey Semple—can you just give me a few particulars so I can write a report?"

"Sure, Chuck. He's a man of a certain age who's used to

running the world—a self-entitled asshole with a big, fat Swiss watch and big, fat hidden assets. And he's never going to pay up. Didn't I put that in my report?"

"Seriously, Mer—"

"Seriously, Chuck. That's it. But you write whatever you want. You're the boss."

I went to my office then, thinking there were things I should take home with me, some personal photos, some of the shoes I kept in the bottom drawer of my filing cabinet. But after a few minutes turning circles, I realized I didn't need any of that crap, so I just grabbed my jacket and my purse and I left by the back door.

III.
BALANCE SHEETS

147.

DAD'S FACE AT my door was a surprise, though he'd phoned first
to say he was dropping by. His cheeks were ruddy, his ears and
scalp still pink and peeling a little. I hadn't noticed that when
I'd picked him up at the airport, but it was early morning
then and he'd been almost incoherent with exhaustion and his
teeth had chattered in the cold air. I'd turned the car's heater on
full blast and explained about Mom, how she'd slipped on the ice
and broken her hand but it was almost healed. Then I dropped
him in the driveway in front of a dark house.

Three days later he looked less brittle though still haggard,
and his hug inside the door was both too loose and too long. I
assumed it was the awkwardness of returning after such a pro-
found time away, but when I reached for the Kodak bag that
held the photos from his trip, he didn't give it up. Instead, he
asked for a cup of tea then watched me watch the kettle, both of
us stiff and silent waiting for the boil.

He knows, I thought, my head madly rushing in search of
the trace of evidence that had tipped him off. I wanted to bang
my forehead against the cupboard to stop the whirling, to
castigate myself for ever agreeing to cover Mom's crimes.

But maybe it wasn't that. Maybe it was worse. Maybe this
visit, Dad's agitation, was about Justin. If Dad looked even
slightly remorseful as he tried to explain why they'd kept the

secret of Gord's son from me, I might not be able to stay quiet, to swallow my own confession. Lately, I hadn't been able to swallow much at all. I'd even tried to exact a pound of flesh from Daneen one night on the phone for keeping Justin—my nephew, for God's sake—from me. But her "Thank god they finally told you," shut me up and shut me down, and I listened to her go on about some cryptic fan mail, which is what she'd called to talk about anyway.

I took down a box of teabags and two mugs and sat across from Dad at my kitchen table. I passed him the sugar bowl but he shook his head. "I find myself content these days," he said, "with less."

I wrapped a hand around my mug just to feel the livid heat. The only sound was Dad's breath blowing across the surface of the tea. Finally he launched. "I understand things have become quite strained between you and your mother." It wasn't a question, so I didn't respond. "She tells me you've been very harsh with her, accusing her of all kinds of mean things."

My face flamed with indignation, which I'm sure looked like guilt. "I stayed with her for two weeks when she broke her hand." My voice shook. "I took care of her and used up all my vacation days—and she sent you here to yell at me for how I treated her?"

"No one's yelling, Meriel-Claire." His quiet voice. His judgment voice. It forced me to lower my volume.

"And did she tell you what I accused her of?"

"Meriel-Claire, I didn't come here to have an argument. I just want to ask you—"

"What did she tell you?"

Dad watched the steam coming off his tea. "She says you blamed her for Gord's death, that you said it was her fault for being a bad teacher, a bad parent."

"That's a lie. I didn't say that. What the fuck is her—"

"Meriel-Claire! Settle down."

I snapped my jaw shut and stared at the wall, reconstructing. When I had it, I spoke quietly. "All I said about Gord—the only thing I said—was that he wasn't here to help her because he never learned to look both ways. That's it. I didn't say anything about Mom."

Dad studied me for a moment and his expression softened. "Meriel-Claire, I'm asking you to be more generous with her. She has never been able to reconcile Gord's death—she still blames herself."

"Herself?"

Something in him slumped, though his posture didn't change. "Of course she does. She taught him to drive."

I'd forgotten that. Dad had taught me, but there was no way Gord would have taken instruction from Dad.

"In the first few years afterward, she must have said it a hundred times—'Why didn't I teach him to stop at the tracks and look? Why?'"

I fiddled with the handle on my cup, wondering how, through all these years, I hadn't known about this.

"Meriel-Claire, you and I know Gord's death wasn't anybody's fault. But I'm asking you to have a little more compassion for your mother. To appreciate the things she does for you."

"Appreciate what? She's never done anything for me." My voice edging back toward petulant.

He set down his empty mug and looked me in the eye. "And she would say you've never let her."

His eyes were bloodshot, the smudges under them so dark it looked as if someone had marked him with coal. I poured more tea into both our mugs. Dad said, "We're both worried about you, you know."

"No one needs to worry about me, Dad, I'm fine." I scooped a heaping spoonful of sugar into my own cup. "I promise I'll be nicer to Mom."

148.

I WAS LOOKING at a taffeta ball gown—a bridesmaid's dress maybe, or a graduate's—in the Salvation Army Thrift Store. I'd never wear it but I was tempted to waste thirty dollars on it just to hang it in my closet as a kind of talisman. I had room, after all. I'd purged my wardrobe that morning, donated a bulging garbage bag of old clothes.

And I'd promised myself I wasn't going to buy used anymore. Some days I just wanted to spend every penny I had left in the bank on new clothes and new furniture, a whole new everything. But of course as soon as I'd dropped off my donation, I waded right into the racks of castaways.

I ran my hand over the gown's scarlet fabric and pictured myself showing up in Chuck's office, swirling around in that taffeta just so he'd know I was still crazy. For weeks, I'd meant to go talk to him—even driven to the parking lot and looked up at the window that used to be mine. But I was afraid to go inside.

I squeezed the heavy fabric of that dress again, weighing the rich folds against the cost of frivolity, considering my regret if I bought it, my regret if I didn't.

There was a light tap high on my arm, then a familiar voice saying, "Wow that's some dress." I turned to find a grinning Addie Sullivan. "Did you get the envelopes?"

"What? No. Oh, but I haven't been at work for a while."

"But I dropped off forty dollars two weeks in a row!"

"It's okay, Addie. It'll be there when I go back." Perfect. I had a reason now to set foot in the building, an excuse to drop by. "So business has been good then?"

Addie didn't answer. She was looking off in the distance, grinning again. She pointed toward the household section. "I come in every week to see if it's still here."

I couldn't tell what it was. "The lamp?"

"The carousel. Like they have at the library or the video store—so I can keep some books off the ground when it's wet." She gestured toward the windows at the front of the store. The rain had stopped but the newly minted sun was glistening on drops that still clung to the pane. I wanted to break away, but Addie was compelling me toward her prize, her hand on my arm. When we got within reach of it she seemed to stop breathing. She just froze, staring reverently as if a spinning wire carousel was the answer to every prayer.

Eventually she remembered I was there. "But don't worry, I won't start saving for this until I've paid you back the last of what I owe, plus the interest of course."

I reached out to spin the empty carousel. It wobbled uncertainly, too light on its feet, then squeaked into a turn. The price tag came into view: $29.99.

"You need this for your business?" I looked at her sideways, cautiously. "Then I'll loan you the money."

"You're still trying to buy your way into heaven." Her smile didn't waver.

Was I?

"No, really, Addie, think about it. The better your business, the faster I make my return. We'll add it to your account."

Of course I had to wrestle the damn thing into my car and drive her home with it. That was the extent of my social engagement for all of May.

149.

I RAN THROUGH my full-salary sick days and onto the rougher pavement of reduced short-term disability cheques. I should have been skimping. Instead, I dipped into my savings to order Chinese every other night, to splurge on expensive night creams. I figured it was okay, that Chuck couldn't do without me for much longer. Anyway, an insufficient cash flow felt like less of a burden than a surfeit of time. Time and more time. I couldn't remember ever having so much of it, unplanned and unfilled hours like a truckload of deflated balloons I didn't have the energy to blow up.

Every minute held its breath, waiting. Waiting for who knows what—I didn't. If I'd been an addict, at least I would have been waiting for rock bottom, the final hard thwack as I hit it. But I wasn't an addict and no one was waiting with me and no one could tell me if I was still plummeting, or if I was already as far down as I could go.

When I couldn't take it anymore, the waiting and not knowing why, I made a counselling appointment. I thought it might be fun to have someone listen to me for a change. But the day before my appointment, I flipped a page in the newspaper and there was Roger, looking the same as he had three years earlier when he'd left—only now he was beaming. Now he was wearing a tuxedo and standing next to his bride.

I scanned the announcement, fast: The parents of...thrilled to announce...married in a ceremony overlooking. I'd never heard of her, Roger's bride, but obviously she was young enough to need her parents to lead the way.

I told my breath to stick around, that we were over him, but my breath left anyway and took its time coming back. I tore the page in half and half again, crumpled it and stepped on it and hurled it at the wall. I left the house, lit a cigarette on the sidewalk, sucked it all down and found no relief. I stormed back inside, swirling, knocking things down. For the first time ever, I understood Gord's frenzied tantrums, the need to stir the air, to crash against things. By two in the morning I was exhausted, but I couldn't bear my bed. I dragged a comforter to the couch and finally, I slept.

I woke up late, still alive, still breathing, so I skipped my appointment with the counsellor and I went to see a travel agent instead. I asked for brochures to just about everywhere I could think to go. She wanted me to sit and look at destinations but I wouldn't. I just wanted to get home with my slippery stack of possibilities.

I spent Saturday morning turning those slippery pages, struck by the sameness of everywhere—the same resort rooms, the same close-ups of exotic bar drinks. The requisite spa shot. Even the unique tourist attractions were indistinct, photographed in soft, balanced light to mask any true significance.

When the phone rang, it snatched me back from that slick world. It was Daneen, calling from Calder where she'd been in full retreat for weeks—not that I'd known she was there.

"Hey, Meriel, come out and see me. I miss you."

150.

DANEEN EMERGED FROM her house as I climbed from my car. She held out her arms and I walked into them, not a word yet between us. She smelled just like herself, like something sweet and sour. The rush of feeling almost knocked me over.

"Doris saw the announcement in the paper and called me. She was worried about you."

I pulled back fast and held up the two bottles of wine I'd brought. "Can I sleep over?"

We ate tinned salmon sandwiches and opened the first bottle of wine. We talked for a while about Portia and why she hadn't come along this summer. Daneen put the back of her hand against her forehead in mock angst. Portia at eleven, she told me, had hit puberty with a vengeance. She hated her mother and the idea of spending the whole summer alone in boring, crappy old Calder was unbearable. "So we're splitting the summer. Bryan can deal with her for a month and I can have some peace."

We were sitting cross-legged on opposite corners of her velvet settee. I'd heard my mother call it that. I ran my hand over the fabric. Its deep, fleshy pink was stiff and ribbed like the roof of a mouth. The whole room, a room so carefully and gradually appointed, reminded me of an old hotel parlour in a movie. Window sheers filtered the west sun so it fell evenly on every surface, on the walnut table and the crystal teardrops dangling from painted lampshades. On the grey hairs that glinted when Daneen tipped her head at just the right angle. So few grey hairs, and no other outward sign of time passing through her.

"She's hardly changed," I thought. And then I thought how I'd known her for half my life, and how from here forward, it would always be more than half.

I took a deep drink of wine. Daneen asked again how I was handling Roger's marriage.

I wanted to let loose, to tell her how bad it hurt. I wanted to tell her everything, tell her about my mother's gambling and my father's gullibility, my leave of absence and how it felt like I'd taken leave of my senses, too. I wanted to spill my crazy all over that serene house, the whole mess of it, to confess and be absolved, but Daneen said, "You must be so angry, the way Roger used you to support him all that time until he got a good job."

I shook my head to clear the fast-growing tumour of that. "That's not what happened, Daneen. He wasn't using me. He just—we couldn't make it work." Tears flooded in, some shuddering relief just within my grasp, but she laughed.

"I think you're being naïve."

I got up and went to the kitchen to open the second bottle of wine. When I returned to the living room with it, Daneen was gone, was moving around upstairs. When she came down, she led with her long white hand, with an envelope dangling from her fingers.

"Did I tell you about the crazy woman who's been harassing me?" I had a vague memory of it, but nothing concrete. "I want your professional opinion on this, whether you think I need to be worried about what she'll do."

I filled both of our glasses to the rim, then studied the envelope like I was searching for clues. Really, I was just prolonging my anticipation. It was hand addressed to Daneen, care of her publisher, *Personal & Confidential* printed very precisely along the bottom edge. The return address caught my eye. Mission, B.C. and the house number: 523, same as mine. The two was dropped slightly below the other numbers, and I wished for some arcane knowledge of handwriting so I could make some pronouncement about that.

I slipped two folded pages from the envelope and settled back to read the letter, blue ink on both sides of lined notebook paper. After a tortuous lead in, the letter's claim was straightforward enough: Daneen had stolen the premise and the plot for *Desperate and Bliss*, had appropriated not just the voice but the very soul of the narrator. Halfway through, I looked up to find Daneen watching me intently.

"What do you think? A weird fan fixation? Do you think she could be a stalker?"

"Daneen, you're a writer, not a rock star." I meant it to be funny. She didn't laugh.

"Listen, it happens. Success is a magnet for freaks like this— it's blood to sharks."

I'd gone back to reading, blood and sharks weaving in and out of the looping script. The letter struck me as needy, pathetic, but that could have been the impression made by the schoolgirl handwriting, the misspellings and bad grammar. The gist of it was that *Desperate and Bliss* was hers—her story, her family, her book. That Daneen was a thief. But the letter writer didn't make that allegation, not clearly or succinctly, anyway.

Nothing was clear until the last line, direct and concise. *I think I deserve to be compensated.* It was signed, *Most Sincerely, Joanne Braun.*

I looked at Daneen.

"Astounding, isn't it?" She didn't give me the space to ask anything precise, and maybe I preferred that. "I knew she was strange when I first met her, but she seemed harmless. I certainly didn't expect this."

"You know her?"

"I was the writer-in-residence at the library in Mission. She came in to meet with me a few times."

"And?"

"And nothing. I met with her, I was nice, the way you're supposed to be. I never thought about her again."

I laid the letter on the coffee table. "Did you respond to this? Or did your publisher?"

"Christ, I didn't tell them." Daneen had gathered herself up into a tight knot on the couch. She was hugging a satin cushion to her chest. "I showed it to my agent, in confidence. I thought she would try to fix it—I mean, isn't that her job?"

I had no idea what an agent's job was, so I just waited for more. Daneen leaned back on the couch, looked out the window and I watched her over my wineglass. Finally, I had to jog her into speaking. "So, what did she do?"

"Nothing—she did nothing. She said to ignore it, and when I pushed she said to just leave it alone, that she didn't want to get mixed up in it. Didn't want to waste her time on it."

"Mmm." I refilled my glass. For once, I was outdrinking Daneen.

"It really pissed me off. I have done so much to help build her career." Daneen set her glass down hard. "I guess that's how it goes. I feel like I've spent my whole life doing things for other people and when I ask for something, nothing comes back."

I closed my eyes and nodded, held a mouthful of wine against the roof of my mouth with a stiff tongue. When I opened my eyes, Daneen was looking off toward the kitchen, a smile playing at the corner of her mouth.

"A fixer—is that what they call it? That's what I need. I need a fixer." She topped up her glass and held it aloft, laid her other hand over the letter. "I know I should just ignore it. That's what you're supposed to do with blackmail attempts, right?"

Blackmail. Nothing in the letter seemed direct enough to warrant such a harsh label, yet hearing it, the word prickled on my skin like electricity.

"So you have no idea why she'd write this?"

"It's utterly ridiculous."

Daneen had shifted back into easygoing, into eye rolling, but I stayed stuck deep in the cloak and dagger of it. "Do you want me to talk to her?"

It seemed like such a good idea. I knew how to defuse a bomb.

Daneen locked her eyes, wide and dead-serious now, on mine. "God no. Absolutely not."

I'd expected yes—a grateful yes, even—and my disappointment registered.

"Meriel, I know you're a genius at this kind of thing, a real snake charmer. But there is no point in opening this door even a crack."

At five thirty in the morning, unable to sleep, I re-read the letter and then read it again until I could see it wasn't at all what Daneen thought. It wasn't some crazy, clumsy blackmail attempt. There was a sharp angle of desperation that made it so much more threatening. But I was, just then, on the ugly side of too much wine, the place where it feels like everything is coming unstitched.

151.

AFTER THE RAIN stopped, it was hot. Steam bath hot. Three nights in a row I slept on the couch because my room upstairs was stifling, the nights too muggy to offer even the solace of a slight breeze. But no matter where I slept it was fitful, and my empty days felt as heavy as the air outside, punctuated with bursts of restlessness.

I tried calling Daneen to ask if I could come stay with her for a while in Calder. I imagined the air in that thick-walled house was cooler, that the Auberge flowing past would offer some kind of mental relief. Her phone was continuously busy, off the hook I guessed, and her cellphone must have been turned off.

So day after day I just traipsed through the city heat, heading nowhere.

One afternoon, after I'd walked past Debt Services but stopped myself from stepping inside and asking for the envelopes with my name on them, adding, "Look how calm I've become," I looped around the park. In the distance I saw Addie, sitting on her red blanket surrounded by her books, that ridiculous carousel perched at one corner of her makeshift establishment. Someone was turning it—I could see just a shoulder, occasionally a hand. Behind her, the city's memorial fountain soared and tumbled.

Addie looked so regal, sitting there. She looked like she owned the whole world.

I started toward her—I could use a book, maybe some cheerful company—but I stopped myself. She'd only think I'd come to collect. There was just no good approach for me to make, no place at all for me to go where I'd be wanted, where I could do some good.

All of a sudden I was desperate for a change of scenery.

152.

I PRETENDED, EVEN to myself, that I didn't know where I was heading, that this was just some sudden, keen interest in the Fraser Valley, a serendipitous marriage of travel brochure and airline seat sale. A longing for less level topography. Anyway, I had some time on my hands.

I picked up a rental car at the Abbotsford airport, checked into a Best Western hotel on the highway and left for Mission the next morning. The sun was brilliant. I bought a cup of tarry coffee at a gas station and settled into my road trip.

I had to remind myself to slow down, to enjoy the scenery, to pay attention to something beyond the asphalt in front of my car. I was almost there but it wasn't even noon and the coffee I'd guzzled burned in my empty stomach, so I stopped for breakfast.

The Country Restaurant beside the highway had exactly what I wanted, the kind of breakfast I'd only order on vacation: eggs and sausage, hash browns and thick, doughy pancakes that would absorb all the acid in me. While I waited for my food, I picked up a visitor's guide from a rack by the door and thumbed past descriptions of fishing holes and golf courses, my eyes glazing until I turned a page and discovered the monastery.

I asked for directions when I paid my bill.

The Benedictine abbey jutted from sprawling green hills. Though the lofty erection of its bell tower suggested I might not be the gender most wanted in this place, I went in anyway. Morning light blazed through elliptical windows that rose over my head, their stained glass a kaleidoscope, every dust particle rendered sacred. It felt like an epiphany, the realization that faith could fashion such a place.

I read all the plaques and then a pamphlet, tangling myself up in Benedict's inner torment, his self-imposed exile, his commitment to forsaking worldly goods. How he banished his lust by tearing at his skin. I revelled in it, really. For a long time, I just stood between pillars and admired the fresco on the far wall—St. Benedict risen, emaciated, temptation defeated by the brambles he still embraced. An olive branch sprung from the stump of an oak at his heels and I held very still, my breath deep and even until the man standing next to me pushed back his baseball cap and said, "Jesus, that guy needs to order a pizza."

Jarred loose, I went back to the main hall and selected another pamphlet, raised my eyes to the ceiling to consider the symbolic reliefs it described: the sacrificial ram, the winged serpent. And then the raven, trusted to dispose of the poison loaf cooked up, so the story went, by a jealous rival who resented Benedict's gifts.

I stared at that raven until my neck hurt. I was thinking I'd finally found the thing I was meant to do. I was thinking: This mission will save me.

153.

JOANNE BRAUN'S FRONT door was painted pylon orange, a peculiar accent against the faded cedar shakes. As soon as I struck the brass knocker, the door opened like she'd been waiting just inside. Bright red lipstick and dark, puffed up hair. Her waist was cinched with a wide belt to compel an extreme hourglass figure. She was right out of a comic book, and that confirmed my expectations of her mental state, even while the gaze she trained on me was solemn and cordial.

I introduced myself as a representative of Daneen DeCario. I wanted it to sound official but not officious, so I made sure to say it with my eyes and my throat wide open, my mouth turned in the shape of friendly and my hands apologizing for this late afternoon interruption.

Her expression shifted immediately to something close to thrilled. There wasn't an ounce of wariness when she asked me in.

"I've come to see you, of course, about *Desperate and Bliss*. About your letter—"

"Please sit down. Can I get you tea or coffee?" Good, I thought, the formality of tea would play in my favour. She bustled off and came back carrying an empty serving tray. From a china cabinet in the corner, she lifted two teacups on their saucers and set them carefully on the tray.

"These were my mother's teacups, one of the few things she brought from Czechoslovakia." Joanne handed me one as if she needed me to examine its bold blue on white pattern, the gold rimming the impossibly slight, scalloped edge. "Just looking at them could make her cry. Anything that reminded her of home made her cry."

It was the perfect opening—there were teacups in *Desperate and Bliss*, too—teacups with yellow roses that had also survived a perilous journey. I remembered that much from the few pages I'd read. But though she'd swung that door wide open for me,

Joanne blocked the threshold with a torrent of details. "She had four to start, but one lost its handle on the way. She tried gluing it but it never took. Sometimes, she'd just hold that little handle and cry."

She took the empty cup from me. The kettle trilled, but she left it on the burner until it screamed from the pressure. When she came back with the tea, she was apologizing for having nothing else to serve.

I was seated on an emerald chair, its fabric worn to a shine. It was the kind of old-fashioned furniture that demands good posture. Joanne perched across from me in its twin, poured our tea and never once stopped talking. She'd just gotten home—she was a receptionist in a chiropractor's office, twenty-seven patients that day and I judged from her tone that this was a lot—this was, in fact, too many, and she was exhausted and hadn't been sleeping well, which was probably hormonal. Which had her worried, since it was ovarian cancer that had killed her mother, a malignancy fueled by estrogen or maybe, probably, by the ravages of homesickness and heartbreak and struggle.

"And bitterness, of course. My father had promised they'd only be in Canada for a few years while he studied, but after the Soviet invasion he said they could never go back. And once he left us, there was never any money for her to take the kids and go home. She never saw her family again."

I sipped my tea and tried to keep up. Joanne was rattling off her story in shorthand, the way you would if you were telling it to someone who already knew it. I started to worry that maybe this was all a mistake.

Before I could steer the conversation back to the purpose of my visit, she veered into a much more detailed monologue about a broken engagement, love smashed on the shores of her obligation to her mother, and that led straight to the family drama that now swirled. "My brother left as soon as he could. Just a teenager off to make his fortune—which he did. He turned out so much like our father."

It kept coming, rapid-fire intimacy designed, I suppose, to manipulate me into sympathy. "When my mother was too sad to get dressed, I dressed her. When she was too weak to eat, I spoonfed her. When she needed someone to care for her around the clock, I quit my job."

In my office, I'd have known how to take charge. Here, I couldn't get a handhold.

"I've lived in this house my whole life, but none of that counts now. My brother and sister get their equal third. They never helped, they never did anything but go on with their own lives. I fought it for two years but the court says I have to—" a shudder, a quelled sob maybe—"I have to sell the house or buy them out, even if it means I end up on the street."

"I'm sorry." I bit back the urge to ask financial questions, to offer to help her remortgage or work out a payment plan.

"It's just that family—well, you know. They're wired in so tight you can love them and hate them at the same time. And then you start to wonder if you're the crazy one."

She must have seen my eyebrows lift because she clamped her mouth shut, rolled her big red lips inward until they disappeared in a seam. Then she released them and said, very softly, "I've gone off on one of my tangents again." She blushed as if this were a terrible social sin, as if tangents were something she'd been accused of her whole life.

Finally I took the reins. "Joanne, can we talk about *Desperate and Bliss*—about your claim to have some entitlement to the proceeds from this novel? In the letter you sent Ms DeCario—" I'd retreated into formality, into that refuge where statements pose as questions—"you indicated that you believe some of your ideas were used in the novel."

She nodded and disagreed at the same time. "Not just some of my ideas, the whole story. I just explained that. It's about my family, my parents coming here from Czechoslovakia, my mother's homesickness. I think she made up some stuff that happens back there, but I don't know about any of that."

It occurred to me slowly, incrementally. She was just filling in the rest of the story, augmenting the book I hadn't bothered to read. It was sloppy and so unlike me, not to have done my homework. It put me at a dangerous disadvantage. Still, I could see now what this was about. And I knew just how such a mistake gets made.

"So your family came here from Czechoslovakia and that makes you feel as if Daneen—Ms DeCario—stole your story. But you know it's not a story unique to your family. She wrote a book of fiction, and you recognize some of it. But she had no way of even knowing your personal story."

I experienced a familiar exhilaration at having untangled a problem knot so handily.

Joanne frowned. "But she did—I told her all of this. I showed her the book I was writing about it, my mother's story." She was talking more slowly, as if she suspected I was easily lost. "I gave it to her and asked if she thought it was a good idea. And she took it."

She clearly believed this version. No one was that convincing a liar.

Before I could ask another question, she was on her feet. "I'll show you." She disappeared down the hall.

Outside it was dusk, a light rain just starting and except for the pool of light from a side lamp, the room was growing dark. Joanne was gone for a long time, and I listened to the opening and closing of cupboards, a rolling drawer, the sudden rush of a toilet flushing. I dug around for what I knew about mental illness, about psychosis and celebrity fixations and people who got caught up in their own fantasies.

There was a phone in the furthest corner from me. I considered tiptoeing over, calling Daneen and whispering where I was—whispering that she should worry if she didn't hear from me in an hour. But by the time I'd formed the thought and willed myself to rise to it, it was too late. Joanne's footsteps were coming back down the hall.

"Sorry, I couldn't remember where I'd put it." She held out a flimsy spiral notebook, teal-covered, pedestrian. The kind of notebook every kid at school uses. "This is what I showed her. It's just the first four chapters in here, and an outline of the rest of the book."

I put out my hand and she passed it to me, then looked like she might snatch it back. I pulled the notebook close, laid it across my lap and opened the cover. *Chapter One* was written neatly on top of the first page. I recognized the looping script from Joanne's letter and I tried to focus, to pretend, at least, that I was reading the page with interest. Then I turned to the next.

There was no mistaking Daneen's flared and confident handwriting in the margins, her signature green ink. I couldn't make sense of the words, couldn't translate either hand into a comprehensible text. Joanne sat rigid, watching me. She'd turned on another light but it was still too dim in the room. My eyes burned with fatigue. It couldn't be much later than seven but I hadn't adjusted to the time difference, to the strangeness of my surroundings.

I checked the time on the watch I wasn't wearing and stood up.

"I really can't stay any longer, Joanne. Can I take this with me and bring it back to you tomorrow evening? I'd like to be able to read it carefully."

A door slammed across her face. Her eyes narrowed and her head slowly, deliberately signalled her refusal. "You can come back tomorrow and look at it, but you can't take it." She put out her hand and I gave back the notebook. She drew it to her chest and crossed her arms over it.

I stepped away from the chair and tried to relax my face,

steady my legs. Smile. I needed her to think I was on her side, to win back her trust. "Okay, tomorrow. What time would be good for you, Joanne?"

We agreed on three.

154.

A LIGHT SHOWER beat an uneven tempo on the roof of the car as I retraced my route from that house with its hazard orange door. The black velvet of the wet road swallowed the light of my low beams. Over the furor of the car's fan, I argued viewpoints, considered angles. I was formulating excuses, looking for an out—for Daneen and for me.

I guess I'd always known she was capable of something like this. We are, after all, better judges of character than we ever allow ourselves to admit. But as I swung onto the highway, my tires a dark hiss on the pavement, it was hard to see just what offense had occurred. Harder still to discern my culpability.

I tried to imagine the conversation ahead—what I would say, how Daneen would respond—but I could only picture her as she was in that newspaper feature my mother kept pinned to the fridge: the full-colour froth of her daffodil yellow dress as she stepped from the stage, plaque clutched tight in one hand, a copy of *Desperate and Bliss* dangling from the other. In that photo she's not looking down at where she's going but she's not looking over her shoulder, either. She's looking straight ahead, her expression an odd coalescence of angles. Desperate and bliss.

I was halfway to the Best Western hotel when the sky lost its grip. Rain pummelled down like a reckoning and I had to fight the urge to accelerate into it. It would be too easy to underestimate the unknown road, to slip sideways and out of sight. And then what? Who would notice? I was alone, accountable to no one.

The road dipped and my tires left the pavement, skidding on top of the water. My hands tightened on the wheel. For the longest of seconds, I had no traction at all before the tires caught hold on a slight rise.

Maybe this was all my fault, this problem with Joanne. Maybe complicity was woven into my acquiescence to Daneen's version of every story. Commiseration had been, after all, my life's work, and if I moved aside my carefully arranged bangs, I would see how calculated sympathy had carved lines in my forehead.

I slowed, tried to focus on my driving, on the freshly painted centre line but I kept drifting over old ground again. I was searching for some obvious error in the ledger, some small miscalculation that had led straight to here.

I was wondering how much it could cost me this time.

155.

BY THE TIME I reached my hotel room, I was stumbling from exhaustion, my limbs unwieldy as I dragged my suitcase off the bed. I wanted to call Daneen, but I thought I should eat something first, recover some strength. In the hotel restaurant, the laminated menu was stiff and sticky. The pictures made me queasy, the thought of chewing and swallowing overwhelmed me. I ordered a beer and drank it fast enough to feel bolstered.

Back in my room, listening to Daneen's phone ring, I pulled the bedspread back. Finally voicemail picked up and delivered its impersonal, electronic invitation to leave her a message. But I couldn't think what to say, how to explain anything, so I just placed the phone in its cradle.

I stripped off the wrinkle resistant slacks I'd put on so many hours before, when I'd been convinced that looking relaxed and unflappable would matter, and wormed under the sheet. As I closed my eyes, I saw a page of lined paper covered in Joanne's foolish squiggles, Daneen's green pen running circles around it.

156.

I WOKE BEFORE six, sunlight creeping in through a slit between the curtains. It was too early to call Daneen in Calder, even with the time change, so I went for breakfast and made up for the meal I'd skipped the night before. My cloak-and-dagger dread, all the anxiety I'd felt watching Joanne clutch her spiral notebook like genuine treasure, had receded.

At seven, I dialed Daneen. She answered on the second ring. When she heard my voice, she asked how I was, but I didn't want to get tripped up in the pleasantries.

"Daneen, I'm in BC—in Mission. I talked to Joanne Bráun last night."

"What? How did you run into her?"

"I went to her house. I was trying to defuse the situation."

When Daneen finally responded, every word was sharpened to a point. "I can't believe you did that. You had no right. What were you thinking?"

"I was thinking she was dangerous, and you needed my help. Daneen, she has a notebook. You've seen it. You wrote comments in it."

"She has a notebook?" Her voice softer now, cautious. "What are you saying, Meriel?"

"She wrote a novel, the start of it, and she showed it to you. I recognized your handwriting in the comments. She says you took the whole story from her?" I made it a question, because it was.

"You think I copied her notebook? Jesus, Meriel. What crap." I didn't know if she meant the accusation or the notebook's contents. "Look, she's crazy. You said so yourself. Dangerous. And she didn't write that novel, I did. If you want to talk about notebooks, come back here and I'll show you piles of them, all my research."

I could feel my arteries open, blood flowing in relief. "I'm going back there today. Daneen, she absolutely believes you stole her novel and that her notebook is proof."

Daneen took a long, slow breath. There was another pause, the sound of water running on her end. Then, gently, "God, Meriel, she's crazier than I thought. I'm so glad you're there. Thank you for helping me."

She was grateful after all.

"You can fix this, right, Meriel?"

"I just wish I'd known—"

"Listen, I know her type. They have an image of themselves, that they'll become famous writers but they won't—they can't write and even if they could, they never do." I thought of Joanne sitting ramrod straight, telling me her hard luck story while her tea went cold.

"You know what I think—I think she should be honoured that some half-baked idea she had actually turned into something of merit."

"Daneen, are you saying—"

"That's it." She'd cut me off. "That's what you should do—flatter her, make her feel proud that she had some small part in the creation of a good book. That would work, right?"

I was too confused to respond.

"Please, just try it, okay? Promise me you'll fix this, Meriel, promise me you'll get that notebook from her." She seemed every bit as desperate as Joanne had.

"Okay Daneen. Relax. Of course I'll do what I can. I'll call you tonight, after I've seen her."

I expected her to hang up, but she didn't. "You're an amazing friend, Meriel. Thanks for doing this."

157.

I HAD HOURS to kill before three o'clock. The library in Mission opened at ten. They had one copy of *Desperate and Bliss* that wasn't out—but it was reserved. I asked if I could sit in the carrel nearest the desk and read it, promising to hand it over immediately if the person who'd reserved it came along. The young woman at the desk practically wept with joy, she was so delighted to have such a simple solution presented to her—one that meant no one would be mad.

To my surprise, the narrator's voice that had seemed so stiff and unnatural when I'd first tried to read *Desperate and Bliss* now seemed captivating. Occasionally I caught myself slowing down, mesmerized, and I had to remind myself I was reading for plot, not pleasure. When the librarian pushed a cart of returns to the back of the library to start shelving, I darted to the washroom, taking the book along. I was back before she noticed my breach.

The next time I looked at the clock, I was fifty pages from finishing the book and it was ten minutes to three.

Joanne opened her door just as quickly as she had the day before, but she looked wary. "I didn't think you were coming." I apologized for being late, though it wasn't even five after, and followed her inside. She wore a blue business suit, skirt above the knee and high-heeled pumps, a red scarf tied at her throat. The whole outfit reminded me of a 1970s stewardess, but Joanne wasn't serving coffee or tea this time and I felt like I'd been bumped from first class when she suggested I sit at her dining-room table. The spiral notebook was waiting there.

For a few minutes she sat across from me, watching me, but when she realized I really meant to read the entire thing, she went to the emerald chair and perched with a magazine on her lap.

I didn't need to read the whole thing, though I pretended to. It was hard going, some sentences impenetrable, the dialogue overwrought and wooden. I skipped quickly through Chapters Two and Three, focusing on the blue ink and ignoring the green, and then I studied the scribbled outline, the notes detailing where Joanne intended to go next. It was as if some ham-handed adolescent had tried to write a summary book report about a novel she'd read.

A novel I'd also read.

It was the same story—exactly the same. It was the same protagonist with a different name, the same family history, the same teacups dressed in some other finery. I kept my face impassive, my breathing even and I turned back to the beginning to read Daneen's comments. They were neutral, not as unkind as I'd expected, and most focused on grammar and word choice. Next to the paragraph about the teacups she'd written *Nice detail!*—the only exclamation point, the only positive remark. Her notes grew less frequent page by page.

In a marginal note at the bottom of a page, I noticed something I'd missed the first time through: Joanne had written *She went back and forth between desperate and bliss-*, the hyphen nearly lost to the notebook's steep edge. Daneen hadn't made a mark anywhere on that page.

At the very end of Joanne's detailed outline, Daneen had written a few careful lines:

> *Joanne, this could be an interesting story, but it's too much for a beginning writer. Your characters aren't alive, and you need to work on vocabulary. Consider taking a course in grammar and style before writing anything else.*

A wave of nausea flooded through me. I closed the notebook and Joanne immediately set aside her magazine, stood up and smoothed down her skirt.

"When did you write this, Joanne?" I placed my hands palms down on the table, pressing them into the honey-coloured, pitted wood to keep me steady.

"Four years ago maybe? More than that I think. When my mother was first sick."

I tried to calculate in my head when Daneen would have begun writing *Desperate and Bliss*. "Is it possible that Ms DeCario told you what she was working on and it reminded you of your family's story, and that's when you wrote this?"

It sounded plausible, but Joanne shook her head. Vehemently. "I wrote this out of my own brain before I ever met her. She didn't tell me anything—she just read it and stole it. When I heard on the radio in the car that she'd won this big award, and they said what the book was about—that's when I realized."

Finally, a firm handhold. "Joanne, that was over a year before you wrote to her."

"My mother had just died. I guess I wasn't..." She trailed off.

"I'm sorry about that. But have you even read *Desperate and Bliss*?"

Joanne looked at her pumps. "I didn't need to. I know the whole story."

I gave her what I hoped was a pleasant and not patronizing smile, but my face felt too taut, like the pulleys beneath my cheekbones might snap. "What you have here is a few dozen pages, a very simplistic outline. The novel is well over three hundred pages long."

"But it's my idea, my story—my family. Right?" She asked the question like she could trust my answer.

I was careful not to nod, not to enter into any tacit agreement. "Joanne, it's a very, very complex novel. This—" I put one hand on the notebook, pushed it away. "This isn't. It's a few short chapters."

"But she has the other two notebooks." She looked at the floor, slid a finger under the scarf at her neck and wriggled as if the scarf were suddenly too tight. "I never went and got those back from her after she said she didn't think I could write it, that it wasn't very good."

"There are other notebooks?" The shock in my voice so undisguised I instinctively ran for cover. "I think it seems possible that something you said, or even something you wrote, stuck with Ms DeCario. Inspired her—" I stood up. My legs felt uncertain. "And you know, that's something to be proud of.

You should be honoured that you influenced a great novel. So many people are reading it."

The words came out like they were mine, formed on my own thick tongue.

Joanne had taken off her scarf and she was twisting it around and around one hand. She couldn't meet my eye. Her voice was quiet and flat.

"I never thought of it like that. I guess it was stupid of me to write that letter."

158.

FOR JUST A second, the reflection I saw in the hotel mirror was a face from long ago, impossibly young and unguarded. Unlined. Then my real face resurfaced with all its wariness, its parentheses bracketing a mouth that had held in so many words. I turned away and dialed Daneen before I could think about anything else.

"I read your book. And I read her notebook."

"Hang on a second." There was no discernible sound through the receiver for several minutes. By the time Daneen came back on the line, I felt dulled.

"Sorry. Say that again—what happened?"

"I read them both, yours and hers. It's the same story, Daneen."

"Is that what you told her?" Fear in her voice. I could have just let her dangle there.

"I told her she should be honoured to have inspired you, and she agreed."

"Thank God." The sound of her smile opening. "Hey, I've got company in the other room so I can't really talk. But thank you, you're so great, Meriel. When you're back home, come out and see me."

"Daneen, I—" She was gone, the hollow air on the phone whiting out every sound in my head. I sat on the edge of the bed, blind and deaf and dumb until I realized the only thing I wanted to do was finish that book. I was still hoping, I think, for some amazing plot twist, some redemptive ending.

It was raining again, almost six o'clock and I was relieved to see cars in front of the library, the sign on the door that said it stayed open until eight on Thursdays. The same young woman behind the desk.

"Can I have that book, *Desperate and Bliss*, again? I'm almost done."

Her expression collapsed into true regret. "I'm so sorry, but the lady who'd reserved it came and took it." She reached for a clipboard. "I can put your name on the list."

I drifted into the stacks as if there was something else I might want to read. My eyes moved over the spines but all I saw were shapes and colours. I was staggered, like I'd suffered a blow to the head.

159.

WHEN MY MOTHER answered the phone, I hesitated. I'd spent the last hour pacing my hotel room, waiting for the sun, for the morning to edge into reasonable before I dialed. I'd rehearsed the conversation in my head but I was so desperate for Dad's voice that the surprise of hers threw me. She waited just a beat beyond her single hello, then she hung up.

I dialed again, a complicated series, the calling card code before their number. "Hi, Mom."

"Was that you before?"

"Yeah, sorry. Bad connection. How are you?"

"What's wrong?"

"Nothing's wrong. I'm in British Columbia."

"What are you doing out there? Has Daneen left Calder?"

"No, she's not here. I'm here. She's there." I looked at myself in the mirror on the wall, rubbed at the deep crevice between my eyebrows as if it could be erased.

"I don't remember you saying you were going anywhere.

What are you doing out there?"

"Just visiting a friend, having a vacation."

"What kind of friend?" Interested now, she polished up those last words.

"Not the kind you hope, Mom. Can I talk to Dad?"

"He's getting dressed." Her voice flat again. "Call back in a while."

I pressed the receiver tighter against my ear. "I really need to talk to him. I can wait, I don't mind."

Her gruff exhale made sure I knew she did. "Hang on." There was a sharp rap as the phone hit the counter.

I wouldn't be able to get at what I wanted with Dad, I thought—not over the phone, not with her in the room. I could feel my throat tightening. But then I heard his voice say my name and instead of crying, I stood up straight.

"I have an ethical question, Dad. I thought you were the right guy to ask." I said it as lightly as I could, as if I was enquiring about how to fix a toilet that wouldn't stop running—a toilet that wasn't even mine, that was someone else's problem and I was just curious about.

"I'll do what I can. Shoot." He sounded pleased.

"Okay. Is it more important—" I hesitated. I wanted to get this right—"to keep your word, and do what you said you'd do. Or to do what you think is right?"

Silence then, the kind that sounds like pondering. It comforted me to know how he was holding his mouth, that he was looking not at the far wall but beyond it. There were two versions of "Hmm," and then, "It seems to me that what you promise and what's right should be one and the same. An ethical person doesn't agree to do something they know is wrong. Right?"

An hour later, standing in the near silence outside the abbey, my father's words rolled over me like waves. He had such certainty, such an ability to sweep away ambivalence.

I'd come back to stand again in the sacred space of the abbey, but I couldn't goad myself into going inside. Instead, I turned to walk the grounds. The air was furred soft, all the colours re-imagined by the recent rain and I was alone with the rhododendrons, a riot of showy flowers, not a bramble among them to throw myself on.

Then, out of the corner of my eye, I saw it, a raven under a bush of scarlet blooms, its head bent to drink from the damp ground, its iridescent body playing tricks with the light.

A raven, and I couldn't remember ever seeing one up close before.

I edged closer, trying not to unsettle the air. There was no sound in the world, not a whisper, though I canted my head to listen closely. A raven, the messenger. I took another steady step and the bird emerged from beneath its bush to turn a beady eye on me.

It wasn't a raven at all. It was a crow, big and bold as every one I'd ever seen picking through the garbage in my back lane. It cawed once, then it took off.

160.

ANYTHING WORTH DOING should at least be easy. Gord's philosophy came to me standing in line—a deceptively short but painfully slow line—at the bank in Abbotsford.

This wasn't easy. None of it was easy. It wasn't easy to convince the teller, who disappeared for an eternity with my driver's license, and it was almost as difficult to convince the account manager into whose office I was escorted. She asked a lot of questions and I answered in an even tone while a maelstrom twisted beneath my ribs. I reminded the manager it was my money, so there was really no way she could say no. Still, she made me wait until my signature was faxed over from my branch, until a final positive identification could be made. While I waited, I kept the soles of both feet flat to the floor and

I moved them slowly back and forth so they'd stop trying to flee.

The next transaction, the exchange, was faster. Joanne opened her orange door just halfway and held me to the front stoop. Everything that passed between us was at arm's length. Still, I thought I glimpsed gratitude beneath her solemnity when I handed over the money order and said, "We've decided this is fair."

161.

IN CALDER, IT was Portia who appeared when I shut the front door behind me. The prickly heat under my skin ebbed a little at the sight of her. She was as tall as me now and possibly thin, but her clothes were too baggy to see any shape beneath them.

In the pictures her mother had sent me when she was young, Portia had always looked like a dark-haired version of Daneen, an imprecise replica, but now I could see so much of Bryan in her—his sharp nose and wide brow, his bold stance. Still, she had none of his affectation. Portia was just herself, just an expanded version of the small child she'd been, in charge of all the air around her.

I said something about how much she'd grown, embarrassing both of us.

"My mother's working. We have to be quiet until she comes out." She turned and loped, quietly, back to the kitchen, leaving me to wonder if her whole life hinged on conciliation, each minute charged with tacit expectations. But something about Portia seemed unconcerned, seemed to stand apart from what might bruise her.

In the kitchen, my mother was pulling a tray from the oven, the smell of her Toll House recipe as familiar as the line of her shoulder, the snap in her eyes when they met mine. I told my face to say it was glad to see her and it complied. And then Mom's expression matched mine, and what welled up inside me felt like hunger.

Upstairs, a door scraped opened and Daneen was announced by steady footsteps. I sidled into the dining room to steel myself for this next part. Laying my hand on the warm surface of the sideboard, I surveyed the room, struck again by how perfectly pulled together it looked, the whole space in balance.

"Doris! You know we don't allow her to have refined sugar."

A snarling half-syllable from Portia. My mother stepped in. "A little sugar isn't going to hurt this gorgeous girl."

Happy for the distraction of their disagreement, I shifted to the kitchen. Seeing me, Daneen stood down, waved her go-ahead to the indulgence. My mother told Portia to get her things. "We'll go eat our contraband cookies at my house and let these two old friends alone."

I wanted to reach for a cookie before they were swallowed by Tupperware, but Mom trained an assessing gaze on me. Before she could say anything, I did. "If you have some time, Mom, I really need to redecorate my house. Would you come over and give me some advice?"

"Of course. I'd love to." She held the cookies out so I could help myself.

162.

AFTER THEY'D LEFT, Daneen strolled toward me in her long-legged, casual way. "Hey, my hero!" Her skinny white arms angled for an embrace. I crossed mine and let her bang into the impasse of my face.

"What is it, Meriel? Did something go wrong?"

In answer, I picked up my bag from the floor and reached into a side pocket, pulled out the teal notebook. Daneen looked at it and relaxed. I wanted to slap the ease from her expression; instead, I slapped the notebook against the counter.

She moved toward it. "So it's all settled?"

"It's settled." I kept my hand flat on the notebook and Daneen's gaze travelled up my arm to my face.

"Then what?"

"Where are the other notebooks, Daneen?"

She looked like she'd walked in on the middle of a movie and couldn't figure it out.

"Joanne said there were two other notebooks. She says you have them, she never got them back."

I could see it surfacing behind her wide open eyes, the memory of those notebooks. "I don't know what you're talking about. She's crazy. Anyway, it doesn't matter. What's-her-name, she's dealt with, right?"

"Joanne Braun is her name." Daneen reached for the notebook but I snatched it away, opened it and pointed to a comment written in her own hand. "This is yours, Daneen. This is you."

"And just what are you planning to do with it?" She didn't look worried or frightened now—she looked bemused.

"I'll keep it I guess, since I paid for it."

"You paid for it?" Her laugh a harsh caw. "I hope you didn't pay more than two bucks for that piece of shit." She opened a cupboard beside the refrigerator, took out a pack of cigarettes. "What am I saying? Of course you didn't."

Eighteen thousand dollars, my hand shaking as I wrote it out on the slip. I'd spent some time figuring out what seemed like the right amount, principle plus compound interest on a loan from more than fifteen years before, a debt too long unpaid. "I gave her what I thought she deserved for conceiving such an acclaimed work."

"Meriel." Daneen lit her cigarette and drew deep. "Meriel-Claire." Her tone way past the ugly side of patronizing. "I guess you think you've uncovered something here, but that's because you only understand simple equations. You still believe everything has to add up to something, don't you?"

"You used her family story, Daneen." I was about to stride across the kitchen and take a cigarette for myself, but I considered the satisfaction she'd take from that, how she'd love being the architect of my vice. Watching her flick her long ash into a cereal bowl, I decided I would never smoke again.

"So what? My God, Meriel, this is not about ownership." She perched her cigarette in the bowl, took out a bottle of wine and twisted the cap off, a second glass pulled from the cupboard as an afterthought. "Even if I was influenced—"

"Influenced? You stole her family story and pretended it was yours."

Her face split into a full-on smile, like she'd won another prize. "So that's what this is about—this and all the years of your simmering hostility." She handed me a glass of red wine and returned to her cigarette. "Bryan always said, right from the beginning, that you resented me, that you were jealous. I told him he was wrong, that you just tended toward severe like your father. I told him you were a good friend."

I set the wine down unsipped.

"All these years I really wanted to believe, Meriel, that grudging was just your natural tendency." A coil of smoke escaped her mouth, twisted around her face. "But you really do resent me, don't you? You think I took something from you."

The heavy air, the smoke—it was too much for me. I went for the window, shoving it as high as its casing would allow. She kept up her barrage. "Don't pretend you have some moral high ground here—this is all about envy. You've always wanted what I have."

Eric's name leapt to the tip of my tongue, pungent and ready. Daneen was looking at me, maybe expecting me to say it but I couldn't be sure which of us that dull old weapon would serve. Besides, she was also moving, bit by bit, toward the teal notebook.

I had no intention of letting her grab that small advantage, and I saw no point in subtlety. I lunged, cutting her off, and snatched up the notebook, knocking over my wineglass in the process. It hit the floor with a satisfying smash. Red wine spread across the expensive white tile but neither of us made a move to clean up the mess.

I side-stepped the shards of glass in their luminous pool. "Daneen, this has nothing to do with me. This is about what you did to Joanne Braun."

"What I did? I did her a favour. I made the story she wanted to tell into something beyond its pathetic beginnings. I adopted it and I raised it. I shined it up and gave it to the world. She couldn't do that—" Daneen drew another cigarette from her package. "Nothing is worth anything if it's kept squirrelled away and safe where no one can have it."

Was that right? No argument came to me, so I slid the spiral notebook into my shoulder bag. But before I did, I tapped it twice with my index finger as if I was making some point too brilliant for words. As if I was laying down some new understanding about the rules.

Daneen chased me to the door. "Meriel, don't leave. I'm sorry. Let's just be reasonable. I'll pay you back whatever you paid for the notebook, and we'll put this behind us. I think you owe me that much."

I turned, one foot already over the threshold. "I don't owe you a thing, Daneen. Not anymore." Then I closed the door behind me without looking at her, without letting her say another word.

163.

DAD LOOKED DRAWN, sitting across from me. Outside it was pouring. Dark splotches had formed on his shirt from his dash into the restaurant and now the wet cotton seemed to weigh him down. After we ordered, he apologized again for being late. "I had to make sure your mother was alright before I left. She's been so down since Daneen and Portia decided to leave early."

He hadn't put on a pound since he'd returned from Malawi, so when our meals arrived, I was relieved to see him tuck hungrily into his meatloaf and mashed. For a while, our chewing filled the chasm between us. When I looked up, he'd decimated his potatoes and was watching me, fork poised over an almost empty plate. "Is there something you want to tell me, Meriel-Claire?"

There were a thousand things I wanted to tell him and I was grateful for the mouthful of chicken that kept them all from spilling out. None of my secrets would straighten Dad's shoulders. And if revelation turned reciprocal, what then? I didn't want to imagine what he might trade. I didn't want to know how it might all add up, or how sad we might be to discover we didn't know each other at all.

"I called your office yesterday. They said you were on leave."

I swallowed. That, at least, was cheap currency. "I took time off to sort a few things out."

I girded for a lecture. Instead, I got his hand reaching out, covering mine, the slightest squeeze. "Good for you. It's important to step away sometimes and take a good look. I wish I'd done it years ago—I might have realized then how little value there was in the way I was choosing to live."

After a pause, he asked, "So have you?"

I looked at him blankly.

"Sorted anything out?"

A minefield, the potential for wreckage in every direction. I took the smallest step I could. "I think so. I'm starting to miss the job." I slipped my hand out from under his before I confided anything else. "Anyway, I'll have to go back soon. I lost a lot of my retirement savings in Narcissus." A letter from the trustee had arrived just the day before, outlining the process now that the assets, what little was left of them, were frozen.

"Investing is always a gamble, Meriel-Claire, but you know that. Hopefully your other investments balance this bad one out."

He looked remarkably unconcerned until I admitted that Narcissus had held almost half of my retirement. "I thought it was a good fund, Dad—worthwhile, I mean, not just solid. I thought my money was doing some good."

I could see a calculation going on behind his tired eyes, a struggle to find the right formula for what he wanted to say. Maybe he'd seen through my pretense of altruism to the tax credits and promised returns. But when he finally spoke, he just said, "Money can do a lot of good in this world, Meriel-Claire, but it never comes with a guarantee. Just be sure you're not trying to buy your way into heaven."

I'd heard that before.

Dad speared the last bit of meatloaf with his fork but left it on his plate, tines poked clean through it. "I've promised your mother I won't go away again, no more international missions."

"Dad—why? You spent so long finding what you wanted. It's so important to you."

He was using two fingers to rub the base of his skull. He turned his gaze to something quite far past the rain. The blade of his elbow looked like it might cut right through his shirt-sleeve.

"What's important, I think, is being sure that you're making the choice, not just going along with a choice made for you." His smile looked as thin as the rest of him. "Anyway, there's enough need right here. I don't have to leave your mother alone again."

I wanted to say, "She doesn't deserve you," to warn him about the cost, but then I saw he already knew. He knew, and he was willing to pay it.

"Your mother tells me you've asked her to help redecorate your house. She could sure use a project right now. I hope you call her soon."

My misgivings had begun almost immediately after I'd asked her. I knew she'd do something great with my small space, but I just wasn't sure I could cope with the awkward silences between fabric samples. Still, it seemed like such a simple thing for Dad to ask of me. "I'll put it on my list," I said and to prove

I meant it, I pulled the list from my pocket and wrote, *Call Mom about house project.*

I'd recently taken to making lists, letting them coerce me into action, into small accomplishments I could tick off to mark the passage of another day. I had my car tuned up, joined yoga, talked to a counsellor. After Mission, time didn't seem the vast, empty space it had just weeks before. Now time felt small and tight, like there was so little of it and I'd already wasted so much.

Dad drew two twenty-dollar bills from his wallet and laid them on the table. It was enough to cover both our lunches and a healthy tip besides. "I suppose I can't buy my way into heaven either, but I can certainly be a cheerful giver."

It came to me like a bell going off.

164.

FOR WEEKS, I tried to convince Addie to accept me as a venture capitalist, to let me finance her bookstore. I offered a full partnership, enough money to lease a permanent location, but she only gave me an emphatic "No." I thought she didn't trust the offer or else she was being proud, so I gave it some time and I went back with the offer elaborated—a storefront, maybe with an apartment in the back where she could live. Shelving, a business license. Stability.

"What's in it for you?" she asked.

"It's an investment. You'll pay me back with interest and we'll both make money."

"You're not gonna get rich off used books, you know." I nodded. I had no illusions. "And I'll lose my welfare cheques— and then what? Then you'll own me."

So that was it. She considered me a bad risk.

The third time I made the pilgrimage across the park, I was armed with numbers, with a business plan and the tape from an adding machine. "We can start small and expand," I told her.

"We?" she repeated.

"You, I mean. You'll be in charge. You'll make it happen." I pointed to the numbers again. "Look, this can work. And look here—my gain. It's really very simple. Rent is cheap in this part of the city but there's a lot of traffic—"

She'd barely glanced at my paperwork before turning her narrowed eyes back on me. "Not everything works like that, you know—credits on one side, debits on the other and a line down the middle that everyone can see. When you're poor, life is more complicated than that."

I sat down on the edge of her blanket. "Look, Addie, I'm not trying to own you. And this isn't charity, if that's what you think. It's—it's an opportunity. For both of us."

The breeze picked up, blowing some of her books open. Flecks of spittle from the nearby fountain spattered against my face. "It's really important to me," I said quietly, though I already felt defeated.

Her carousel started to turn and then to teeter. Addie struggled to her feet to anchor it more securely in the grass. That done, she examined the darkening sky. Finally she turned back to me. "I guess it's time to get inside."

She knelt to gather up the books and I knelt to help, though I didn't think she wanted me to until she said, "Thanks." Said, "So what will it be called, this bookstore? I guess you get to name it, since you're the patron."

I considered suggesting we name it *Gord's* since his money was financing it, but the thought was ridiculous. The name was all wrong for a bookstore and besides, Gord had never willingly read a book in his whole life.

"Name it whatever you want, Addie. I'm hands off, remember? It's an investment, not a relationship."

"You expect me to believe you're just giving me the money and letting me steer?"

I nodded. Vigorously. That's exactly what I was doing.

"Well, you might just turn out okay after all."

165.

I ROLLED IT over for days before going to the drawer where I'd
stashed the stack of paper my mother had given me to shred.
To get to them, I had to flip Joanne's teal notebook off the top—
I didn't like to touch it. Even the colour made me queasy. Near
the bottom of that pile of all Mom's debt, I found what I was
looking for: the letter from Darla's lawyer about bounced
cheques, a name and address embossed in the top corner. I
dashed off a note quickly, before I could change my mind,
slammed a stamp in the corner and walked it to the post office.

I had a response in less than a week. Then I called the bank
for an appointment.

Dylan greeted me at the door to his office as if we were old
friends. "Meriel, wonderful to see you." He grasped my hand in
both of his like a much older man might. Behind him, I could
see my file spread across his desk, along with graphs and charts
and shiny fund brochures.

His face hardly registered surprise when I told him: "That's
right—another twenty-five thousand."

"Another business venture?" he asked but I just shook my
head.

"Personal."

It didn't matter if I thought it was fair or reasonable; it just
mattered that my parents would get to spend time with the boy
who looked so much like Gord, the boy they wanted desperately
to be their grandchild.

After I'd signed the money order for Darla and tucked it
into my purse, Dylan rose to his feet but I scooted my chair
forward and folded my arms on his desk. "There's something
else. I need some money for a home renovation."

He sat back down.

"Okay. This is what you have left in this account—" Dylan
pointed to the balance on his computer screen as if he couldn't
bear to bring himself to speak such an insignificant number. I

leaned in to see better, then blinked at the digits. There were so few of them, so much of Gord's money already gone. The surprise was a satisfaction so acute it was almost elation.

I withdrew it all, emptied the account. Had Dylan close it.

"One more thing, Dylan. My retirement savings—I need to start investing more aggressively."

He lit up like a little boy but caught himself and dimmed his bulb. Then he outlined some options, some market trends, handed me some brochures and I agreed—not to every recommendation, but to everything that felt right.

I was almost thirty-seven years old, nearly broke, and tremendously optimistic. Thirty-seven was a prime number comprised of prime numbers, an age attached to nothing else. It seemed like just the right time to be starting again.

166.

ADDIE DIDN'T HAVE anything as extravagant as a grand opening. She just called and said she was finally, officially open for business. I'd been waiting for that call; I had a gift ready—something I knew would be worth a great deal to the right person.

After we'd signed the lease and made the banking arrangements, I'd left Addie alone to set up the store. On the surface, I suppose it seemed reckless, turning over so much money and walking away but I wasn't worried. I'd even resisted the temptation to go past, dropping by just once to deliver a box of books I'd cleaned out of my house while Mom measured walls and windows. I cautioned Addie that some of them might be no good—my mother had written *Merry Christmas, Meriel-Claire!* on the inside cover of each and every *Nancy Drew Mystery*.

"People love inscriptions," Addie said. "It's part of a book's charm, the hands it's passed through."

The gift I was taking to her store was inscribed, too: *For M, loyal reader and friend*, and then the big flourish of the author's signature, ink a verdant green. But I wasn't just presenting Addie with my copy of *Desperate and Bliss*. Inside a plastic bag, I was also carrying that teal spiral notebook. I had in mind a kind of boxed set, a collector's item for the right buyer.

It was a hot afternoon and I'd left the office on foot after my last appointment. The plastic bag made my hand sweat and I had to wind the handle around my palm to keep a solid hold of it.

Addie had warned over the phone that she'd named the shop for me after all, but she'd added, "Kind of," which made me hope she was kidding, or at least hadn't used my first and last name. Two blocks from the shop, I started praying hard for a metaphor—for something appropriate but unidentifiable.

I steeled myself for the worst and then I looked up at the sign. Delicate red lettering announced CLAIRE'S BOOK-SHOP, its old-fashioned hyphen an elegant grace note.

I couldn't believe my eyes. It was like stumbling across something lost a long time before, a small thing packed away and now uncovered and found to be worth something after all.

A couple came toward me and then parted to walk around me on the sidewalk. "Here it is," the woman said to the man. "I told you it was on this street." They disappeared inside and I hurried off, away from the store, the corner of that hardcover book poking me in the leg every few steps.

At the drugstore I bought a gift card and a manila envelope and took them to the post-office counter. I slid the notebook into the envelope and wrote on the card in a neat hand: *Dear Joanne, This belongs to you so I am returning it. Sincerely, Meriel-Claire Elgin.*

167.

"SHE LIVES IN these parts, doesn't she?" Addie was turning over the signed copy of *Desperate and Bliss* I'd just given her.

I ignored that and took in the shop. "You've done a beautiful job, Addie." I guess I'd expected someplace faded and musty, like a box of books found in a basement, but Claire's hummed with colour and life. She'd hung stunning woven mats—"A friend of mine makes them from scraps"—on the wall, accepted displays of jewelry from local artists to sell on commission. When I'd come in, she was restocking the wire carousel with paperbacks. I looked at the sign and bit back the desire to suggest pricing them at more than a dollar apiece.

Addie let me stay while she closed up shop, let me ask questions and touch everything until I realized my touching might seem proprietary. When I turned to her, she held up Daneen's hardcover and asked again: "She's a local author, isn't she?"

"Not really."

"Too bad. Those sell well, local authors."

"Oh. In that case, I suppose you can say she is. She's got a place out in Calder," and then I added, "a big gothic monster of a place."

If I'd stopped sooner, if I hadn't given in to the urge to overstate it, Addie wouldn't have wanted to see it so much and I wouldn't have had to drive her out there.

After we cleared the overpass, Addie said it had been years—years and years—since she'd been out in the open, away from the city. Then she fell silent. When I glanced her way, she was staring at the ditches and fields as if enraptured. There was blue sky behind and ahead and it was that perfect time of year when everything's come to fruition and you can't imagine it will ever fade.

Though I knew the place was empty, Daneen long gone, I didn't take Addie up the driveway. I just couldn't do it. Instead, we drove to the best vantage point, a spot by the river below that big old house. It offered the best face, anyway. Looking up and from a distance, an onlooker could see that house's true character, how crooked and out of place it was on that minor bluff.

Addie, after coming all this way, only glanced at the house. She was suddenly much more interested in the Auberge River, rolling by fat from rain and placid in the September warmth. As soon as I brought the car to a stop on side of the road, she flung her door open. "Come on, I'll teach you to do a mermaid's dive."

"A what? Wait!" But she was already gone, clambering down the slope toward the river with her arms stuck out like poles for balance.

I chased after her, worried she'd slip, go down and under but she stopped at the water's edge. I caught up to her there. "What are you doing, Addie?"

"Mermaid's dive. I'll show you—" She stooped and came up examining something in her hand. It was just a rock, smooth and shaped like an anvil. Without a word, she pulled back her arm and I saw that rock rise into the sky and out over the river. It dropped straight into the water like a knife cutting clean. No sound, barely a ripple.

"Where'd you learn that?"

"I grew up beside a lake, four brothers and not a lot else to do. Haven't been back there in thirty years but some things you never forget." She was grinning to beat hell when she bent down again, searching for just the right specimen, fingering curves and angles, weighing heft in a loose hand. She stood up holding two stones and handed one to me.

"I don't know how—"

"Just hold it like this—" she demonstrated the placement of thumb and forefinger, "then open your hand and let it spin away." Addie let hers fly, another high-climbing acrobat that paused, mid-air, and dove straight into the water.

She looked at me expectantly. I squared my shoulders and mimicked what I thought she'd just done, but my stone floundered and splashed, loud and clumsy, just a few feet from the water's edge. Addie shook her head like I was the most disappointing creature to ever cross her path. Then she ducked down again.

"Here, this one. This one's perfect." She held the prize out to me. It wasn't much bigger than a quarter but fatter and perfectly smooth except for one cleaved edge. "You just have to relax— let your hand open up and release it." She unfurled her small hand in illustration. Her palm was surprisingly pink. My hand tightened reflexively and I felt the bite of that fractured edge.

Addie frowned at my fist and reached to take back what she'd just bestowed. "Here, let me show you again—"

I drew the stone to my chest, protecting it with both hands. "Don't you dare take this away from me."

"Then open up, let it go."

I gathered in my breath and pulled back my arm. The world hung in balance. Then I hurled that stone and watched it make an imperfect arc, saw it pause and fall. It struck the water almost as cleanly as Addie's had.

I picked up another stone, this one slightly bigger than the last, and let it fly, too. It was true. It was so easy when you just opened your hand and let go.

ACKNOWLEDGEMENTS

To Jessica Grant, I owe an incalculable debt of gratitude—for early encouragement and later, for deep wisdom, for walking right into these rooms, turning on the lights and checking under all the cushions for loose change.

Thank you to Rebecca Rose, James Langer, Megan Coles, Rhonda Molloy and Elisabeth de Mariaffi at Breakwater Books for giving MC and me such an enthusiastic yes, and working so hard to bring the book to life.

I am grateful to have in my corner Shaun Bradley of Transatlantic Agency—thank you for unwavering support and good counsel, for perception and determination.

Gratitude also to the Canada Council for the Arts and to the Newfoundland and Labrador Arts Council. Both of these organizations provided funding.

Thanks to Lynn Coady and Greg Hollingshead, who muscled through an early draft of this book at the Banff Writing Studio and gave solid advice when there were mountains left to climb. Thanks also to Danine Farquharson, Heather Norquay and Brenda Leifso, whose perceptive feedback improved the story, and to Paul Rowe for discerning, finally, the title.

A lot of the work on this book happened at Kilmory, so a nod to my extended Piper's Frith family, every single one of you, for such inspiration and so many memories.

To Billie, Ralph, Bruce and Doug Vryenhoek, thanks for being funny, smart, loving and so easy to hold dear that there is room to imagine other, less easy families. (Seriously, Mom, not even remotely you.) And thanks to the Norquays for introducing me to the prairie small town.

Thanks to Caitlin and Raquel for coming with me to Mission years ago, and for letting me see through your amazing eyes, and to Peter and Philip for tiptoeing—more than any young fellows should have to—while I worked.

Finally, immeasurable appreciation and love to Russell, who never keeps score but always keeps me safe.

The biblical epigraph is from *The Holy Scriptures* (Jubilee Bible 2000), ©2013 Life Sentence Publishing.